Surrendering HIS Heart

A BUENA HILLS ROMANCE

ALLISON GYGI

Published by Castlerod Press

Chicago, IL

Cover design by Raneé of Sweetly Us Book Services

https://allisongygi.com

ISBN: 979-8-9860561-4-2

✻ Formatted with Vellum

For Finn
You make the world brighter just by being in it.

Author's Note

Surrendering His Heart explores themes that may be upsetting to some readers. These themes include emotional trauma caused by parental and spousal abandonment and parental death (off page). Like in all my books, the implementation of these themes is handled in a delicate way that inspires hope and healing to the characters involved, and ideally the reader too.

Chapter One

September

"Why is this so hard?" Hallie Abernathy groaned under her breath, careful not to disturb the other library patrons. Closing her laptop, she dropped her forehead onto it. *Build a website, she said. It'll expand your reach, she said.*

It had seemed like a good idea when her sister suggested it over the phone last month. But what Elise failed to realize was that neither of them knew a thing about website design. And Hallie's ambitious assumptions of her own abilities had refused to consider it too. She could barely figure out how to use gifs while texting. Did she really believe she could make an entire internet space look professional?

Her side hustle, Hallie's Cakes, had made an okay name for itself around Buena Hills since its inauguration during her second semester at USC. But five months after graduation, simply supplementing her academic scholarship no longer cut it. Now her livelihood depended on her ability to scale up. If she didn't figure out how to expand her customer base soon, she'd have to rethink her career goals.

Needless to say, the idea of paying someone thousands of dollars to create a website for her stomped on a little piece of the confidence she had in her future.

She couldn't do it.

That was the purpose of the internet, right? She may not be a tech wiz, but she did know how to work a web browser. Anything could be figured out with the help of YouTube and pure determination.

Or so she'd thought.

She'd certainly met her match with this problem. The whole reason for buying this website theme in the first place was because the demo showed exactly what she needed. But what she'd managed to create looked nothing like it. What was the point of paying for it if she couldn't get her site to look the way she wanted it to?

Was this the computer gurus' way of keeping themselves in business? It made sense. If a tech illiterate like Hallie could figure out how to do it, the world wouldn't need geniuses like them. A smart business tactic, for sure.

An annoying one, but smart.

She rubbed her nose with the back of her hand, willing the pointless tears away. Sheesh, her family always called *her* the voice of reason. There was nothing reasonable about breaking into tears in the middle of a public library after three hours of limited progress.

With another strangled groan, she slid her laptop into her bag. Leaving her secluded corner, her path to the exit took her past the youth section. She waved at the librarian sitting behind the desk. "See you later, Mrs. Hawthorne."

The woman, with both sides of her ginger bob clipped behind her ears, looked up from the computer. "Hallie! I'm so excited you'll be providing the treats for our Halloween gathering this year. The cake for my son's graduation party was absolutely to die for. All our guests had something to say about it. Delicious and gorgeous, they all said."

"Thank you." Hallie's spirits lifted a bit. Speaking with a satisfied client always turned her day around, no matter that Justin's graduation party was over three months ago and the woman still brought it up whenever she saw her. "I'm glad you loved it."

"Oh, I did!" Mrs. Hawthorne clapped her hands together. "I told Lawrence that very night we needed to hire you for our next gathering. Between the cake and those raspberry cream puffs you brought to the school carnival last year, you've become a favorite of ours. Yes you have."

The praise wasn't all that surprising. Lawrence Hawthorne, the principal at the school they were speaking of, had sampled many of those cream puffs himself. But Hallie still gave the librarian a pleased smile.

"Before I forget," Mrs. Hawthorne continued, "Is it too late to add a few dozen of those amazing macarons you sold at the Summer Kickoff event?"

This must be some party. Mrs. Hawthorne had already added two dozen double chocolate cookies to the order since placing it back in August. Hallie had no room to complain, though. This event might be the key to keeping her in business. If Mrs. Hawthorne talked her up to her friends, it could lead to some fresh customers.

"Not at all." Hallie made a mental note to check her stock of business cards when she got home. "I'll be in touch to confirm everything a few weeks before the party."

Mrs. Hawthorne smiled. "Thank you, dearest. You're an absolute godsend."

"It's my pleasure."

Ending the conversation, Hallie turned toward the exit, but she only took a few steps before a small child darted past her, almost colliding with her legs. She stopped short so she wouldn't trip. The girl continued toddling along, pausing by the fish tank along one wall of the youth section.

Shouldn't there be a parent following that child? Hallie looked around but saw no one. The girl seemed way too young to be without supervision.

Granted, she knew nothing about kids. In high school, while her friends were padding their wallets with babysitting money, she was working as a waitress in her mom's café. Her one foray into the world of childcare didn't go well.

This child wasn't in Hallie's charge though, so she continued toward the stairs leading down to the self-checkout stands. But those stairs only triggered more concerns. What if this girl wandered to the first floor by herself? She could easily walk out the automatic doors and get lost. Or worse.

Hesitantly, Hallie approached the fish tank unnoticed. The child stood on the wooden stool, her face pressed to the glass, staring at the colorful neon tetras swimming around artificial hardscape and book ornaments.

"Hey, sweetie," Hallie said cautiously, looking around for any parents nearby. Would they appreciate a stranger talking to their daughter? "Are you lost?"

The girl pulled her focus away from the glass, her wispy, light brown pigtails bouncing with the movement. She smiled, revealing dimples on both cheeks.

What an angelic child. With twinkly blue eyes and naturally rosy cheeks to offset her porcelain complexion, even dolls didn't come cuter than this little girl.

"Fish so pwetty." She giggled.

"Penelope!"

Hallie startled at the frantic voice.

A young woman about her age emerged from between two stacks of middle grade books. She placed a hand on her chest in obvious relief. "I couldn't find you, Nell. Why'd you run off?"

Penelope looked at the woman without a care in the world. "I not lost. I see fish."

"Next time tell me where you're going first, okay? I need to know where you are." The woman patted Penelope's shoulder as she addressed Hallie. "My niece has no fear. She'd wander anywhere and think it's an epic adventure." She gave a breathy laugh that held a hint of exasperation. "I hope she wasn't bothering you."

Hallie gave her a reassuring smile. "No worries. I just wanted to make sure she was safe."

"Thank you."

"Of course." Hallie turned to go, only then noticing Penelope studying her computer bag.

"What's dis?" she asked, coming down from the stool and touching the bright keychain hooked to the strap.

Hallie knelt on one knee, looping the bag off her neck to give Penelope a closer look. "It's a llama. I got it in Chile years ago."

The llama, with a colorful blanket draped over its back, had been a gift from Señor and Señora Morales to remember the six years she'd lived in Santiago as a child. The older couple had owned the panadería near her family's home. Though they weren't blessed with their own children, they claimed all the expat kids as their unofficial sons and daughters. Whenever an expat family moved back home, the kids always received a small gift.

Even thirteen years after the Abernathys' return to the States, Hallie still thought about the sweet couple a lot. If not for the time she spent in their store, she never would've aspired to open her own bakery. She'd loved spending hours helping there after school. Her parents still didn't know the man had paid her ten pesos to restock the pastry cases every afternoon.

"I like it," Penelope said, touching the key chain again.

Hallie smiled. "Thanks. I like it too."

The woman took Penelope's hand. "Come on, Nell. We still need to check out our books, and your dad just texted that he and Isla are on their way home."

As the woman and Penelope walked away from the fish tank, Hallie headed downstairs to the exit. A warm breeze whipped at her when she stepped outside the library. Thank goodness the late summer heat had worn off this week, leaving the days pleasantly in the mid-seventies.

With the distraction of the library gone, her computer woes festered in her mind all the way home. Not even passing her favorite building in the whole town brought her out of the nagging annoyance. She normally slowed down whenever she passed the two-story Victorian with its gorgeous windows and a porch on both levels. Especially during the Christmas season with its elaborate light display. But today, she barely spared it a glance.

Why hadn't she had the foresight to take a few classes in website development at USC? After meticulously planning her courses to get the most of her degree, she'd grossly underestimated that hole in her education.

Once on her street, she pulled into the driveway of the two-story home she shared with her cousin and two best friends. Lugging her backpack from the passenger seat, she spotted her brother's Honda parked at the curb.

What's Tyler doing here?

He only lived across town, though family responsibilities, and a frequent travel schedule at work often kept him too busy to stop by during the week.

Voices carried to her from the kitchen when she stepped inside. Intending to join them, she kicked off her flip flops, tossing them onto the bottom step of the staircase leading up to the bedrooms. She paused. It only took a few extra minutes to put them away.

Her room was the first at the top of the stairs. She placed her flip flops in the shoe rack hanging from her closet door, then crossed to the window and set her bag on the antique wooden chair at her desk. On her way out, she picked up the pjs she'd somehow forgotten to put away that morning. Folding them neatly, she set them on top of the dresser. Satisfied with the cleanliness of her living space, she headed back downstairs and pushed through the swinging kitchen door.

Her brother stood at one side of the center island, a hip resting against the counter, his eight-month-old son in his arms. Their honorary sister, Kendall, sat on a stool on the adjacent side, a text-book open at her elbow.

"You brought Will with you?" Hallie approached them and ran a hand gently over her nephew's soft, yellow curls. "Hey, Williekins. I haven't seen you in forever."

She scooped the infant from her brother's arms and pressed a kiss to his chubby cheek. Will's blue eyes twinkled even more than usual, and he offered his aunt a dimpled smile, showing off the tiny tooth poking out of his bottom gum.

"You saw him on Sunday," Tyler said in feigned annoyance. "How come you never get this excited when it's just me?"

"Don't you realize your most important job is to get your son to his aunts?" Kendall asked with her usual snark. "That's what happens when you have a baby."

Hallie pulled her attention away from Will only long enough to give her brother an exaggerated nod of agreement.

Tyler chuckled. "I'm beginning to figure that out."

Technically, Kendall wasn't related to them, but she'd come to live with the Abernathys at fourteen, making her as much Will's aunt as

Hallie or Elise. And though she swore she didn't love kids, no one could spend even a few minutes with the baby and not become absolutely smitten.

He was perfection in a squishy, adorable package.

The kitchen's swinging door burst open, clattering against the counter behind it. Hallie jumped at the sound as her cousin Bridget, known by everyone as Beej, entered the room. Her nostrils flared in a good impression of an angry bull ready to charge.

"That was the worst. date. of. my. life." She thumped her purse onto the countertop so hard it sounded like an anvil hitting the granite. What did she have in there?

Will squawked from Hallie's arms, so she handed him back to Tyler before he got too agitated. She lowered herself onto the stool next to Kendall. "What went wrong this time?" Her cousin had been on a string of bad dates since breaking up with her last serious boyfriend almost a year ago.

Beej groaned, dropping onto her own stool. "First, he made fun of my name. *What kind of nickname is Beej? Do people call you that because Bridget is an old lady name?* Who says that? Then he proceeded to low-key insult me for the next two hours."

"Why didn't you leave?" Tyler asked, rubbing Will's back. The baby settled on his shoulder.

"I couldn't help being curious about what creative insult he'd throw out next," she admitted with dry amusement. "I can't believe he had the *audacity* to ask me out again. I mean, seriously."

Kendall's eyes narrowed. "Please tell me you said no."

Hallie hoped that as well. Beej's dating choices were questionable at best.

"Of course I said no. I didn't actually enjoy being insulted." Beej shook her head, and her countenance flipped in an instant to something lighter. "Did you figure out your website issue?"

"You're making a website?" Tyler asked.

Hallie blew an errant strand of blonde hair from her face. "*Attempting* to make a website. I can't seem to get it to work."

"My buddy works in tech. He might be able to help you. You've met him, actually. Remember Christian?"

"Wasn't he one of the groomsmen at your wedding?" Kendall touched the side of her head with her fingers. "Light brown hair, kind of broody?"

"That's him."

Beej gasped, bolting upright on her stool. "I remember him. He's *cute.* If I hadn't had that thing going with Tim, I would've asked for his number."

Kendall cast her brown-eyed gaze to the ceiling, though her mouth tipped upward. "Of course you would."

"How come you never invite him to hang out with us?" Beej asked, ignoring the slight. "He's got to be better than all the losers I've gone out with lately."

Tyler bit his bottom lip, looking visibly uncomfortable with the suggestion. He swayed Will from side to side, lulling the baby to sleep.

"Please don't go after my friends," he said finally.

"Why not? Is he married?"

"No."

Beej tilted her head to one shoulder. "Mysterious. Oh no. He still lives with his mom, doesn't he? I dated a guy like that once. Never again."

"He's probably a serial killer," Kendall suggested matter-of-factly. "Have you dated one of those?"

"Ha ha." A broad grin crossed Beej's face. "Ooooh, I know. What if he tells everyone he's a computer guy, but he's really a CIA agent on a secret mission?"

Kendall wagged a finger in her direction. "That's probably it."

"Girls."

Only Hallie noticed Tyler's attempt to butt in, though she couldn't resist joining the round of guesses. "What if he's an alien disguised as a human?"

"I could understand why you wouldn't want me to get too close." Beej nodded like the possibility of Christian being from another planet made the most sense. "One kiss and his face might fall right off."

"Girls!" Tyler called over the raucous laughter erupting from Hallie and Kendall. Will startled, rubbing his eyes with both fists. Tyler dragged his free hand down his face as the three women blinked at him. "*Anyway.* I'm planning to see Christian tomorrow. I'll ask if he has time to help you."

Hallie drummed her fingers on the countertop, considering her brother's suggestion. "I don't know, Ty. I can't pay him much, if anything at all. That's why I'm doing it myself. I don't want him to think I'm just using him for the family connection."

"It wouldn't hurt to ask. I'll let you know what he says."

"Thanks," she said, reluctantly agreeing with her brother's advice. She refused to take advantage of his friend, but she couldn't deny she'd hit rock bottom in her desperation. And cluelessness. She'd be a fool not to explore every potential avenue. "You're the best."

"No problem." He pulled his phone from his pocket, glancing at the screen. "Gotta go. Gemma's on her way home."

His wife worked as a math teacher at the middle school in town.

Bouncing his son a little in his arms, he cooed, "Are you ready to see Mama?"

Will's gummy grin and responding squeal provided answer enough.

Tyler touched his pointer finger to his temple and flicked it forward in a half salute directed toward the women. "See you guys later."

Hallie joined the chorus of goodbyes following him out, feeling more hopeful than she had since purchasing her domain. Once she got her website running, she could refocus her efforts on what she did best.

If only her baking skills were all that determined the success of her floundering business.

Chapter Two

Christian Gustafson placed his breakfast plate in the sink, ignoring the other dirty dishes underneath. *I'll worry about them later.* That had been his motto the last few years. He'd worry about it later. The dishes. The laundry. His life ... Everything seemed to be on that list.

Everything except simply surviving.

More than three years had passed since the worst day of his life, and he still barely managed to keep his head above water most of the time.

He stared out the kitchen window, past the back deck, at the trampoline, its black mesh netting blowing in the light breeze. Right behind it, the morning sun shone on the wooden swing set he'd built for the girls last Christmas. Pushing out a centering breath, he mentally prepared himself for another day.

Penelope's giggles broke the quiet, and he turned in time to find his youngest daughter leaning over the side of her booster. She held her hand out, about to drop a bite of chocolate chip pancake into the open mouth of their golden retriever.

Christian let out a strangled groan, hurrying over to remove the food from the three-year-old's fingers. "Let's save the pancakes for the humans, Nell. Princess Pumpkin can't eat chocolate." He tossed the sticky bite back onto Penelope's plate, bending to kiss her equally sticky cheek.

"Booberries," she demanded in her sweet voice, lunging for the bowl just out of reach on the table.

He dished out a small helping. She'd already had seconds, and he didn't want to think about the state of her pull-up once the berries passed through her.

"Daddy?"

Christian glanced at his older daughter sitting on the other side of the square table. She'd pushed her empty plate to the side and held a picture book open with her elbow.

"What's up, kiddo?"

Isla pointed to the bottom of the page. "What's this word?"

He came around the table to read over her shoulder. "Ghost."

"Oh yeah. Ghost." She went back to sounding out the words in a whisper.

Christian reached around her to grab the bottle of syrup and carried it to the fridge before turning back to his daughters. "If you're finished, I need you to go get dressed. Aunt Dani will be here soon to take you on your special girls' trip to the park while I'm gone."

"Park!" Penelope's whole body shook in anticipation of her favorite place. She strained against the strap holding her hostage in the chair, her wild limbs flinging out, knocking her sippy cup off the table.

And that's why we still use leak-proof dishes. Mealtime was already messy enough without any spilled milk.

The clatter of plastic on the wooden floor startled the dog, who'd sprawled out on her side near her water bowl. She trotted over to investigate, the tags on her collar tinkling a metallic melody.

"I thought you'd be happy about that. Here, I got it." Christian rescued the cup from Pumpkin's interest, then freed his daughter from the constraints of her seat before her frantic movements toppled over the chair. Scooping her into his arms, he peeked over at his oldest child.

Isla's brown eyes had darkened, and she'd slouched back in her seat. "Why can't I go with you to your appointment, Daddy?"

"You don't want to come, sweetie. It'll be super boring. You'll have way more fun at the park with Nellie and Dani." He set the bowl of berries on the counter, snapping a lid on the glass container with his free hand before Penelope could help herself to a fistful. She'd have blueberry juice oozing through her fingers in no time.

Isla's bottom lip puckered, her brows drawn down in a deep scowl. She played a mean pouting game when she wanted to.

Christian let out a silent sigh. His daughter hadn't always been anxious about being separated from him. What happened to the young toddler he couldn't take his eyes off of in public without her wandering away?

Scratch that. He knew exactly what happened. And it killed him that he couldn't do a thing to change the past. Isla wasn't the only one who'd been drastically affected the day their family fell apart.

But she'd made great strides since beginning her appointments with the child psychologist—a recommendation from her preschool teacher last year. Her anxiety still crept up now and again, usually as a result of sudden changes being thrown at her. Christian tried to be as upfront about their schedule as possible. When he'd told her of the plan two days ago, she hadn't seemed too bothered about the prospect of him leaving for a few hours on a Saturday. What had caused her fears to suddenly reappear?

"But you'll come back?"

The pleading in her brown eyes sliced through his heart. And stirred up the frustration constantly lingering under the surface of his composure, though not because of her. *What were you thinking, Sabrina? Do you even realize what you've done to this family?*

Probably not. His ex likely didn't stop for a second to consider the ramifications of walking out on her two daughters—the youngest only a few weeks old—or the fact that she'd left her husband to pick up the pieces.

"I always have," he said, swallowing his anger. No good would come from dwelling on it. Sabrina wasn't coming back, and he didn't want her to. Her selfish choice had shattered their family. No apology would put it back together. "And I always will."

"Annelise isn't coming back." Isla stared at the table while kicking the legs of her chair with her heel. "She left just like my mom."

There it is. The reason for this sudden relapse into anxiety. The college-student he'd hired three years ago to watch the girls in the afternoons had recently graduated and gone on to greener pastures. They'd said goodbye to her two weeks ago.

He set Penelope down and the child toddled over to Pumpkin,

who was lounging in her dog bed by the back door. Pulling Isla's chair out from the table, he crouched in front of it, taking a few seconds to consider his words. She was smart, so smart he often had to remind himself she was still a child, incapable of understanding the motivations of those around her.

"You know Annelise didn't want to leave, right?" he asked, placing his hands on the base of her chair on either side of her legs. "She went to grad school in a different state. But I know she misses you too."

Isla's bottom lip trembled, twisting the dagger of guilt even more into his side. Any moment, she'd add tears, and Christian would really be done for.

What am I supposed to do, Dad?

Dad didn't answer. He never did, but these one-sided conversations with him had become second nature since the early heart attack that took his life fifteen years ago. Christian had been twelve, but his sister hadn't been much older than Isla. He vaguely remembered watching her experience the same feelings of abandonment his daughter often did.

"Do you still have your heart?" He stroked the tight blonde curl framing her face.

"It washed off." Isla held her hand up for him to see.

Giving her small fingers a gentle squeeze, he wandered to the junk drawer next to the sink. He dug through it until he found a ball-point pen, then returned to kneeling in front of her.

"While I'm away," he said, uncapping the pen and drawing a small black heart on the back of her thumb, "just look at this heart whenever you miss me. Remember how much I love you." He drew a matching heart in the same place on his right hand before replacing the cap.

"Wait! You forgot the best part."

"Right. First, we need to seal in the magic." He pressed a kiss to her heart while holding his up for her to do the same.

"I love you, too, Daddy."

"I know." Christian smiled. "Tell you what, as soon as I get home,

I'll take you to the Halloween store to get your costume. Do you still want to be a gymnast?"

She'd been planning her costume since watching the prestigious Global Elite Games over the summer. McKenzie Bowman, an athlete from Buena Hills had headlined the gymnastics competition, winning multiple gold medals. A true local hero, and the object of Isla's fascination for the three months since. She'd been practicing her flips on the trampoline ever since.

"A zombie gymnast," she said with finality.

That detail was new, though not surprising. "Sounds like you've got it all figured out. Maybe we can grab some ice cream after?"

Penelope squealed, jumping up from Pumpkin's dog bed. "Ice cweam!" Her little feet pitter-pattered across the floor as she ran from the room.

Christian shook his head with a chuckle. It never took much to please her. He turned his focus back to Isla.

"Two scoops?" She held up two fingers.

"Two scoops," he confirmed with a decisive nod.

"And sprinkles?"

He huffed out an overdramatic sigh. "And sprinkles."

"How about gummy bears?"

"Gummy bears?" His voice rose a few notches in pitch.

This ice cream date would lead to a major sugar rush if he wasn't careful. *It's my own fault.* No one could accuse him of being above bribing his kids.

"You drive a hard bargain, little lady." His horrible attempt at a country accent made Isla giggle. "Fine, you can have gummy bears."

That brought a smile to his daughter's face. "Okay, I'll go to the park. Can I bring a book?"

"Sure. Go get dressed."

As Isla left the kitchen, Christian ran a hand down his face, the day-old stubble on his jaw scratching at his palm. That could've gone a lot worse. He constantly walked a fine line with her. She resembled that superhero baby in *The Incredibles*. One moment, sweet and cooperative. The next, she'd burst into flames. Not real flames, obviously.

But still just as hot. Luckily, he'd navigated through this difficulty without getting torched.

Within an hour, Christian found himself twisted in an unnatural angle, his cheek flattened against the plush fibers of the pink shag rug on Penelope's floor.

"Ah, there you are," he muttered, spotting the glittery sneaker underneath her crib. He attempted to fit into the tight space far enough to grab it from the farthest corner. How had it gotten there? She'd worn it yesterday.

Grabbing it, he carefully shimmied out from under the crib, tossing the shoe next to its mate on the rug.

"Let's remember to put your shoes away next time." He spoke the words out loud, even while directing them more toward himself. Sitting back on his haunches, he glanced at the spot where his daughter had been a moment ago. The empty glider chair underneath the collage of Penelope's baby photos swayed gently back and forth on its base. "Nellie?"

Where'd she go? That sweet girl had more energy than she knew what to do with.

"Christian?" Danica called from downstairs. "I'm here."

Just in time.

He grabbed both shoes and left the room, finding Penelope outside the door playing with the shape sorter blocks she'd left in the hallway. Princess Pumpkin, her loyal follower, sniffed at the colorful shapes scattered on the floor.

Although Christian had originally agreed to the idea of a dog to help with Isla's anxiety, he was pretty sure the retriever preferred the youngest Gustafson because of the likelihood of pilfering a treat. Dogs really were the smartest animals.

"Come on, Nellie." He picked her up before continuing to the stairs, Pumpkin trotting behind them. "Aunt Dani's here."

"Yay!" Penelope bounced in his arms. "Let's go!"

Once downstairs, they found Danica sitting next to her niece on the couch in the living room. Their heads were bent together watching a show on the tablet in the younger girl's lap. Isla's headphones hung around her neck, and she pointed at something on the screen, drawing a laugh from her aunt.

"Hey, sis." Setting Penelope down, she scurried around the couch to climb up next to Danica. He gave his sister's shoulder a squeeze. "Thanks for coming on such short notice."

Danica leaned her head back to look at him. "I'll never pass up an opportunity to hang with my favorite nieces." She poked Penelope in the side, and the toddler bent over giggling.

"We're your only nieces," Isla said, scrunching her face in confusion.

Danica smiled at her with genuine auntie devotion. "You're still my favorites. Besides, my roommates decided they wanted to dye their hair in our bathtub. I thought it was best to leave before they tried to convince me to become a redhead. Can you imagine *me* with red hair?" She flipped a honey-colored strand back from her ear and shuddered.

"That would be a mistake, for sure." Christian tossed Penelope's shoes onto the floor in front of the couch. "Have you talked to Mom recently? She hasn't answered the last few times I've called."

Danica wiggled her way out from between the girls. Penelope filled the gap quickly, scooting over to cuddle with her big sister.

"I saw her last night." Danica followed him into the kitchen where they could converse without interruption. "She's looking forward to her cruise."

"Mom's going on a cruise?"

Danica's face lit up like she was about to reveal a juicy secret. "Her friend talked her into going on a"—she made her fingers into quotation marks, bending and unbending them to emphasize her statement—"two-week singles cruise for middle-aged adults."

A low guttural snort escaped Christian's throat. "A singles cruise?

Really?" When he caught his sister's scowl, he softened his tone. "That's cool, I guess."

"She deserves to be happy, Christian," came Danica's mild reprimand. "I think it's sweet. She's finally getting back out there. You know how long it's taken her to be okay with the idea after Dad died."

"Sure, whatever." He still didn't like the prospect of her possibly dating again. It had been just the three of them for so long. "By the way, I told the girls I'd take them to get ice cream when I got home. You're invited, of course."

"Hey, I'll never pass up free ice cream. Especially with crushed cookies on top."

"This trip is beginning to cost me one of my limbs," he muttered, scrunching his nose at her. "Don't take it personally if Isla's a little moody. She's still sad about Annelise leaving."

Danica glanced into the living room. "I understand. I'd be grumpy too if my nanny left. Annelise has been a constant for over half her life. It's not easy having that suddenly disappear."

Christian followed her gaze to the girls still snuggled up together on the couch. "I wish I could change things for her more than anything. She's way too young to have to deal with these issues." The anger he tried so hard to squelch flickered again.

His sister touched his arm. "So are you. But you're doing your best for these girls. Remember that."

Sometimes Christian forgot that Danica was only twenty-one. She spoke with more wisdom and experience than many people her age, maybe as a result of growing up too fast after Dad's death.

At least she had enough brains not to elope at twenty, then get blindsided by a surprise baby a year later. Only Christian would make that mistake. Love sure caused a guy to make questionable choices.

Love. *Ha.* Yeah, right.

"How's the nanny search going?" Danica asked, rescuing him from his spiraling negativity.

"I'm interviewing two candidates next week, but I'm not holding my breath that either one will amount to much." A few applicants had seemed promising during the interview, but one look at them with the girls made it obvious they weren't a good fit. "Annelise has spoiled us."

Danica reached over and squeezed his wrist in a show of support. "Hang in there. There has to be someone out there who'll care about the girls as much as we do."

Christian thought about that as he kissed his daughters goodbye and left the house a minute later. He'd contemplated offering the job to his sister on more than one occasion. But she had a hefty course load—with some of her classes scheduled into the late afternoon—plus a part time job, and her own social life. It wasn't fair for him to dominate all her time. And Mom couldn't do it—she was still several years away from retirement.

Would he ever find someone suitable enough to fill Annelise's purple low-top Chuck Taylors?

He drove the five minutes to Tyler's sister's place on a street he'd avoided for years. Too many memories were tied up in that place. Ones he wished he could forget. As he pulled up in front of the familiar house, he couldn't suppress the tsunami of images bombarding his brain.

Why couldn't Hallie live in a beat-up old apartment like a typical early-twenty-something year old woman?

Answering the question took no time at all. The house belonged to Tyler's aunt and uncle, who lent it out to their children, nieces, and nephews to live in during college. Christian had benefited from that generosity by virtue of his friendship with Tyler and his cousin, Brad, long before Hallie had moved there. That had been a fun six months.

Let's get this over with, he thought, forcing himself to leave the car. Trudging up the walkway, his eyes landed on the stone balustrade lining the front porch at the top of the steps. It looked over the small rose garden in the yard below. A vivid memory he hadn't thought about in years hit with such force, it almost knocked him backward.

"He just doesn't understand," Sabrina said, snuggled up against his chest, her head nuzzled into his neck.

Christian leaned his back against the stone pillar holding up the porch's awning. Tightening his protective hold around her, he listened to her as she poured out her frustrations.

"I'm an adult now. I should be allowed to date whoever I want. He's never happy with any guy I'm with. If it were up to him, I'd be sent to a convent."

Christian knew not to say anything. Her relationship with her father was a complicated one. As much as Sabrina complained about him, she'd defend him to the moon and back if anyone spoke a word of criticism.

"If he'd get to know you," she continued, "I'm sure he'd realize what I knew from the day I met you."

Christian leaned forward again, resting his mouth against her raven hair. "What's that?"

She raised her face to glance at him, keeping her cheek pressed against his chest. "That you're the perfect guy, and I'm the luckiest girl in the world to get to be yours." She sat up and placed a lingering kiss on his lips.

"Nobody's perfect, Sabrina," he murmured when they'd broken apart. He brushed his lips against the tip of her nose.

She smiled sweetly at him. "You're perfect for me. And you're the only one I want to spend my life with." She gasped, her eyes bright with an idea. "Let's get married."

"What?" Christian choked on his laugh. "We can't get married. Our parents would freak."

Sabrina grabbed both his hands in hers, bringing them to his chest. "So? It's our life. We can elope. We both know we're destined to be together. Why wait?"

He should've shut down the idea immediately. Shouldn't have let her talk him into it. But he couldn't deny the way he'd fallen hard and fast for the flirty ray of sunshine who'd become his dance partner during his first practice with the ballroom team on campus. They'd been inseparable since day one.

It had only taken a few weeks to see a future with her. Not long after, she'd promised to love him forever.

"Forever." Christian snorted. Her forever lasted about as long as the time between their courthouse wedding and the day the pregnancy symptoms kicked in. She'd had one foot out the door ever since, despite his many attempts to fix their marriage.

He continued up the stairs to the porch, furious with himself for indulging in the past. If his marriage had taught him anything, it was that forever love didn't exist. *Romantic* love didn't exist. It was all an illusion people created to make themselves feel good.

But not him.

Not anymore.

He'd learned his lesson. All that mushy stuff was for the other chumps. He had enough on his plate already to get mixed up in foolish delusions again.

Chapter Three

"You wouldn't believe how beautiful it is here, Hal. I've never seen so many fall colors this early in the season."

Hallie listened to her sister gush about how amazing autumn in Connecticut was.

Again.

"New England is known for its fall foliage, so I believe it." Rolling onto her stomach on her bed, she hooked her arm around the stuffed fox her parents had given her before moving the family to Santiago for Dad's research trip years ago. At five years old, she'd been terrified to go on what was deemed "their big adventure."

Hallie still remembered her mother tucking her into bed the night before the flight. "No matter what changes come into your life, you'll always have a friend," Mom had said, sliding the stuffed animal under her arm.

The fox had seen Hallie through many changes, from moving back to Florida after six years as an expat, to college on the other side of the continent, and everything in between. No matter what the big event, Foxie had never let her down.

"The hiking trails are insane." Elise's comment brought Hallie back to the present. "Rory and I find a new one almost every weekend. Seriously, pinch me now. This place is a dream."

"Sounds like paradise." Did that sound bitter? She loved talking to her sister, but it was hard not to feel a little sad at the same time. Only eleven months separated them in age, and she could count on one hand how many times they'd lived apart. There was the year between their high school graduations, of course. Then came Elise's study abroad in Dublin. And last fall when she and Kendall backpacked around Europe for a semester.

This time was different, though. Elise had moved on to greener pastures, which included graduate school and marriage to her Prince Charming, whom she'd met during that stint in Ireland.

Hallie couldn't be happier for her sister. Still, she had a hard time not feeling left behind. It was silly, really. She'd always known they wouldn't live together forever. But no matter where they both ended up, they'd be sisters for life. The best of friends. Their relationship didn't have to change much, right?

"I'm sorry I won't be there to help with the Autumn Festival," Elise said, reminding Hallie that she'd tuned out the conversation again.

She gave Foxie a squeeze to push away the feelings of sadness that often came when she realized she and her sister were heading in different directions.

"That's okay. Kendall will be there. And Zee offered to work a shift one of the days," she added, referring to the fourth woman who lived in the house. "I'm sure I can rope Tyler into coming too."

Planning for the weekend-long festival celebrating all things fall had already been a lot of work, and Hallie needed all the help she could get. She'd never manned a booth at the event before, but the anticipation of it caused her to vacillate between wanting to back out and bouncing around with excitement. Practically the whole town stopped by the Autumn Festival during the two days of operation, and usually some folks from neighboring suburbs showed up too. Hopefully, it would add a nice boon for her business.

"You could ask Brad," Elise said. "He might be able to help if you still need people."

"I wasn't planning on asking him," Hallie admitted, even though she knew their cousin would be willing to help. "He has enough to worry about with Cassie so sick."

"She's still not feeling better? She has to be past the first trimester by now."

Hallie slid off her bed before arranging Foxie neatly in front of her pillows. "Yeah, but she still can't keep anything down. They're in the hospital almost every week getting fluids."

The pregnancy announcement had been a shock to the whole family, considering the short time since Brad and Cassie's wedding last spring. And the toll it had taken on her ever since worried everyone, especially Brad. The guy was a mess.

"Poor thing," Elise said. "I wish they'd move from the city. They'd have more than enough help in Buena Hills."

"We keep telling them that, but Cassie refuses. She insists she's not ready to settle in a small suburb after living in New York for so long." Hallie stepped into the hallway, leaving her door open and crossing to the stairs.

"Even without them, I know the festival will be great," Elise said optimistically. "You'll sell lots of goodies and pick up more customers than you know what to do with."

"I hope so." Desperately. Hallie's options were running out otherwise.

She reached the bottom step as three knocks came at the front door. That must be Christian. She pulled the phone away from her ear to look at the clock above the call log. Ten a.m. on the dot—exactly the time they'd arranged to meet when they spoke on the phone. The man was punctual. She appreciated that.

"Elise? I have to go. Tyler's friend is here to help with my website."

"Let me know how that goes," Elise said. "I hope he can get it the way you want it to look."

Hallie said goodbye, sliding her phone into the back pocket of her capris. After a quick breath, she pulled the door open.

Christian stood on her front porch, his hands shoved deep into the pockets of his jeans. He looked different than she'd pictured. Granted, the last—and only—time she'd seen him was at Tyler's wedding two years ago. He'd been wearing a tux, and a guy couldn't go wrong dressed in formal wear. His sandy brown hair hadn't changed since then: trimmed short and neat on the sides and back with slightly longer tips on top. Facial hair graced his angular jaw, which couldn't be classified as a full beard—more like he'd chosen not to shave before leaving the house.

She didn't remember the deep scowl claiming the bottom half of his face, though. And she understood why Kendall called him broody. The guy gave off every impression that he'd rather be anywhere other than standing on Hallie's porch. She could practically see the storm cloud hovering over his head.

This should be fun. She pasted on her friendliest smile. "Christian, right? I'm Hallie."

"I remember." He offered a curt nod.

And that was it. No "It's nice to see you again," or "How's it going." Not even the barest of smiles. What a grump.

He hadn't seemed standoffish during their phone conversation two days ago. Had something happened to put him in a bad mood? Or was it *her?* Either way, she was seriously rethinking asking for his help.

"Oh...kay." She cleared her throat. "Thanks for taking time out of your day to meet with me. Come in."

Christian stepped inside, and Hallie realized she hadn't fully appreciated his height the first time they'd met. Despite being on the lower end of average, she wasn't a tiny woman by any means, but she still had to tilt her head back to look him in the eye. Hmm, she'd always been attracted to tall men.

Not that she'd checked him out or anything. That would be weird. She didn't know the guy. Besides, she wasn't into grumps.

"I think the kitchen would be the best place to work," she tried again, pushing aside her own growing testiness.

He stretched out his arm, gesturing for her to go first. "Lead the way."

Silence accompanied their walk through the hallway, and Hallie grew more uncomfortable with each step. She pushed through the swinging door into the kitchen to find it already occupied. Her roommate, McKenzie, sat at the center island. Her thick, copper braid hung down one shoulder as she hunched over a cream-colored envelope. On her far side, her fiancé, Mitch, stuck postage stamps on the stack of matching squares in front of him.

"Wedding invite time?" Hallie asked, leaving Christian's side to peer over McKenzie's shoulder.

McKenzie nodded as she handed the envelope she'd finished addressing to Mitch before setting down her calligraphy pen. She swiveled to face her roommate. "These are the last of them, I hope." She flexed her writing hand into a fist, then relaxed it again. Nudging Mitch, she added, "You don't have any more obscure relatives to invite, right?"

Amusement flashed in his brown eyes as he placed the last stamped envelope onto the stack. He was the epitome of tall, dark, and handsome, thanks to the Latin features he'd inherited from his Ecuadorian mother. "I think we got them all. But you never know with my enormous family."

Hallie spared Christian a glance. He'd wandered to the fridge to study the collage of photos plastered to the front. Though he probably didn't appreciate her wasting his time with idle chit chat, she needed this little break from the awkwardness that tethered them. She turned back to her friends.

"Why didn't you use labels?" There had to be over a hundred envelopes on the counter. Way too many to address them all by hand.

Mitch poked his fiancé affectionately in the side. "That's what I said but she shot that idea down as soon as I suggested it." He flashed McKenzie his usual teasing smile and kissed her cheek.

"Handwritten looks so much classier," she said matter-of-factly. She leaned closer to Hallie and added in a whisper, "Who's your friend?"

Again, Hallie's attention shifted to Christian at the same time that he turned away from the fridge. He'd obviously heard the almost silent question. Did the guy have bat ears? Or an especially high radar for when people were talking about him?

Their eyes locked, and Hallie caught a pained look in his features seconds before he disguised it with his usual stony mask. That was odd.

Before allowing herself to analyze the reason behind his change of expression, she gestured toward him. "This is Tyler's friend. He's here to work on my website."

Mitch stepped over to him, sticking out his hand. "Hey. Mitch Skaggs. Nice to meet you."

"Likewise," Christian said, returning the handshake. Standing next to each other, he was only an inch or two shorter than Mitch's six-foot-four.

Mitch was one of the most charismatic people Hallie knew. His natural ability of making everyone feel like a million bucks minutes after meeting them had been the main reason he'd succeeded in winning McKenzie's quiet heart. But even he couldn't crack Christian's icy exterior.

Maybe he was one of those strong, silent types. There was nothing wrong with that. But he didn't intend to stick with one sentence answers the whole time, right? That would make things difficult once they got down to business.

"We were hoping to work in here where there's more space," Hallie said, swallowing her frustration. "But it seems you've beat us to it. We'll go somewhere else."

McKenzie scooped up a stack of invitations from the counter. "No, no. Stay. I have to get to work anyway." She dropped the pile into the box at the corner of the island before removing one from the top and handing it to Hallie. "It's just a formality since you'll be in the wedding, but this is for you. I hope you don't mind sharing with Kendall and Beej."

"Of course not." Hallie slipped the matte invitation out of the unsealed envelope, studying the photo of the happy couple snuggled together under a maple tree amidst the setting sun. "Ugh, you both are so photogenic. This will go right next to Elise's."

She set the invitation on the counter behind her before turning back to Christian. "Have a seat. Do you want anything to drink? Water? Juice? I think we have some coffee around here somewhere."

"Uh, no. Thanks." He sat down, sliding the final stack of envelopes off the counter and handing them to McKenzie. *At least he has some manners.*

She thanked him with a smile before easing the invitations into the only space left in the box. Lifting it from the counter, she dropped it into Mitch's open arms. "Will you mail these on your way to practice? I have to get to the gym. There's a group of overly excitable three-year-olds waiting to be molded into cute little gymnasts." After retiring from competitive gymnastics following the Global Elites, she'd slid right into her role of coaching beginning classes at her old gym.

"I'm on it." He shifted the box to one arm and placed his free hand on her back, allowing her to lead the way from the kitchen.

Before passing through the swinging door, McKenzie turned back. *He's cute!* she mouthed, pointing discreetly in Christian's direction and wagging her ginger brows. Thankfully, her fiancé's tall body hid her from his view.

Hallie rolled her eyes. The assessment was accurate, but she'd never been one to go gaga over attractive men. Christian's good looks didn't mean anything. No love match would develop in this kitchen today.

"Was that McKenzie Bowman?" Christian asked once they were gone.

"You know Zee?" Surprising. Neither of them had shown any indication they'd recognized each other.

Christian coughed. "No, I remember her from the Global Elites. My ... uh ... I watched the US win the team finals."

Gymnastics was one of the most popular events so that tracked. "Have you heard of Mitch too then? He's also a Global Elite champion. In beach volleyball."

Christian blinked twice. "No."

Okay, so he was back to the one-word answers. Great. A few beats of awkward silence followed, and Hallie rushed to fill it. "I left my laptop in my room. Wait here, I'll be right back."

"We can use mine." He bent toward the messenger bag he'd set on an adjoining stool.

Hallie hesitated a few seconds before sitting. She watched him type in the password to unlock the screen. Could he sense the tension swirling in the kitchen right now? Because she was practically drowning in the thickness of it.

"Go ahead and pull up your site," he said, turning the laptop toward her. "I'll take a look."

As he removed his hand from the keyboard, she noticed a small black heart at the base of his right thumb. Interesting. A flirty token from a girlfriend, perhaps?

It doesn't matter, Hal. You're not the nosy type.

"Right. I'll do that," she said, shaking the thought from her head. "Because that's why you're here. To look at my website." She groaned at herself for stating such an obvious fact.

Clamping down on her jaw to stop herself from continuing this string of ridiculous comments, she navigated to the admin dashboard for Hallie's Cakes.

"I've been working on this for weeks and it still looks like something a first grader came up with. I'm afraid I'm hopelessly lost when it comes to technology." She glanced at him nervously, unsure what he'd think about the amateur drivel on the screen before him.

But his brown eyes weren't on the computer. Instead, they scanned the kitchen, slightly narrowed. She couldn't read much in his expression, though it didn't look good. What about her home did he find so lacking?

"Is something wrong?" she asked, unable to keep the frustration from her tone.

His gaze snapped to her, his brows jumping toward his forehead. "No. The house ... It just looks ... different since the last time I was inside."

"You've been here before?"

"I used to live here."

Hallie gaped at him. "You did?"

He blinked at her, his judgy expression replaced with confusion. "Yeah. For part of my sophomore year. I thought you knew that."

She shook her head. "I knew my brother and cousin had another roommate for a while, but I still lived in Florida back then, so I didn't know who it was."

"It was me," Christian said with a shrug. "I had the bedroom at the top of the stairs."

"Wait! That's mine." She gave an ironic laugh. "How crazy is that? So, you must be the one responsible for the disco ball hanging from the ceiling when I moved in. Do you have some weird *Saturday Night Fever* obsession I should know about?"

He barked out a laugh. A small one, but definitely a laugh. So, he *was* capable of displaying some positive emotions.

"I swear that was Brad." A light shade of pink stained his tanned complexion.

Hallie bit back the urge to smile. "Oh, it was Brad, huh? You're saying he was responsible for damaging the ceiling *and* lighting the microwave on fire?"

"He wasn't very bright back then." The corners of Christian's mouth twitched up as he delivered the assessment of his former roommate.

Hallie's laugh bubbled from her throat. "Actually, I believe you. Was the fire really as dramatic as Tyler and Brad made it sound?"

"Oh yeah." Christian drummed his fingers against the island's granite countertop. "The whole chili can burst into flames. Luckily, we had the extinguisher under the sink, so he was able to put it out before it ruined the whole microwave. Is the burn mark still there?"

Hallie nodded. "My uncle put in a new stove and countertops, but he left the microwave. Something about wanting it to be a lesson for young tenants. I guarantee Brad never made that mistake again. He's grown up a lot since then. You know that he's going to be a dad in a few months, right?"

Christian's face clouded over, a noticeable sadness marring his eyes. "No, I didn't." At Hallie's confused look, he added, "We don't talk much anymore."

That's odd. Tyler had mentioned the three of them used to be close. But it was none of her business, so she didn't press.

Christian turned back to the computer. "So, what's this problem you need me to look at?"

"Right, the website." *Gah, why am I being so weird right now?* "I'm trying to make it look similar to the demo, but I seem to have bitten off more than I can chew. Why do you people make website design so hard?"

Oh great, now she sounded whiny.

The quiet chuckle emerging from Christian's chest surprised Hallie, and it made her feel a little better about her petulant comment.

"If it were easy, anyone could do it," he said, keeping his attention on the computer while he scrolled through the homepage.

"I knew it. Is it job security you're worried about? Or do you people just want to prove that you're smarter than everyone else?"

Warmth trickled down her spine at the look on Christian's face when his attention shifted to her. She couldn't put a finger on it, but for a split second, that hint of a smile stirred something inside of her. Like butterflies in her stomach without the nerves that usually accompanied them. Or a warm jacuzzi with bubbles and all. Whatever it was, she found herself leaning closer to him as he turned back to the screen.

Except this only brought her into smelling range of his sharp scent. It was like mint with a hint of something spicy she couldn't identify. Which was weird since she loved working with spices when she baked. No dull flavors allowed in her kitchen. But spices often took on different smells when mixing with the oils on a person's skin. Whatever it was, this particular ingredient worked *really* well for Christian.

Excuse me? Time to come back down to earth now, Hal. She backed up a smidge before he caught her crowding his personal bubble.

"You did this yourself?" he asked, clicking onto a different page.

Hallie leaned forward, placing her elbow on the counter and resting her chin on her palm. Unfortunately, that brought her back in range of his yummy scent.

Yummy? She'd never used that word to describe a person before. *Stop being ridiculous.*

"I know. It's terrible." She squirmed a little on her stool. She'd tried her best to create a clean, professional interspace, but looking at it now made her want to scrap it all and *not* try again. "I don't have the money to invest in something better right now. My business brings in enough revenue to cover only my basic costs, but nothing more than that. And I'd really like to start saving for a downpayment on a traditional bakery."

Christian bobbed his head once in acknowledgment before clicking to another page and scrolling to the bottom. "Actually, it's not bad for someone who doesn't know a lot about website design."

Were they looking at the same website? "Thank you?"

He stopped scrolling and directed his focus to her. "I'm serious. It's clean and organized and easy to navigate." He slid the laptop further away from him before clasping his hands together on the counter.

Hallie's attention again dropped to the heart on his thumb. Why did that symbol capture her interest so much?

But Christian's next comment pushed that little heart to the furthest crevices of her mind. "I could make it better, though."

Her brows drew together. "What?"

Christian appeared equally as surprised, like he couldn't comprehend the words coming from his own mouth. After a long second, he said, "Yeah, if you'd like me to."

Did he have some ulterior motive she hadn't picked up on before now? She didn't think Tyler would intentionally volunteer his friend if he'd thought Christian would try to lure her into using his services. But maybe her brother hadn't known either.

"That's okay," Hallie said. "I wouldn't be able to pay you."

Christian shifted on his stool, not looking her in the eye. "I don't expect payment. Let's just say Tyler has helped me out a lot in the last few years. I figure I owe him some favors."

Not that her brother would ever consider taking any kind of payment when aiding a friend. Even in the form of favors. Accepting Christian's help still felt like taking advantage of him, though. But delegating this task would free up her time to go back to the part of her job she loved the most. She'd be an idiot to refuse his offer.

"Thank you," she said finally, giving him a genuine smile. Maybe he wasn't the grump she'd originally pegged him to be.

"Sure. Do you have a piece of paper?"

"Uh..." Hallie looked around, spotting Mitch and McKenzie's wedding invite resting on the counter. Rising from her stool, she picked up the envelope and slid the invitation back out, once again admiring the gorgeous photo before sticking it to the fridge with an *I heart Miami* magnet. She handed him the envelope with a pen. "Here you go."

Christian started scribbling on the paper. "Here's my email. Send me all the pictures and graphics you want included. I'll need yours as well, if it's okay with you. The company I work for has a question-naire we send to all our clients to fill out during the onboarding process. It helps me get an idea of what you want as far as color schemes, vibe, and all that. I'll get that to you within a few days." He tapped on the mouse pad before turning the computer and gesturing for her to add her address into the blank contact form he'd pulled up.

"Wow, you're really thorough," she said, filling out the form.

"It makes the process a lot simpler." He closed his laptop and slid it into his messenger bag.

With their task out of the way, Hallie walked with him to the entryway and said goodbye. As she shut the door behind him, she leaned her back against the white wood, puzzling at the change that had come over him toward the end of his visit.

Christian likely didn't realize how much of a burden he'd taken off her shoulders. He'd mentioned doing it as a favor to Tyler, but could he really be that altruistic? What was the real reason he'd offered to help her?

And why did his intoxicating scent linger in her memory long after he was gone?

Chapter Four

What was I thinking, Dad? Christian's one-sided conversation with his father had been spinning in circles since meeting with Hallie two days ago. It often did during moments of intensity and stress. *I don't have time to build an entire website for her right now. Or ever, really.*

Blowing out a heavy breath, he pushed his foot on the brake, slowing to a stop at the light heading into Buena Hills' downtown area. He drummed his fingertips against the steering wheel as he waited for the light to change.

His eyes strained against the rain pelting against the windshield of his Highlander, scanning the array of mom-and-pop restaurants and boutiques on the right side of the street. The window display of the indie bookstore the girls loved to visit already showcased a selection of Halloween and fall recommendations, even though October hadn't yet begun.

In fact, many of the shops in this part of town had begun to decorate their storefronts for the season. Downtown Buena Hills was a favorite of locals and visitors alike for a reason, after all. The town put a lot of effort into celebrating every holiday. From cozy décor in the fall to the off-white icicle lights during December and the giant Christmas tree in the Village Green at the end of Main Street, Park Management always went all out.

Out of nowhere, a memory of strolling aimlessly along the sidewalk with Sabrina accosted his mind. She used to love snuggling close to his side while peeking through store windows, searching for quirky finds. She was a master at that. His personal favorite had been the dance-inspired ornament she'd given him for Christmas one year —a token of their time as partners on the ballroom team at USC.

That ornament was one of the first things to go after she'd left. So much of his prior identity had fled out the door with her.

He squeezed his eyes shut to block out the scene. It was moments like this one that reminded him why he avoided this part of town whenever possible. So much of their happier times occurred on this very street, and he never enjoyed the walk down memory lane.

Honks from multiple cars behind him startled his eyes open. He stomped on the gas, peeling through the intersection while shaking the lingering remains of the memory from his mind. Why couldn't he move on from the past? He'd thought finalizing the divorce, which gave him full custody of the girls, would provide the closure he needed to move forward. But he couldn't keep the anger over Sabrina's abandonment from remaining front and center in his life.

He clenched down on his jaw to keep the growl from escaping his throat. Not that it mattered—the girls weren't in the car. But he really needed to calm himself down before he arrived for pick up.

Main Street ended at the Village Green. He flipped on his blinker, about to turn left toward Penelope's all-day preschool when a figure emerged from the copse of trees at the edge of the park. The woman walked quickly in the opposite direction from where he needed to go. She reached the street, turning her head to check for cars before crossing.

Squinting against the rain, it only took a split second to recognize her. *What is Hallie doing out in weather like this?* What had started as a slight sprinkling had grown to a near downpour since he'd left his office, and she was several miles away from home.

He glanced at the clock on the dashboard. His boss had held him up at work, so he'd left his downtown office later than usual. But one look at Hallie tugged at his sympathies. Her lightweight hoodie was already drenched, her blonde hair plastered to her body like wet crepe paper. Christian couldn't leave her to battle the elements any longer. If he swung by Isla's school first, which was closer to Hallie's, he'd get there a few minutes just as Kid Care ended. Then he'd pick up Penelope from the other side of town before heading back this way toward home.

Pulling up to the curb where Hallie was walking past an empty shop with a *For Sale* sign, he lowered the passenger side window. "Want a ride?"

She whirled in the direction of the car, placing a hand to her chest. "Oh, hi. I didn't see you there. I guess I picked the wrong time for a walk."

Something stirred inside his chest, sending warning flares zipping through his body. He'd felt a similar phenomenon at her house on Saturday when she'd talked about her struggling business. What was it about her that made him want to help her?

He didn't know, and he couldn't back out now. "Hop in. I'll take you home."

Hallie waved away his offer with both hands, though her whole body shook. "That's okay. I don't want to inconvenience you. It was nice seeing you though." She started into a slow jog.

Part of him wanted to take her at her word. Whatever she was doing to his psyche created so much discomfort inside of him that he'd like to put as much distance between them as possible.

You can't leave her like this. She looked cold. If either of his daughters were caught in a rainstorm, he'd hope someone would stop to help.

He took his foot off the break and the car rolled forward. "It's not an inconvenience. Get in." Tugging his computer bag off the passenger seat, he moved it to the back, painfully aware of all the random toys and garbage littering the girls' domain. It was past time to clean out the car. Hopefully the storm's veil of darkness would camouflage the clutter.

At first, Hallie looked about to resist again until thunder clapped loudly overhead. Eyes widening, she glanced at the tempestuous sky before hurrying to the car and yanking the door open.

"Thank you," she said, sliding inside. She angled her body so close to the door, she practically hugged it. "I'll just stay over here. I don't want to get the seat all wet."

Throwing the gearshift into drive, he checked his side mirror before pulling away from the curb. "That's the exact reason I picked leather interior when I bought this car." Not to mention, the material made it easier to clean sticky spills from the backseat. "I'll just towel it off when I get home." He glanced at her sidelong and winked.

Why did he wink? He wasn't some suave ladies' man, turning on the charm.

The smile she aimed at him pushed his confusion from his mind. She had a lovely smile. Easy. Natural. He'd noticed that on Saturday too. She exuded a peace and calm that somehow freed him from the bad mood he'd been in after thinking about Sabrina. And here she was again doing the same thing.

Don't think about it, buddy. It means nothing.

They drove a few blocks in silence before Christian spoke again. "Do you make a habit of walking in the rain?"

She gave a shaky laugh. "Not usually. Walking helps me work through things that are bothering me. Unfortunately, my weather app let me down this time. It wasn't predicting rain when I left the house."

Christian grunted in commiseration. "Those apps are notorious for being wrong. You walked pretty far."

She shrugged. "My mom used to say she could predict my stress level by how far I walked."

He eyed her briefly before returning his focus to the road and making a turn. Was her business causing her more stress?

"Thanks again for the ride," she said, shaking off the heaviness in her tone. "I can handle a little rain. But lightning ... no. And thanks for taking over my website too. I'm sure you're probably already swamped with your paying clients."

"It's no big deal."

A slight exaggeration on his part. Hence his spinning thoughts and endless conversations with Dad ever since. Sure, he'd thought about taking over Hallie's website, but he hadn't expected to speak the offer out loud. And he'd spent the rest of the weekend wishing he could take it back. His boss was already annoyed with him for leaving early every day for the last two weeks, even though Christian had assured him it would be temporary.

Plus, he stacked so much onto the daily task lists that Christian already had trouble getting it done while juggling his parental responsibilities. As soon as the girls went down for the night, he often had several more hours of work before he could crash too. When would he find even a few spare moments to build an entire website?

"I know you said you didn't expect payment," Hallie continued. "But I feel like I should give you something. What would you like? I make a mean chocolate cake. And I'm not trying to brag, but people rave about my cookies too."

Christian fought against the smile threatening to take over his mouth. How was it that she had the ability to lighten his mood with the simplest comment? "That's not necessary. Really, I'm happy to help."

Are you happy? No, but she had nothing to do with that.

"I want to. You're seriously coming through for me. Now that I don't have to worry about my website, I can focus on getting ready for the Autumn Festival. It's coming up fast."

"You have a booth?"

Hallie nodded. "It's my first year. I want it to be perfect. You ever been?"

"My family used to go every year, but I haven't been back since my dad died." Christian didn't realize he'd squeezed the steering wheel until his knuckles had turned white. Thinking about Dad would do that.

She was quiet for a minute before responding. "I'm sorry to hear that. About your dad, not the festival."

"I figured." Christian chuckled, though he couldn't keep the sadness out of it. Would talking about Dad ever not hurt? "It was a long time ago but thank you."

"You grew up here then?"

"I'm a born and raised Buena Hillian. Not to be mistaken with a Buena *hellion,* although a few of my elementary school teachers would vouch for the accuracy of that description of me as a kid."

Hallie laughed, and the happy sound lifted the melancholy stirring deep in his chest. "I can't picture you as the wild one."

His mouth ticked into a smile. "I've mellowed out a lot."

"Apparently."

"You know that house across from the library? The Victorian one?"

"I love that house," she said. "Every time I drive by, I wish I could go inside. It has to be just as gorgeous as the outside."

Christian raised his brows but kept his eyes on the road. "Meh, it looks like a regular house. Sometimes a little messy, with a lot of windows to clean..."

She turned her full body toward him, her back pressed against the door. "That was your house?"

This time, he couldn't keep the smile off his face. "My mom still lives there."

"Wow. Do people ever sit outside and stare at it? Because I do. Especially during the Christmas season with all the lights. Too bad it doesn't snow around here. It would make the perfect Christmas card. Does she hire someone for that? She couldn't possibly do it herself. Sorry, I don't usually ramble this much."

Christian glanced at her in time to catch her cheeks pink, which only contributed to her natural beauty. Nope, not going there. "If by hire you mean volun*telling* me to do it for free, you've got it right."

Hallie laughed again, and Christian's heart stuttered. "Wow! I'm learning so much about you. I didn't realize you had a talent in Christmas light design."

Christian snorted. "More like she stands in the yard and tells me exactly where to string them, and I do all the manual labor."

"Ah, so you've got brains and brawn?"

Did he detect a little flirtation in her voice? Impossible. She didn't seem like the flirty type. And Christian couldn't encourage it anyway. He didn't understand how she'd broken through his walls again. That barrier was iron-clad.

"I don't think anyone would ever describe me as brawny. But thank you for stoking my ego. I'm just trying to live up to my dad."

"What do you mean?"

He took a minute to answer, sadness returning to his tone when he did. "He loved Christmas. The lights were his favorite part. Every year he did something different. He'd start designing in October and putting them up the day after Thanksgiving. And he'd never let my mom see the finished product until December first."

"That's really fun."

Christian swallowed hard. "A lot of our traditions stopped when he died. Not intentionally, but my mom worked multiple jobs to support me and my sister, so there wasn't time for them anymore."

"How old were you when he died?"

"Twelve." His voice cracked, and he cleared his throat. "Christmas lights were the one tradition my mom stuck to every year. She always wants them exactly the same as the last time my dad put them up."

"Your parents must have adored each other."

"They did."

A lot of good that did anyone. Dad was dead. Sabrina left. Love only brought pain. And Christian was tired of hurting.

He sucked in a breath as he pulled up in front of Hallie's house. "Sorry, I didn't mean to get all sentimental on you." He glanced over at her as she wiped her eyes with the back of her hand.

Oh, no. He made her cry? Why did knowing that make his gut twist?

She shook her head. "Don't be sorry. Thank you for sharing that. And thanks for the ride."

"You're welcome," he said softly, forcing himself not to look over at her as she let herself out of the car.

But he did turn to watch her hurry across the grass and take the porch steps two at a time. Only after she'd slipped inside the house without looking back did he pull away from the curb.

What had compelled him to open up just now? He hadn't allowed himself to let down his guard since Sabrina left. Especially to a woman.

A beautiful woman at that.

He couldn't let it happen again.

Chapter Five

The next day, Hallie sat on a stool at her kitchen's center island, sketching a maple leaf on a piece of white paper to recreate on her pumpkin spice cookies for the Autumn Festival. A few more potential designs fanned out around her on the counter.

Thanks to Christian, she could finally focus on preparing for the two-day event. By early evening, she'd decided on all the bakes to have on hand. She planned to offer a few kinds of cookies, as well as cupcakes and her favorite fall sweet bread flavors. Since most of her larger products were special ordered by her clients, she'd have only a handful of generic cakes on hand to sell by the slice. But her portfolio was up-to-date with her best products to showcase her abilities.

While she sketched, her thoughts turned to Christian, as they often had since their car ride chat the day before. He didn't have to stop. The fact that he did spoke of a kindness that would've surprised her if he hadn't willingly taken over her website. She couldn't let his generosity go to waste, even if he'd brushed off her attempts at a thank-you offering.

Plus, baking for him would give her an excuse to see him again, though she refused to analyze what that desire meant. But what to make him? He hadn't exactly been helpful when she'd tried to gauge his preferences.

"It smells amazing in here," Kendall said, entering the kitchen through the swinging door. "Like baked Nutella in a cupcake. Mmmm."

Hallie laughed without glancing up from her sketch. "Chocolate and hazelnut—two foods that always go together."

"We'll never need air fresheners while you're living here." Kendall's keys jingled as she thumped them on the counter. She eased her backpack off her shoulders, setting it flat onto a stool on her way to investigate the culprits of the aforementioned aroma. All two dozen freshly decorated cupcakes were set out on multiple cooling racks next to the stove, waiting to be boxed and delivered. "Look at the cute little bears! Who're these for?"

"The Pattersons down the street are having a gender reveal party tonight." Finally satisfied with her maple leaf, Hallie stacked it on top of another design before gathering the rest in a neat pile. "I'm delivering them in a bit."

She'd modified her original chocolate-hazelnut cupcakes to accommodate the French vanilla cream—dyed blue for the announcement—piped into the middle. She'd geeked out a little when Kristin and Troy came to her with a sealed envelope containing the sex of their baby. Until sometime after seven o'clock tonight, she and the ultrasound tech were the only people who knew the Pattersons were having a boy.

"That's fun." Kendall retrieved a glass container full of some kind of leftovers from the fridge. Pulling off the lid, she stuck the whole thing in the microwave and the appliance whirred to life.

"What're your plans for tonight?" Hallie asked, crouching in front of the cupboard next to the oven while Kendall filled a glass of water from the tap.

"I have a big test on Friday, so I plan to lock myself in my room with my textbook and notecards. Why did I go to grad school again?"

Hallie paused in folding the first box to shoot a humorous glance at her friend. "Because you're super smart and love school."

"Somehow, I don't think that's it."

Hallie set the first folded box on the counter and picked up the second. "Do you need me to grab some reinforcement snacks after I deliver these?"

"No thanks. I stocked up on caffeine yesterday to get me through." The microwave timer beeped, and Kendall headed over to check her dinner. Steam rose from the broth slopping against the side.

"Text me if you change your mind." Hallie began placing the cupcakes inside the assembled boxes. "You have mail, by the way."

Kendall set her dinner on the counter. "What is it?"

"Something forwarded from my parents," Hallie said, tugging off her plastic gloves before thumbing through the pile of mail on the counter until she found the mentioned item.

Kendall took the oversized envelope from her, turning it over and breaking the seal. She slid out another, this one the size of a standard letter. Scowling at the front of it, she crumpled it into a ball and delivered it to the recycling bin underneath the kitchen sink.

"With that reaction, I don't need to ask who it's from," Hallie said, stacking the two cupcake boxes on top of each other. "This is the second letter in a month. She obviously wants to talk to you. Aren't you at least a little curious about what she has to say after all this time?"

"No," Kendall said emphatically, plopping back onto her stool. "I haven't heard one word from my mother since I came to live with your family in ninth grade. A few letters aren't going to make up for that. The woman is dead to me. It doesn't matter what she has to say."

Hallie couldn't imagine running away at fourteen. The fact that the woman didn't do anything to convince her daughter to come home made her want to track her down herself. What kind of mother did that to her child?

"My life is much better with Roxy Parr out of the picture. I intend to keep it that way." Kendall ran her finger along the delicate gold bracelet lining her wrist, betraying her unbothered tone. It was the only piece of jewelry she ever wore, and Hallie had often noticed her fiddling with it during stressful situations.

Hallie resisted the urge to wrap her friend in a hug. Kendall hated being coddled. Her childhood left some heavy scars, giving her a fierceness and independence that made her reluctant to get close to anyone. Yet she'd become almost feral in her loyalty to the small circle of people she truly cared about.

Balancing the bakery boxes in one hand, Hallie headed for the door. "I'll see you later. Good luck with your studying. I can help run through your flashcards when I get back."

"Thanks," Kendall said, waving her off with her spoon. "I'd appreciate that."

After delivering the cupcakes to the Pattersons, Hallie stopped by Tyler's on her way home. The house, located in a cute neighborhood with picture-perfect lawns and tidy homes, belonged to Gemma's grandma. The couple had acted as caretakers for the spunky old woman since her stroke four years ago.

Darkness hadn't yet fallen when Hallie parked on the curb in front of the two-story home. Her brother and sister-in-law occupied the front porch, cozily snuggled together on the hanging swing Tyler put in a few years back. With his arm draped around her shoulders, he lazily rocked them back and forth with his feet.

As Hallie stepped onto the porch, a quiet, electronic hum reached her ears from the baby monitor propped up on one side of the swing.

Tyler stopped rocking, lifting his head from his wife's hair. "What brings you to this neck of the woods on a Tuesday night?"

"I had a delivery to make, so I thought I'd drop by. I wanted to ask if you'd be in town for the Autumn Festival." He traveled a lot for work, so she never knew whether he'd be around or not.

Thankfully, Tyler nodded. "We were planning on taking Will one of the days. Do you need me for something?"

"I'd love some help running the booth, if you're willing."

"Just tell me when." He glanced at his wife, flashing her a flirty grin. "Do you think you can spare me for a few hours on a weekend?"

Gemma rolled her eyes with a smile. "I think I'll manage. It'll give me a nice break." She laughed when Tyler scoffed in feigned offense.

Hallie watched the playful exchange that followed, shifting a little uncomfortably on her feet as she worked out the words to bring up her next request. "There's something else I wanted to ask."

Tyler looked at her expectantly. "Name it."

"I was ... uh ..." *Just spit it out.* "Can I have Christian's address?"

Her brother's eyes narrowed. "Why?"

She had no reason to be nervous about this perfectly reasonable question. Still, maybe texting him would've saved her from the awkwardness. This was one time her preference for face-to-face conversation complicated the situation.

"I ... um ... wanted to bake him some cookies." She rubbed the bottom of her flip flop across a small pebble on the porch. "For helping me with my website."

"No way." Tyler shook his head forcefully. "I've been around the block enough to realize a woman delivering any kind of baked goods to a guy is girl code for 'I like you.'"

"What?" Hallie took a step back, and her heel teetered off the porch. Her stomach swooped to her throat at her near fall. "That's not it at all."

She was curious about him, sure. After yesterday, she could even say she enjoyed his company. True, the way her body reacted to his scent when she was within smelling range was a little weird—it had happened in the car yesterday too. As was the way he entered her mind at random times, or how the prospect of seeing him again made her stomach bubble over with anticipation.

But no. She didn't like him. That would be silly.

"Ty, I'm a baker. Delivering cookies is literally my job." She wasn't even a little bit interested. No matter that Christian was super hot.

Wait.

What?

No.

Tyler stared at her with squinty eyes that made Hallie want to squirm. And defend herself. Why did her brother always have to get all protective of her when it came to men? It was the one drawback of living so close. "I have to do something to repay him. He offered to build me an entire website for free."

"He did?" Tyler's eyes were now tiny slits, and the blue in his irises had disappeared. "That doesn't sound like something he'd do."

"Hence, why I want to give him something in return."

Gemma nudged Tyler gently in the side, drawing his attention away from Hallie long enough for her to breathe. "I don't think there's any harm in it."

They shared a silent conversation before he sighed and turned back to his sister. "Fine. I'll text it to you." The intensity in his stare didn't lessen. "But I need you to promise me one thing."

"What's that?" Hallie asked.

"Please don't get involved with him."

Hallie sputtered out a laugh. "You have nothing to worry about on that score." Did her voice sound pitchy?

"Good."

"Good," she repeated, bobbing her head once in finality. Except her curiosity wouldn't let this conversation die. She swung her arms back and forth a little. "But ... uh ... why exactly ... don't you want me to get too close ... to ... him?"

Sheesh, she needed to work on her acting skills.

Her brother tilted his head to one shoulder, suspicion returning to his face. "It's not my place to dig up his demons."

Demons?

Hallie's mouth tipped upward. "With that vague reference you're giving credence to Kendall's suggestion about him being a serial killer. You know that, right?"

Gemma laughed, but Tyler barely managed a smile.

"Why is he your best friend if he's such a bad guy?" Hallie asked.

"I never said that. Christian is one of the best men I know. He's just been through some pretty traumatic things, and I don't think he's capable of being the kind of partner you deserve. Not right now anyway." Tyler snapped his mouth shut as though he'd already said too much. "Look, I don't feel comfortable airing his dirty laundry, so I'm only going to say this. Please be careful. I don't want my little sister getting hurt."

Well, that didn't clear anything up. "That's not going to happen, so stop worrying about it. I have to go. I'll text you the details for the Autumn Festival. Give Will a big, squeaky kiss for me, and say hello to Grandma June."

Gemma waved to her, and Hallie headed toward the car. At the curb, she made the mistake of glancing back at the porch before sliding behind the wheel. Gemma's head was back against Tyler's shoulder, but his attention remained on Hallie. She was too far away to read his expression, though she practically drowned in the concern radiating from him.

They'd always been close, and as annoying as he could be with the whole protective older brother stance, she'd never doubted he only wanted the absolute best for her. If he felt it necessary to be cautious, she'd keep her distance.

Starting tomorrow after she delivered some thank-you cookies.

Chapter Six

Christian pulled into his driveway and threw the gear shift into park, letting the Highlander idle as he jabbed the button on the dashboard to turn off the stereo. The kids' playlist filling the car the whole way home stopped mid-song, the hum of the motor becoming the only sound. He swiveled to face the girls in the backseat.

"Once we get inside, I need you to wash your hands. After your snack you'll have to entertain yourself while I meet with someone about the nanny position."

Isla groaned. "I don't want another nanny." Her already stormy face grew even more tempestuous. Slouching low in her seat, the safety belt provided the only barrier keeping her from sliding entirely off her booster.

Facing forward again, he pushed a breath out through his teeth. "I know you don't," he muttered under his breath.

But he summoned his patience, letting the conversation drop. She'd been in a mood the whole way home from school, and he'd let her grumpiness get to him. No good would come from rationalizing with her right now. They were already in for a long afternoon.

Christian stared out the windshield at the garage door. He didn't want to hire another nanny either. Annelise had been a godsend the last few years, not only taking care of the girls, but easing the household load on him as well. Isla and Penelope weren't the only ones sad to see her go.

But what other option did he have than to keep looking? His boss had handed Christian more backhanded comments less than two hours ago when he'd left the office early to pick up the girls. Even after working out his situation with HR—not to mention the extra hours he logged once the girls went to bed every night—he couldn't shake the feeling that Jim would latch onto any little reason to give him the ax.

Yanking at his tie, he shut off the car's engine and grabbed his work bag from the passenger seat. Once outside the vehicle, he opened Isla's door, then circled around to the other side.

"Hey, sweet girl," he said, unbuckling Penelope's five-point harness. "You ready for a snack?"

Penelope kicked her feet, anxious to be freed from the constraints of her car seat. "Okay!"

He chuckled and helped her down from the car. "What sounds good?"

She made an adorable thinking pose with one finger covering her mouth. "I want applesauce."

"How about some toast with honey too?" Grabbing her hand, they walked toward the porch.

Penelope bobbed her head with exaggerated movements.

"Okay, little lady. Applesauce and toast coming right up."

Isla waited for them on the porch, her backpack flung onto the welcome mat. Curly blonde strands stuck out from her ponytail, and she reminded Christian of someone who'd had a long day at the office.

Hmmm... she looked the same way *he* felt.

He unlocked the front door with the keypad above the handle. The clinking of metal dog tags welcomed them in as Princess Pumpkin bounded toward the entryway, barking out a greeting. She jumped, her front paws landing on Christian's stomach.

"Did you miss us, girl?" he asked, giving her a long scratch behind her ears with both hands. "Let's go inside. After my meeting, we'll take you for a good walk. Would you like that?"

Christian grabbed her collar and guided her into the house. Isla followed, dragging her backpack inside by one shoulder strap. She was going to wear a hole in the bottom of that thing with how many times she towed it across the floor instead of carrying it on her back.

Pick your battles. Fighting this one right now would only make her testy mood worse, so he let the issue drop.

As he moved to shut the door, Pumpkin sprang to attention, bouncing her front paws on the hardwood floor. Her long whines filled the entryway.

"Pumpkin," Isla said, petting the golden retriever's side. "Are you hungry too?"

The dog's airy whimpers turned to barks, and she continued to dance around the entryway.

"What's gotten into you, girl?" Christian glanced out the door, unable to see anything on the grass in front of their porch. The Highlander blocked his view of the other side of the yard. "Let's move away from the door so I can close it."

Before anyone moved, Pumpkin broke out of his hold, taking off through the open door. Her tail whipped Penelope as she passed, knocking the child off her feet.

What had gotten into that dog? She was so mellow most of the time.

A low growl escaped Christian's throat as he followed her out the door. Chasing their dog down the street hadn't been in his plan for the day. Penelope's cries reached his ears, and he backtracked to her. Swiftly lifting her into his arms, he resumed his purpose.

"Princess Pumpkin!" He winced. Why hadn't he vetoed that name when Isla suggested it? Bella was a nice name for a dog. Or Boomer. But no. It had to be Princess Pumpkin. "Yo, Pumpkin!"

He rounded their car in time to see the retriever bounding toward a woman making her way up the driveway. The candidate for the nanny position, most likely. He gave her props for being punctual.

A little too punctual. She was a whole fifteen minutes early.

Princess Pumpkin jumped onto the newcomer, her tail whipping back and forth in her excitement. Hopefully, the woman liked dogs.

By the way she shrieked and pulled into herself, that would be a hard no. She turned her back to Pumpkin, raising a green-and-white box above her head.

Sticking his thumb and forefinger in his mouth, Christian let out a piercing whistle. "Down, Pumpkin!"

The dog lowered her paws to the ground.

"Sit," he commanded, and she obeyed, though her tail still thumped against the concrete. "Good girl."

He crouched in front of her, ruffling the fur on her head, then moved to scratch below her chin. Penelope did the same and was rewarded with a lick on her hand.

"Sorry about that," Christian said without glancing up from the dog. "She doesn't bite. In fact, she's a real softy. Her only flaw is getting overexcited around new ... oh."

As the woman turned back around, he finally got a good look at her. His stomach flip-flopped over itself. Instead of the nanny applicant he'd expected, Hallie stood in front of him, her blue eyes wide as though she was questioning every life decision she'd made up to this point.

His breath caught, a silent curse running through his mind. He'd never sworn in front of his kids, and he refused to start now.

What's she doing here? How does she know where I live?

"I'm sorry." Apparently, that was the only thing his muddled brain could come up with right now. He stood. "Did she hurt you?"

Hallie shook her head a little too quickly. "Uh ... no. It's fine." But she hadn't relaxed, and she eyed Pumpkin warily.

The dog inched forward, sniffing at the newcomer's flip flops. Hallie took a step back.

Christian's tongue felt too large for his mouth. He hooked a finger underneath his collar, attempting to pull it away from his neck. "What're you doing here?"

Oh, real smooth, buddy.

Where did all these nerves come from? It didn't help that Penelope kept patting his cheek with her hand and giggling. She was obviously oblivious of the tension swirling around them all. They were caught in this weird cringey snow globe waiting for someone to come by with a hammer to break the glass and free them all.

With a small shake of her head, Hallie seemed to snap out of her frozen state. She held out the green-and-white box. "I know you told me not to but ... I wanted to thank you for helping me." Her eyes darted from Christian to his daughter and back. "I hope you like cookies."

"Cookies!" Penelope lunged for the box.

Christian circled his other arm around her to keep her from toppling out of his hold. "This one does, as you can see."

Hallie gave a hesitant laugh, but she said nothing more. She became fixated on something at his side, and he realized that Isla had emerged from the house.

"I washed my hands, Daddy. Can I have a snack?" Her expression turned suspicious when she noticed Hallie. "Who're you?"

The smile Hallie gave the child was polite, but her obvious discomfort grew. "My name is Hallie. What's yours?"

Isla ignored her question, instead looking up at her father. "I don't like her."

"Isla," Christian warned.

Hallie's brows shot up to her hairline. "Oh ... um ... it's nice to meet you too."

Isla glared at her. "Are you my new nanny? Our last one quit, and we don't want another one."

Christian set a hand on his daughter's shoulder. "Isla, that's enough."

This is not going well. She made it sound like Annelise left for some horrible reason, not because of her educational pursuits. He summoned all his calm, despite his desire to scoop both girls up and disappear into the house before this escalated further. Good thing he'd had lots of practice remaining composed around people.

Isla was bent on testing every ounce of it, however. Yanking her shoulder from his grasp, she spun toward him. "No! I won't have another nanny. She'll leave just like everybody else!"

Christian opened his mouth, but Isla wasn't finished.

"Go away!" she screamed, turning on Hallie. "We don't want you here! You'll never be my nanny." She lunged forward, landing a swift kick in the middle of Hallie's shin.

"Isla!" he gasped.

Hallie winced in pain at the same time Isla took off toward the house. Pumpkin's barks echoed through the air as she sped after the girl. In all the chaos, Penelope broke down crying.

Tilting his head to the sky, Christian pinched the bridge of his nose with his free hand. Was it too much to ask that someone else be the problem solver for once? He was tired, dang it!

He rubbed Penelope's back, *shhhing* softly in her ear. Once her wails had downgraded to quiet sniffles, he switched his focus to solving the next problem.

But when he turned to Hallie, his eyes landed on another car parked at the curb. A woman, who looked to be in her late thirties, stood frozen outside her vehicle, watching the commotion.

The real nanny applicant. How much had she seen?

By the alarm written across her face, Christian knew she'd witnessed the entire unfortunate event. And she did not like what she'd seen.

Fantastic.

She yanked the door open, hastily folded her ample body inside, and started the engine. Her tires squealed as she peeled away from the curb.

"Awesome," Christian muttered bitterly. Blowing out a breath, he faced Hallie. "I'm sorry. My daughter is ... she's having a hard time right now. Are you hurt?"

"No. Of course not." She held out the box again. "You seem like you could use this."

He pushed out a desperate laugh as he took the offering. "Thanks." He stole a glance toward the house, then back at her. "Uh..."

"Really, I'm fine. Go." Hallie shooed him away with both hands.

Christian didn't need more encouragement than that. He nodded briefly at her before stalking back toward the house. Once inside, he set the box on the coffee table before carrying Penelope upstairs to her room. She didn't object when he set her on the pink shag rug with some toys.

Leaving her door open, he returned to the hall, approaching Isla's open door. He stopped for a moment to figure out how to address what had happened outside. She was so smart for her age, but she was still a child, and he needed to approach this delicately.

Isla's bedroom resembled what Christian would expect from a princess's Halloween party. A mural of a giant black witch's hat, complete with gold ribbon circling the inside of the brim, took up most of one wall above the purple wainscoting. A collage of ballerinas in tutus decorated for the holiday adorned another, while a pink silhouette of a castle hung on a third. Christian couldn't take credit for the creativity of the space. Both girls' rooms were the products of Mom's and Dani's imaginations.

Isla sat cross-legged on top of the purple-and-pink puffy bedspread, partly shadowed by the open teepee canopy draping across the bed from the ceiling. Arms wrapped tightly around their dog, her shoulders shook.

Pushing out a centering breath, he knocked softly on the purple doorframe. "Can I come in?"

She nodded but buried her face deeper in Pumpkin's fur.

Christian approached the bed, tossing aside a pink stuffed jack-o-lantern—one of many pumpkins decorating the room. He sat down on the edge of the mattress. "Will you explain to me what happened out there?"

He held his breath, waiting for her explanation.

And waited.

And waited some more.

Finally, his daughter sniffed. "Why am I so different?"

He hadn't expected that answer. "What do you mean?"

Isla removed her face from Pumpkin's fur but still refused to look at him. "Sammy Pritchard told everyone in class not to be friends with me because I don't have a daddy *and* a mommy. Everyone knows a family is supposed to have a daddy and a mommy."

Christian sighed. Not Sammy Pritchard. For some reason, Isla's former best friend had developed a personal vendetta against her. *I guess I'll be having a conversation with her mother.* Again. The thought made him want to scream. Talking to the neighborhood gossip was never a pleasant experience for any normal person.

Not that he came close to normal. Most twenty-seven-year-olds—particularly those working in his office—were enjoying their single lives, partying at a new club every weekend or spending their vacation time in exotic places with friends. They weren't doing a lousy job of raising two kids on their own, that was for sure.

He dropped a hand onto his daughter's knee. "Isla, look at me."

She raised her head. Tears hung on her long lashes, twisting the proverbial dagger right through his heart.

"How many times have I told you not to listen to Sammy?" he asked gently. "She's wrong. Families come in all shapes and sizes. I guarantee some of the kids in your class come from families that look a little different."

Isla didn't respond.

"Heck, Marcus Taylor doesn't live with a mom *or* a dad. He lives with his aunt." The Taylors lived on the next street over. Both of Marcus's parents had died in a car accident while he was still a toddler. "But you know what?"

"What?"

"It doesn't matter what a family looks like. What matters is that the people in it love and take care of each other."

Isla moved another jack-o-lantern plush—purple this time—from her side and scooted toward Pumpkin, an unspoken invitation for Christian to slide into the vacated spot.

Accepting it, he tucked his little girl close to him. "And you have something Sammy Pritchard doesn't have."

"I do?"

"Yeah. You have a pretty awesome sister, for one thing." As if on cue, a crash of toys came from the next room, followed by Penelope's squeal. "And a grandma who lives nearby."

"And Aunt Dani."

He smiled down at her. "We can't forget about Aunt Dani. All of them love you so much and want you to be happy. And so do I."

Hope mingled with the sorrow lingering in her eyes. "I love you too, Daddy."

Untangling herself from Princess Pumpkin, she climbed onto his lap and wrapped her arms around his neck. Burying his face in her curls, he soaked in all the comfort her hug provided. Despite being the adult tasked to soothe and protect, it never ceased to amaze him how any affection from his girls had the effect of calming his own emotions.

"But Isla," he said after a minute, sliding her backward on his legs enough to look her in the eye, "it's never okay to kick people."

She dropped her gaze to the bedspread. "I know. I just ... don't want another nanny. I miss Annelise."

Christian tucked her securely back in his embrace. "So do I."

"Why can't *you* stay home with us?"

"I really wish I could." He meant that more than anything. "But it's my responsibility to take care of you. You know what responsibility means, right? We've talked about it."

She thought for a few seconds. "It's doing the things you have to do, even when it's not fun, and you'd rather do something you love."

"That's right." He tapped the end of her nose with his finger. "And part of my responsibility is making money so you and Nellie have all the things you need to grow big and strong. That means I have to go away sometimes and someone else has to care for you, even though I'd rather be here. But I won't stop looking until I find a nanny who thinks you're the coolest kid on the planet."

"Pinky promise?"

He held up both fists with only his little fingers extended. "Double pinky promise."

Her smile finally broke free and she locked her pinkies with his. She kissed her fist as Christian leaned forward to do the same with his. He couldn't remember the origins of their little ritual, but their pinky promises were as binding as signing a legal document.

"But you need to make me a promise too," he said, arching an eyebrow.

"What's that?"

"No more kicking. Okay?"

She snuggled into his chest. "Okay."

They sat for several minutes, the sounds of Penelope playing in the next room the only thing breaking the silence. Christian leaned his head back against the headboard and closed his eyes. He'd handled this crisis, and he appreciated the momentary pause from the chaos.

Because he never knew when the next storm would blow through, but it always did.

It always did.

Chapter Seven

Christian had a daughter.

No, he had *two* daughters. That would've been nice to know before showing up at his place unannounced. Why hadn't Tyler told her?

Sure, Hallie could've figured it out if she'd just looked in his backseat the day he'd given her a ride. In her defense, the rain had made the inside of the car darker than normal, and she was more focused on her wet clothes than snooping around Christian's space.

Once she'd come down from the panic of being accosted by his dog, she'd immediately recognized the cute little girl from the library last week. Who could forget those angelic cheeks? She was Christian's daughter? Oh, the irony.

Hallie's shin throbbed as she pulled into her driveway a few minutes later. She limped up the steps to the porch. Man, Christian's older child packed a mean kick for someone so little. The girl couldn't be more than six years old.

The house was quiet when she let herself inside. Beej's shift at the hospital ran until eight, and Kendall no doubt had decided to study late at the campus library tonight. Hallie didn't know what McKenzie's plans were, but with Mitch on break from tournaments this week, she was probably at his apartment. He'd recently relocated from his old place in Long Beach to be closer to his fiancée.

Hallie didn't bother turning on a light to chase away the growing shadows inside the house. She took the stairs at a jog in the dark, sliding her phone from her back pocket once she'd made it to the upstairs landing. Crossing through her open bedroom door, she hit the first speed dial and anxiously tapped her free hand against her thigh, waiting for Elise to answer.

"He's got kids!" she blurted as soon as the call connected.

"Who's got kids?" The man's Irish brogue immediately announced his identity.

"Oh, hey Ror." Hallie pulled the phone from her ear to make sure she'd dialed the right number. Elise's name scrolled across the top of the screen. Why was her fiancé answering her phone? Had something happened? "Sorry, I thought you were my sister."

"Ah, no bother at all," Rory said. "She was in the other room when you rang, so she asked me to answer. I'll fetch her for ya. You sound like you're in need of some ear bendin'."

It had taken a while for Hallie to get used to Rory's Irish phrases, but she had no trouble understanding him now. "I could use a good chat." She dropped onto her neatly made bed. "How's work? Any new projects?"

"Yeh, it's grand altogether. Right now, I'm finishin' up a romance score for an independent flick due in a few weeks. That's what's takin' up most of my time. Here she is." A short, muffled conversation followed before Elise picked up the phone.

"What's up, Hal?"

Hallie let out a squeaky moan.

"That doesn't sound good," her sister said through a chuckle. A door slid shut on Elise's side of the line, and Hallie wondered if her sister had stepped outside.

Turning onto her stomach, she slid Foxie under her chest, resting her chin on the soft but worn fur. She needed the comfort the stuffy provided right now. "You know how I told you Tyler's friend was coming over to work on my website?"

"Yeah. Was he able to fix the problem?"

"Oh, he fixed it," Hallie confirmed. "And he offered to create a brand new one."

"That's nice of him."

Hallie was anxious to unpack the events of the afternoon—and figure out why they bothered her so much—but first, she needed to catch her sister up to speed.

"I don't get it. He was so stand-offish at first. Like he'd rather be anywhere else but helping me. Why would he go out of his way to do something like that?"

"This is the same guy from Ty's wedding, right?" Elise asked.

Hallie nodded before realizing her sister couldn't see it. Old habits died hard, and she still hadn't adjusted to having these conversations over the phone instead of face-to-face. "Kendall called him broody, and I can totally see why. But then he started opening up, especially in the car the other day. He's ... I don't know ... not what I expected." Warmth sped up her neck.

"Wait, why were you in the car with him?"

Hallie shrugged. Again with the nonverbal communication. Would she ever get used to having an entire country between them? "I was caught in the rain, and he drove by, so he gave me a ride home. It was kind of ... nice." Seriously, why couldn't she stop blushing? People offered rides all the time.

"So, he's a good guy," Elise said.

"Yeah, he is."

"Why do I get the feeling that's a problem?"

Hallie considered the question. Was it a problem? "I just can't get a read on him. Even Tyler said he wouldn't go out of his way to take on a project for free, and now that I've tried to do it myself, I know what a big deal it is. I mean, sure, it's his job. He can probably build a website in his sleep. But after what I learned about him today, I doubt he has the time."

"Oooooo, intriguing. Continue."

"He has kids."

She still couldn't believe it. Of all the reasons Tyler would refuse to talk about Christian, or invite him to hang out with them, or take it upon himself to warn Hallie not to get involved ... She'd never considered this as the reason why.

So what? Lots of people had kids. This shouldn't be an earth-shattering discovery.

Then why are you making it one?

The question came out of nowhere. And she didn't have an answer to it.

"Awww," Elise gushed. "Are they cute?"

Did she not realize the big deal here? Hallie sat up, pulling Foxie onto her lap. "One of them is. The other one..." She cut off her assessment of Christian's older daughter, refusing to speak ill of a child. Instead, she rubbed her shin. It no longer throbbed, but the bruise still hurt when her fingers traced the mark. "She seems like a handful."

"What do you mean?" Elise asked.

Hallie took the next few minutes to fill her sister in on everything that occurred at Christian's. When she got to the part where Isla came in—was that her name? Through the chaos, she couldn't be sure she'd heard him correctly—Elise gasped.

"She kicked you? Why?"

"She screamed something about not wanting another nanny," Hallie explained. "The only thing I can figure out is that maybe she thought I was her? Seriously, can you picture me as a nanny? I'm terrible with kids."

Elise scoffed. "No, you're not. I'm willing to bet you're Will's favorite aunt."

"But Will's a baby. All you have to do is smile at him and he's your best friend. I never know how to relate to older kids. Remember that time I watched the Matheson kids? Sam rode his big wheel right off the deck."

"You were fourteen," Elise said, laughing. "And the deck was less than a foot off the ground. Sam was fine."

Hallie tried to stay indignant but couldn't resist smiling at her sister's amusement. "He still cried the whole time. Believe me, it was traumatic. And proof I shouldn't be trusted around other people's kids. That's the whole reason I never babysat again. Plus, Christian has a dog."

Elise slid right into the topic change like she always did during these heart-to-hearts. "That would be a red flag for you." No sarcasm touched her tone. Hallie's deep-seated fear of dogs went back years, ever since the golden retriever up the street chased her every time he escaped his house. Which happened way too often.

That devil canine loved to dig his way out of his yard just to torment her.

At least the owners moved away after a year, but those twelve months were the longest of her entire life. And they gave her a permanent unease around all dogs. Especially golden retrievers.

"Does it matter though? He's only doing you a favor. It's not like you're dating the guy. Unless—" Elise gasped again. "Do you like him?"

Hallie bolted upright, tossing Foxie to the side. "What? No!"

"You totally like him. You're way too practical to get all bent out of shape over something that doesn't have anything to do with you. Has my logical sister finally found a guy who makes her knees weak?"

"Of course not." Hallie shook her head so hard her neck popped. She tilted it from side to side to stretch it out. "I can't like someone I barely know. A warning that I needed to protect my shins would've been nice though. I could've put on pads before going over there."

"Is that all?"

Okay, now her sister was getting annoying.

"Yes, that's all." Wasn't it? But Elise's noise of disbelief made her pause. "I mean, sure, he's … handsome." She could state the obvious.

"He *is* pretty cute," Elise agreed. "And tall. I remember that from the wedding."

Hallie nodded. She'd always preferred tall men. Especially when they came with an angular jaw and piercing brown eyes. And just enough facial hair to look sexy without resembling a mountain man.

"Okay, maybe I am a little attracted to him." Not that she ever put a lot of stock into looks. So many other factors determined whether a relationship could work. Kindness, loyalty, responsibility, to name a few. Good looks faded, but the essence of what made a man attractive should not. "But I don't *like him* like him."

"It just seems a little strange that you're making such a big deal about this if there aren't feelings involved."

Elise had a point. And Hallie's confusion was the reason she'd called in the first place. This whole thing with Christian didn't make any sense. It was so unlike her to go crazy when it came to men.

"Honestly, I don't understand why this bothers me so much," she admitted, hoping her sister could provide some explanation for her swirling emotions. "I barely know him. And yet, it's like I'm ... disappointed, or something. Yes, I realize I'm being ridiculous."

"No, you're not," Elise responded gently. "Sometimes our hearts try to tell us things our brains aren't ready to comprehend. You're a rational thinker, and that's not a bad thing. You make decisions with your brain instead of your heart. It's totally understandable to be shocked about his situation, even if you weren't actively wanting to date him."

"I don't have time to date anyone right now." Hallie had enough on her plate worrying about her business. Now that the Pattersons' gender reveal was over, she didn't have any events coming up besides the Autumn Festival and the Hawthornes' Halloween party. She had all she could handle trying to market her business.

"And you're only twenty-four," Elise said. "You've got your whole life ahead of you. Dating someone like him would look a lot different than a typical relationship for people our age. Not wanting that right now is totally fine. But it's also okay to be disappointed about letting the idea go, even if it was a small one."

Hallie blew a strand of blonde hair from her face. "It's probably for the best. Please don't tell Tyler we talked about this. I kind of promised I wouldn't get involved with Christian anyway."

Was that the reason for these confusing emotions? The off-limits thing, and all that?

"Hey, we younger sisters have to band together against protective older brothers." Elise laughed. "I know what it's like to date someone Ty doesn't approve of. Hello? Remember Carter?"

Hallie smiled at the mention of the guy who'd proposed to Elise after three dates. Tyler had been right to hate him. She hadn't been a big fan either. "At least now you have Rory. It's impossible not to like him."

"He is pretty amazing, isn't he?" Elise gave a dreamy sigh before returning to the topic at hand. "What Tyler doesn't know won't hurt him. Your secret is safe with me."

They'd shared so many secrets over the years that Hallie knew she could trust her sister not to share this conversation with anyone. That should've made her feel better.

Yet something still nagged at her. In some ways, Elise had shed light on Hallie's dilemma about Christian. Unfortunately, she'd also realized that she might have a teeny tiny crush on him after all.

But if she gave in to it, that teeny tiny crush had the potential of changing the entire trajectory of her future.

What a terrifying thought.

Chapter Eight

From the floor in Isla's room, Christian stared at the computer screen. The website updates he'd been working on for the last hour blurred in front of him. Giving in to a yawn, he rubbed his palms against his eyelids and closed his laptop. The soft glow of Isla's nightlight—a quirky, non-scary replica of a haunted house to go along with the Halloween princess vibe—replaced the harsh blue light of the screen.

Scrubbing a hand down his face, he listened for any sounds indicating his daughter had fallen asleep. Quiet snores coming from Pumpkin lying on the shag carpet next to him reached his ears instead, so he leaned his head against the wall for a minute to rest.

Was he enabling Isla's sleep troubles by hanging out in her room until she fell asleep every night? Mom seemed to think so. But she'd never experienced raising a child with challenges as severe as Isla's. Bedtime was far less painful if he didn't have to redo the routine a dozen times.

After several minutes of silence coming from Isla's bed, he slid his laptop off his legs and pushed himself from the floor. He arched his back, and a satisfying pop eased the crick that had settled in his spine from sitting for so long.

Approaching his daughter's bed, he watched her for a moment, willing the frustrations of the day to melt away. Too many times, his anger toward Sabrina had made him wish he'd done things differently in his life. Like not eloping, for one thing. If they'd continued to date instead of rushing into an impulsive marriage, her red flags would have surely come out before it was too late. He could've spared himself the agony their divorce had created. And his children could've come under happier circumstances too.

But that was the catch, wasn't it? Without Sabrina, he wouldn't have the girls. And he couldn't imagine his life without them.

With a weary sigh, Christian turned from the bed, nudging Pumpkin with his foot on his way to the door. The dog lifted her head long enough to huff out an annoyed grunt.

"Come on," he muttered, digging his toes deeper into her side. Pumpkin let out a low whine and Christian froze, darting a glance in Isla's direction. If she wasn't deeply under, he'd be back on the floor to start the process all over again. Her breath stuttered, but she only rolled over and settled deeper into her pillow with a sigh. Pumpkin reluctantly stood and followed him into the hall.

Tucking his laptop under his arm, he closed Isla's door partway, then poked his head into Penelope's room. The child slept soundly, her legs tucked underneath her belly, and her arm hooked around her favorite blanket. Thank goodness he had one champion sleeper. It never took more than a story and a few minutes of snuggling in the glider chair to get her down.

With both girls finally asleep, the weight he carried around every day lifted somewhat. Rolling his shoulders, he headed downstairs, not bothering to turn the lights on in the living room. The one from the upstairs hallway provided enough of a glow for him to see. He lowered himself onto the couch and propped his legs up on the coffee table, crossing his bare feet at the ankles. Hoping to get in a few hours of work before crashing himself, he opened his laptop.

Princess Pumpkin jumped up beside him, turning in a circle before lowering herself onto the couch cushion and resting her head on top of Christian's computer keys.

"Needy mutt," he cooed, scratching the retriever behind the ears before nudging her head off his lap so he could work.

Pumpkin curled her face into her chest next to him, and they settled into their typical evening ritual of him catching up on work while she dozed. He'd always pictured spending these kid-free hours cuddling with Sabrina—not the dog—and reconnecting after work. Or slow dancing in the kitchen while doing the dishes. Even talking while folding laundry had once seemed like the perfect way to end a day.

But now he knew what marriage really involved. Those desires were only for the naïve saps who hadn't yet fallen from the clouds.

"It could be worse, right?" he muttered to himself. At least he wasn't shackled to that misery any longer.

Princess Pumpkin snored in her sleep, and Christian's eyes flicked to her. Silly mutt. She didn't seem to mind his shortcomings. And she wasn't trying to find new reasons to blame him for their circumstances. It only took a full food dish, lots of walks, and a little affection to keep her happy.

As he turned away from the dog, he noticed the box Hallie had delivered earlier, illuminated by the upstairs hall light. He'd forgotten all about tossing it onto the coffee table after coming inside. Even more surprising was that neither of the girls had spotted it either. They were like bloodhounds when it came to sweets.

A nighttime snack sounded kind of nice right now. He moved his laptop to the couch cushion on his other side so it wouldn't slide off his lap as he reached for the box. Pumpkin startled awake, snorting as she jumped off the couch and padded into the kitchen.

Christian stared at the box, his mind drifting back to this afternoon when Hallie had appeared in his driveway. The shock of seeing her had wiped clean the rational side of his brain, rendering him incapable of having a normal conversation. He couldn't recall what he'd said to her, or anything else about the interaction, for that matter. Except the part where Isla had physically assaulted her, of course. Who could forget that?

A wave of guilt turned his stomach. Should he reach out to her to make sure she really was okay? He thought he'd muttered an apology in the moment, but again, in his mentally blacked-out state, he could've asked her what she liked for breakfast for all he knew. It was safe to say he wouldn't be seeing her again.

Ignoring the surprising disappointment that realization caused, he flipped open the box and pulled out a cookie—chocolate chip, on closer inspection. He returned his attention to the website on his computer screen. As he toggled to the page's html code, he absent-mindedly took a bite, and...

Whoa.

He stopped typing, glancing at the cookie with wide eyes. He'd eaten a lot of chocolate chip cookies in his twenty-seven years of life, but apparently, not all were created equal. And *this* was a little slice of heaven. Crisp on the outside, chewy on the inside, with a little kick of spice to make it unforgettable.

Was everything Hallie made this fantastic?

He finished off the cookie, immediately reaching for another. If more people knew of her talent, she'd have enough clients to keep her bakery running for years. Yet she'd admitted that her business was struggling. Impossible. The people of Buena Hills didn't know what they were missing.

Popping the last of the second cookie into his mouth, he slid his laptop back onto his thighs. He clicked out of the legal website he'd been working on—with its straight lines and boring colors—and logged into the dashboard for Hallie's Cakes. Although she hadn't sent him a full list of products she wanted displayed on the menu page, he at least had enough information and photos from what was already there to get started.

His eyes burned with fatigue. Tomorrow would be rough if he didn't get to sleep soon, but he needed to follow this motivation train while it accelerated down the track. Staying up a few minutes longer wouldn't make much difference in his ability to function tomorrow.

Just a few minutes of work and then he'd go to bed.

"Daddy?"

The little voice, followed by someone jabbing at Christian's cheek, jolted him from slumber. He grunted, turning his face to the side to evade the poking.

"Daddy?" A second voice, then the fingers found his cheek again. "Daddy!"

His eyes flew open, and he glanced around the room. *What am I doing on the couch?* And sitting up, no less?

Sunlight shone through the small windows above the front door, bathing the living room in a morning glow. Raising his head from where it had been resting against the back of the couch, he spotted his open laptop laying haphazardly on the cushion next to him, the screen dark. He must've fallen asleep before making it upstairs to bed.

More fingers poked his cheek, and Christian finally registered his daughters standing in front of him.

"Hi, Daddy." Penelope smiled at him as she climbed onto his lap, all cozy in her white fleece footie pajamas. Her mousy brown hair stuck out in all angles. The child always woke with the best bedhead. "I hungwy."

He scrubbed a hand over his face, his three-day-old stubble scratching his palm. "Morning, sweetheart," he mumbled. "How'd you get out of your crib?"

"I climb out." Her words were perky like she'd been up for a while.

Wait, she climbed out? "I guess it's time to turn your crib into a real bed. Why are you awake so early?"

Isla sat down on his other side, pulling on the hem of her nightgown so it covered her legs. "My clock turned green. That means it's time to get up." She shoved the clock from her nightstand in his face.

You choose now to follow that rule? Christian blinked at the green light surrounding the device before taking it from her, half glancing at the digital numbers.

What he saw on the screen sent a jolt of panic zipping down his spine. "Oh—" He swallowed the curse that almost burst from his mouth, barely managing to secure Penelope in his arms before flying from the couch. "We have to go. Now."

They should've been out the door fifteen minutes ago. At this rate, no miracle could get both girls to school before the tardy bell.

Isla scrambled up the stairs behind him. "What about breakfast?"

"We'll take something in the car," he said, rushing into Penelope's room. "Get dressed."

They were ready in record time but still didn't make it to Isla's school before the car line attendants had gone inside. Once he'd signed her in at the office, then dropped Penelope off at preschool, it was already ten minutes to nine. There was no way he'd make it to the office downtown on time.

Jim will have my head for this. What number infraction was this? He couldn't begin to guess. How many more would the man put up with before he used it as an excuse to fire him?

Christian should've known it wasn't a good idea to help Hallie. Bad things happened when he didn't stick to the exact plan.

He sure hoped his decision wouldn't cost him his job.

Chapter Nine

When Christian slunk into the conference room at work almost an hour later, his team's morning meeting was already in full swing. Jim scowled at him from the front of the room.

"You're late," he snapped. Several of the team swiveled to look at Christian as he headed for the only empty seat at the large oblong table.

"Sorry, sir. Rough morning." Christian sat down next to Pamela, who worked in the cubicle next to him. She offered him a commiserating smile, her gray eyes full of pity. She'd been the target of Jim's demonstrative unhappiness. They'd *all* been targets at one time or another.

His excuse only made the vein in Jim's forehead stick out more. And red splotches broke out over his shiny round head as he launched into the lecture he gave at almost every team meeting. "Your family crises aren't my concern. That goes for all of you. Deal with your problems on your own time, not during working hours. You are easily replaceable, and your role in this company is dependent on you being here."

Yeah, he really inspired team morale.

"Christian," he continued, looking down at the piece of paper on the table in front of him. "You're on debugging duty today. I'll send you the list of clients' sites."

Christian nearly groaned. Debugging was Jim's favorite form of punishment whenever someone wasn't following his expectations with exactness. Probably because he knew everyone hated it. Who *would* enjoy going through the list of client websites to identify and eliminate all the reasons that could've crashed their systems? And on top of all the other tasks Christian had on his plate?

Yeah, this day was going to be rough, and it wasn't even ten.

Once the meeting concluded, everyone filed out of the conference room to their various workspaces in the maze of cubicles spaced in the otherwise open room.

Pamela followed on Christian's heels, rising on her toes to speak quietly so their conversation wouldn't be overheard. "Debugging? What's biting *his* butt? That's harsh, even for him."

Christian grunted in response, his annoyance rising. Jim demanded punctuality, but it wasn't like Christian was the only one to walk in late to a meeting. It always annoyed the boss, though he seemed extra peeved today. Was it because of Christian's arrangement with HR, allowing him to leave early? There was nothing he could do about that until he found a replacement nanny for the girls. Being punished for arriving late for the first time in three years was way out of line.

Besides, his never-ending task list was punishment enough.

He rubbed two fingers along both of his temples, pushing out a frustrated sigh. "I think I'm slowly going insane."

"Aren't we all in this place?" Pamela spoke a little louder now that they were out of their boss's earshot. The laugh that followed bounced off the cubicles they passed. "I was planning to approach him about taking a day off next week, but after the smackdown you just received, I think I'll wait."

"Day off?" Christian entered his cubicle and swiped his finger across his computer mouse to wake up the screen. "Doing something fun?"

"Only if you consider interviewing for a new job fun."

"After working in this nightmare? Yeah, an interview somewhere else would be like Spring Break in Miami."

Pamela's infectious laugh warbled again. Christian threw a smile in her direction before sitting down. Her ability to lighten the mood would be sorely missed if she left. But he understood her desire to go. Honestly, he was a little jealous too. Not in a malicious kind of way. He wished he could follow her lead. But his kids depended on him to give them the world, and his crushing workload made it impossible to find a spare moment to even look for something new.

Maybe that was Jim's plan all along.

At least this virtual slave labor paid well.

"Christian," Jim barked, suddenly appearing in his cubicle. How did he sneak up like that? For someone with the finesse of a rhinoceros, he could slink around as quietly as a cat stalking a mouse.

Christian's throat tightened with his next thought. Had Jim overheard his conversation with Pamela just now? He'd thought they were far out of ear shot, and he didn't want to consider what other monotonous tasks the boss had in store if he knew what they'd been talking about.

Pamela scurried back to her side of their shared cubicle, suddenly very interested in her work.

A growl forced up Christian's throat, and he swallowed it before it escaped. "Did you need something else?" he asked, glancing up at his boss. That didn't sound insolent, did it? The last thing he needed was a drawn-out lecture about respect in the workplace on top of everything else.

"It's your turn to clean the break room this morning," Jim said, a smirk forming at the corner of his mouth.

You've got to be kidding me. The break room? Christian had worked in this purgatory for three years and he'd been late one time. *One!*

Part of Christian's brain expected his boss to turn that smirk into a grin before yelling, "gotcha!" and sprinting back to his office.

But no. Jim never joked around. Maybe if he did, people would respect him more. Unfortunately, he was all business all the time, and often hostile and unpleasant to be around. At least Christian didn't have to live with him. His poor wife.

"I wasn't aware we had turns," Christian said, unable to keep the dryness from his tone. Never once had he been handed kitchen duty. His boss's intentions were clear. He was still getting back at him for being late. And Christian suspected the punishments were just getting started.

Jim crossed his arms over his chest. "It's up to all of us to keep this office clean."

When did that become a thing?

"So, you're up today. Get it done before you leave today."

Christian barely managed a "yes, sir" before Jim was gone. Once out of ear shot, he dropped his head into his hands and growled. It was a quiet growl. An under his breath kind of growl. But a growl, nonetheless.

Pamela's head appeared from around the makeshift wall separating their cubicles. "Wow. He's really mad. You didn't even miss that much of the meeting."

"That man's going to give me an aneurism, I swear," Christian muttered through his hands.

Pamela sighed. "On the bright side, the staff room actually isn't that bad."

That was true. Most of their coworkers were pretty good about cleaning up after themselves. They were adults after all. Of course, a small few refused to throw away their old leftovers or wash their dishes after using them, but that was true everywhere. And in reality, Jim was the type of boss who micromanaged everyone. Taking any kind of break was a joke, really. Christian spent most days scarfing down his lunch at his desk. He'd only stepped foot in that room a handful of times in the entire three years he'd worked here.

With a sigh, he pushed back his chair. He might as well get it over with early so he could prepare for the next task of menial labor his boss threw his way.

"If you need me, I'll be in the break room," he told Pamela, then stepped out of his cubicle for the walk of shame past the rest of his coworkers.

Not even thirty minutes after arriving home with the girls the next afternoon, Christian found himself dangling over the top of a ladder, his body outstretched as he hung the string of lights to the house. It would probably be safer to climb down from the rungs and move the whole ladder over a few inches. But with only one more clip needed to fasten the interwoven orange-and-purple bulbs to the gutter, he just wanted to be done.

If it weren't for the girls constant begging since the beginning of September, he wouldn't bother decorating for Halloween at all. But with October right around the corner, he figured they wouldn't let him put it off very much longer.

Behind him, Pumpkin's happy barks cut through the early evening, Penelope's giggles joining them as they chased each other around the yard.

"Where should we put this, Daddy?" Isla asked as a warm breeze whipped against Christian's back. He grabbed onto the ladder to keep from losing his foothold on the second rung down. Once he'd steadied himself, he secured the lights to the gutter before turning to his daughter. She held a giant, hairy spider that took up half her height. Its eight beady eyes were a vivid shade of red, which only made it look creepier than it already was.

It's going to be fun staring at that thing for a whole month, he thought climbing down from the ladder. "Where do you think we should put it?"

Isla tossed the spider onto the bushes underneath the porch railing. "How about right here?"

"I couldn't have picked a better place myself." Christian stopped untangling the remainder of the lights and walked over to the bushes, straightening the ugly thing over the branches.

The yipping of small dogs announced the arrival of one of their neighbors. Pumpkin barked out a greeting. Christian turned, barely managing to stop the groan from escaping his mouth.

Carrie Pritchard, of all people, stood on the sidewalk in front of their yard. Her three yorkies strained on their leashes in their effort to get to Pumpkin. Tail wagging, the golden retriever trotted over to say hello.

"Hey, Christian!" Carrie called, dragging her yipping dogs across the lawn toward him.

His smile felt more like a grimace, and he fanned his hand out in front of him in an unenthusiastic wave. "How've you been, Carrie?"

The only upside to being caught in an unexpected conversation with the head of the neighborhood gossip chain was that her daughter wasn't with her. Sammy had caused enough grief for his family this week. Which reminded him, he still needed to address the child's latest grievance.

"I'm hanging in there," she said, flicking a strand of shoulder-length black hair behind her. Dressed in tight leggings and a racer-back tank top, she gave the appearance of someone coming back from the gym, minus the sweat and flushed complexion. She narrowed her heavily mascara-lined eyes at the spider decoration hanging off the bushes. "Did you hear about Lorie and Bill?"

Christian pursed his lips before giving his head a slow shake. "I haven't seen them in a few days."

What beef could she possibly have on the couple who lived in the house between theirs? They mostly kept to themselves, the only signs of life occurring as they came and went.

Carrie dropped her voice to a loud whisper. "I'm pretty sure they're having marital problems. I heard them fighting in the back-yard last night."

"Every couple argues sometimes. I didn't hear anything out of the ordinary." Christian searched his mind desperately for a reason to abandon the conversation. He could only take a few minutes with her before the exhaustion kicked in. And the irritation. Most days he tried to avoid her and all the neighborhood dirt she managed to uncover. He had enough problems of his own.

Carrie didn't seem to catch on to his diplomatic attempt at curbing the gossip. "Now that their kids are gone, I wonder if their differences are being aired in the light. A lot of marriages fall apart once couples become empty nesters."

He wouldn't know. His marriage never made it past the baby

stage. "Well, whatever it is, I'm sure they'll figure it out." He began wrapping the lights around the drainage pipe.

"Have you heard from Sabrina?"

The question came out of nowhere and practically knocked him off his feet. "No." *And it's none of your business if I had.*

When would Carrie get the picture that his ex wasn't coming back?

She was a few years older, and she'd taken Sabrina under her wing from the time she and Christian first joined the neighborhood, which hadn't been his idea in the first place.

If it weren't for his wife's insistence that a house in the suburbs would make her happier than staying in their shoebox apartment close to campus, he never would've moved back to Buena Hills when they did. Fresh off receiving his bachelor's, it had taken most of his entry level income just to pay the rent. But back then he'd do anything to fix their marriage.

Except it hadn't. Not even close.

And once their relationship ended, the idea of moving again seemed like too much of an undertaking. Especially when the original owner approached Christian about buying the place, an option that only became available after he'd landed his current job.

"I tried calling her the other day, just to see how she's doing, you know, but I think she changed her number," Carrie continued.

"Mmmm." He ground his teeth to keep the words he wanted to say from coming out of his mouth. Her information digging might work on the other street gossips, but it wouldn't on him. She already knew way too many details about his failed marriage, thanks to Sabrina. This busybody wouldn't receive any spilled tea from him.

Not that he held any tea to spill. No word had come from his ex since the note he'd discovered on the kitchen table the day she left. Even when the finalized divorce papers arrived in the mail—unsigned by her, thanks to California's abandonment clause—nothing. He had no clue where she was, and he refused to dwell on it with his nosy neighbor.

"Sabrina? Wasn't that my mom's name?"

Shoot. When had Isla come up beside him? Pushing a hand through his hair, he bit down on the inside of his cheek to keep a curse from escaping. "Go find your shoes, kiddo. We need to leave soon."

Isla's brow furrowed, and for a minute, he thought she was about to argue. She'd tiptoed around the subject before, sometimes bringing up specific memories of her time with her mother. She wasn't old enough to recall much, and their conversations usually ended in tears, which was why he went to great lengths not to talk about Sabrina in front of the girls. Thankfully, his daughter's mouth only formed into a deep pout this time. She turned with slumped shoulders.

Christian latched onto Pumpkin's collar as the dog sauntered by him. "Take the dog with you, please."

Isla backtracked, beckoning for Pumpkin to follow, before continuing toward the house. She passed Penelope playing with one of the gourds lining the porch steps.

"You really should encourage your girls' curiosity about their mother," Carrie said once Isla was out of ear shot, adopting her usual I-know-everything-about-parenting tone.

Sure, because I'm really looking forward to the day I have to break the news that their mother didn't want them. No child deserved that weight on their shoulders.

"I'm handling the situation, thank you." Christian's jaw hurt from clenching it. Sometimes keeping his composure could be a real test of self-control. He wasn't sure how long he could keep it in check today.

One of Carrie's dogs nipped at his legs while another tangled itself in the remaining lights. Christian scowled at them both.

"They really deserve to know what happened to the woman who gave birth to them," Carrie said, shortening the dogs' leashes.

Christian didn't comment, going back to wrapping the lights around the drainpipe.

"Those girls already struggle so much, they should at least know they had a mother who loved them."

Were they talking about the same Sabrina? Mothers who loved their children didn't abandon them.

He continued wrapping, not falling for her concerned air. There was nothing sincere in her syrupy-sweet tone.

Circling the lights tighter with each rotation around the metal, he tried to tune out Carrie's unsolicited advice. Her words swirled through his head like the grownups in the Charlie Brown movies, mixing with her dogs' yipping at something outside his peripheral vision.

"I think she just felt trapped in her marriage," Carrie said as though she weren't talking to the very husband her friend had been married to. "But she really did love those girls."

Christian circled the lights into another loop around the pipe.

"They deserve to know that," Carrie continued. "Don't you agree?"

One of the bulbs shattered against the metal pipe, slicing his finger and his composure in one swoop.

"No, I don't," he snapped, dropping the lights. "Sabrina's not dead. She chose to leave. I refuse to subject my girls to that reality."

He started toward the house before whirling to face her again.

"And while we're on the subject of children, I'd appreciate if you'd tell yours to stop bullying mine." Lifting Penelope into his arms, he stalked toward the front door, leaving a stunned Carrie in the yard with her annoying mutts.

That could've gone better. He slammed the door behind him and set Penelope down. She toddled off to play with some toys she'd left in the living room before going outside.

Resting his back against the door, he sucked on his finger to stop the bleeding while reeling in his anger. He shouldn't have lost his temper out there. His name would be as good as mud by tomorrow.

Was it too much to ask for someone—anyone—to give him a break for once? He'd made one impulsive choice seven years ago. And no matter how hard he tried to move on from it, he couldn't get away from the constant reminder of what a dumpster fire his life had become.

Chapter Ten

A rare bout of dread hovered over Hallie as she sat at her desk chair, entering the last expense to the budget software she used to track her business finances. She'd just returned from shopping for the Autumn Festival, and the chunk of cash it took to purchase everything she needed for those two days had made quite a dent in her already declining bank account.

She blinked at the number displaying the remaining total at the bottom of the screen. At this rate, she only had a few more months until the money she'd meticulously saved during college ran out.

"You'll make it up next weekend," she muttered to herself, drawing as much optimism as she could from speaking the assurance out loud. She didn't doubt her baking skills. It was the businessy stuff —the branding, marketing, finances, etcetera—on top of the baking that proved more difficult than she'd realized. In the five months since finishing college and transitioning into the real world, she'd figured out quickly that she wasn't super woman. There just weren't enough hours in the day to do it all.

Closing out of the budget software, she sighed at the job listing for an assistant baker at Crème de la Crème, a bakery near her alma mater. She'd found it on a job listing site she'd perused before leaving for the store. She didn't love the idea of fighting the city traffic to get to work every day, but she'd managed it while going to school. And maybe working there would give her a few years of valuable experience. That would be good in the long run, right?

"Are you ready for girls' night?" Beej asked, breezing through the open doorway into Hallie's room. She still wore her light pink nurse's scrubs from her shift on the pediatric floor of Buena Hills Hospital, and her tight blonde curls were piled in a messy bun on her head.

Kendall entered behind her, and they both made themselves at home on the bed.

Hallie swiveled in her chair to face them. "Is that tonight? What're we doing?"

"Manis and pedis." Kendall's nose scrunched like she'd smelled something foul. "Not my choice."

Not Hallie's either. Like she really needed to spend more money right now. "Why don't you guys go without me tonight? I'll come next time."

"Hal, you can't bail," Beej whined. "Girls' night is a time-honored tradition."

Back in college, maybe. But now that Elise had moved to Connecticut and Beej frequently worked the night shift at the hospital, it seemed they barely managed two Fridays a month.

"Besides, this is Cassie's choice," Beej continued. "Brad's coaching in Inglewood tonight and doesn't think he'll get home until late. They're staying at Grandma June's, so I invited her and Gemma to join us."

Beej's sister-in-law hadn't felt well enough to leave her apartment for weeks. And Hallie hadn't stopped by to help out since last month. She'd love to see her. But still, the expense. "I don't think it's smart to splurge on something so frivolous right now. Some of us don't have a thriving career yet."

"You've been working on your finances, haven't you?" Kendall lowered onto her stomach, using Foxie to prop up her chest. "You always get in your doom-and-gloom mood whenever you have to deal with money."

Hallie threw a side eye in the direction of her friend. "I do not. I'm being cautious until I get my business off the ground. And you should be too. I have my doubts that the campus biology lab pays enough for a lot of extras."

"Don't worry about me." Kendall shrugged. "One time isn't going to destroy my bank account."

Beej pulled her legs into a crisscross position. "Hal, you *will* get your business off the ground. I know it. It'll just take time. And you know we're here to help with anything."

Hallie dropped her gaze to the floor, embarrassed by the random tears stinging her eyes. She didn't doubt her cousin's insistence—all her roommates were fierce supporters of her ambitions. "I didn't realize it would be this hard."

"You know what you need?" If Beej's last statement had been delivered in a compassionate tone, this one could only be described as perky cheerleader.

"What?" Besides a long walk to clear her head, which she wouldn't be getting tonight.

A bright smile slid onto Beej's face. "A night out with the girls to take your mind off your business troubles. Kendall and I will cover your bill."

"We will?" Kendall's dry tone made it obvious that this was the first she'd heard of the plan.

"I'm not letting you pay for me," Hallie insisted. Kendall's financial situation wasn't all that different from hers. And despite Beej's full-time salary, it wasn't fair to expect her to pay for everything. Although Hallie knew her cousin wouldn't mind, she refused to set that precedent now.

Her adamance didn't dim Beej's determination in the slightest. "Fine. I have another suggestion."

"What's that?" Hallie joined the others on the bed.

Beej pulled her phone from the pocket of her scrubs and swiped her finger across the screen before holding it out for Hallie to see. "I have a coupon. I'd planned to use it myself—I have a date with a hand model tomorrow, so you know my nails have to look perfect."

"Yeah, because you know he'll notice." Kendall rolled her eyes with a smile.

Beej ignored her. "I think you could use it more."

"Why do you want me to go so much?" Hallie asked.

Sure, girls' night was tradition, but it wasn't like no one had ever skipped in the past. So why the importance of this one?

Beej's jaw worked as she swallowed slowly. "It's just ... Remember the old days when we used to do everything together? With Elise gone and all of us done with school—"

Kendall loudly cleared her throat.

"Well, the two of us done with school," Beej corrected, gesturing to herself and Hallie. Kendall still had over a year left of her PhD, and McKenzie wouldn't start her undergrad program until January after putting off college to pursue the Global Elite Games. "I miss the old days when we were all together."

They never talked about the dynamic shift that had occurred in the house with Elise's absence. Hallie had simply thought she was the only one who'd felt it. She sighed. "Fine. I'll get my feet done. I hate having nail polish on my fingers anyway. I always pick it off before it has a chance to dry."

Beej clapped her hands. "Perfect! I have to change and Zee's in the shower. As soon as she's ready, we'll head out." She picked up her phone from the bed. "I'll text Cassie and tell her and Gemma to meet us at the salon."

With that, she popped up from the bed and left the room, a slight skip in her step. Kendall gave Hallie a commiserating glance before following.

Alone again, Hallie rose to her feet, smoothing out the bedspread and straightening the pillows before arranging Foxie in her rightful place in front of them. Returning to her computer, she slid her finger back and forth across the mouse. The job application greeted her as the screen lit up again.

She hated the idea of giving up on Hallie's Cakes. But her financial situation had never been this dire before. And her year of culinary classes had required a hefty tuition. At USC, her full-ride academic scholarship allowed her to save much of the money she'd earned from her on-campus job and her baking business.

What good had all that saving done her now? It was vanishing before her eyes.

She stared at the application for several long seconds, the blinking cursor mocking her. *Maybe it's time to admit defeat.*

Sighing, she clicked on the first section and started typing.

Chapter Eleven

"Can we do this again, Daddy?"

Christian glanced at Isla, partially hidden by the giant leather chair dwarfing her small body. Her feet were propped up on the matching footrest, her toes separated by purple foam dividers.

The smell of acetone mixed with whatever flowery lotion the woman in front of him massaged into his feet. "Sure, sweetheart."

He didn't mention that this would probably be the last time they splurged on their occasional daddy-daughter dates until he knew whether his job was truly at risk. They weren't considered wealthy—especially stacked against Carrie and her CFO husband—though Christian's salary provided a comfortable life with a few splurges when necessary. If he weren't so uncertain about his permanence at the company, this outing wouldn't concern him. But Isla didn't need to know all that.

His daughter smiled at him before returning her focus to the nail technician at her side. The woman had painted Isla's fingernails in alternating orange and black for Halloween with tiny pumpkins on both her thumbs.

Before becoming a girl dad, he'd never dreamed of stepping foot in a nail salon. So when Isla had suggested manis and pedis for this special outing, naturally he'd had reservations. But then she'd mentioned how all the other girls in her kindergarten class went with their moms. Really? Taking five-year-olds to a salon was a thing now?

But maybe it had always been a thing, and he just didn't know it. Put this on the list of situations he never expected to deal with as a parent. How could he deny his daughter the experience simply because he wasn't a woman?

Simple answer: he couldn't. He'd give her the moon if it fit in her bedroom.

And bringing Isla to get her nails done turned out to be just the distraction Christian needed. Jim's lecture from yesterday about being late—and the subsequent "consequences" that followed—didn't gnaw at his mind right now. Nor did the unfortunate conversation with Carrie earlier. It had taken the entire ten-minute drive to the nail salon to unclench his jaw from that encounter.

The technician dug her thumb into the arch of his foot, jolting him from the uncharitable thoughts forming about the entire Pritchard family. Christian relaxed his shoulders, only then realizing how tense they'd become in the moment it took to rehash the conversation.

She signaled the end of the massage with a light tap on his calf, and he slipped his wallet from his back pocket, pulling out a twenty-dollar bill. "Thank you."

She bowed her head before walking away. After unrolling his pant legs, he slipped on his socks. Once the other technician slid Isla's flip flops onto her feet and removed the foam dividers, he tipped her as well.

"You ready to go, kiddo?" he asked, tying his shoes. The trays of pedicure tools left in front of him looked like a colorful Jackson Pollock of smeared lotions and body scrubs. He walked around them, holding his hands out for his daughter.

"Yep!" She reached up and Christian lifted her from the chair, setting her on the floor. "I'm hungry. Can we go to dinner now?" She swung their connected hands back and forth as they walked up the middle aisle to the entrance.

It warmed his heart to see her carefree like this, so he swallowed his hesitation at spending even more money. He'd just have to keep his head down at work so Jim wouldn't find additional reasons to let him go. And after tonight, he'd tighten his wallet to be on the safe side. "You're in charge tonight. What're you in the mood for?"

Isla pursed her lips, thinking. "How about french fries?"

"The Burger Stop it is, then." Buena Hills' family-friendly restaurant was a town legend with its burger that easily fed at least four people. He'd never ordered it before, but he'd always been curious about the truthfulness of that claim. "How about a milkshake to go with those fries?"

"You can't have french fries without a milkshake, Daddy."

Christian chuckled at her exasperated tone. "Silly me."

After signing the receipt, he grabbed Isla's hand again. The bell above the door announced their departure as they stepped out of the salon into the dim evening light.

"Hey, Christian."

He turned to find Tyler's wife approaching from his right side, her sister half a step behind. Though twins, their appearance was a study of opposites. Gemma's dark curls cascaded haphazardly over her shoulders, and she wore jeans and a zippered hoodie. Cassie's blonde locks were pulled back in an immaculate ponytail, thin curly tendrils framing her face.

"Hey, Gemma," he said, then turned to the other woman. "Cassie."

She gave a little wave and a smile that didn't quite reach her tired hazel eyes.

Gemma reached down and tapped Isla lightly on the shoulder. "Hi, Isla. Are you on a special outing with your dad?"

Isla lifted her free hand up for the women to see, wiggling her fingers. "I got my nails painted."

Cassie made an *oohing* sound.

"They're so pretty. I like the pumpkins." Gemma glanced back at Christian. "Did you get your nails painted too?"

One side of his mouth flicked up in a smirk. "Not this time."

"Your loss," she said, then tutted her tongue against her teeth.

His smirk transformed into a grin. Turning to Cassie, he noted how much paler her skin appeared than he'd remembered. Granted, he didn't know her that well. He hadn't seen her since she'd married Tyler's cousin back in May. And that had only been for the few minutes he'd stopped by the reception. "How're you feeling?"

"Awful," she groaned, placing a hand on her tiny baby bump,

barely detectable through her lightweight sundress. "Ask me again in March. Hopefully, I'll have a different answer for you."

His heart went out to her. "Has Brad been taking care of you?"

Mention of Cassie's husband brought an unexpected twinge of guilt to Christian's stomach. During their USC days, especially the several months they lived together, he'd considered both Tyler and Brad his best friends.

Unfortunately, his friendship with Brad was just another shattered glass ball in his screwed-up life. His former buddy hadn't even told him his wife was pregnant. Christian found that out from Hallie.

It was his own fault though. Sure, his friend's vocal objections to Sabrina had been without tact, but once her true colors came out, he'd realized Brad's real intentions: to save him from inevitable misery. Christian hadn't wanted to believe the red flags presented to him. How could he have been so blind?

"He's great," Cassie said, distracting him from the pity party thrown by his conscience. A soft smile appeared on her wan face. "I've never been so spoiled, actually. He works really hard, and I feel so lazy. How can something the size of an avocado wreak so much havoc on my body?"

Gemma squeezed her hand. "You'll forget all about that as soon as this baby is born."

"You keep telling me that, but I don't know if I believe you." Cassie grimaced. "You weren't this sick with Will. At least we'll get an adorable baby out of it."

A heavy weight dropped into Christian's gut. Neither of his daughters would ever know what it felt like to be loved so completely by their mother. Sabrina had spent both pregnancies blaming him for her condition. A time that should've bonded them as husband and wife had only driven barbed wedges between them.

Isla didn't seem to care about the adults' conversation. An orange-and-black caterpillar inching along the pavement had captured her attention, and she crouched down for a closer look.

He pulled his gaze away from her, landing on the sedan at the far end of the parking lot as Hallie emerged from the driver's side. His heart stuttered.

Stop it, he commanded the organ. Why did it keep doing that every time she unexpectedly appeared?

"I should give Brad a call," he said, turning back to Cassie. "To see how he's doing."

He didn't love the idea of approaching his former best friend, despite getting back on speaking terms after reconnecting at Tyler's wedding two years ago. Every conversation had the potential of bringing up past grievances, and he didn't need any more grief in his life.

Cassie's face softened, tempering some of Christian's guilt. "You should. He'd love to hear from you."

Did she know the extent of Christian's strained relationship with her husband? How much had Brad told her? Christian was sure he'd only received an invitation to their wedding as a formality. His appearance had certainly been one. Could he have it wrong in thinking that way, though?

As Hallie and her roommates approached, Cassie gave an audible sigh of relief. "Oh good, you're here. I need to sit down."

With a small wave to Isla, she skirted around the group and into the salon. Gemma said goodbye as well, catching the door before it closed and holding it open for Beej.

Christian ignored the pointed look she shot at Hallie and nodded to Kendall as she passed. He almost stopped McKenzie before she stepped into the salon. Isla would love an autograph. But his daughter was still fascinated by the caterpillar, and he didn't know the gymnast well. She'd seemed nice enough the other day, but he couldn't predict whether she enjoyed interacting with fans. And he'd do anything to prevent disappointing his little girl.

Besides, his attention had zeroed in on Hallie too intently to give the other women more than a passing nod. "Hey." He flipped his hand up in a weird half-wave.

"Hey," she repeated.

Isla stood, and Hallie's eyes flicked to her, wariness crossing her lovely face. She took a step back, the subtle movement almost imperceptible. Her mouth lifted a tiny bit as she greeted the girl. "Hello."

His daughter blinked back at her, and Christian held his breath. He gave her shoulder a light squeeze. "Do you have something to say to Hallie?"

Isla turned pleading eyes onto him, and he arched his brows.

Once more, she faced Hallie, not quite looking at her, and took a shaky breath. "Sorry for kicking you."

Surprise sparked in Hallie's eyes, but she masked it quickly as she shifted her weight from one foot to the other.

Please be kind, he silently pleaded. He stepped forward to intervene, wanting to save his daughter from unnecessary chastisement.

But before he could excuse them from this situation, Hallie bent to Isla's level, placing her hands on her thighs. "It's okay. You seemed to be having a hard time. I hope you're feeling better now."

Her words had a visible effect on Isla. A small one, but Christian noticed it. The child finally met Hallie's eyes, and the rigidity in her posture relaxed. She may have smiled a little, though he couldn't be sure from his angle.

So many people dismissed Isla's needs without taking the time to see the vulnerability underneath her fight. Did Hallie realize the magnitude of this small kindness, not only for Isla but for him too?

Pulling his keys from his pocket, he pushed the unlock button on the fob twice and patted Isla's back. "The car's unlocked. Go buckle yourself while I talk to Hallie for a minute."

Isla ran off without another word. Christian watched to make sure she got to the car a few feet away.

"Uh..." he muttered once she was inside. He rubbed a hand along the back of his neck as words tumbled through his brain, none spilling from his mouth.

"I'm sorry," Hallie said, beating him to the apology he was attempting to make. "I should've called before coming over the other day. I didn't mean to upset her."

How could she think the incident was her fault? "No, you're ...

fine. Thank you for the cookies. They were gone in a day." His chuckle morphed into an awkward throat clearing.

She smiled, pulling another stuttering response from his heart. "I'm glad they were a hit."

More silence followed, and Christian berated himself for contributing to the weird vibe between them. But after swearing off dating following Sabrina's abandonment, he could hardly be blamed for his lack of practice talking to gorgeous women.

Yikes, did he just consider Hallie gorgeous? She *was* beautiful. But he had no business thinking of Tyler's sister that way. There had to be something in the Guy Code about it.

Rule #34: No making googly eyes at your best friend's sister.

Googly eyes? Yeah, he'd lost it.

"Listen," he said finally, trying to ignore the way his nerve endings zapped out of control. His eyes strayed toward the car to check on Isla. He could barely make out the silhouette of her frizzy curls in the backseat. "About the other day. I'm the one who's sorry. Isla had a horrible day at school and—"

"Really, it's okay." Hallie held his gaze, and he couldn't look away from her captivating blue eyes. "Adults have big emotions too. We can't expect a child to know how to handle their feelings if we also struggle with them."

Who was this woman? She'd practically recited a direct quote from Isla's therapist. Did she have some invisible Cyrano de Bergerac camping out in the bushes somewhere, telling her what to say? Every word emerging from her mouth had the effect of easing the burden Christian had carried for years. How did she do that?

He blew out a heavy breath. "She didn't used to be this difficult. But then her mom..." He stopped himself. Just because Hallie had shown some unexpected kindness didn't mean she wanted—or needed—the entire life story of his children.

Goosebumps scattered across his skin when she placed her hand on his arm, and his heart pounded.

"You don't owe me an explanation." She gave his arm a light squeeze before letting go, leaving Christian wishing she'd keep it there a little longer. He followed her attention to the rest of her group occupying comfy chairs inside the salon. "I should go."

Did he detect some hesitation in her voice? Was he wrong to think of it as reluctance to leave their conversation?

Of course you are. He'd barely said anything to her. Why would she rather stay out here with him?

"Me too," he said, pushing that thought far away where it belonged. "Isla will start shouting out the window any minute now."

Hallie laughed, the sound light and void of the discomfort that plagued *his* body. "Where's your other little one?"

"Penelope."

"That's cute. Where's Penelope?"

"She's with my sister. I try to take the girls out on their own sometimes to give them some individual attention." Again with the unnecessary info dump.

"That's really nice." A whimsical smile came over Hallie's features. "I'm sure they love it."

The break in conversation offered the perfect exit opportunity. But neither of them made any move to leave until the sound of a car door opening cut through the evening.

Isla's head popped out of the back seat. "Daddy! I'm hungry! My tummy is making noises."

He squeezed his eyes shut. "That's my cue."

Amusement flashed across Hallie's face when he opened them. "You shouldn't keep her waiting. My mom used to say that once the tummy starts making noises, it means the stomach monster is emerging from its cave, ready to eat everything in its path. You might be next."

A sharp crack of laughter burst from Christian's gut, prompting another gorgeous smile from her. His heart rate kicked up a few more notches. Dang, when was the last time a woman smiled at him like that?

"Daddy!"

Isla's voice snapped the bubble of enjoyment growing inside him, and he actually jumped. He shot an annoyed side-eye toward the car.

"I'll see you around, Christian." A chuckle surrounded Hallie's words. She hesitated briefly before stepping past him to grab the door to the nail salon.

He turned, watching her walk down the center aisle inside until a row of oversized chairs blocked her from view. Standing on the curb for a long moment, he tried to still his racing breaths while his thoughts spun in an endless loop of confusion.

For some reason, Hallie stirred up so many feelings he hadn't experienced since his marriage ended. Long before, perhaps. Was it simply because for the first time in years he hadn't been expected to solve anything? Instead of demanding he provide an explanation for his daughter's behavior, she'd given him a pass instead?

Or did his reaction to her stem from an entirely different reason? A more sentimental reason? One from the heart?

What do you think, Dad?

He was only left with his own terror that it might be the latter.

Chapter Twelve

The smells of popcorn and Christian's childhood hovered in the air at the Autumn Festival a week later. On both sides of a marked walkway, booths selling everything from fall crafts to artwork to candles filled the soccer field behind Buena Hills' community center. Metal poles wrapped in burlap stood between each vendor, white lights and colorful maple leaves twining around them to provide more illumination once the sun went down.

Festive music mingled with kids' laughter and shouts of glee, stirring up memories of attending this same event with his parents and sister years ago. He used to love how Dad would whisk him off to play carnival games. It hadn't dawned on Christian back then that his father always let him win. The realization of that now put an additional sting on his absence.

Sadly, they'd stopped coming to this event after Dad died. A lot of things went away during that horrible year. Christian suspected it was just too difficult for Mom to face all those happy memories she'd had with her husband. And once she'd come to terms with her new reality, this particular tradition had already been buried underneath the others she no longer had time for with raising her kids on her own. Boy did he relate.

Holding onto his daughters' hands, he browsed a booth selling hand-crafted jewelry. If he'd known he'd spend the whole time missing Dad, he wouldn't have come. Today, as it had many times in the almost-six years since Isla's birth, the unfairness of it all hit him. Dad wouldn't be around to see the girls grow up. And Isla and Penelope were being deprived of knowing a man who'd love them with every piece of his soul.

But it wasn't only his father's absence plaguing Christian's emotions today. What bothered him almost as much was how much Sabrina would've loved the Autumn Festival.

No, Dating Sabrina would've loved it.

He often referred to his ex in stages. Dating Sabrina was all sunshine and blue skies while frolicking in fields of daisies.

Not that Christian had, or would. ever frolic. But that was beside the point.

Next came Married Sabrina, where that field became a little rockier. Once Pregnant Sabrina entered the chat, their whole relationship had been thrown off a cliff.

Was it insensitive to think of her that way? Maybe. But it kept him from diving too deep in analyzing what went wrong. Channeling the anger in his heart prevented him from dwelling on how much her abandonment still hurt.

Penelope tugged on his arm, slipping her small hand from his grip. Christian latched on again. "You need to stay here, Nell. There are too many people around for you to wander."

"I'na go over dere." She jabbed a finger toward the booths on the other side of the soccer field. "I see toys."

Christian could see the booth of handmade wooden toys from where they stood. "We'll go over there in a minute."

He tightened his hold on her hand. He'd rather not spend the next hour searching for his kid. *I should've brought the stroller.* But the soccer field was so packed it would be difficult to maneuver it through the crowds. He wouldn't be surprised if Buena Hills' entire population, plus the surrounding suburbs, had decided to show up on opening day.

"Oooh, I like this one." Isla pointed at a gaudy mood ring in one of the displays. "Look at the swirly colors!"

He gave the ring a passing glance. "I think it's too big for you, kiddo." She didn't need any more useless stuff. It would surely end up in her pile of forgotten junk two days from now.

"I know," Isla said with a shrug. She moved to a display of beaded bracelets. "This one's pretty too."

As he looked at where she pointed, Penelope managed to free her sweaty hand from his grasp.

"Nellie!" Christian called after her, but she slipped through a gap of people, blocking her from view. Hastily, he grabbed onto Isla, tugging her away from the jewelry. "Come on."

They left the booth. His heart pounded as they crossed the central path toward the toys, skipping several beats when he didn't see any sign of her. Seriously, where could she have gone in only a second?

Hurrying his steps, he scanned both sides of the path, relief flooding his senses when he spotted her two booths past where they'd come. She stretched on her tiptoes, reaching toward a crate of cookies. Man, that girl was quick.

"Come here, you little cookie monster," he play-growled, plucking her off the ground. He tossed her in the air, and her infectious giggle cut through the commotion around them.

As he caught her and pretended to gobble her cheeks, awareness pricked at the back of his neck. Shifting his daughter to one arm, he took a good look at his surroundings, realizing for the first time whose cookies Penelope had attempted to snitch.

Christian's heart thumped against his chest. He hadn't stopped thinking of Hallie since their conversation outside the nail salon last Friday. Why did seeing her cause him such a gut reaction? She'd told him herself she'd have a booth this weekend. Had that been the reason he'd brought the girls in the first place?

Don't encourage this, he reprimanded himself even as his feet brought him closer to the table of baked goods.

Hallie stood behind it, a soft smile on her lovely face as she watched him approach. He tried squashing the subtle stirrings taking root in his heart. This strange preference to his buddy's sister couldn't make him surrender the choke hold around the organ. Doing so would only bring more pain he didn't need and certainly didn't want.

Speaking of that best friend, Tyler stood a few feet away, chatting with an older couple who looked familiar. Maybe Christian had seen them around town. The woman carried most of the conversation, her ginger bob bouncing as she talked. None of them noticed Isla surveying the sweets, her nose inches from a display of cakes sealed in plastic containers.

Confident that she wouldn't wander off, Christian stopped directly in front of Hallie. "You have quite the set up here."

"Thanks. Can I interest you in something sweet?" Her tone held a slight teasing quality, and she swept her arm above the orange-and-white checkered tablecloth filled with pumpkin bread, cupcakes, and other sweets. Three wooden crates of cookies took up the right side, each set at varying heights created by small hay bales. Leaning into the whole fall theme, she'd scattered miniature pumpkins around the table. It all looked very ... festive.

"Based on those cookies you dropped off last week, that's a pointless question if you ask me. Which is your favorite."

She opened her mouth to respond but didn't get the chance before the red-haired woman cut into their conversation.

"Hallie, these are simply marvelous," she said, holding up a partly eaten cookie shaped like a maple leaf. "I could eat a dozen of these right now."

Christian stomped down the prickle of annoyance percolating in his gut. He'd finally succeeded in starting a normal conversation with Hallie. Couldn't he have a few minutes to talk to her without being interrupted?

What would it be like if he just pulled her away for a few minutes? Maybe an hour? Isla and Penelope loved Tyler. And he could handle the customers too, right? Getting to know Hallie while browsing the booths together sounded like the perfect way to spend the afternoon.

You shouldn't want to get to know her better. Still, the noose around his heart eased a little more.

"Thank you, Mrs. Hawthorne." Hallie flashed the woman a pleased look. "You've always been one of my favorite customers."

Hawthorne! He knew he'd recognized the woman. She worked in the youth section at the library.

"That's good to hear. We're ecstatic to see the finished order for our Halloween party. Aren't we, Lawrence?" Mrs. Hawthorne leaned toward her husband, her hair brushing forward slightly to reveal the festive leaf clip pinning her locks back from her face.

Mr. Hawthorne mumbled an agreement around a mouthful of his own cookie.

"I'm saving my calories for all the yummy treats." She patted her already plump stomach.

I'm pretty sure caloric intake doesn't work like that. Though Christian secretly loved the way Hallie glowed at the praise the woman gave her cookies. As she should.

Mrs. Hawthorne finally seemed to notice they weren't alone in the booth. "Well, we won't take any more of your time. I think sweet Penelope needs a treat."

"Thanks for coming by," Hallie said to the Hawthornes. "It was good seeing you both."

"You as well," Mrs. Hawthorne waved her cookie in farewell. "We're off to catch the hayride."

Munching on their sweets, the couple walked away, heading in the direction of the community center where the horse-pulled trailer waited out front to take passengers on a leisurely ride down Main Street.

With the booth now empty besides Christian and the girls, Tyler came around the table, holding out his hand. "It's good to see you, man."

Christian accepted the greeting as his friend slapped him on the back.

"Hey, Nellie girl," Tyler cooed in what his wife always deemed his *kid voice*. His face scrunched up as he tickled Penelope's neck, making the child giggle. She lunged forward, and he caught her before she flung herself from Christian's grip.

Securing her in his arms, Tyler reached his closed hand toward Isla. "Pound it." She knocked her smaller fist against his.

After all the times Tyler had come over to help with various house repairs and projects the last few years, he'd become like a favorite uncle to the girls. In fact, Penelope had latched onto him like he was her second dad. Even Isla had taken to him, though her affections were more understated than her energetic sister's.

Tyler had every reason to hold a grudge by the way Christian had pulled away following his and Sabrina's courthouse wedding. He hadn't meant to, really. But he'd been so wrapped up in Sabrina at first, then balancing a new baby while finishing up his degree. Only sheer desperation had driven him to reach out to his former buddy the day he'd returned from work to discover his wife gone for good.

But Tyler had come running with no hesitation at the call, thus solidifying his best friend status. He'd willingly sacrificed precious hours with Gemma during his summer break from Berkeley to help Christian through his grief. And he'd proven his loyalty time after time since then.

Christian didn't only trust him with the girls; he trusted him with *his* life.

"Gemma didn't want to come?" he asked.

Tyler shrugged. "We're bringing Will tomorrow, but today, I'm here for Hallie. She's been taking me to task all afternoon."

"I have not." Hallie gave her brother a look of exasperation that every sister on the planet must have stored in her wheelhouse.

Christian ignored how adorable the expression was on her face. *She's your best friend's sister.* And that wasn't even the biggest reason to stay away. "You should've brought Will. He'd be a nice sales pitch."

She snapped Tyler's arm with the back of her hand. "See! That's what I said."

"I'm not letting you use my son as free advertising." Her brother paired his indignant tone with a cheeky grin, proving that no offense had been taken.

"Why not?" Hallie asked simply. "No one can resist those chubby cheeks."

"That's true."

Isla tugged on the hem of Christian's shirt. "Daddy, can I have a cupcake?"

"Sure, kiddo. Choose whatever you'd like. Nellie can have one too." He nodded at Tyler to help Penelope choose.

Isla stretched onto her tiptoes to get a closer look at the cupcakes on the left half of the tablecloth. "What kind are they?"

Hallie pulled a plastic glove from a box behind her then pointed to the orange-and-white frosting that swirled a good two inches on top of the cupcakes. "These ones are apple spice." She gestured to the ones with the tiny bit of dark cake peeking out from underneath the serrated cone of all-white frosting. A shimmery leaf was pressed to the side of each one. "And these are chocolate."

"Chocolate!" Penelope's voice raised to an almost unnatural pitch, even for her. She bounced excitedly in Tyler's arms.

"A girl after my own heart." Hallie slipped on the glove. She selected a chocolate cupcake, delivering it to Penelope's outstretched hands, before turning to Isla. "And what about for you?"

Isla pointed to the selection of apple spice. "I want that one. The frosting is pretty."

"One with the pretty frosting for the girl with the pretty curls."

A small smile passed over Isla's face as she accepted the offering. Christian searched Hallie's expression for any sign of teasing. Even after the kindness she'd shown his daughter at the nail salon, he had a hard time believing she'd look past the whole kicking incident. Wouldn't someone hold on to that kind of thing? But her countenance showed complete sincerity.

"That'll be eight dollars," Hallie said, catching Christian in his stare.

The warmth in his stomach caused by her gentle eyes on him rose into his chest, radiating outward to his extremities. His breathing challenged his heart to a race. It was anyone's guess which would come out victorious.

"Christian?" She looked at him expectantly, and his name on her tongue snapped him out of his momentary gaze. She had such a lovely voice.

Lovely voice? What a strange thing to be attracted to.

Stop it. "Right, sorry."

Reaching into his back pocket for his wallet, he noticed the orange binder on an easel to the left side of the table. The cover had a picture of an elaborate three-tiered square cake.

Taking a step toward it, he studied the picture even closer. The three layers were shaped and decorated to look like presents wrapped in shimmery paper of alternating pink and blue. A glittery striped bow of the same colors decorated the top layer.

He lifted his eyes to Hallie. "You made this?"

She still watched him, expecting his payment no doubt. But finishing the transaction meant leaving, and he couldn't ignore the overwhelming desire to stay at this booth a little longer.

"I did," she confirmed with a nod. "It was for a gender reveal last year."

"Very impressive."

Her mouth stretched into a stunning smile. She had to stop doing that. "Thanks."

"She made my wedding cake too," Tyler said off-handedly, setting Penelope down to assist the young family entering the booth.

Christian turned back to Hallie. "Did you really?"

"I've improved a lot since then." She shrugged.

"What are you talking about? It was amazing."

Truthfully, he didn't remember the cake. Tyler got married over two years ago. And Christian's head had been filled with too many unpleasant things to recall details from the wedding. The first anniversary of Sabrina's abandonment had loomed, leaving him raw and full of heavy emotions. On top of that, he'd bowed out of all the wedding week festivities besides the actual event because Penelope was sick and teething. He'd left the reception before the newlyweds had even cut the cake.

But he'd give Hallie all the encouragement in the world, even if it meant lying through his teeth. Hopefully, his kids never found out their dad didn't always practice what he preached.

Christian felt Penelope's small hands tug on the back of his shirt and he lifted her into his arms. Chocolate smeared across her face, her hands not much cleaner.

Resigning himself to the impossibility of leaving the festival with a clean shirt himself, he opened the binder. The cake on the first page was shaped like a wooden ship with *Happy Birthday!* scrawled on the sail and a skull and crossbones underneath.

He bent closer to the page to study the details. "This is incredible. It actually looks like a ship. How do you make the wood so lifelike?"

Hallie's cheeks flushed a light pink. "Lots and lots of practice."

He flipped through a few more pages, each cake blowing his mind a little more. Every single one was as detailed as the one before, bringing objects to life in baked form. They reminded Christian of the cakes on *Food Network,* created by bakers with decades of experience. She had just as much talent.

Puffing out a breath, he focused again on Hallie. "I knew you were an amazing baker, but I didn't realize you were an artist too."

"The best ones always are."

"Are you saying you're the best?" he asked, his mouth ticking upward.

Her coy expression was too exaggerated to be real. "That's the goal."

"I have no doubt you'll get there, if you're not already." Christian turned another page of the book, revealing a simple castle with pink turrets, sparking an idea. "Isla, how would you like to have Hallie make your birthday cake this year?"

Isla moved beside him to look at the cake book. "I thought Grandma was making my cake."

"Don't you want something better than one from a box?" No disrespect toward Mom or anything. She was a whiz when it came to cookies, but cakes had never been her strong suit. And Hallie's were, in a word, spectacular. His daughter deserved the best.

Sure, that was the reason nagging at him to hire her.

The *only* reason.

"Really?" Isla asked, her voice full of hope.

"Would you be okay with that?" he asked Hallie. "It's on the twenty-ninth. We'd pay you, of course." Was that a given? He wanted to make it clear he wouldn't expect her to do it for free because of their existing connection.

So much for tightening your wallet. After this purchase, he'd definitely stop splurging until he got his job back on track.

She pursed her lips, drawing Christian's attention to them. He sucked in a breath as the picture of kissing that irresistible mouth popped into his mind.

Nope. Definitely not going there.

He hadn't thought of kissing anyone for years. He forced his eyes away, refusing to start now, especially with Tyler's little sister.

"I should be able to make that work," Hallie said. "Do you have anything specific in mind?"

Isla hopped up and down in her excitement. "I want a really spooky haunted house. With ghosts and witches and a graveyard in the front."

Hallie's blonde eyebrows jumped to her forehead. "Oh my. That'll be … something."

"Isla's a big fan of Halloween," Christian explained.

"I guess you were born in the right month, then." Hallie scrunched her nose at Isla. "Maybe you can help me design something really cool?"

The girl pondered the invitation for a moment before answering. "I think I can do that."

"Awesome." Hallie slid a sheet of paper from a manila envelope, attaching it to a clipboard before handing it to Christian. "This is my order form. I'll call you later to discuss the details. For now, just fill out the top with your contact information and when you'd like the cake ready. And I'll need you to put a deposit down before you leave."

"Sure."

Christian shifted the clipboard into the hand that held Penelope to fill out when he finished flipping through the binder. He stopped on the next page.

"Aw, look at the bunnies, Nellie." He pointed to his youngest daughter's favorite animal, captured mid-hop on top of a forest-themed cake. "Could you … make a cake like this?"

Hallie leaned over the table to see which cake he pointed to. "I did that one, so ... yeah. I could easily recreate it or do something similar."

"Great. We'll add a bunny cake to our order."

Her brows drew together. "Really?"

"Yeah." Christian flipped the page. Before he could stop himself, he made another request. "And while we're at it, let's add this ghost cake too. You know, to stick with the Halloween theme."

What am I doing?

"Dude, how big is this party?" Tyler asked, his hand frozen over the bakery box he was packing with cupcakes.

Not big enough for three cakes, that was for sure. But Christian couldn't stop his mouth from running away from him. It possessed a mind of its own, and he had no say in what came out of it.

Tyler's blue eyes narrowed in an expression of confusion. Or suspicion, perhaps?

Christian's laugh sounded forced even to him. "That should do it."

Hallie blinked several times, apparently too stunned for words. "Um ... okay. How'd you like to pay the deposit?"

"I'll put it on my card and pay for the cupcakes in cash." Setting the clipboard down on the table, he pulled his wallet from his back pocket and handed her a ten-dollar bill.

She placed his money in the cash box on the chair behind her, then turned back to him. "Here's two dollars in change for the cupcakes."

As she placed the bills on his outstretched palm, her fingers brushed his hand. Sparks sizzled up his arm, and he sucked in another breath. His eyes flew to her face, locking with hers, holding her gaze. Time froze, everything around them fading away. Even Penelope seemed to disappear from his arm, leaving a cozy haze surrounding only Hallie and himself.

What was this connection that sparked between them? He couldn't begin to read the expression written across her beautiful features. But she didn't look away.

Finally, after an eternally long minute, she gulped in a lungful of air, yanking her hand away. "Do you want a cookie?" Her voice squeaked. "It's on the house, of course. As a thank you ... for your generous order."

She spun to the side to grab one from a crate, smacking hard into her brother's chest. Tyler bobbled the box of cupcakes in his hand.

"Whoa," he said, righting it before he decorated the astro turf with chocolate and apple spice. "Are you okay?"

Hallie hurried around him to grab a maple leaf cookie. "Yep. Fine. All good."

Did she really believe that? Because after what passed between them just now, Christian was anything but all good.

He felt like the captain of the ship cake from Hallie's portfolio. And he was barreling straight into dangerous waters.

Chapter Thirteen

"He bought three full-sized cakes." Hallie couldn't keep the bewilderment from her voice while recapping Christian's visit to her booth to Kendall and Beej at the conclusion of the Autumn Festival Sunday night. "Three!"

Kendall turned from her closet, shoving a hanger into the sleeve of a sweater. "He must really love cake."

"I doubt it, unless he hides his cake belly well," Hallie said from the bed. "He doesn't exactly have a dad bod underneath his clothes." Warmth raced across her face. She'd never actually seen the state of his stomach, but her imagination was forming a very nice image of chiseled abs to compliment his tall, trim figure.

Do not entertain that picture. She resisted the urge to feel her cheeks, hoping the direction her mind had taken didn't show on her face.

"Hello ... isn't it obvious?" Beej looked at them both like they were clueless teens in need of direction only she could provide.

Kendall flipped a pair of dress pants over the bottom of a hanger and hung it in the closet. "Isn't what obvious?"

Beej forced out a groan. "Do you know nothing about basic human attraction?"

"Is everything always about dating for you?" Kendall shot back with the same inflection.

Pushing her friend's wadded up pjs to the corner of the bed, Beej pulled her legs into a crisscross position. Kendall wasn't a complete slob—she contributed a lot to the cleanliness of their shared living spaces. But her bedroom was an experiment in controlled chaos. She had her various piles on her desk, her bed, and shoved in her closet, though she always knew exactly where everything was. Her organizational style clashed with Hallie's need to have a place for all her belongings though they'd lived together long enough that their differences didn't matter. At least as long as the piles stayed out of the rest of the house.

"I've dated a lot, *as you know*." Beej added a sarcastic spin to the last few words, an acknowledgement of the way the family lovingly teased her about her dating habits. "But I've picked up a thing or two about how guys act. He's interested."

"No, he's not." Hallie looked at her cousin like she'd sprouted two heads. "He hardly talks to me when we're together. He's not exactly screaming his undying devotion to me."

Her doubts failed to dampen her cousin's enthusiasm. "He's probably nervous. With two kids, I'd imagine his dating opportunities aren't exactly plentiful. Maybe he was showing his interest in the only way he knew how."

"By spending close to five hundred dollars on baked goods?"

Not likely. Christian seemed like a rational guy. Even if there was any interest on his part, she couldn't imagine him spending that kind of money.

And yet, he did, proving Hallie knew absolutely nothing about him.

"It's possible." Beej's upper body shimmied in her spot on the purple bedspread. The idea of someone—anyone—making a love connection always made her giddy. "I'd jump on that."

Hallie hoped her cousin didn't mean anything beyond taking advantage of the chance to date him, but with Beej, she couldn't be completely sure. "I can't *jump on that*. Even if Christian did like me, nothing can ever come from it. He has kids."

Besides, Tyler had already warned her not to get too close to his best friend. He'd been on the verge of bringing it up again yesterday. He didn't actually say anything, but Hallie could feel the worry radiating off him once Christian and the girls left the booth.

"So what if he has kids." Beej tossed one of Kendall's pillows in Hallie's direction. You've said you wanted to be a mom eventually."

Hallie threw up her hands. "Not right now. It would be irresponsible to start something with him when I know I'm not ready for that kind of commitment."

"Why do you insist on doing the practical thing all the time?" Beej asked, in close to the same exasperated tone Hallie had used. "If you ask me, you have a golden opportunity here. We know he's good with kids. That'll serve you later when you're ready to—" She cupped a hand around her mouth, lowering her voice to a stage whisper "—take things to the next level."

"Why are you whispering?" Kendall asked, sticking her empty laundry basket in the closet before sliding the door closed.

"I don't want to jinx it."

Hallie huffed out a sigh. "You're not jinxing anything because there won't be a next level."

Her cousin might be okay with raising someone else's kids. Even though she already had a fulfilling career as a pediatric nurse, her biggest aspiration in life was to find her soul mate and birth a gaggle of chubby cheeked kids. Hallie wanted that too ... eventually. But taking on the responsibility of children had never been part of her perfect dating scenario.

Not that she had a perfect dating scenario, but if she did, kids wouldn't be in it.

Besides, what happened to the girls' actual mother? Was Christian widowed? Divorced? Did he share custody with an ex? The possibility of having to coparent with another woman gave Hallie serious red flags about the matter.

Which was a good thing, really. She had all she could manage getting her business off the ground. Dating in general would be too difficult, especially once she got her real bakery. She wouldn't have time for kids if she spent her whole life at work.

Then why did the memory of him playing with Penelope or the gentle way he talked to Isla stir up warm fuzzies inside her?

And what about the sparks that flew up her arm when their hands touched? She'd had a few boyfriends over the years, and none of them had ever caused such an instant reaction to an accidental hand touch. Maybe her body was rebelling against Christian's off-limits status.

Off-limits. Yes, she needed to keep reminding herself of that.

Hallie rose from the bed, tossing the pillow onto the mattress. "We're jumping to major conclusions here. Maybe he's just throwing a really big party."

Beej flipped onto her stomach and slid her cousin's abandoned pillow under her chest. "Big enough for three cakes? That would be A LOT of kids."

"Sounds awful." Kendall shuddered.

She wasn't as anti-kids as her comment made her sound, but she'd been very vocal in the past about not wanting them. Especially since she adamantly claimed she had no intention of ever getting married.

"Why be shackled to a loser when I can live my life the way I want on my own?" she always asked whenever their conversations steered toward men. It would take a very secure man to break through Kendall's fierce independence. Not that she needed one to be happy. But if the right man wanted to win her heart, he'd have his work cut out for him.

"I should call Christian and give him a chance to back out of the order." Hallie sighed. She could really use the money those cakes would bring into her business. Still, she didn't feel right about being the cause of his buyer's remorse.

Beej's eyes lit up and she sat up a little straighter. "Or you could put that poor man out of his misery and ask him on a date."

"I will *not* be doing that," Hallie said as she rose from the bed and headed for the door. "And before you say it, you better not find a way to stalk him to do it for me." She knew her cousin too well.

Without turning back to witness Beej's reaction, she stepped into the hall. The jitters returned to her stomach as she reached her own room. Perhaps settled wasn't the right word, though. Her nerves were performing complicated steps like a whole company of tap dancers. She'd never been this nervous to call a customer before. But Christian wasn't any customer. Against her better judgment, he might be rivaling the Hawthornes as her favorite.

She grabbed her binder full of client contact forms and plopped down on her bed. Foxie, standing sentinel in her usual spot right by Hallie's pillow, fell over with the sudden movement.

After locating Christian's order form, she dialed his number, stopping before initiating the call.

Her finger hovered over the screen as she blew out a breath to calm the stomach flutters. Before she could talk herself out of it, she jabbed at the green call button. Immediately, she second guessed her decision not to wait until morning to contact him. It was after nine o'clock. He could be putting the girls to bed. What time did kids that age even go to sleep?

As her brain began forming the message she'd leave once his voicemail kicked in, she heard a click on the line.

"Hello?"

The flutters took on a new round of dances as the deep timbre of Christian's voice vibrated all the way down to her core. How could one word sound so sensual?

Sensual?

Ugh ... Absolutely not.

"Hey, Christian. It's Hallie. Sorry to bother you so late. Is this a bad time?"

"No, I just got Isla to bed." A hint of fatigue touched his voice. "What's up?"

Hallie bit her lip, unsure of how to bring up her concerns. "I'd like to double check your order."

"What's the problem?"

"There's no problem." She hurried to explain. "Three cakes is just kind of a lot, more than most people order for a single party. I wanted to make sure you still wanted them all."

"Is it too much work for you?" he asked, and Hallie immediately picked up on the hesitation in his voice. Oh man, did he think she was lazy now, like she couldn't handle making that many cakes?

She lifted her shoulders to her ears then lowered them again, hoping the movement would relax the tension seizing her body and slow her mouth. "No, of course not. I'm not bothered by the work. Obviously, there is a time constraint. It takes several hours to make one cake, with the baking and the assembly and the decorating. But I can figure that out. I'm more concerned about the cost. And what would you even *do* with that many cakes?"

A soft chuckle cut through the line. "Do you always analyze your customers' orders?"

Great, she *was* analyzing. How unprofessional and inappropriate. What he did with the cakes was none of her business.

"Before you write your scathing review, citing your atrocious customer service experience, let me tell you that no, it isn't like me to question what my clients order. But I also haven't had anyone spend almost five hundred dollars on only cakes."

"What can I say? I'm just extra," he deadpanned.

Hallie swallowed the snort trying to force its way out, which only caused her to choke on her spit.

"Are you okay?" he asked, sounding like he was also having a hard time holding back his amusement.

Thumping herself on the chest, she cleared out the liquid invading her trachea. "Yep. I'm great." She coughed. "I can't picture you ever being extra."

"Isla must be rubbing off on me. She comes home frequently with new words. I didn't realize the use of slang started so early. She's only in kindergarten. They're still working on learning grammar. Sure, it's a great idea to throw in a bunch of generational colloquialisms."

This time, Hallie couldn't rein in her laughter.

A metallic thump clattered from Christian's end of the line, followed by a rhythmic humming that sounded like a dryer. Her heart thudded. Thinking of him doing domestic things like laundry provided a strangely attractive picture.

Sheesh, what was wrong with her? Everyone did laundry. She needed a serious reality check.

"The girls seemed to be enjoying themselves when you stopped by my booth yesterday," she said, partly to prevent her brain from inserting herself into that picture of domestic bliss. Dropping onto her stomach on her bed to get comfier, she kicked her feet up behind her.

"They loved it, especially the hayride. No surprise there." The whirring in the background grew softer as if he'd moved away from the dryer. "It was always one of my favorite parts. Not much has changed, actually. The whole thing brought back a lot of memories."

"Good ones, I hope."

A long pause followed. "Mostly. Being reminded of my dad always makes me sad, especially when I think about my girls never getting to know him."

Hallie's heart hitched at the subtle reminder of their conversation in the car. "That must be really hard." She couldn't imagine having to live without either one of her parents.

"Yeah." A heaviness crackled across the line. "But things got better after a bit. It was kind of fun being there with the girls. I'm sure they'll beg me to take them next year."

"Of course they will. It's the happening place to be."

"Apparently." Christian's quiet chuckle brought a smile to Hallie's face. "How did today go for you? Anyone crazy enough to top my order?"

"I wish. I'd be so much closer to my bakery if that happened. At this rate I'll be retirement age by the time I save enough."

"I'm sure you'll get there before then."

"Let's hope." Hallie's eyes stretched wide. "Wow. I don't know what came over me. Telling a client about my financial struggles is completely unprofessional. I totally deserve that scathing review now."

He laughed again, and Hallie's cheeks hurt from all the grinning she'd been doing during this conversation. Not only was he highly intelligent, a good dad, and one of the most gorgeous guys she'd ever met, she could add a quick wit to his list of attractive qualities. Was it any reason her crush grew every time they were together?

No. Maybe the one-word reprimand would succeed in putting her heart back in its place. Because every other gentle reminder hadn't done the trick.

"Tell you what, I won't slam you on the Better Business Bureau if you'll stop referring to me as a client," he said. "Think of me as more of a business consultant. I am taking care of your website, after all. I can't effectively work for you if I don't have first-hand knowledge of the products you sell."

"I guess I'll have to keep baking for you." Yikes, did that sound flirty? *Please, for the love of all the pastries in the world, stop talking!*

"I wouldn't say no." He let that hang in the air for a few seconds. "Speaking of baking, what're you doing tomorrow?"

Thank goodness, a safe topic. "I'm working on marketing and event research. And I have a client call to make. Why do you ask?"

Silence sizzled between them.

"Christian?"

He cleared his throat, then responded quickly. "Doyouwantto-comeover?"

"What?" So much for a safe topic.

"To talk about Isla's cake?" he hurried to clarify.

Hallie didn't normally do house calls with clients. And with the way her heart was overreacting toward him, it wouldn't be smart to give herself the opportunity to fall head over heels for him. Sticking to the normal protocol of sending designs by email for feedback would be best.

"Sure. That sounds great." Wait! Those words weren't supposed to come from her mouth. She pinched her nose with the fingers of her free hand. Great, now her mouth was in cahoots with her heart. They were both fired.

"Awesome," Christian said. "I'm picking up the girls from their after-school care at five. Would five-thirty be good for you?"

No.

Not good.

Not good at all.

"Sure, sounds great."

"Perfect. It's a date then." He cleared his throat again. "I mean, not a *date* date. A business date. A meeting."

The mention of a date sent Hallie's insides jumping on an inflatable bouncy house. They were still doing flips when she hung up the phone shortly after, and she stared at the call log for several long minutes, wondering what just happened. The timestamp listed their phone conversation as lasting for forty-five minutes.

Forty-five minutes?

She'd made a lot of calls in the three years since starting Hallie's Cakes, and not once had she spoken on the phone with a client for that long. And she'd never enjoyed any of them as much as this one.

The screen went dark, waking her from her temporary daze. She tapped the phone to light it up again and opened a new contact. She'd need to reach out to Christian again for feedback on the other cakes he'd ordered, so she put a permanent place for him in her phone.

And that was the *only* reason, though she couldn't explain why she labeled his number as *Christian: My favorite client.*

Chapter Fourteen

The prospect of having a woman over for the first time in three years forced Christian to take a hard look at the state of his house.

Technically, Hallie wouldn't be the first woman to ever step foot inside the front door since Sabrina left. Mom and Dani made frequent visits. And sometimes Gemma accompanied Tyler when he came over too.

But those women didn't cause his heart to beat against his rib cage in its attempt to leap from his body. This visit felt different.

And why would that be?

He refused to consider the reasons. Still, what he learned in his panic-induced assessment was that he couldn't let Hallie see his place like this. He wasn't a slob, per se. There were just only so many hours in the day. Between caring for the girls, earning a living, and all the baggage that came with that, the house fell to the bottom of his priority list on more days than not.

Perhaps it was time to hire a cleaning lady to take that burden off his hands. Of course, that wouldn't do him any good right now. Hallie was due any minute to discuss Isla's cake. Nothing but his own desperate attempts to straighten up would save him this time.

"What you doing, Daddy?" Penelope asked, kicking her legs against her booster seat while she and Isla finished their goldfish crackers and string cheese. They both stared at him as if emptying the sink of dirty dishes was an unusual task.

"I'm cleaning up a bit." Christian strode over to the table, tripping over Princess Pumpkin—again—as she got under his feet. She didn't know what to do with all the nervous energy buzzing in the house. She flitted around, barking like she couldn't contain her anticipation that something exciting was about to happen.

Exciting? Or terrifying?

"Isla, after you finish your snack, I need you to help Nellie take the toys in the living room upstairs."

Isla mumbled something through the crackers in her mouth. Little bits of orange crumbs flew onto the table.

"I didn't catch that," he said, making a mental note to wipe it down when he finished the dishes. "Chew and swallow your food and try again." Unclipping Penelope's booster seat, he set her down on the floor. "Go take your toys upstairs."

She sped from the room.

Isla washed her snack down with a drink of water. "Can I help with the cake?"

"Sure, it's your cake. Ugh ... Pumpkin." His groan sounded more like a growl when the dog zipped by him, knocking one of his legs out from under him. Lurching forward, he braced his free hand against the sink to catch himself, miraculously holding onto the stack of dishes in his other arm. "Don't you have somewhere better to be?"

While Isla brought her snack plate to the sink, Christian retrieved the giant dog bone laying on the floor by the back door. He held it up for Pumpkin to sniff, then tossed it onto her bed. The retriever trotted over, took it in her mouth, and got comfortable in the cotton-covered memory foam.

High-pitched squeals of laughter from the other room reached his ears. The girls were not taking his instructions seriously. They'd probably stopped to play with the toys instead of taking them upstairs. At least they were occupied, allowing him to tackle a couple more tasks before Hallie arrived. The rest would have to be good enough.

He jammed Isla's snack plate onto the top rack of the dishwasher in the only spot it would fit. This wasn't the most organized loading job. It fell under the pack-as-many-dishes-in-as-he-could method, so Hallie wouldn't see how many days he'd gone without doing them. Sliding the rack inside, he bent over to make sure the height of the dishes cleared the spray arm.

Success.

The doorbell rang as he fumbled under the sink for a detergent pod. Christian's heart jumped to his throat. *Keep it cool, man.* Hallie was here for Isla, not for him. Even though the idea of having Hallie in his living space was setting off romantic notions in his brain.

Romantic notions?

Absolutely not.

Princess Pumpkin launched into another round of excited barking. Abandoning her bone, her feet slid on the hardwood as she raced toward the living room.

He started the dishwasher, the machine whirring to life with a swooping hiss. Then he wiped his hands with the towel hanging over the stove before leaving the kitchen.

"Stop it, Pumpkin," he said exasperatedly, entering the living room. "Do you want to scare off our guest?"

The dog alternated between frantic barks and high-pitched whimpering, pawing at the front door like that would make it open.

Crossing the living room with wide strides, he picked up Penelope's shoes, the jacket he'd discarded upon entering the house, and a few random toys scattered on the floor. He dumped the pile into Isla's arms. "Take these upstairs."

"But Daddy," she whined. "I wanted to open the door."

Christian held up a finger. "Just toss them on my bed. We'll sort through them later. Then you can come back down."

She huffed as she stomped up the stairs. He cast a tired glance at the ceiling, shaking his head. *Just wait until she's a teenager.*

Another knock interrupted that unsettling thought. "Okay, okay. I'm coming," he muttered.

Approaching the entryway, he pulled Pumpkin back, holding her by the collar to prevent her from accosting Hallie. But once he opened the door, his nerves deflated like a limp balloon.

"Geez, what took you so long?" Tyler asked, holding Will. "Pumpkin was about to have a conniption from barking so much." He gave the dog's head a good rub with his free hand. "Weren't you, girl?"

Pumpkin went wild, sniffing and pawing at Tyler with short, happy barks.

Taking advantage of his friend's distraction, Christian stepped one foot onto the porch to check for Hallie. Besides his Highlander in the driveway and Tyler's Honda parked behind it, the only other car in sight was a decades-old pickup belonging to the teenaged son of the neighbor across the street.

He came back inside and shut the door. "What're you doing here?"

Tyler followed him further into the room. "I'm on my way home from picking this little guy up from daycare." He bounced his son a bit, drawing a giggle from Will. "I figured it's been a while since I've checked in."

Christian worked hard to keep his eyes from rolling. It wasn't abnormal for his friend to come over on his way home from work. But usually, he texted first. The unexpected visit put Christian on edge.

"So ... what's up?" he asked, trying not to let his annoyance show. Hallie would be here any minute, and he'd rather Tyler not be around when she arrived, though he didn't stop to consider why the idea bothered him.

Tyler made himself right at home on the sofa. "I should ask you the same question." He set Will on the carpet, and the infant scooted on his bottom toward the girls' play kitchen set up underneath the front window.

Christian narrowed his eyes. "What do you mean?"

"Like you don't know? Three cakes? What's going on with you and my sister?"

Christian almost groaned. Not the cakes again. He'd already spent most of Saturday night replaying how much of a fool he'd made of himself with that situation. Not to mention the cost of those cakes. He had no idea custom cakes were so expensive.

"I get it, my sister's an amazing baker," Tyler continued when Christian didn't respond. "But no person in their right mind would order that many cakes for a six-year-old's birthday party. And let's not forget about how you offered to build her website for free..."

Hallie must've told him about that. Christian shrugged,

attempting to play it off as no big deal. "She seems like she could use the support."

"Uh huh. Sure."

Christian dropped beside his friend on the couch. "Ty, we're just friends. Not even friends. Acquaintances, really. Nothing more."

Is that what you want to be, though?

Seriously? He didn't appreciate his brain's third degree. Of course it was what he wanted. Sure, he'd thought about pulling her away from her booth on Saturday for an informal date at the Autumn Festival. And if he were being honest, he'd wondered if she'd be open to the idea of going out with him.

But no. They could never be anything more than friends.

Besides, he couldn't jump to conclusions. Just because Hallie had brought him cookies and showed so much kindness toward his daughters didn't mean she reciprocated his feelings. She seemed like the type of woman who treated everyone that way.

"You know I'm not ready to date again." Why was he working so hard to explain himself? "I don't think I'll ever be."

Any notions he'd had about the existence of unbreakable romantic love scurried out the door the day his marriage ended. He'd let that belief slip the last few days with this ill-advised crush on Hallie. Now was the best time to recommit.

Tyler's shoulders relaxed and he slouched into the couch cushion. "You know I love you like a brother. But Hallie's my actual sister. I don't want to see her get hurt because you can't give her what she needs."

They were on the same page on that score. "Trust me, I'm not stringing her along. I promise you that."

It wasn't just about his lack of trust in love. He was a father now. Every decision he made had to be done with his girls in mind. He couldn't even go on a date with a woman without considering their well-being. These romantic thoughts about Hallie had to stop.

Outside, a car door slammed. Speaking of Hallie...

Electricity sparked in his veins. Obviously, the reminder he'd just given himself about not getting carried away with her hadn't had time to sink in.

And in the next instant, an opposite, yet equally strong, charge engulfed him. Tyler had warned him to stay away from his sister, and not five minutes later, she showed up at his house?

Not good. Not good at all.

Christian glanced at his friend as the knock came at the door.

Oh boy. Things were about to go down.

Chapter Fifteen

Clutching the handle of her crossbody bag, Hallie waited on Christian's porch for someone to open the door. Heat raced up her spine, and she squeezed her eyes shut to focus on blocking out the repeated barking coming from inside the house.

You can do this. She untangled one hand from her bag's handle and wiped her clammy palm on her jeans. *Christian won't let it hurt you.*

"Easy, girl," Christian said as the door opened.

Hallie's eyes flew wide. Was her terror that obvious?

It only took a second to realize he'd been talking to the dog. His head appeared at waist level from behind the door, but he rose as much as he could while still latched to the collar. "Hey, thanks for coming."

"Sure." Hallie stepped inside, casting nervous glances at the retriever straining against Christian's hold, her tail whipping from side to side like the old-fashioned metronome her grandma used to have sitting on her piano. Back and forth, back and forth. If Hallie's anxiety level wasn't at an unnatural high, the motion would've lulled her into a peaceful contentment.

As the situation stood, contentment wouldn't be achieved today.

"Sorry, she loves people," Christian said. "Have a seat while I take her out back."

She gave him a tight smile, though she didn't breathe until he and the dog had retreated several steps away. His path from the living room led him past the couch where her brother, of all people, shot him a glare. Christian returned it with a glance that Hallie couldn't even begin to interpret.

This looks bad. VERY bad.

Had Tyler known that Hallie planned to come over today? Or was this just a horribly timed drop by to check on his friend?

"Hey, Ty. What're you—"

A crash and a squeal distracted her from finishing the question. She turned to find her nephew pulling the baskets of plastic fruit off the pink kitchen set underneath the front window. She hurried over to him, her unease over Tyler's presence dissipating for the moment.

"How's my little Williekins?" She scooped him up, hugging him tightly.

Offering her one of his gummy smiles, Will brought his chubby hand to her face, attempting to shove his fingers into her mouth. She showered it with kisses instead.

Tyler made his way over to her. "I'm surprised to see you here." That sounded almost like an accusation.

"Relax, Ty." She may have tolerated his overprotective side as a seventeen-year-old, but at twenty-four, she was over it. Shouldn't she, a full-fledged adult, be trusted to make her own decisions about the men she spent time with? "I'm only here to work on Isla's cake. You can drop the whole bodyguard visage."

Her brother's eyebrows jumped up his forehead. "I'm just watching out for you."

"Really, it's fine." Hallie glanced toward the kitchen to make sure Christian wasn't about to enter the room. "I haven't forgotten your warning. And what I told you still stands. I'm not—"

Thumping footsteps on the staircase behind the couch interrupted her assurances. "Tyler! Tyler!"

Penelope barreled toward them, her wispy brown hair bouncing around her shoulders. Isla walked a few paces behind her. Tyler caught the younger girl right before she collided with his legs.

"Hey, sweet pea!" Tyler kissed the girl's cheek.

"You stay for dinner, Uncle Tyler?" Penelope asked, her little voice slurring the r's and l.

He tapped the little girl's nose with his pointer finger. "Sorry. I have to get dinner on at my own house. I only stopped by to see my two favorite girls." He squeezed Isla's shoulder.

The girl tilted her head to the side, studying Hallie. "Are you related to Tyler?"

"He's my brother."

"And we're making my cake today?" she asked, as though that were the only acceptable reason for Hallie to cross into her domain.

"Well..." Hallie attempted to find words to explain her purpose here. "I won't do the baking today. But I've come up with a starting design that I want to show you. Maybe you can help me make it better."

Isla seemed to accept that answer and walked to the couch. She sat down, lifting her legs into a crisscross position, then looked at Hallie with expectant bossiness.

Okay then. Hallie passed Will off to her brother—who set Penelope down to accept his son—and joined Isla at the couch.

When the three-year-old dragged Tyler up the stairs, chattering about the dolls in her room, Hallie felt the quiet that followed deep in her core. She resisted the urge to drum her fingertips against her thigh as Isla continued to watch her with equal parts curiosity and skepticism.

Where was Christian? How long could it take to put the dog outside? It was one thing to talk to his kids at the Autumn Festival when he'd been right there. He'd guided the interaction, and Hallie knew how to act when there were baked goods involved. Without him, she didn't know the first thing about children.

Thankfully, Christian reentered the front room then, restoring her breath. A frazzled gleam pierced his eye. "Sorry about that. I had to refill Pumpkin's water bowl. And then my neighbor stopped by to ... chat. Did Tyler leave?"

Hallie didn't miss the relief that entered his posture at the possibility. *I wish.* "He's upstairs with Penelope. I was about to show Isla the sketch I made for her cake."

Christian sat down next to her. "You came prepared."

"It's just an idea." She slid a file folder from her bag. Inside was a single sheet of paper, which she handed to him. "Anything about it can be changed or adapted to fit what Isla wants." Turning to the girl, she flashed what she hoped was a friendly smile. "The birthday girl should always get what she wants."

Some of the wariness left Isla's face.

"Well, I have to go," Tyler said, returning from upstairs.

Both Hallie and Christian swiveled in their seats to face him. Sparks zipped across her leg when her knee brushed his.

Tyler had Will in one arm and Penelope in the other, though he set the girl on the floor once they'd reached the downstairs landing. He stopped short, his attention bouncing between Hallie and Christian. She stared back, trying not to appear guilty.

Seriously, she had nothing to feel guilty about. So why was she holding her breath?

Finally, Isla reached over Hallie to snatch the sketch off Christian's lap. "Can we talk about my cake now?"

That snapped the awkward spell hanging over the adults, and Tyler headed for the door.

"I'll leave you to it then. But remember, I'm watching you both." Touching two fingers to his temple, he flicked them forward in a peace sign salute.

Kill. Me. Now.

It was just like her brother to deliver one last warning in the cringiest way possible.

To make matters even more mortifying, he signaled for Christian to join him in the entryway. The men exchanged a few words that Hallie couldn't hear but a look passed between them that made her wish she was the lucky one leaving.

Once Tyler and Will had stepped outside, Christian shut the door, keeping his back to her. She watched his shoulders go up and down as he took a deep breath. Then slowly, he pivoted to face the room.

"I'm sorry my brother is so weird," she hurried to get out before he said anything. "He was totally out of line. I hope you know I don't ... like you ... that way."

Oh shoot, did she just make things worse? Maybe she should've just pretended the whole thing never happened. Not to mention the little fib she just told.

The air sparked with tension when he met her gaze. And it had nothing to do with Isla sitting next to her or Penelope banging around at the play kitchen.

Christian cleared his throat. "Don't worry about it." He scrubbed a hand across the back of his neck, scrunching his nose as if he didn't know what else to say. The look was oddly ... hot.

Why did everything he did end up being attractive as all get out, even when he clearly wasn't meaning to be?

Get a grip, girl.

Perhaps his hotness stemmed from the fact that he was one-hundred-and-fifty percent off-limits. For multiple reasons, not just because her brother said so. And yes, she realized the possibility of getting over a hundred percent didn't exist in this scenario. But seriously, it had never been this difficult to ignore a connection with a man.

Christian approached the couch, and all she could do was stare. "So, about that cake..." he said.

Right, the cake. She gave her head a little shake. "Of course, that's why I'm here. The cake." Because why not make things more awkward by restating his exact words. Beej would eat this story up when they rehashed it later. There weren't enough facepalm emojis in the world to cover this unfortunate moment.

Isla seemed to be devouring the drawing in her lap when Hallie turned back to her. "What do you think? We can keep any details you want, or scrap the whole thing—"

She stopped mid-sentence when Christian's thigh brushed against hers as he sat down beside her. Electricity tripped up her leg at the light touch.

Her head whirled toward him. Their eyes met and his shot wide. As one, they jumped apart.

With Isla on her other side, Hallie didn't have much space to go. Christian, on the other hand, landed on the opposite side of the couch, leaving at least a foot between them. Lots of nervous fidgeting accompanied the next few long seconds.

"Look, Daddy." Isla held the sketch up for Christian to see. "I don't think Grandma could do anything like this."

He took the paper from her, going to great lengths not to brush his arm against any part of Hallie's body. "You came up with all this in less than twenty-four hours?" he asked, studying the drawing.

The pencil sketch included a simple outline of a rickety old house set behind a field of tombstones with a few bones poking out of the dirt. Some ghosts danced around the outer walls of the structure, and a twisted tree with a broomstick stuck in its leafless branches tied the whole thing together.

"I can't take all the credit." Directing her comments to Isla felt much safer to Hallie than having to look at Christian's face. That attractive man beside her had taken a sledgehammer to her self-control. "My sister helped me come up with it. She's the real artistic genius in the family."

"I highly doubt that."

Hallie wasn't sure if Christian had intended to say the words out loud, or if they were meant to be mumbled under his breath. Either way, she heard them, and her face flushed at the compliment.

"No really," she said, turning to him. Bad idea. He studied her with the same intensity that his daughter had studied the sketch. Except his brown eyes appeared way broodier, and did she detect some longing in them?

Excuse me? Earth to Hallie. Christian isn't pining for you.

That would be ridiculous. Tyler's departing warning must be putting ideas into her head that didn't belong.

"Elise studies art," Hallie explained. "Many of my abilities came from her teaching me different techniques. It's really helped with my baking."

Isla reached over to snatch the paper back from her father. "Can you put a witch flying over the house? Right here?" She pointed to the empty space above the dilapidated chimney on the weathered house.

Man, Christian hadn't been kidding when he mentioned his daughter's love for Halloween.

Hallie rotated the page toward herself, pursing her lips as she considered the idea. Since starting Hallie's Cakes, she'd stretched herself past what she thought she could do many times. Those instances had helped her grow as a baker and taught her not to back down from any challenge. Attempting to create something suspended in the air would be a first though.

But looking at Isla's hopeful face made up her mind. If the girl wanted a flying witch, Hallie would make it happen, one way or another.

"I can try." She dug through her bag until she found a pencil.

"How can you make a witch suspended on a cake?" Christian asked skeptically. He'd moved away from the end of the couch and was leaning over to get a better look at the drawing.

"On a broomstick," Isla and Hallie said in unison.

"Duh." Hallie added, shooting a teasing smile at Christian.

Another bad idea.

Her eyes were at exactly the right angle to study his chiseled jaw, which led to lingering admiration all the way down to the way his t-shirt pulled slightly against the muscles of his chest. That spicy scent she'd come to associate with him swirled around her head, giving her unrealistic notions of bottling the smell to enjoy it later. She'd call it Eau de Christian, said in a fancy French accent with extra phlegm.

Was that creepy?

Yes. Yes, it was.

Christian held his hands up in surrender. "My bad." He smirked, though something sparked in those enchanting eyes as they passed from Hallie to his daughter and back. "You seem to have everything under control, so I'll let you girls handle the planning."

That's probably wise. Having him on the same couch, even when they *weren't* touching, was putting her heart in severe danger of cardiac arrest.

He slapped his palms against his thighs once before standing. "If you need me, I'll be making dinner."

The mention of food pulled Penelope from her play, and she abandoned the kitchen set to follow her father.

Except she didn't follow him. Instead, she headed straight for Hallie. Climbing onto the couch beside her, Penelope reached her arms up to be held.

Hallie hesitated before lifting the child onto her lap.

"You stay for dinner?" Penelope's voice rose in pitch on the last word.

Oh, the sweet girl. Hallie's heart melted at the tender way the child twirled a strand of her blonde ponytail around her small finger. "Aww, that's a nice invitation, but I think it's up to your dad."

Penelope bobbed her head once. "You stay for dinner." Sweet *and* bossy.

Hallie held back a small chuckle, glancing at Christian who stood frozen in the doorway to the kitchen.

"I'm sure Hallie has other plans tonight," he said.

"Please, Daddy?" Isla's pleading surprised Hallie even more than the original invitation. Two weeks ago, the girl didn't want anything to do with her. How quickly things changed, though Hallie wasn't naïve enough to think she'd become Isla's favorite person.

Christian ran a hand down his mouth, bringing Hallie's unwanted attention to it. His jaw held enough sandy-colored scruff to give him that rugged, irresistible look.

Again ... hot.

"I guess I'm outnumbered," he muttered, pasting on a smile. "Would you like to stay for dinner?"

Hallie's mind recalled the grandmother's response in *Mulan* when that question was asked of Li Shang. *"Would you like to stay forever?"*

Maybe not forever, but Hallie wouldn't mind staying for a long time. Which meant she shouldn't stay at all. But how could she leave when two little girls watched her with such hopeful expressions?

"Sure, I'd love to."

Chapter Sixteen

"I still feel bad for the way my brother acted earlier," Hallie said near the end of dinner, setting her fork across her empty plate. Although she'd already apologized, she wasn't able to let her brother's words go. And she couldn't force away the curiosity to find out what he'd said to Christian right before he left.

Christian stopped cutting the last of Penelope's noodles to look at Hallie from across the table. The child had spaghetti sauce smeared across her cheeks and more smashed in between her fingers.

Gross.

"You have nothing to feel bad about." He slid the pink plastic plate back in front of his daughter. "Besides, He was very ... illuminating."

Okay, what did THAT mean?

"It's just that Tyler has a way of making things awkward around the guys I date," Hallie explained.

Christian's hand froze, his fork hovering above his plate. Heat burst across her face. Of all the explanations she could have made, how did *those* words fly from her mouth?

"Not that we're dating. We're just friends. Are we friends? Maybe we're more like business acquaintances. We're clients. I mean, I'm not a client. You're the client. My client." Hallie hadn't known she could talk this fast.

Christian stared at her in alarm, like he didn't quite know what to do with the word vomit spewing from her. Apparently, he didn't realize she could talk this fast either. He started to respond but her overworking mouth cut him off before he could utter a word.

"Technically, you did take over my website. So maybe I'm your client after all?"

Just. Stop. Talking.

"I'll do the dishes." She stood abruptly. Too abruptly. Her thigh knocked against the metal expander on the underside of the table. She sucked a breath in through her teeth as her skin throbbed out a steady pulse in time with her heart.

Christian's brows pulled together as he watched her carefully. "Are you ... okay?"

"Yep. Perfect."

She set her plate on top of the saucepan soaking inside the sink. Was she okay? Physically, sure, despite the mark that would surely greet her when she changed her clothes tonight.

Emotionally? It was too soon to tell. She threw on the faucet to rinse her plate.

Christian joined her at the sink. "Please, don't clean up. I'll handle the dishes later." He ran a paper towel underneath the faucet once before wringing out the excess.

Returning to the table, he began wiping Penelope's cheeks. The girl squirmed away from her father's attempts to clean her.

"You happen to be looking at an expert busser. Are these clean?" She yanked open the door to the dishwasher to find a chaotic jumble of kids' plates and cups on the top rack. A few child utensils stuck out haphazardly from the container in the center. It looked like an explosion went off in there. She tossed Christian an exasperated side eye.

At least he had the decency to appear ashamed. "Yes, but really, you don't have to clean up."

Oh yeah, she did. Someone had to save him from himself. Who loaded the dishwasher like this?

On the other hand, at least he had one flaw. Between his gorgeous looks, brains, and mad dad skills, Hallie had begun to think the man was perfect.

"And you didn't have to feed me." She pulled out the bottom rack and found a similar arrangement as the top with larger plates and bowls. "It's the least I can do. Besides, my mom owns a café but hates doing dishes, so she always left them to the rest of us. It's second nature to me."

"We grew up with similar childhoods then. My mom cooked, and my sister and I had to clean up afterward." Christian tossed the soiled paper towel onto his plate and turned to Isla. "If you're done, take your dishes to the sink please."

Hallie stacked four cereal bowls on top of each other. "Where do these go?"

"To the left of the fridge," he said, freeing Penelope from her booster. Setting her on the floor, he crossed to the dishwasher and plucked the silverware tray from the bottom rack.

Hallie slid the bowls into the cabinet he'd indicated. "And did your after-dinner cleanups turn into impromptu dance parties? Because ours always did."

Those were some of her favorite memories. So much laughter and joy occurred during times her family spent together, even doing monotonous activities.

"Huh," Christian muttered, his back to her. "I've never pictured Tyler as a dancer."

"Would you believe he's better than me?" Hallie chuckled. "I have zero rhythm."

"Daddy can dance," Penelope said from the corner of the kitchen where she'd flung herself onto the dog's bed. Thankfully, the retriever —Princess Pumpkin, as Hallie had learned—was still in the backyard.

Christian whirled to face his daughter, his movement punctuated by clattering metal. "Where'd you hear that, sweetheart?"

Isla spoke for her. "Grandma told Aunt Dani she misses watching you dance. The last time we went to her house."

His mouth puckered into a grimace, and he returned to sorting the last of the silverware.

Hallie didn't have time to contemplate his odd reaction before Penelope jumped up from the bed. Dog hair dotted her blue tunic and white-flowered leggings. "Let's dance!" She extended her arms to the side and twirled.

"I'm sure Hallie doesn't want to dance right now." Christian flicked his gaze in her direction, his mouth set in a firm line. "Besides, there's no music."

As if on cue, Taylor Swift's voice cut through the tension in the kitchen. Penelope squealed, her movements intensifying.

Christian's head whipped to Isla holding his phone as he patted his back pockets. "Where'd you find that?"

"On the counter." She set the device on the table before joining Penelope's dance.

Christian turned back to the half-unloaded dishwasher, muttering under his breath.

Penelope hopped over to Hallie and reached up to her. "You dance. Like dis." She demonstrated a little hip shimmy.

"Now, even I can do that." Hallie laughed as she mimicked the movements.

At first, she felt silly showing off her lack of grace in front of Christian. Dancing with her family was one thing. They loved her no matter what. The man across the room, pointedly trying to ignore the rave taking over his house, proved an entirely different matter.

One look at Isla pushed all that aside, however. Her smile stretched wide as she let loose, a carefree expression easing the underlying suspicion she so often carried around Hallie.

"You dance too, Daddy!" Penelope hollered, twirling up to her father.

He eyed her, tension rounding his broad shoulders. His hands didn't stray from the spaghetti pot rinsing under the water. "That's okay, sweetheart. Someone needs to finish the dishes."

Man, Hallie hadn't seen him scowl like that since the day he'd come over to her house. Did he hate dancing that much?

The tinkling of Isla's laughter cut through the music, which had changed to a Justin Bieber song. Instant surprise took over Christian's face before transforming into something more tender as he eyed his daughter.

He was softening, Hallie sensed it. Maybe they could lighten him up even more. Ignoring her lack of dancing skills, she performed an atrocious moonwalk toward him, bumping his hip with her side.

"Come on, dance with us. Please? Just one song. You know you want to."

He gave her a sidelong glance, and she alternated her arms up and down in a fluid wave. Jutting her hips from side to side, she probably looked more like she'd been electrocuted than anything. The thin line of his mouth ticked up in the barest of smiles.

Totally worth the embarrassment. Any minute, he'd crack.

"Hey, if I'm forced to make a fool of myself with my two left feet, I should be able to see these amazing dance skills you're rumored to have." She swallowed the laugh bubbling up from her gut.

His smile grew as he obviously struggled to hold back his amusement. "Flattery doesn't work on me."

"How about the pouty face?" She stuck out her bottom lip.

The debate clearly raged in his head as he watched her for a drawn-out second. Finally, when Justin proclaimed himself gone in the last strains of "Baby," Christian gave a dramatic sigh and flipped off the faucet.

Drying his hands on the towel hanging from the oven, he held out his arm as the musical vibe switched from playful to reflective and gentle, with Jason Mraz's voice taking center stage in the kitchen.

Wait, what? He wanted to dance *with* her? She stared at his outstretched hand, Tyler's warning ringing in her head. *I don't want you getting hurt.* And then directly after: *I'm watching you both.* She suspected getting up close and personal with his best friend fell under the category of getting too close.

"Do it!" Penelope giggled, her hands clutched in her sister's as they half danced, half watched the scene unfolding before them. "Dance with Daddy!"

"I have no rhythm," she warned. She'd leave the rest of her hesitations out of it. "I'd probably step on your feet."

He moved toward her, his hand still extended. "You wanted to dance, so let's dance."

She hesitated another second as Jason crooned "I Won't Give Up" around them.

Could one dance really be so tragic? Tyler wasn't here, and Christian's walls were actually coming down. Who knew, maybe these moments would become a regular thing in this house. If sharing one slow dance helped him connect with his daughters, was there really any harm in the long run?

Isla bounced up and down, flapping her arms. "Dance with him, Hallie."

Her encouragement sealed Hallie's decision, and she set her hand in his. He stepped closer, placing her left hand onto his upper arm before sliding his to her back, right below her shoulder blade. Her skin scorched at his touch.

Slowly, he swayed to the music, getting her used to the movement of the song. At the chorus, he guided them into a simple waltz. Only two steps in, her toes jammed into his. He winced.

Hallie jumped out of his hold. "Sorry. Two left feet, remember?"

He reached for her again. "Just relax and follow my lead."

She took a breath and stepped back into his hold. At first, she clung to him, not trusting her own abilities to carry her through the length of the song. But as they flowed in rhythm to the music, Christian's murmured instructions helped Hallie relax. The fluidity of his movements, the confidence of his steps invited her to trust him. In his arms, she knew exactly where he was leading her, pushing her to do more, give more, be more. All the while, her heart urged her not to tread lightly.

It urged her to take a flying leap.

Into what? Her logical side feared the answer. But her heart refused to let go of this feeling. Like floating on air.

Her heart raced much faster than the beat of the music. His intoxicating scent swirled around her, making her lightheaded. And when was the last time she took a breath?

Dancing with Christian was a full body experience, each of her senses stimulated to maximum level through the remainder of the dance. As the song played its final gentle chord, he tightened his hold on her back and slowly lowered her into a dip.

Hallie squeaked in surprise, and she clung to his neck as if she'd land flat on her back if she let go even a little. Then a quiet hush fell over the room, that brief pause before a new melody began. Isla and Penelope stilled, seemingly aware that something was happening, though too young to grasp exactly what.

Hallie wasn't sure herself, only that something had shifted. Slowly, her eyes rose from his neck to his face, locking on his piercing, soulful eyes that in the moment held nothing but warmth. And maybe a little fear.

Yep, there was definitely some fear there.

His gaze flitted to her mouth, then back up to her face. *Is he going to kiss me?* Did she want him to?

The magical moment poofed into nothing the instant Christian raised her back to standing and stepped away. "I think that's enough dancing for one night." He turned away from her.

Confused at the mixture of disappointment and relief at his sudden distance, Hallie took a deep breath. "Where'd you learn to waltz?" she asked. The confidence in his steps, the way he'd positioned their hands, and the grace in which he'd carried himself spoke of more than just a basic knowledge of the dance.

"Ballroom," he mumbled.

"What?" Did she hear him correctly?

He swiveled around again. "I was on the ballroom team in college."

She coughed, reeling back her surprise at his odd look. "You were?"

"Why is that so shocking?"

Hallie crossed the room to stand next to him as the girls resumed their dancing. "I just took you as more of the nerdy type. Or a jock. I hadn't decided which." She smiled at his sudden crack of laughter.

"I *am* a big nerd." He flashed her a self-deprecating look. "But I like sports too. Growing up, I wanted to play hockey. So naturally, my mom put me in ballroom lessons instead."

"I'm sure your teeth thank her," Hallie said.

His smoldering half-smirk sent her heart racing again. "I think they're more grateful for the four years of braces."

"Four years? Yikes."

His laughter sliced through the last bit of tension in the room. "Yeah. The teenage stage wasn't kind to me."

The years were kind to him now. Way too kind. "It seems she made the right call."

Christian shrugged. "It was fun while it lasted."

"While it lasted?" she repeated. "You don't dance anymore?"

His forehead creased as pain flashed across his handsome face. And then, just as quickly, he steeled his composure once again. "No. Not with all the baggage."

She pondered that through the rest of dinner cleanup. Her mind momentarily dropped it when Penelope insisted she only wanted Hallie to help her get ready for bed. She couldn't pinpoint why the toddler had latched onto her so quickly, but Hallie was finding it impossible not to give the adorable girl everything she wanted.

But when Hallie finally made her escape—was escape the right word when she was actually enjoying herself?—Christian's words latched onto her brain again.

Too much baggage? What did that mean? What could've possibly caused him to abandon something he was obviously so good at?

Chapter Seventeen

Christian had lost his mind.

How else could he explain the way he'd let down his guard so completely by waltzing with Hallie the other night? The last person he'd danced with had left a giant hole in his heart, and he'd feared sharing such a vulnerable act with anyone else would feel like a constant reminder of their tragic love story.

Why did Hallie get to him so much? Was it the way her stunning eyes sparkled with a mischief he'd never seen in them before? Or maybe it was the adorable way she was so bad at dancing. Whatever the reason, the moment Hallie set her hand in his, something shifted inside him.

He'd felt it instantly.

Undeniably.

Contrary to his long-standing fear, it wasn't Sabrina filling his head during that impromptu waltz. And she wasn't in his head now as he stood by the big twisty slide at Village Green Park.

Three days had passed, and the sensation of holding Hallie in his arms still lived in his head rent free. Dancing with her had been a mix of heady exhilaration and gentle contentment. But also terrifying as realization struck him in those moments.

He was no longer just attracted to his best friend's little sister.

He was falling for her.

And he had to put a stop to it before he stumbled too deep. Especially now that the girls were involved. Penelope had refused to let Hallie leave the house until she'd gone to bed, for crying out loud. She wouldn't even let Christian brush her teeth or read her a story. Isla hadn't claimed the woman as an unsuspecting bestie like her sister had, but even she'd warmed up to the idea of having Hallie around.

Continuing down this road wouldn't just hurt him, but his girls as well.

Because all romantic relationships eventually stumbled onto the twisty path toward heartbreak. He couldn't risk it. Whatever was happening with Hallie had to end before he took another step.

"Daddy, watch this!"

Christian pulled his head back to his surroundings to find Isla, standing at the top of the twisty slide. "I'm watching."

As she flung herself down the slide, Penelope and her preschool friend, Charlotte, ran past him toward the rope climbing wall. Those girls were living their best lives this afternoon. Except for the one time she'd asked for a snack, his youngest daughter had been too busy playing during this playdate to even glance his direction.

Isla tumbled out of the slide's bottom, her giggle bringing a small smile to Christian's face. These glimpses of the joyful little girl she'd once been always gave him hope that she'd eventually be okay.

"Did you see me, Daddy?" She hopped up to him, her curly ponytail bouncing behind her. "I went so fast!"

Christian held up a hand for a high five. "You were so fast, I could hardly see you."

"Oh, Daddy, you're silly." Isla spun back toward the jungle gym. "I'm going to do it again."

He waved her off. "I'll be here."

While she ran toward the wobble bridge leading up to the twisty slide, Charlotte's mom approached, her infant son in her arms. "I think we're going to take off. This one's getting tired. I really hope he falls asleep on the way to Charlee's dance class."

Christian checked his watch. "Yeah, we should get going too. Thanks for organizing this. Penelope's having a blast, as you can tell." On cue, a high-pitched cackle came from the wood chips at the foot of the climbing wall.

Charlotte's mom laughed. "She's adorable. We need to get the girls together again soon. Charlotte talks about Penelope all the time."

"For sure. They play really well together." Sticking two fingers in his mouth, he let out a shrill whistle, capturing the attention of all three girls. "Nellie, it's time to go!"

Isla groaned from the top of the slide. "Can't we stay for five more minutes, Dad?"

How could he resist her simple request when she was having so much fun? "Fine, five more minutes."

At first, he thought Penelope's timely squeal spawned from her excitement over more park time. But instead of heading back to the playground, she took off running toward the copse of trees at the edge of the park. Christian hastily said goodbye to Charlotte and her mom before jogging after his daughter, wanting to catch her before she reached the sidewalk. The number of times that girl gave him heart palpations had already taken at least ten years off his life.

Fortunately, Penelope stopped before jutting into the street. However, when he saw who'd captured her attention, he squeezed his eyes shut. How could he possibly put a stop to his developing feelings for Hallie if the woman showed up wherever he was? Was she intentionally trying to drive him mad?

Oh, gosh. Was she a stalker?

He almost laughed out loud at himself. *You're being paranoid.*

"Hallie! Hallie!" Penelope tugged on the hem of the woman's hoodie.

"Hey, sweet girl." The way Hallie smiled down on her bathed Christian's chest in a pool of delicious warmth. Like a hot tub on a cool evening.

Stop it. You just said you were ending this. Pulling his eyes away from their interaction, he checked to make sure he still had Isla in his view. She'd exited the slide and was heading their way.

When he turned back to Penelope, she'd slipped her small hand into Hallie's, dragging the woman over to him. "You have cookies today?"

"Nellie ..." Christian began.

"No, sorry," Hallie said with a light laugh. "I don't have any treats today. But maybe the next time I make cookies I'll drop some off for you. How does that sound? Hi, Isla."

Isla gave her a silent wave—not a glowing hello, but a far cry better than previous greetings.

It seemed like forever before Hallie finally acknowledged him. And when she did, her friendly expression turned to uncertainty. Had she thought about the other night as much as he had?

She dropped Penelope's hand, clasping both of hers in front of herself. "We keep running into each other, don't we?"

He nodded. Too much. And yet, not enough.

"Is your business stressing you out?" Wow, what a conversation starter.

"What do you mean?"

"You're out walking again." He swallowed his concern. He couldn't end this ill-conceived crush if he kept inserting himself into her troubles. *It's not your responsibility to fix them.* Then why did he want to so badly?

Hallie tilted her head to one shoulder, considering him. "Something like that."

By the way she said it, he deducted that whatever was on her mind had more to do than just her business. But it wasn't his place to press the issue.

"I like walking over here," she continued, bouncing on the balls of her running shoes. "There's an empty storefront across the street."

Christian nodded. Like a dumb bobblehead. "I've seen it."

"I come down here a lot to think about how great it'll be when I finally get my bakery. I'm manifesting my goals, I guess." She gave a shaky laugh. "I know, that sounds silly, but it actually helps."

"Whatever keeps the dream alive." At least she had the opportunity to dream, which was more than he could say about himself.

"Wouldn't that storefront be a perfect location? Think of all the families stopping by on their way to and from the park. I don't think Buena Hills has ever had its own bakery." Hallie squinted up at him. "You grew up here. Is that true?"

Christian shrugged a shoulder. "As far as I know. My mom would be a better judge though. She remembers further back than I can."

"It doesn't really matter, I guess." She sighed, the sound full of longing. "This place will be long gone by the time I come up with the funds to put down a deposit."

"Sounds like you need an investor. Or a partner."

She made a noise that was half desperate laugh, half groan. "Where do I find either of those? You don't have any rich friends hiding in the woodwork, do you?"

The corner of his mouth turned up at her attempted levity. "Sorry."

He didn't miss the sagging of her posture as she stared in the direction of the empty storefront, not visible through the trees.

"I'm sure you'll figure it out." Her discouragement tugged at his heart, providing more than a little discomfort. It wasn't his responsibility to be her cheerleader, and yet he hated seeing her so down. "Wherever you end up, it'll be perfect. Don't give up."

Hallie startled a little and looked down at the space between them. Christian did too, confused to find her fingers resting in his. When did he reach for her?

Her eyes traveled slowly to his face again, their light blue depths full of questions. "I'm not."

A lengthy pause followed her words, during which he couldn't look away. Neither did he pull his hand from hers.

This is dangerous, he reminded himself. Dangerous for the girls. And dangerous for him. He shouldn't let her get under his skin like this.

Hallie cleared her throat, slipping her fingers from his. She turned to Isla, her tone regaining its lighter nature. "Are you looking forward to your birthday? What're you doing to celebrate besides your party?"

Isla's face lit up as it always did when talking about her birthday. "I wanted to go to my first haunted house, but Daddy said no."

"I can't take you to a haunted house, kiddo," Christian said dryly, though grateful for the topic change.

"Why not?"

"I don't want to have nightmares after." Not to mention, Carrie Pritchard, and the entire neighborhood gossip chain, would have a hay day if word got out that he took his kindergartner to a place over-flowing with "satanic creatures." Carrie's words, not his. But he did agree with the wisdom of steering Isla away from things that might terrify her. His daughter talked a big game about loving the scary side of Halloween—should he be concerned or find it endearing?—but her anxiety already caused enough bad dreams. She didn't need anything else disrupting her sleep.

Isla let out a giggle. "Oh, Daddy, you don't get nightmares. You're not afraid of anything."

"You must be really brave to want to go." The amused twinkle reentered Hallie's eyes. "My brother took me to one once and I had to sleep with the light on for weeks."

"When was that?" Christian asked, holding back his own amusement.

"I was twelve. Tyler thought it would be funny." She chuckled. "Newsflash, it wasn't. For either of us."

"What did you do?" Isla asked, hanging onto every word.

Hallie shrugged. "I clung to his side the entire time. I don't think he anticipated I'd be *that* scared. He definitely regretted it after when our mom made him sleep on my bedroom floor until I felt safe enough to make it through the night by myself."

Christian was about to respond with a comment about teenage brothers when Penelope tugged on her hand. "Hallie! Hallie! You push me please?"

"Uh ... I have a couple minutes." She looked at Christian uncer-tainly. "If it's okay with your dad."

Her statement gave him the perfect exit opportunity. He wanted to take it; really, he did. His decision-making abilities suffered when-ever she was near.

But one glimpse of Penelope's hopeful face weakened his resolve. The child just wanted to play. Her thoughts didn't run any deeper than that.

He jutted his chin toward the swings. "Go on. Just for a minute before we go."

"Yay!" Penelope tugged Hallie to the bucket swing before reaching her arms up for help.

Christian followed with Isla at his side, his stomach twisting. It worried him how readily his sweet daughter trusted Hallie. Yep, he definitely needed to put a stop to this.

Before disaster struck.

Chapter Eighteen

Christian struggled to stay focused at work on Monday. Even the simplest tasks led his mind to wander back to Hallie. Reclining in his uncomfortable swivel chair, he closed his eyes. Visions of her danced across his eyelids—at the park, in his kitchen, with Penelope—and he snapped them open again.

His willpower had failed to keep him from falling for her, so the situation now screamed for the initiation of Plan B: stone cold avoidance.

But how could he avoid her when she popped up everywhere? She was like some freaky magnet, attracting him to her energy. Not that *she* was freaky. No, Hallie was gorgeous. Kind. Thoughtful. Radiating sunshine—

He groaned out a long sigh.

"Christian," his boss barked from the opening to his cubicle.

Christian jerked upright, a natural reaction whenever the man came near.

Jim didn't wait for a verbal response before launching into whatever order he'd come to deliver. "I scheduled a meeting with the Lawson Group for four-thirty today. We need to go over expectations for their website expansion. Make sure you're there." He left as swiftly as he'd entered.

Four-thirty? Christian groaned again. Pushing back his chair, he followed his boss. "Sir, I'm not available at four-thirty. I have to pick up my kids from school."

Jim strode into his office. "Haven't you figured out your nanny situation yet?" His eyes narrowed, and he pressed his mouth into a thin line. "It's been weeks since the last one quit."

"I hope to have one lined up soon. Until then, you know I can't attend meetings past three."

Christian hesitated in the doorway. His boss hated when the employees presumed an invitation into his hallowed space. Sunlight, streaming in through the floor-to-ceiling window, reflected off Jim's bald head. Downtown Los Angeles provided a canvas of concrete and glass outside the office.

"Your childcare arrangements aren't my concern." Jim leveled Christian with a serious look. "I need you in this meeting. The Lawson Group is our longest standing client. They have very specific requests, and as my best employee, you're the only guy I trust to get it done."

That was a rare comment from a man who never dished out complements.

"Thank you, sir," Christian said, recovering from his momentary surprise. "I understand. And under normal circumstances, I would absolutely be there. But I've already worked it out with HR—"

"No buts." His boss held up a finger as he took a seat behind the mahogany desk. The chair groaned under the weight of his ample rear end. "You'll be there. I don't need to remind you that you're already treading on thin ice with your recent infractions."

Recent infractions? Did he mean the baseless ones he pulled from his own ears? Sure, Christian would own up to arriving late two weeks ago after staying up to work on Hallie's website. But the rest?

Completely bogus.

He couldn't argue with his boss though. And no matter what arrangements Christian had set up with HR, Jim had the ability to twist the knife any way he wished with those suck ups. They'd do anything to stay in his back pocket.

"Do I make myself clear?" Jim's tone held no room for argument.

"Yes, sir," Christian muttered, staring at the picture of Jim's wife and kids sitting on the desk. Judging by the hours he spent in the office, those four people had to be leading completely separate lives from their workaholic patriarch.

Christian hoped he never became so obsessed with his job that it had a negative impact on his family. If the opportunity arose, he'd ditch this place so fast for something with more flexibility, and a much better home-work life balance.

The man jiggled his mouse to wake up his computer. "Good. You're dismissed."

What is this, the Army?

Christian returned to his cubicle. Collapsing into his chair, he bent forward and dropped his face onto the desk. Pamela was out for the day, leaving him free to groan to his heart's content. He did a few times as he bounced his forehead on the faux wood surface.

What was he supposed to do? Isla wouldn't be happy with the change of plans. Heck, *he* was furious about them. Perhaps it was finally time to start looking for another job. Of course, that wouldn't help him today.

Feeling sorry for himself would get him nowhere, so he stopped his silent pity-party and reached for his phone.

"Hey, Dani," he said when his sister answered on the second ring. "Can you pick the girls up from school today? I'm stuck at work."

"You know I would if I could," she wheezed into the phone, clearly out of breath. "But I have a biology test this afternoon. I'm on my way to a last-minute study session right now. I'm sorry."

Christian puffed his cheeks before emptying them of air. *Strike One.* "Don't worry about it. I'll figure something out. Good luck on your test."

"Thanks. Hey, I gotta run. I hope you find someone. Too bad Mom's still on her cruise, huh?"

Yeah, too bad. While he was stuck at work, she was probably living up her middle-aged single life with new friends. Christian caught himself before the bitter thought went any further. Mom deserved to be happy. Just because he didn't have the luxury of taking a vacation, didn't give him the right to judge the woman who'd sacrificed so much to raise him.

He called Tyler next. Perhaps his buddy was working from home today. He'd picked up the girls a few times on those days, though never last minute like this.

His voicemail clicked on immediately, dashing the flicker of hope left in Christian's mind.

Frantically, he scrolled to the top of his contact list. There had to be someone suitable to watch the girls for a few hours until he escaped the office. His breath caught at the first entry on the list.

Sabrina Abbott.

A piercing ache sliced through his heart. He'd worked hard to purge her from the rest of his life. Why hadn't he deleted her contact from his phone?

For a moment, he allowed the lingering grief and anger over her abandonment to fester, using it as a reminder of what could happen if he let himself get carried away with the little crush he'd formed on Hallie. He'd learned his lesson once. He couldn't surrender his heart to it again.

But as he lowered his finger to delete Sabrina's number, the name right below hers forced another jolt through his heart.

Hallie Abernathy.

Was this some kind of sick joke? His former love's contact directly above the woman he couldn't stop thinking about?

Something urged him to tap on her name, but his phone buzzing in his hand stopped him. Christian opened the text.

> Tyler: In a meeting. What's up?

> Christian: Stuck at work. Need someone to get the girls from school.

> Tyler: Won't be home in time. Gemma could possibly do it, but I don't know what she has after school.

Gemma had never watched the girls by herself before. That might make things difficult with Isla.

Christian: That's ok. I'll find someone.

Christian went back to his contact list, his eyes landing on Hallie's name again. No, he wouldn't call her. There had to be someone else.

He scrolled through the list. Bill Carter from next door? Naw, Christian didn't know him or his wife well enough to trust them with the girls.

Molly Denmark from across the street had filled in for him once when Annelise was sick. That had worked out fine. Maybe she'd be willing.

No, the Denmarks were out of town on an anniversary trip, leaving their seventeen-year-old son home alone.

The Halls couldn't do it; all their kids had after-school sports. He hadn't talked to Jack Lewis, his best friend from high school in years. And he wouldn't call him even if he had. Not a chance. Christian doubted the guy's ability to keep *himself* alive most days.

Carrie Pritchard. Absolutely not.

He briefly considered calling Josh Robinson. The two of them had hung out a lot back before Christian's marriage was on the rocks. But he'd pulled away from him after the divorce due to the man's relationship status with Sabrina's best friend. Calling him now wouldn't be helpful.

Dread lodged in his stomach as he reached the end of the list. He scrolled back to the top, his eyes snagging on Hallie's name once more.

I can't. Reaching out to her would be the worst thing he could do right now. Not only for himself, but the girls too. Penelope had already handed over her loyalty wrapped in shiny paper and a pretty bow. Even Isla had warmed up to her in her reserved way. He couldn't give Hallie the opportunity to get even closer, only to break their hearts later.

But what other choice did he have?

Opening his messages again, his thumbs hovered over the screen before he typed out another text.

> Christian: Do you think Hallie could do it?

Three dots appeared underneath his message, signaling Tyler's impending response.

> Tyler: Hallie?

> Christian: Yeah. I don't know who else to call. Would you trust her with your kid?

He stared at the screen, waiting for his friend's reply as his stomach filled with dread. He was supposed to be avoiding her, not handing her an invitation to become even more ingrained in his family.

> Tyler: Yes.

> Tyler: You can trust her.

There was a brief pause before another text came through.

> Tyler: Is there something between you two that I should know about?

Christian dropped his head onto his phone. He knew his friend would be skeptical. Heck, he was skeptical too. Especially by the way he couldn't get her out of his head. And how his heart pounded in both exhilaration and contentment every time she came near. It wasn't smart entertaining any sort of ideas involving her though. Not with her obvious discomfort around the girls.

But that discomfort had become less each time she'd been with them. It was practically nonexistent at the park last Thursday. Still, he couldn't leave the girls with anyone he hadn't vetted first.

And he'd put his life in Tyler's hands without hesitation at this point. He knew Christian's situation, and how protective he was of the girls. If he trusted his sister enough to give her the green light, then Christian could too.

Christian: Only desperation on my part.
Thanks, man.

Despite his buddy's endorsement, Christian went back through his contacts for another option. Asking Hallie for this favor had the potential of sending them all into a tailspin of chaos.

Was he really prepared for that?

Chapter Nineteen

"Is that Christian?" McKenzie asked, peering over Hallie's shoulder at the laptop on their kitchen's center island.

Hallie jumped. Perhaps she should've picked a more discreet place for her deep dive into Christian's dancing career via YouTube. She peeled her eyes from the video of three couples in the middle of a lively jive playing on the screen. How long had her roommate been standing there?

"Yeah," she said as McKenzie slid onto a stool next to her and turned the screen enough to see.

What had started as a mere curiosity about Christian's time on the ballroom team in college had turned into a week-long obsession to find every YouTube video available of him dancing.

Obsession is such a strong word. Hallie checked the clock above the web browser. *Two hours?!* Today's indulgence had lasted longer than the rest.

Maybe *obsession* was a more accurate term than she thought. This curiosity had derailed her entire afternoon. And turned her into a stalker.

Yet she couldn't stop herself from starting just one more video, this one a dance with only men from what appeared to be a show on campus.

Hello, shirtless Christian. Nice to meet you. Hallie groaned inwardly. *Stop ogling him. He's not a cupcake.*

But she still had to use an exorbitant amount of willpower not to fan her face.

He was, for lack of a better word, incredible. His dancing, not his abs, though those were nothing to scoff at either. Other descriptors could include graceful yet masculine. Powerful yet gentle. This younger version of Christian made the perfect leading man.

"I didn't know he was a dancer," McKenzie said after several moments of silently watching.

At least she didn't comment on Hallie's obvious loss of sanity. If Beej had been the one to discover Hallie stalking old YouTube videos of the guy, she would've gone crazy over a potential love match. Kendall would've rolled her eyes. But McKenzie was more subtle.

Thank goodness.

"I didn't know either." Hallie started another video.

This is absolutely the last one. It was her favorite because it featured only one couple. She'd watched it four times already, but after exhausting all the content she could find, what else could she do?

Besides turn it off altogether, because she'd already proved she didn't have the control to do that.

Christian and his partner—a shockingly beautiful woman named Sabrina Abbott, according to the caption—began an Argentine Tango that was both elegant and sensual. Their obvious chemistry came through in the dance, and Hallie, as much as she loved it, felt an uncomfortable twinge near her navel.

You're being ridiculous. This obsession wasn't healthy.

McKenzie leaned forward, resting her chin on top of her forearms. "He's good. Too bad we didn't know him while I was still competing. I could've used his help with my floor routine. I hated the dancing elements."

Hallie's phone buzzed on the countertop between them, interrupting any response she could've made. McKenzie glanced at it as *Christian: My Favorite Client* scrolled across the screen.

A glimmer of mischief twinkled in her blue eyes. "Speak of the devil." She waggled her ginger brows.

Hallie snapped the laptop closed. Face burning, she waved her arms over the computer. "This never happened."

"My lips are sealed." From McKenzie, that promise was like making a blood oath.

Hallie snatched her phone off the counter and rushed from the kitchen, answering the call only when she'd reached the entryway.

"Hello?" She tried to keep her breath steady as she jogged up to her room.

"Hey," Christian grunted. "Sorry to interrupt. You busy?"

Not unless you count cyberstalking you for the last two and a half hours.

"Nope. What's up?"

He exhaled deeply, and Hallie's stomach twisted with dread. She closed her door before dropping onto her bed.

"Everything okay?" she asked.

Christian puffed out another breath. "Actually, not really. My boss set up this mandatory but totally unnecessary meeting for this afternoon. I don't know what to do with my kids. My sister usually watches them but she's taking a test."

Where was he going with this?

"Tyler is working Downtown today, and my mom's on a cruise. The girls' nanny moved, and I haven't found another one. There's no one else to take them. I know this is probably crossing so many boundaries—and I wouldn't ask if I wasn't desperate—but your brother said I could trust you, so ... would you be able to watch them?"

He wanted *her* to stay with his girls?

Alone?

Wait, her *brother* said that? *Oh boy, I'm going to hear about this later.*

Christian trusted her—the girl who, at fourteen, had let a kid ride his big wheel off the deck—to take care of his precious children? Her, the one who'd spent her teenage years hustling for tips as a waitress in Mom's café instead of building up her babysitting skills?

The queasiness turning her stomach thickened. Sure, she'd grown more comfortable around the girls lately. She didn't feel so out of her element, and even Isla seemed okay with her around. But...

"I don't know, Christian," she said. "I've never watched them alone before. I'm not sure it's such a good idea."

"Please, Hallie?" The distress in his voice cut straight through her heart. "I've exhausted all other options. I'll pay. Whatever you want."

"You can't afford me." Wow, that attempt at a joke sounded arrogant. So much for lightening the mood.

He pushed out a breathy laugh. "It would be worth it. I'm that desperate."

No kidding.

And she could use the money that came from watching the girls. It wouldn't solve her need of finding more clients, but every little bit helped.

Her shoulders sagged. "What time should I pick them up?"

He exhaled again, the relief coming through the line. "Isla's school gets out at three-thirty, but she's been going to Kid Care the last few weeks, which ends at five. You can pick up Penelope any time after four."

He explained the pickup process, promising to text her the addresses of the girls' schools, and reminded her to bring her ID.

"I'll call the schools to put you on the pickup list," he continued. "Thank you *so* much, Hallie. You're an angel."

Angel? No one had ever called her that. And coming from him made the flutter in her stomach transfer to her heart.

"What about car seats?" Sticking with the conversation kept her from analyzing the nickname too much. Or her body's reaction to it.

"There's an extra set in the garage. The high-backed booster is for Isla, and Penelope's is the five-point harness. You should be able to clip both into the anchors in your backseat."

"I know how to do it. I've installed Will's before."

"Great." She could feel his weight lifting through the phone. "I'll text you the code to the garage and the front door. And there's one more thing."

"What's that?"

Christian's silence triggered Hallie's lingering uncertainty. It felt like he was about to drop a major bomb.

"Isla struggles with separation anxiety," he finally said. "It's gotten a lot better, but she's hit a bit of a relapse since her nanny left. I know she won't be happy with the change of plans."

"Oh." Nausea rippled in Hallie's stomach. "How can I help her?"

Christian considered that for a moment. "When I call her school, I'll ask to talk to her directly. They're pretty good at allowing that, given her condition. So, she won't be blindsided when you show up. Also, if she's having a hard time, you can remind her of our heart promise. She'll know what that means. It's this little heart on her thumb."

Hallie remembered the matching icon on his hand the day he came over to help with her website. What she'd thought had been a token from a flirty girlfriend had been a sweet way of helping his daughter. How adorable.

"And she likes to chill in my bed sometimes too," he continued. "I guess the pillows smell like me. It comforts her."

That made sense. "Heart promise. Pillows. Got it."

"I'll call once I'm done, so you know I'm coming home. And if you need anything, please text me. Thank you. You're a lifesaver."

Hallie swallowed. "Of course. Don't worry about us. We'll be fine."

If only she believed that.

Beads of sweat slid between Hallie's shoulder blades as she wrestled Isla's booster seat into the back of her car. She'd attached the first strap to the anchor easily. The second? Not so much.

"Come on," she groaned, twisting herself into an unnatural angle to push the seat's claw against the metal anchor. "Go in!"

Installing Will's infant seat was a lot simpler than this monstrosity. Then again, her nephew's Graco had two parts, allowing the carrier to be removed during installation. Dealing with the lighter weight made manipulating the base into place much more manageable.

Hallie let out a long grunt and thrust the claw into the space between the two sections of the back seat. The most beautiful sound in the world filled the car: the thwack of the buckle clicking into place.

"Success!" She moved her arms in the only celebration dance possible while crammed into the tight space. "You're no match for me!"

"Do you need help?" a woman's voice asked, followed by a series of high-pitched yipping.

Hallie stopped her celebration, warmth rising up her back that had nothing to do with the unexpected workout. Backing out of the car, she poked her head around the door, meeting the curious eyes of a woman in tight leggings and a long-sleeve athletic tee. Her brightly lipsticked mouth twitched in amusement while she ignored the four yorkies straining at their leashes.

Hallie couldn't ignore them, though. Did everyone in this neighborhood have dogs?

Her chest tightened. Christian's was waiting to terrorize her when she returned with the girls. She'd been so focused on listening to his instructions on how to help Isla that she'd forgotten all about that major complication.

She kept the open door between herself and the dogs. "I was trying to install these car seats. But I got it. Thanks."

Hallie turned to open the driver's side door, willing the woman to leave so she could be on her way. It was already after four, and she wasn't sure how long it would take the schools to verify her identity and release the girls to her care.

"I'm Carrie, by the way. Carrie Pritchard. I live in that house over there." She made a grand show of pointing to the immaculate mansion two doors down—the only home on the street free of at least some Halloween decorations.

"Hallie. Nice to meet you."

"Are you the girls' new nanny? I haven't seen you around here before."

Hallie almost laughed at the idea of her being a nanny to anyone.

"Uh, no. I'm just a ... friend. Christian is stuck at work, so I told him I'd watch the girls until he got home."

One of the dogs had broken through Carrie's hold, lengthening its leash enough to meander around the wall of Hallie's temporary sanctuary. She sidestepped his attentions.

Carrie pulled on the leash to get the dog back in line. "Well, you can't blame me for making that mistake. Christian likes to hire the *young* nannies. The last one was barely out of high school. And gorgeous, if you know what I mean." She wiggled her dark brows.

Something about this woman rubbed Hallie the wrong way. The easy way she gossiped about Christian, and her implication of inappropriate relations with his former employee sent an icky sensation skittering across Hallie's skin.

"I think she left because of a broken heart." Carrie gave a smug shrug. "Not that I blame her. I wouldn't stick around either, given the state of his kids."

"Excuse me?"

"I thought you'd know, being his *friend* and all." Carrie gave an exaggerated wink as though she knew exactly what was going on between Hallie and Christian.

How can you when I don't even know?

Carrie continued in a conversational tone. "Well, if you're not aware, I guess it's my obligation to warn you before you get in too deep. You know—" she leaned in closer to Hallie, dropping her voice to a whisper "—woman to woman. That family has problems."

Hallie's defenses elevated.

"Penelope is a doll, of course," Carrie continued. "So sweet, like my Sammy. But Isla has some real psychological issues that need serious intervention. I heard she lashed out at a woman last week. Full on assaulted her."

Hallie's guard took an even larger spike, turning into a full-blown case of indignation. Assuming she wasn't mistaken, *she* was the woman Carrie referred to. How dare she spread gossip about a situation she knew nothing about?

Assault? Please.

"The worst part is, her dad enables her. Just the other day, I spoke to him as a concerned neighbor, and he immediately turned it onto me like it was somehow my daughter's fault that Isla is ostracized at school. I refuse to let my Sammy play with her anymore. Why would I subject her to such a dangerous child?"

Okay, Hallie really disliked this woman. Did Carrie just enjoy stirring up trouble everywhere she went? Or were her claims about Christian's daughter valid? Perhaps the kicking incident hadn't been the only—or worse—outburst Isla had committed. Was her behavior really as bad as Carrie made it seem?

She pushed those thoughts from her head. Sure, she didn't know Christian very well, but Tyler did. And she trusted her brother way more than this neighborhood gossip.

"Christian is doing the best he can," she said, refusing to listen to Carrie disparage his family any longer. "We can't all be so perfect. Excuse me."

Carrie's mouth dropped open in shock seconds before Hallie slid into the driver's seat, ending the conversation. She plugged the address to Penelope's preschool into her phone, giving Christian's busybody neighbor a chance to clear out of the driveway before backing out.

The woman was nothing but the worst kind of gossip—one who didn't care about having the facts correct or not. Hallie couldn't take anything she said with more than a grain of salt.

That didn't stop doubt from creeping into her mind on the drive to the girls' schools. It shrouded her already confusing feelings over Christian into darker shadows. Maybe it was wise to step back even further from this thing developing with him.

If only she'd taken her brother's worry more seriously.

Chapter Twenty

"Do you need help buckling your seatbelt?" Hallie asked, stepping out of the front office of Isla's school with both girls at her side. She pulled her key fob from her front pocket to unlock her sedan parked at the far end of the lot.

"I know how to do it," Isla answered quietly. The poor girl's bottom lip puckered like she was holding back tears.

Christian had been spot on when he'd warned of his daughter's likely reaction at the abrupt change of plans. They'd managed to get through pick up without any meltdowns, especially the kicking kind. But now Hallie had the strangest urge to scoop the little girl into a hug, despite the doubts swirling around her as a result of Carrie's gossip.

Hallie grabbed Penelope's hand as they crossed in between two SUVs waiting in the pick-up lane, their hazard lights flashing. When she arrived at the school, she'd contemplated joining the line—it certainly would've been easier with Penelope in the car—but she hadn't known how long it would take to verify her ID. Parking had seemed the best option this time.

This time? There wouldn't be a next time.

Once the girls were buckled into their seats, they drove to Christian's house in silence, except for Penelope's occasional gleeful exclamations over what she saw out the back window. The quiet only intensified the nerves doing a jig in Hallie's stomach.

What am I supposed to do with them until Christian gets home? She didn't even know when that would be.

Her heart thumped in her throat as they pulled into the driveway. Carrie wasn't in sight, thank goodness, though the reminder of their interaction—and the four yorkies yipping at their leashes—stirred up unpleasant feelings about what she'd find inside the house.

Maybe he put the dog in the yard. Owners didn't usually keep their pets inside when they were home, did they? Wouldn't leaving them to run free be recipe for disaster? Certainly a big mess, at the very least.

"Let's go inside," Hallie said, sliding from the driver's seat. She helped the girls from the back, and they walked up the path to the front door, decorated with a display of pumpkins in various colors and shapes.

Isla thumped her backpack onto the porch while Hallie looked up the text Christian had sent with the front door code. Summoning all the good vibes she could muster that Princess Pumpkin wasn't in the house, she typed the numbers into the keypad above the handle and pushed the door open.

No such luck. The golden retriever came bounding toward them from the kitchen as soon as they stepped inside. Flinching, Hallie pulled into herself. Images of her neighbor's dog danced through her mind as her breath came in short gasps. Her pulse sped out of control, and she turned, bracing for the attack.

"Pumpkin, sit," Isla commanded.

No paws collided with Hallie's back; no teeth marks broke her skin. Could she really be safe?

After a few seconds, she braved a look over her shoulder. The dog sat a few feet away, tongue hanging out, tail whipping against the hardwood floor. But it was still baring its teeth.

Or was that a smile?

Either way, she appeared safe for the moment. She turned all the way around but kept her guard up. Dogs could attack at any time.

"Pumpkin no hurt you," Penelope said in her adorable three-year-old voice. "She say hi."

Hallie didn't want to say hi.

But Penelope took her hand and led her to the canine. Extending her own arm outward, she allowed the dog to sniff her palm. "Hold your hand like dis."

Hallie followed Penelope's lead, marveling at the way the sweet girl was able to ease her anxiety even a tiny bit. Were all three-year-olds capable of showing such compassion? Or was Penelope just special?

Princess Pumpkin pressed her snout into Hallie's palm. She jerked her hand away. This would take some getting used to. Forcing herself to push past the nerves, she brought her hand forward again, allowing the dog to continue sniffing. Seconds later, the dog's soft, sandpapery tongue scratched her skin.

Penelope giggled. "She like you."

Hallie hesitantly patted Pumpkin's head. The retriever nuzzled into the touch, panting happily as she inched closer.

"You're not so bad," Hallie said, growing a little more confident in her strokes.

Penelope reached out to pet Pumpkin's fur as well. "Her hair is soft. Good for hugging when you sad."

Hallie smiled at her. "I'm sure it is."

Finally convinced she wouldn't be mauled by a rabid dog tonight, she stood, wiping her hands on her pants. "Okay, what would you girls like to do?" *After washing the dog slobber off my skin?*

Isla ignored her and sprawled onto the couch with her face in a picture book. Hallie would receive no suggestions from that corner. She turned to Penelope.

"Snack time?" the girl asked.

Hallie looked at her watch, realizing it was getting close to dinner time, and she hadn't asked Christian what he'd planned. "Sure, let's get you a snack to hold you over while I figure out dinner."

Heading through the living room, she startled when a small hand slipped into hers. Penelope smiled up at her. *I guess we're holding hands tonight.*

Once they'd passed into the kitchen, Hallie's eyes stretched wide. Had they been robbed? The whole room was a disaster. Breakfast bowls littered the table, with more dishes stacked in the sink and surrounding areas. A pile of clutter took up most of the counter by the back door.

This wouldn't do.

She helped Penelope into her booster seat, then cleared the table of the leftover dishes, setting them on the counter on top of an electric skillet that had bits of what looked like melted cheese stuck to the black surface. Then she searched the cupboards for a suitable snack. Isla hadn't followed them into the room, so Hallie didn't push her. She'd come when hunger struck, right?

In her search of the cupboards, she came across flour and sugar, giving her an idea of how to pass the time with the girls. She set a small bowl of pretzels and a yogurt pouch in front of Penelope, before returning to her task of gathering the ingredients to make her favorite snickerdoodles. She even found a bottle of cream of tartar wedged in the back corner of the spice cabinet. The expiration date was smudged beyond recognition, but the powder still held its white color, and no strange odors rose from it when opening the lid. It would have to do for now.

She gathered all the ingredients in the one counter spot not taken over by dirty dishes. "Would you like to help me make some cookies?"

"Okay!" Penelope bounced in her chair. "Isla! Come make cookies!"

Isla offered no response. Hallie paused in her search through more cupboards for mixing bowls to peek her head into the living room. Her heart hitched to find Isla still on the couch, her arms around Pumpkin.

"Isla?" Hallie slowly made her way toward her. "Are you hungry?"

The girl shook her head, and she traced a finger over the small heart on her thumb. The same icon Hallie had seen on Christian's hand weeks ago.

Hallie watched her for a moment, the small hiccup indicating Isla's tears pricking her heart. Again, the urge to hug the child came over her but she took a step back instead. "We're in the kitchen if you need us. You're welcome to join us if you want."

Isla nodded, and Hallie returned to her search for the bowls in the kitchen. Finding two that worked, she placed them on the table since there wasn't room on the counter. All the while, her thoughts remained on Isla, wishing she could do something to help her.

"First, we need to sift the flour," Hallie said, opening the bag. "You don't suppose your dad has a sifter, do you?"

Penelope blinked back at her.

"Probably not, huh? We'll just do the best we can." Hallie located some plastic measuring cups and plunged one into the flour. "Here, sweetie. Go ahead and dump that into this bowl."

Penelope held the measuring cup high in the air before tipping it over and letting the powder fall. The force of the thump caused some of it to poof out onto the counter. She brought her free hand—which was already coated in white—to her mouth to cover her giggle.

"It's snowing," she squealed, setting the measuring cup down and swirling her fingers through the flour.

Hallie tore a paper towel off the roll hanging from an upper cupboard and got it wet. "Let's not make a mess, okay?"

She'd never been a messy baker. In culinary school, when her fellow students' stations were a disaster of mixing bowls and spatulas, with batter smeared all over their countertops, her station was always pristine, even by the end of class.

Except, this kitchen hadn't started out immaculate. A small pile of salt was gathered along one edge of the stove, with something sticky on the counter. And what was that crusty burnt spot on the front left burner?

She thought back to the times she'd baked with Mom, finally appreciating the difficulty of baking with a small child. Yet Hallie only remembered the feeling of love present in the kitchen during those special times. Perhaps there were worse things than making a mess.

"You know what? We'll clean it up later." She tossed the paper towel in the garbage.

The next few minutes saw them measuring ingredients and mixing them together.

In between whisking the dry stuff and creaming the butter and sugar, Isla abandoned her perch on the living room couch. Hallie smiled at her when she entered the kitchen, wanting her to feel welcome but not overwhelmed with a grand show.

Isla still wore a frown as she sat down at the table to eat her snack, though the rest of her face had softened to wary curiosity, and she darted occasional glances at the bakers.

The electric mixer whirred to life and Hallie beat the ingredients together. A small clump of sugar-coated butter escaped the bowl, landing on Penelope's cheek.

"Whoops," Hallie said over the noise, scrunching her nose at the child. "How did that happen?"

Penelope giggled, reaching her tiny fingers to her cheek to wipe off the smear. Popping it in her mouth, she shimmied her shoulders as she swallowed. Adorable.

"Now what?" she asked after they'd mixed the eggs in with the butter and sugar.

"We need to add the two bowls together." Hallie picked up the flour mixture. "Can you help me dump this in?"

Together, they poured the dry ingredients into the wet ones.

Isla appeared at their side just then. "Can I mix?" Her expression turned wary as though afraid Hallie would say no. Nothing in her posture spoke of the monster Carrie had made her out to be. Only a sweet child in need.

Hallie didn't know how to help beyond deciding right then that she wouldn't put stock into any of Carrie's "warnings."

She smiled down at Isla. "Sure. It's a little tricky, so let me help you keep it stable."

Isla placed both hands underneath Hallie's on the beater. Her lips tucked around her teeth as she concentrated on keeping the base steady while moving the beater around the glass bowl.

"There you go," Hallie encouraged as the mixture turned from a powdery-topped goo to the consistency of raw cookie dough. "I think that's good. Who wants to lick the beaters?"

Their eyes grew wide. "We can eat it?" Penelope asked.

Hallie scoffed. "You've never eaten cookie dough from the beater? It's the best part."

"Daddy never makes cookies," Isla stated matter-of-factly. "And Grandma says the eggs could give us fish flu."

Fish flu? Once she'd interpreted the meaning, Hallie bit down on a laugh. "You mean salmonella?"

Penelope scrunched her nose. "What's salmon-lella?"

Hallie brushed the flour from her hands into the sink. "It's a bacteria caused by food. But I've been eating dough off the beaters my whole life, and I've never gotten sick from it. Here." She handed each girl a beater.

While they happily licked the metal tools, Hallie covered the bowl with the plastic wrap she found in a bottom cupboard. As she slid it into the fridge, her phone buzzed in her back pocket. An unfamiliar number scrolled across the screen. She swiped to answer it. "Hello?"

"May I speak with Hallie Abernathy please?" the woman asked.

"I'm Hallie." She used the professional tone she always adopted when clients called. "What can I do for you?"

"This is Melanie from Crème de la Crème Bakery."

Hallie's breath caught. Before getting trapped down the rabbit hole of Christian's ballroom videos several hours ago, she'd called the bakery to check on the status of her job application. No one had answered, so she'd left a message. "Thank you for getting back to me."

"No problem at all," Melanie said. "I'm sorry I wasn't available to take your call earlier. I've reviewed your application, and while your portfolio is impressive, we're looking for someone with more experience in the field."

Hallie's heart sank. "Oh. Of course. I understand."

"However, one of our servers will be leaving for a summer internship out of state. If you're still looking then, we'd love to have you apply for that position."

Hallie's experience in Mom's café made her fully qualified for the job, though serving only customers didn't thrill her. She already felt like she was giving up her dream by applying to work for someone else. Would she really have to sink even further from her goal?

"Thank you. I'll consider it."

She hung up and set her phone on the table, slumping into one of the kitchen chairs. Why couldn't she go back to four years ago when she first started Hallie's Cakes? Back when she had nothing but optimism and excitement in this new entrepreneurial endeavor. Owning a home bakery was a fun side project as she made her way through school.

But turning it into a sustainable career was starting to feel downright impossible.

"What's wrong?" Isla's blonde eyebrows turned down toward her nose.

The last thing Hallie wanted was to alarm the girls. Not when they'd started to feel comfortable with her in charge. "Nothing. I just received some disappointing news."

"Don't be sad." Penelope climbed onto Hallie's lap, wrapping her small arms around her neck. "I make you feel better now."

Oh, this sweet child. She was quickly claiming a place in Hallie's heart. Even Isla had come a little closer as though her nearness was meant as a comfort.

For a moment, they all sat in silence while Hallie worked through her disappointment. Then she steeled her composure and forced herself to smile. "Who wants pizza for dinner?"

Both girls cheered.

Hallie slid Penelope off her lap and picked up her phone again. "That settles it. I'll order it now." Normally, she would've made it herself but if they waited for the dough to rise, they wouldn't be eating dinner until tomorrow. And eventually, the girls did need to go to bed.

Focusing on dinner, she made a conscious effort to let her disappointment go for now. Her dilemma would still be here when she chose to address it. But tonight, she knew exactly where she needed to be.

Chapter Twenty-One

Eight-thirty had come and gone by the time Christian pulled up next to Hallie's sedan in the driveway. He leaned his head against the headrest for a minute to let his frustration ease before going inside.

The conference with the Lawson Group ran excruciatingly long. It hadn't taken more than a few minutes to realize that every point the representative addressed—in painfully monotonous tones—could have been outlined by email. But pointless meetings were Jim's bread and butter. Why take care of things in writing when he could waste everyone's time by hashing it out in person?

And after they'd wrapped up, Jim insisted that Christian get a jump on the project. By the time he'd left the office, traffic on the 110 was so congested, it took him thirty minutes to go half a mile. He spent that time listing all the reasons not to quit on the spot.

There were only two. And they waited for him inside the house.

The girls depended on his steady income, and he didn't have the time or energy to go through the effort of finding another job.

Christian snatched his bag from the passenger seat before pushing the door open. He unfolded himself from the car and headed up the walk.

No one had thought to turn on the porch light. Using his phone's flashlight, he punched the code into the keypad at the door. The lights on the thing had burned out last week, and he never remembered to switch the battery except for the times like now.

The faint aroma punctuating the air hit him first when he stepped inside. Like sugar and vanilla with a hint of cinnamon. Some of the weight of the day lifted from his shoulders with that comforting smell.

When was the last time his house smelled like cookies? Probably the time Dani spilled that liquid air freshener on the carpet in Penelope's room. The whole upstairs reeked of vanilla for weeks.

He set his bag by the door, freezing when he flipped on the inside light. *It's so clean in here.*

The living room hadn't been a complete disaster when he'd left this morning, but he could've sworn there'd been a few toys lying around. As well as a pile of picture books on the coffee table.

They weren't there now. Someone had arranged the throw pillows immaculately on both ends of the couch too. Was this really his house?

A giggle from upstairs captured his attention. *Yep, definitely my house.* He'd worry about the state of it later. Taking the stairs two at a time, he headed toward Isla's room.

His gut clenched at what he found inside. Hallie sat in between the girls on Isla's bed, a picture book propped against her bent legs. She had one arm around Penelope, who slouched against her side, completely passed-out. Isla, though not quite touching, leaned toward her, fully invested in the story. Pumpkin lay across the end of the bed, part of her head wedged between Hallie's feet.

Christian's heart thumped hard against his chest. The warm glow of Isla's lamp bathed Hallie in a radiant light, somehow making her even lovelier than ever. Like the angel she was.

Before his marriage ended, he'd sometimes imagined coming home from work to exactly this: his wife reading a story to their children, making funny voices to match the characters.

"Ah ha!" Hallie read in a crackly witch voice, adding to the feeling of déjavu coming over Christian now. "There you are, my child. I'm ready for you."

Isla giggled, and Hallie joined in for a second before continuing to read. Christian smiled too.

They were so engrossed in the story they hadn't noticed him in the doorway. Leaning against the trim, he marveled at the way Hallie's calm presence fit so well in the room. As if she belonged there.

The realization hit him hard, and he sucked in air just to keep breathing. An ache split through his chest, so deep he had to use the door frame to keep his balance. Squeezing his eyes shut, he focused on calming the jarring panic seizing his joints.

"You're home."

At Hallie's voice, his eyes flew open.

Meeting his gaze, which was no doubt wild with panic, concern crossed her angelic face. "Is everything okay?"

Christian gave his head a little shake, pulling the safety blanket of his composure over himself once more. "Yeah, sorry. I was ... thinking." He stepped further into the room.

"Can we read another story?" Isla asked, drawing the woman's attention away from him, allowing him to breathe again.

Hallie carefully reached over Penelope's sleeping form to place the book on the nightstand. "It's up to your dad."

Isla turned her pleading brown eyes onto him. "Please, Daddy? Just one more?"

Approaching the bed, Christian gently lifted Penelope into his arms. "Sorry, kiddo. It's already past your bedtime, and it's a school night."

Hallie's face twisted into an apologetic frown. "I didn't know what time you usually put them to bed."

"It's fine." He shifted Penelope into one arm, using the other to squeeze Hallie's shoulder. Bad idea. The touch only set off more panic racing through him.

Isla's bottom lip stuck out in a pout. "I don't want to go to bed. I'm not even tired."

"How about I come read you a story another time?" Hallie bumped her side.

"Promise?"

"Promise." Hallie patted her blanket-covered knee. "Goodnight, Isla."

She shimmied off the bed, leaving space for Christian to take her spot. He adjusted the blankets over his oldest daughter. "I'm going to put Nellie to bed and then I'll come back to tuck you in."

"Okay, Daddy."

Hallie had already gone downstairs when Christian slipped from the room. Good. The distance would give him some time to regain control over his racing pulse.

Once in Penelope's room, he lowered himself into the glider chair underneath the window. Rocking his precious daughter in his arms anchored him in the moment as his thoughts ran away from him.

He'd already told himself not to encourage whatever he felt for Hallie. He was no longer the naïve sap who hung out with a woman a few times before recklessly taking a flying leap into romance.

Then why couldn't he get past these overwhelming urges that made him want to pursue something with her, despite the impossibility of it?

And why did the image of his girls snuggled up to Hallie continue to dance across the backs of his closed eyelids? They were so comfortable with her, which made it hard to push away the spark of hope challenging everything he'd come to believe since Sabrina left.

Maybe there could be something there. Maybe someday in the future it wasn't impossible to imagine someone becoming a more permanent fixture in their lives.

No, not just someone.

Her.

Don't get ahead of yourself, pal, he reminded the hopeless romantic that fought to reemerge from his younger self.

He couldn't risk letting that guy resurface.

No matter how much his heart wanted him to.

Chapter Twenty-Two

Hallie flinched when Princess Pumpkin's nose pressed against her bent elbow. Despite knowing the dog wouldn't maul her tonight, old habits died hard.

"You don't like dogs?" Christian asked, following the golden retriever into the kitchen. He still wore his work clothes, though he'd abandoned his tie, and his top button was undone.

She placed the last snickerdoodle into a plastic container she'd found in a cabinet. "They're not my favorite." She spared him a glance before setting the dirty cookie sheet into the sink. "I had a bad experience with one in my neighborhood growing up. I haven't gotten over it."

"No problem. I'll put her outside."

Hallie grabbed the sponge from behind the faucet, running it through the stream of water. "It's okay. We've reached an agreement." She patted the dog's side. "I'll keep scratching her behind the ears in exchange for her not biting my head off."

The sound of Christian's tired chuckle hatched a single bee buzzing in her stomach.

"You won't bite Hallie's head off, will you, Pumpkin?" He dropped to one knee and cupped the dog's face with both hands. "No, you wouldn't. You're a good girl."

Hallie continued wiping the stove, hiding the smile caused by his baby talk.

After a moment, he came up beside her, and the bee in her stomach invited its friends to come play. Ugh ... she shouldn't find him so irresistible.

"When I asked you to babysit my kids, I wasn't hiring a maid."

"I know." Hallie placed the sponge back in its spot before turning to face him. "We made cookies, and things got pretty messy in here. I had them help me clean up after we finished."

"How does that explain the living room?"

She flashed him an amused side eye in response. "You hungry?"

"Starving." His stomach growled in confirmation.

Hallie opened the microwave and pulled out the plate she'd heated up a few minutes ago. "I wasn't sure what you'd planned for dinner, so I ordered pizza. I hope that's okay." She placed two snickerdoodles next to the slice and held it out to him.

"That's great." He took the meal from her. "Thanks for being here. How were they?"

After securing the container's lid on top of the cookies, she joined Christian at the table. "They were fine. Isla wasn't happy to see me at first, but she seemed to warm up after a while."

"How'd you work that magic?"

"What can I say? I have a talent for luring young children in with baked goods." Heat rose up her neck. "Forget I said that. I'm not the witch from *Hansel and Gretel*."

Christian barked out a laugh, almost choking on his pizza. "I sure hope you don't intend to eat my kids. I'm kind of attached to them."

"As you should be. They're adorable."

The small tilt of his head to one shoulder made it clear that her comment caught him off guard. And the slight smile softening his features as he studied her turned her body temperature up several notches.

Pull yourself together, girl. You're not ready to be a mom. Acting on her instincts when it came to Christian would only lead to heartache later when she realized she couldn't have him.

"You're probably tired," she said, placing her hands on her thighs. "I'll leave you to your dinner."

His hand on her arm stopped her before she could make her getaway. And dialed up the heat even more. Pretty soon, she'd need a fan to cool herself down. Or a bucket of ice water.

"I promised to pay you." He reached for his back pocket, but Hallie shook her head.

"That's not necessary." A little piece of her heart lodged in her gut at refusing his money. She needed the boost, small as it was, but she didn't feel right about it. "I did this as your friend."

Christian's lips pursed into a thin line as he pulled out his wallet. "At least let me spot you for the pizza."

"Absolutely not." Hallie slung her purse over one shoulder. "Especially after your generous order at the Autumn Festival."

Throwing his head back, his groan morphed into an embarrassed laugh. "You had to go there, didn't you?"

"Of course." A grin slid onto her face. "And you're taking care of my website. Trust me, we're more than even."

Christian tossed his wallet onto the table. "Do you want to see it?" he asked eagerly before shoving the last bite of pizza into his mouth.

"It's done?"

"Not completely, but I've gotten a good start on it." He stood, wiping his mouth on a paper towel. "Hang on, I'll get my laptop."

A tug-of-war between Hallie's head and heart took place as he exited the room. If she left now, maybe she could prevent her crush from turning into the kind of feelings that didn't go away without copious amounts of heartbreak.

Perhaps it already had.

On the other hand, she wanted to stay. To see her website's progress, sure. But if she were honest with herself, her feelings were plunging way past the infatuation stage already.

Christian reentered the room a minute later, his laptop open in one hand while he typed with the other. He placed it on the table in front of her. "Take a look at this." Remaining behind her, he planted one hand flat on the table next to the computer while the other gripped the back of her chair. The position was unsettlingly intimate, and way too tempting.

Hallie scrolled through the home page, pretending not to notice the way his spicy scent permeated her senses in deliciously inviting ways.

Focus on the website, Hal. Not on how good he smells.

The homepage was created with a warm cream color as the background. Photos of her favorite bakes—outlined by shapes resembling pale green doilies—were placed at pleasant angles with a few lines of description beside each one. Christian had included links to order for special occasions in prominent positions throughout the site. The whole vibe captured the exact look she'd been unable to create herself.

"I love it!"

"It's a starting point." Even knowing he stood right behind her, Christian's voice came closer than she'd expected. "We can change anything you're not happy with."

Shaking her head, she clicked to another page from the menu at the top. Though unfinished, the start looked as beautiful as the homepage. "This is amazing, Christian. Thank you."

Shivers danced across her spine as his breath tickled her cheek. Turning to look at him, she forgot all about the website when their eyes locked, only inches apart.

Look away. Her brain urged her heart not to plunge deeper into this hole it had created.

But when Christian's captivating gaze dipped to her mouth, just as it had during their impromptu dance, her heart declared all-out war. Her brain had no control over the situation.

It would be so easy to kiss him right now. Her pulse accelerated as the temptation to close the short distance between their lips magnified the longer he stayed there.

She wanted to. So much.

Why was he hesitating?

You're an independent woman. You make the first move.

As her heart urged her to take a leap, her brain fought back with a strong counterattack, listing all the reasons why she shouldn't. Her brother would hate it, for one thing. She was past the point of listening to him, though.

No, the strongest arguments against starting anything with Christian were fast asleep in their beds upstairs. A kiss with him carried more weight than any other relationship she'd had before. She couldn't sacrifice her boundaries to appease her romantic appetite.

Still, she didn't pull away. Maybe one little kiss wouldn't hurt. It might even take some of the edge off all this tension. Slowly, she began to move toward him, closing the gap inch by agonizing inch.

Christian sucked in a breath. The fragile string pulling them together snapped in two. He backed away, rubbing a hand down his face before taking a seat next to her.

Hallie's heart dropped to her gut as he slid the chair further away. A heaviness rushed into the empty space.

"It's taking longer to finish than I'd hoped." His tone was forced as though trying to ignore what had almost transpired between them. "My boss has piled on the workload pretty thick lately."

Hallie had to take a few seconds to reorient herself with the conversation. "No problem. It's probably a lot to manage on top of raising the girls."

Yeah, remember the girls. If she kept them firmly in mind, perhaps she'd finally convince herself that dating Christian could never work. She wasn't ready to step in as a mother figure. Babysitting them, sure. Once she'd warmed up to the idea, she actually had fun today. But watching them for a few hours was a lot different than bearing the responsibility of raising them.

He sighed. "Sometimes it's really hard not to be resentful towards my ex."

Whoa, they were treading into heavy topics now. Hallie took in the twitching of his jaw, the way his nostrils flared.

"What happened?" She winced. That question had to be crossing some serious boundaries. "Don't answer that. It's none of my business."

He didn't look at her. His Adam's apple bobbed slowly as he swallowed. "She left."

"What?" Something cracked inside Hallie's heart at the strangled way he said it.

A pained expression crossed his face when he looked at her. "She dropped the girls off at daycare one day and never came back. When I got home from work, her things were gone, and there was a note." He jabbed a finger toward the center of the table. "Right there."

"What did it say?"

A bitter edge caressed his laugh. "Not much. Basically, that she deserved more out of life and needed to go find herself. Maybe I should've seen it coming. She always blamed me for everything. But I didn't realize she could be so ... selfish. I mean, Nellie was only six weeks old. I haven't heard from her since."

Hallie brought a hand to her mouth, as though that would ease the tightening in her chest. She could feel the devastation he must have felt discovering his wife's abandonment and knowing he'd have to hold it together for his kids. How traumatizing.

Christian kept his focus on the tabletop in front of him. "We'd planned to wait for several years before having children. We were just kids ourselves. But birth control isn't one hundred percent effective. Keep that in mind when ... you know."

"Maybe you should remember to mention that when it comes time to give your girls *the talk*," Hallie said to cover up the blush traveling up her neck.

He winced, pushing out a breathy laugh as he shook his head. "Why'd you have to bring *that* up? I can't even cope with the idea of handling their first periods."

Well, this conversation had certainly taken an unexpected turn. Of all the topics she'd imagined discussing with him, menstrual cycles weren't on the list. Yet their shared laughter, though subdued, managed to cut through the heaviness entrapping the room, an oddly peaceful calm replacing it. The calm that came when friends shared their burdens.

Friends. That sounded nice. Regardless of his off-limits dating status, she couldn't deny wanting him in her life.

"I didn't want to be a father at twenty-one." His smile dropped. "But it's the way my life turned out. And I still can't grasp why Sabrina would just take off like that."

Wait. Hallie recognized that name. "Sabrina. Your dance partner?"

Christian shot an alarmed glance her way. "How'd you know?"

Whoops. She hadn't meant to let that comment slip. And now

wasn't a good time to admit she'd spent the entire afternoon stalking him on the internet. She shook her head. "You're still angry with her."

Thankfully, Christian didn't press for an explanation. "It's been three years, and I can't let it go. And despite that anger, I keep running in circles, wondering if I could've done more to fix our marriage. That maybe I drove her away somehow."

His words came faster, as if his brain literally ran in circles as he spoke.

"Or what if we hadn't eloped? What if I'd insisted on waiting a couple years like my gut was telling me. Maybe I never would've married her in the first place. But I thought I loved her." He dropped his head into his hands. "Now I don't know what love is. Or if it even exists."

Against her better judgement, Hallie placed a hand on his knee. "Of course it does. You love your daughters. Anyone around you can feel that."

"That's different."

"How?"

He didn't answer. "I regret so much of my marriage, of my relationship with her." He dragged his head from side-to-side. "But I *can't* regret my girls. They mean everything to me."

Hallie rubbed her nose with the back of her hand, willing her eyes to contain their moisture. A tear slipped down her cheek anyway, though she didn't notice until the salty taste reached her top lip. Why was she crying? Was it because her chest quite literally ached for him and the trauma he'd been through? Or was a little bit of her heart breaking, realizing this man she couldn't forget about was so emotionally out of reach?

He didn't believe in love?

Tyler had warned her that Christian wasn't ready to get involved with anyone. His concern made complete sense now, though she was in too deep to listen to that advice.

Rising from her chair, she stepped to Christian, wrapping her arms around him from behind. At first, he didn't move. He seemed frozen; in shock or indecision, she didn't know. Then slowly, he pushed back his chair. No words were spoken as he got to his feet and returned her hug.

Hallie nestled her cheek onto his chest, circling her hands to rest underneath his flexed shoulder blades. So many questions bombarded her mind. Did he still have feelings for Sabrina? Could doubting love's existence only be his hurt talking? Was he waiting for her to come back?

Even the slightest possibility of that gave Hallie more reason to run for the hills. Yet she couldn't abandon him. Not after what he'd just told her.

She squeezed her eyes shut, willing her thoughts to calm. His heartbeat pounded against her cheek, in sync with her own racing pulse.

"Sorry." He stepped back. "I didn't mean to burden you with all my problems."

He ran his hand down her arm, tangling his fingers with hers. Hallie didn't have the heart to let go as she reclaimed her seat. Christian scooted his own chair closer until they sat with their knees touching.

"Don't be sorry." She placed her other hand on his thigh. "Sometimes, it helps to get things off your chest. Have you talked to anyone about this? Like a therapist, or Tyler even?"

"I've told Tyler some. And my mom." His shoulders lifted then dropped heavily. "Other than that, when would I have the time?"

Shifting her knees to the side, she leaned forward and wrapped her arms around his neck. "Maybe you should find the time. It's not fair to carry this burden forever. The girls deserve more. *You* deserve more."

She meant that completely. And she wanted him to be happy. Even if she couldn't find her own happiness with him, despite realizing that part of her wanted exactly that.

His arms came around her for a moment, and he rested his face in her hair, his breath hot in her ear. They sat holding each other for a moment, until he lifted his head, and his arms fell away from her.

"Hey, kiddo. What're you doing out of bed?"

Isla stood in the doorway leading into the living room. Sleep marks lined her face, her hair a haphazard array of curls.

"I had a bad dream," she said groggily, looking at them with her head tilted to one shoulder. Was that suspicion in her eyes?

In an instant, Christian resumed the role of compassionate father. "Come here, sweetheart." He stood, lifting the child into his arms.

The sight of him tenderly clutching Isla to his chest sent another surge of emotion swelling inside Hallie. Her heart threatened to burst with affection from witnessing their sweet interaction while simultaneously shattering for herself.

"I'll let myself out," she said, hoping to make it to her car without crying in front of them. "Goodnight, Isla."

The child gave her a sleepy wave, her head resting on her father's shoulder. "I had fun making cookies today."

Hallie reached out to squeeze her hand. "Me too. Maybe we can do it again sometime."

She glanced at Christian, immediately wishing she hadn't. His brows furrowed in concern. Not for his daughter, that much was clear with the way he studied Hallie. How much of her emotions showed on her face?

Grabbing her purse from the floor by her chair, she let herself out of the house. The emotions spilled from her as she slipped into the driver's seat. She covered her face with her hands, and her body convulsed in torment as the tears rained down her face.

Her ugly cries lasted the entire drive home. She wept for Christian and the trauma he'd experienced. For the girls, knowing their mother didn't want them. And in the middle of it all, she cried a little for herself, because she had to stop her rapidly growing feelings but couldn't turn her back on this family she'd grown to care about.

She'd never been so conflicted. What was she supposed to do?

Chapter Twenty-Three

Hallie was upset.

She'd been on the verge of tears when she'd excused herself from Christian's kitchen. And the look on her face still haunted him as he sat in the darkness of Isla's room, waiting for his daughter to fall asleep.

What did I do wrong this time, Dad?

An immediate thought jumped into his brain. He shouldn't have confided in her about his problems. She'd seemed fine until he started talking. His past was a heavy burden, one that he'd held inside for years. Only Mom, Dani, and Tyler knew the extent of his trauma, and what he shared with them only had to do with the girls. He refused to talk about how Sabrina's abandonment still affected him every single day. They'd only tell him it wasn't his fault, that he'd done his best to fix things.

Logically, he knew they were right. But logic didn't stop the pain.

Talking to Hallie tonight had been ... refreshing in a strange sort of way. She didn't try to heal him or convince him to let it go.

She'd just listened.

And when talking had become too difficult, when the bitterness and grief threatened to spill out, she'd held him. Only some strong sorcery could push out the negative emotions he'd dragged around for years, replacing it with peace.

Peace.

That was the effect her touch had on him. Like he could finally breathe after being held underwater. It hadn't fixed anything, yet for as long as she hugged him, he began to feel like he could eventually find healing.

Still, he shouldn't have dumped his problems onto her.

He crept silently from Isla's room, leaving the door partly open to let the hallway light illuminate a path to her bed. He always kept it on in case of any nighttime wanderings, which more often than not ended with her crawling in with him.

Entering his room, he crossed to the window overlooking the street. His car sat alone in the driveway, which didn't ease his concern. He'd noticed her sedan still parked next to his Highlander when he'd locked the door on his way upstairs with Isla, several minutes after she'd made her exit.

He pulled his phone from his pocket and sent off a quick text.

> Christian: Thanks again for watching the girls. Did you make it home okay?

He set his phone on his dresser to change out of his work clothes, continuing his one-sided exchange with Dad. *She's okay, right? I was imagining her tears.* He'd simply been projecting his sorrow onto her.

His self-assurance didn't stop him from abandoning the shirt he was about to put on and snatching the phone from his dresser as soon as it buzzed. Hallie's name lit up the screen.

> Hallie: Safe and sound. Heading for bed.

> Hallie: Btw … I still have the girls' extra seats in my car. Sorry I didn't take them out before I left.

> Christian: No worries. I'll grab them tomorrow.

Now he had an excuse to see her again. Not that he should want one. But his mouth slid upward as he walked into the master bathroom to brush his teeth. While spreading toothpaste onto his brush, his phone vibrated again.

> Hallie: I was thinking about something on the way home.

> Christian: Yeah?

Three dots performed the wave below his message before disappearing. They reappeared only to go away again. Whatever she wanted to say was causing some hesitation.

> Hallie: Remember when you asked me to babysit? You said you haven't found a replacement nanny, and you were desperate.

He vaguely recalled mentioning that somewhere in the word vomit spewing from his mouth during their phone conversation.

> Christian: Yeah...

More vanishing dots. They danced across the screen three times before a message appeared.

> Hallie: What if I watched the girls?

She couldn't be serious. Hastily, he rinsed the toothpaste from his mouth before jabbing the icon at the top of the text thread to dial her number.

"I can't ask you to do that," he said once she'd answered.

"You're not asking. I'm offering."

He dropped onto his bed, kicking his feet onto the mattress. "Hallie, I really don't feel right about imposing on you with this. Watching the girls five days a week is a lot, and you have your own obligations. I can't expect you to solve my problems too." Not to mention she was already invading his thoughts most of the time. He'd do well to distance himself from her, a difficult feat if she was in his home every weekday afternoon.

And what about his girls? It wouldn't be fair to allow them to get close to Hallie and have her inevitably disappear. It would break their hearts.

"It would only be temporary until you find someone else," she said.

That didn't make him feel better considering the way Isla had regressed following Annelise's departure.

"I can handle a few hours on weeknights," Hallie continued. "At least until I find a job."

"Job?" Christian asked, momentarily pushing his reservations about her offer aside. "What about your business?"

A sigh laced her words as she responded. "My savings are running out really fast. And I don't have any orders coming up besides the Hawthornes' and yours. I'm not exactly rolling in the dough right now."

"I see what you did there." Her unintended pun pulled a chuckle from Christian before he realized how insensitive it sounded. He cleared his throat. "I'm sorry, Hal."

"Thanks." Despondency hung in her voice. "Who knows, maybe working for someone else for a while will be a good thing. It'll give me valuable insight to take with me if I finally get my bakery."

If? She must really be worried if she'd downgraded her dream status to *if*.

"I applied for a position as a baker's assistant," she continued, "but I found out today I didn't get it. Not enough experience. So, it's back to square one."

Had that been what had bothered her before? As bad as it sounded, Christian hoped her discouragement had only been due to her disappointment rather than the things he'd told her. "If that's the direction you want to go, I'm sure you'll find something. But I get your discouragement."

"You do?"

More than she knew. "Believe me, the job I have now isn't my dream job."

"If you could have any job in the world, what would it be?"

He'd spent hours thinking about his previous career goals. At night while snuggling Penelope in the peaceful quiet of her dark room. After every agonizing team meeting or lecture from Jim. Still, he rarely, if ever, spoke them out loud.

"I wanted to form my own tech startup. Nothing big, just me and maybe one other person. Something with a flexible schedule so I can spend more time with the girls. I hate having to miss so much by being in the office all day. They're growing up so fast."

Not to mention the wonders that would work on Isla if he didn't have to leave all the time. "But I never had the luxury of building it up before the girls came, and they kind of need to eat." He pushed out a breathy laugh.

"You're a good dad," Hallie said softly. "Isla and Penelope are really lucky to have you in their corner."

When was the last time anyone had told him that? He was sure Mom had from time to time. But she was his mother; she had to say stuff like that. Dani may have mentioned something similar too. But had anyone outside his family ever made an effort to ease his doubts?

I'm lucky to have you, Hallie.

He squeezed his eyes shut. No, he didn't have her. And he shouldn't want her.

He shook away the unsettling reminder of his ill-advised crush on his best friend's sister. "I really can't complain. I have a good job that pays well with full benefits. And besides my lackluster boss, I love the people I work with. Many college graduates just starting out aren't so lucky. But I understand the discouragement that comes from having to pivot away from what you'd rather be doing."

"Yeah. I'm sure I'll figure things out." She sighed, and he could feel her mood shifting with the sound. "In the meantime, I'm free to help you."

"I don't know." There had to be a million things she'd rather be doing on a weekday than hanging out with little kids.

"It makes sense. The girls already know me. Even Isla warmed up after a while, and I know you're super stressed about her. Let me take this off your plate."

Christian stretched out onto his bed, bringing his free hand to rest behind his head. She made all valid points, especially about the girls responding well to her. *That's what I'm worried about.*

But wouldn't he have the same problem no matter who he hired? As much as Annelise had felt like part of their family, she wasn't. And her life goals had made it necessary to say goodbye. Nannies, by design, were a temporary fix. They didn't replace the fact that his girls don't have a mother. Perhaps he could use this as a teaching opportunity, especially for Isla. If he prepared her early, she'd have an easier time transitioning to someone new. Hopefully.

And on the good side, letting Hallie step in for a while would get his boss off his back.

He exhaled a resigned sigh. "Fine. If you're willing to watch them, I won't say no. But I have ... stipulations." More like boundaries. Barriers to keep his heart in check.

"Like what?"

"You are not, under any circumstances, allowed to clean my house." He'd let her watch his kids, but he wouldn't add maid service to her duties.

Her strangled groan brought a smile to his face. "The sight of a messy kitchen gives me hives."

Christian chuckled. "I can't tell if you're joking, so for the sake of your physical health, I'll add an exception to that rule. You can *straighten* the kitchen after using it. But nothing else."

"I don't know," she deadpanned. "I've seen the state of your laundry hamper."

"Don't touch my laundry, Hal," he barked, more sternly than he'd intended.

She laughed, and the melodic sound reached all the way inside him, bringing peace to his heart, the same way hugging her had earlier. "Okay, okay. I won't touch your laundry."

"Good." Christian's smile remained plastered to his face. "There's one more thing."

"Fine. I won't clean your bathrooms either."

"They're not even that messy." Aside from a little clutter of bottles on the counters, the bathrooms were the cleanest rooms in the house.

"But that's not my stipulation. I want to pay you. Twenty-five dollars an hour."

"Twenty-five?" She sputtered. "Christian ... uh ... That's too much. I can't ... ask you ... for that."

"It's a good thing you're not asking, then."

She laughed again, though more subdued than a minute ago. "I see you throwing my words back at me."

"And I'll keep doing that until you agree." He turned onto his side, propping himself onto his elbow. "You're taking a huge load off my shoulders. I want to help you too. So please let me."

"Why?"

Because you deserve it. Because even though I don't know why, I want to ease your burdens. Because just being near you makes me feel more alive than I have in years ...

"It's a fair rate. I paid our last nanny that much, and I'll pay the next one the same. And because we're friends, I refuse to take advantage of you."

"You want to be friends?"

"I really do." The words left a funny taste in his mouth.

"Me too." Why did her response sound so sad?

Christian could sense the mood shifting, returning to the foreboding that plagued him earlier. "Hey, are you okay?"

"Yeah, why?"

"You seemed down when you left my house. Is it your job situation?"

"Not exactly," she admitted. "I'm working through some things right now. I'll be fine, though."

She didn't sound fine. And that bothered him more than it should. He almost said as much, but stopped himself. "I guess I'll see you tomorrow then."

"Yeah, see you tomorrow."

After hanging up, Christian set his phone on the nightstand and clicked off the light. Laying on his side in the darkness, a weight clung to him as he ran through their conversation. The words they said, Hallie's despondent tone, and her admission of having to work through some things. Knowing that she grappled with anything, whatever it was, triggered his protective instincts. He was already doing everything he could think of to help her business. But was he doing enough for *her*?

It hurt seeing her struggle. Despite his own rising doubts about letting her get close to his girls—and him—he could no longer fight the fact that he cared about her. And he wanted to help her feel the peace that she'd brought to him.

But was he capable of opening his heart enough to try?

Chapter Twenty-Four

The next day, Isla didn't throw any celebrations when she found Hallie waiting for her in the office at school pickup, but she didn't seem disappointed either. And though she spent the entire drive home staring at the heart on her hand, her deep pout never made an appearance. All things considered, Hallie counted it as a win.

"What do you girls want to do today?" she asked, stepping onto the porch and letting go of Penelope's hand.

The girl spun in a circle with her arms out to the side. "Park! Park!"

Hallie laughed at her infectious enthusiasm. "I think we have time for a quick park trip before the sun goes down." And it might wear them out enough to make bedtime easier for Christian. "What do you think, Isla?"

"Can we have a snack first?"

"Of course. We'll have a quick snack and then head out." Hallie nudged the three paper bags out of the way of the front door. Christian had texted her earlier about having some groceries delivered around the time they got home to make dinner prep easier. Again, his thoughtfulness touched her.

After punching the code in the keypad, she pushed the door open, ushering the girls inside while she grabbed the groceries. Princess Pumpkin bounded toward them, and Hallie congratulated herself for not flinching at the sensation of the dog's wet nose sniffing her hand. At least Pumpkin didn't jump on her. They were both making progress.

While carrying the groceries into the kitchen, she passed the laundry room door. Someone had shut it since she'd been here last, and she stepped closer to read the piece of paper taped to the wood.

STAY OUT!
I mean it, Hal.
Resist the urge.

Despite her amusement, Hallie's heart squeezed at the reminder of their phone conversation last night. She'd liked the easy way they'd communicated, as if the heavy conversation in this very kitchen had broken down the barriers of their friendship.

But their playful banter had only tightened the vice grip squeezing her heart. She hadn't lied about wanting to be friends. She really did want that. Except was that really possible when her feelings for him were becoming so much deeper?

Yet she couldn't turn off her desire to help this little family. Perhaps the arrangement they'd set up would make it easier to keep an emotional distance. She now worked for Christian. He was her boss. If she kept that in mind, maybe she could convince herself not to do something she'd eventually regret.

Who was she kidding? She was walking on eggshells here, some of which were already jagged and broken, slicing into her feet. But it was too late to back out of the arrangement now.

While the girls finished their snacks, Hallie grabbed the leash from the hook by the back door and clipped it to Pumpkin's collar. "There's a good dog. Maybe we can be friends, after all."

The dog responded with a breathy yip.

Once they bundled back into their jackets and shoes, Hallie strapped Penelope into the stroller, and they set off for the park. Isla walked a few steps ahead, kicking at the pebbles on the sidewalk.

Frantic yipping immediately greeted them as soon as they reached the almost deserted playground. Hallie yanked on Pumpkin's leash to keep her from toppling the stroller in her effort to say hello to the four yorkies. She swallowed a groan, recognizing the dark-haired woman sitting on the bench immediately.

Carrie arched a single ebony brow as their entourage approached. "The girls didn't scare you away, I see."

"Not at all." Hallie bit back her immediate annoyance and offered no other response. Unclipping Penelope from the stroller, she helped the child down. "Go ahead, sweetie."

Penelope needed no further encouragement and ran off toward the smaller of the two jungle gyms. Hallie searched the playground for Isla, spotting her over by the swings with another child.

"I'm glad you survived having to watch Isla." Carrie pierced Hallie with a look of pointed interest. "You must be a strong woman."

Hallie's eye twitched in annoyance. *Who does this woman think she is? She's talking trash about a child.* Did she have any decency at all?

The temptation to set Carrie in her place with one verbal put-down raged inside her. Instead, she held her head high as she unwrapped Pumpkin's leash from the stroller's handlebar. "We had a great time."

Carrie's attempt at a sugary sweet smile fell flat. "That's wonderful. Christian is so lucky to have a *friend* like you. Sammy, sweetie," she called to her daughter, who sat in the swing next to Isla's. The girls weren't exactly speaking to each other, more like occupying the same general area. "Come play in the sandbox. I brought some new toys for you."

The dark-haired girl jumped off the swing and ran over without a backward glance at Isla.

Carrie's true intention in redirecting her daughter's play didn't go unnoticed. It was impossible not to after the disparaging remarks she'd made about Isla over the last two days.

What did she find so lacking in the child? Isla wore her heart on her sleeve, sure. And she had trouble handling big emotions. But didn't everyone? Why did Carrie feel the need to protect her daughter from a child who clearly needed extra love and kindness?

Leaving this conversation behind became Hallie's most important task. With little more than a word of farewell, she pulled on Pumpkin to get her to follow. "Come on, girl. Let's go over there." She stopped at a bench near the swing set and looped the leash around the metal armrest, making sure to give the dog room to move.

Isla didn't notice her approach at first. She stared at the ground, her feet waving in lazy kicks, making the swing jerk out in all angles except the direction it should be going. Her hunched shoulders gave away her melancholy.

"Hey." Hallie crouched in front of the swing, gripping the chains to stop its frantic movements. "You okay?"

Isla stopped kicking and lifted only her eyes. "Sammy used to be my friend. But now she's not, and I don't know why."

A small chasm split inside Hallie's chest. Isla wasn't yet six years old, and she'd already experienced so much loss. First her mother. Now her friend. Life could be so cruel.

"I'm sorry," Hallie said gently. "It's hard to lose people you care about, huh?"

Isla sniffed. Her mouth puckered in a deep pout, not out of defiance, but of sadness.

Hallie considered her words for several long seconds before speaking them out loud. "Can I be your friend?"

"Really?"

She nodded, surprising herself with how much she really meant the offer. "Really."

Some of the weight in Isla's posture lifted. "And you'll be my friend forever?"

Hallie didn't want to lie but her complicated relationship with Christian made forever a tough promise to make. But she genuinely wanted to be an influence for good in Isla's life. "I'd like to be, if you're okay with that."

For a moment, Isla only stared at her. Then without warning, she lunged forward so suddenly, Hallie barely had time to catch the girl as she launched off the swing.

"I take that as a yes." She scooped the child into her chest.

Isla wrapped her arms around Hallie's neck in a tight hug. "It is a yes. I want to be your friend."

Hallie unwove herself from the child's hold and squeezed her hands. "It's settled then. How should we seal the deal?"

Isla thought about it for a second before extending the little finger on her right hand. "Pinkie promise."

Hallie raised hers as well, and they linked them together.

"Kiss your hand," Isla demanded. She brought her mouth to her thumb, eyeing Hallie expectantly until she did the same. "Now you're stuck with me."

Hallie scrunched her nose with a smile at the girl's bold declaration. "No getting out of it. How would my new friend like a push on the swing?"

"Can I have an underdog?"

"Absolutely. Let me just check on your sister first." After locating Penelope inside the tunnel slide on the big jungle gym, Hallie went back to Isla at the swings. "Ready?"

Isla nodded, and Hallie pulled the swing back.

"One for the money," she called, running forward without letting go. She pulled the swing back again. "Two for the show." Forward and back. "Three to get ready. And four to go!" She ran forward, propelling herself underneath the swing as she let go.

Isla's laughter cut through the calm of the early evening. Hallie's heart swelled with joy at the happy sound, and she brought a hand to her chest. This sweet girl needed this moment of relief from the heaviness that followed her everywhere she went.

Penelope flew from the tunnel slide. "My turn! My turn! I want one!"

"How about the baby swing so you don't fall?" Hallie slid her into one of the bucket swings on the other side of the set.

For the next several minutes, she ran back and forth between the girls, giving them one underdog after another. As she grew tired from all the running, their enjoyment fueled her motivation, keeping her going. The sound was infectious; even Pumpkin stood on all fours, dancing around on her leash. With each new underdog, the girls called for another until Hallie feared she'd pass out if she pushed any more.

"Phew, I'm worn out." She bent over to catch her breath.

"More! More!" Penelope kicked her legs gleefully.

Hallie waved her hands in front of herself. "Let me rest for a minute and then I'll give you both another one." How could she resist their sweet laughter? She'd give them a thousand underdogs if it meant maintaining their happiness a little longer.

The girls giggled as she flopped down on the artificial turf. Real grass and dirt made up the baseball field, but the playground was lined with the fake stuff on top of rubber to prevent injuries.

With her eyes closed, Hallie didn't notice Isla hop off her swing until she plopped down on the ground next to her.

"I'm glad you came to play with us today, new friend." She dropped onto her back, staring at the rosy sky.

Hallie's heart melted a little more. She sat up, only then noticing that sometime during their play, Carrie and Sammy had left the park.

Good riddance.

She nudged Isla's side with the back of her hand. "I am too. You're a special kid. And so is Penelope." She meant that with all sincerity, marveling at how quickly she'd gone from not wanting anything to do with Christian's kids to genuinely enjoying being around them.

Sitting with Isla, watching Penelope gleefully try to pump her legs, she realized something. Nothing could come from her relationship with their father, and she didn't know how long she'd need to act as their temporary nanny. But she could still love these girls for however long she had the privilege.

I won't let them down. Her vow didn't chase away all her confusion surrounding Christian, but it would have to be enough for now.

Chapter Twenty-Five

A week into their arrangement, Hallie stood in Christian's empty kitchen while the girls were at school, piping purple macaron batter into circles on a baking sheet. She'd texted him a few hours ago for permission to use his oven to test a new recipe she'd created. Her food handler's permit only allowed her to sell products baked in her own kitchen, but it didn't prevent her from experimenting elsewhere.

And as her own countertops were currently occupied with supplies for his cake order and the Hawthornes' Halloween party, Beej, Kendall, and McKenzie were already threatening to force her out of the house if she tried to cram one more thing into the kitchen.

They wouldn't really, but Hallie sympathized with how annoying her business could be for her roommates.

Taylor Swift's musical genius accompanied her while she worked, and she stopped piping batter long enough to turn up the volume on her phone. Mumbling along to the lyrics, she bopped her head to the beat as she returned to her task.

There was something freeing about being here alone. She thrived on rational, logical conclusions to all of life's problems. It had served her well.

Yet lately, that personality trait had fled to who knew where, leaving chaos and confusion in its wake. Her feelings for Christian were anything but rational, and the speed at which she'd become attached to his girls after insisting she couldn't relate to them didn't make any sense at all. Even her struggling business and lack of job prospects were giving her more unresolved questions and not enough answers.

But none of that mattered in this empty kitchen. The girls still had a few hours left of school, and Christian wouldn't be home from work until at least five. For the moment, Hallie could do what she loved with no complications.

With the baking sheet full, she set the piping bag down on the granite countertop. She added a little shoulder shimmy to her head bop as she slid the macarons inside the oven. After setting the timer on the stove, she moonwalked over to the table to pick up the bowl of French buttercream she'd whipped up earlier.

Her movement brought her attention to the rest of the room, and her heart skidded to a stop at the figure leaning against the entryway between the kitchen and living room.

"Christian!" She pressed a hand to her chest to suppress the sudden panic surging through it. The bowl clattered back onto the table. "You're not supposed to be here. I mean, you're allowed to be here, of course. It's your house. You just ... surprised me."

He splayed his hands out in apology, though his mouth stretched into the widest grin she'd ever seen on his face. "Sorry to startle you. But I have to admit, that reaction was probably my favorite ever."

She tossed a side eye in his direction, which lost its edge as he sauntered into the kitchen, his steps transforming effortlessly into a flirty cha cha, complete with flowing arm movements. Hallie's eyes slid to the rhythmic sway of his hips before she caught herself and snapped her focus back to the charm decorating his handsome face.

The dancing world was robbed of a lot of talent. She could watch him all day, as evidenced by the rabbit hole she'd fallen down last week while obsessively stalking every YouTube video she could find of him. But seeing him dance in person was so much better. It was like a private show meant only for her. One she didn't intend to share.

Boundaries, Hal. Yes, she needed to remember them. Now that Christian was paying her to watch his kids, she had more reason to keep her feelings in check. If the rest of her red flags didn't do the trick, the ethical ramifications of getting involved with a man who was technically her boss absolutely had to.

He added a casual spin to end his performance, complete with popping the collar of his pressed white dress shirt. "Oh, yeah, I've still got it," he said with a cheeky smirk.

He certainly did. A little too much.

And not only with his dancing skills. She shouldn't enjoy seeing him like this. He almost seemed like a different person since she'd started watching the girls. Like he didn't constantly have the weight of the world on his shoulders. She wasn't naïve to think that his troubles were over simply because she'd eased this one burden, but she had to admit, it was nice seeing him lower his guard a little.

And she couldn't stress enough how much she loved his smile. He could woo any woman he wanted with the level of charm he displayed now. If only she could be that lucky lady.

She was playing with fire by even entertaining the idea.

Space. She needed space.

Stepping around him, she made a beeline for her phone to pause the music. "With moves like that, I find it hard to believe you weren't the one that hung the disco ball in my bedroom."

"I already told you. Brad did that."

"Uh huh." She willed her face to cool down. "What's the real story?"

He chuckled, the lighthearted response disarming her further. "He put it up the day after watching one of my performances on campus. We did this disco number to Bruno Mars complete with a white, sequined bodysuit. I didn't live that down for weeks."

"Oooh, I saw that one." Hallie almost slapped her hand to her mouth.

Christian arched an eyebrow. "Uh ... what?"

She wasn't about to admit that she'd watched that video three times because of the amount of screen time he'd received. That information was classified.

"So Brad loved it so much he honored you with a disco ball?"

Each second he studied her turned up Hallie's internal thermostat. She avoided eye contact, afraid that if she looked at him, he'd be able to tell how hard she was working to keep her feelings from showing.

Finally, he conceded. "Okay, I'll honor your tragically obvious redirection tactic. For now."

Hallie laughed in spite of her embarrassment.

"But quoting my jerk of a boss, we will circle back to this conversation."

Not if she had anything to do with it. The only person who knew about her temporary lapse of reason was McKenzie, and Hallie had no doubt she'd keep the secret.

"Anyway, yes. Brad hung it up while I was in class a few days later."

Her mouth twitched. "Weirdo."

"We were always messing with each other. I got him back the next day by inverting his computer screen. It took him hours to figure out how to put it back." His face scrunched as he let out an uncharacteristic giggle. The high-pitched sound was so at odds with his deep voice that Hallie's heart stuttered at this brief moment of unguarded pleasure. "Ah man, I miss those days."

Hallie retrieved the bowl of buttercream and carried it to the counter. "What happened to you guys? I remember you saying you don't talk much anymore."

"More like not at all." He sat down at the kitchen table.

Hallie paused in her task of spooning buttercream into an empty piping bag. "You seemed to get along at Tyler's wedding."

"Oh, we're on speaking terms." He clasped his hands together, tapping his knuckles with his interconnected fingers. "We just ... don't anymore."

"Why not?"

Christian puffed out his cheeks, held them, then exhaled a big breath. "Sabrina."

"Your ex."

He confirmed her statement with a single nod. "She hated Brad. And he wasn't a fan of her either. When I told the guys about getting married, he didn't hold back. Some of the things he said were pretty harsh. Of course, I took her side, and our friendship kind of ... blew up after that."

Christian pursed his lips around his teeth as though holding something back. Hallie stood frozen in her spot, torn between maintaining her boundaries and giving him the physical comfort she yearned to provide.

"It wasn't until my marriage ended that I realized he was spot on in his judgment." He shook his head. "He'd only been trying to protect me."

Abandoning the buttercream, she sat down in the chair next to his. "Brad has never been known for his tactful approaches."

That pulled a dry chuckle from him. "Tell me about it. I've sometimes wondered why I never reached out to him like I did Tyler. We were all practically brothers. Maybe I was too embarrassed. Or ashamed it didn't work out with her. I don't know. My emotions were so raw back then. I guess I didn't want him to say 'I told you so.'"

Hallie dropped her hand on top of his where they rested in his lap. "My cousin can be really pig headed sometimes, but he rarely holds grudges, especially with people he cares about."

"I've wanted to talk to him about it for a while. It just seems silly to bring it up after all this time." He turned his palm up, weaving his fingers through hers.

A spark zipped up her arm, reminding her of the boundaries she'd just obliterated by taking his hand. "No, it's not. You should talk to him. I'm sure you'll feel better once you do."

"Maybe you're right."

"Of course I am."

He snorted. "Are you always this rational?"

Not lately, especially when it came to him. "There's a solution to every problem if you look at it logically."

"I don't know if that's true, but it's a nice thought."

Hallie placed her other hand on his thigh, leaning forward to look into his face. "I'm not saying the solution always comes easily."

His gaze didn't hold the same sadness she'd seen the night he'd told her about his divorce. Instead, he seemed thoughtful, as though pondering something he hadn't thought of before.

He brought his other hand down to hers. Then, to Hallie's surprise, lifted it to his lips, kissing the backs of her fingers.

Her pulse performed a jig against her neck. He couldn't expect her to interpret a gesture like this as anything but romantic, right? If he felt comfortable kissing her hand, he couldn't be as callous to love as he claimed.

Or maybe he didn't see it as romantic. Then what could it mean?

It doesn't matter. He's still your boss now.

The oven's long beep brought the relief she needed. "The macarons are done," she squeaked, letting go of his hands faster than the time she'd accidentally pulled a cake pan out of the oven without a hot pad. Her hand burned where he'd placed the kiss just as much as it had back then.

Popping up from her chair, she hurried to the oven, holding her breath to make her heart rate slow. Once she felt more like herself, she asked, "What're you doing home anyway? I didn't think you'd leave work until five."

Christian followed her, leaning against the fridge as she pulled the baking sheet out of the oven. "My boss's wife called with an emergency that apparently only he could handle. He wasn't happy about it, but he left early, so I did too. I wanted to see—" His face turned a light shade of pink. "I thought I'd work from home this afternoon."

His blush, and the way he'd abruptly redirected his answer, made it evident his purpose hadn't been to spend the afternoon with his kids. Was he here to see her?

Oh, please no. She didn't think she'd be able to resist him if he admitted to coming home early for her.

"That smells really good." He leaned in for a closer look, bringing his tantalizing scent into her personal space. "What kind are they?"

"Blueberry lavender." Hallie set the baking sheet on top of the stove.

"Lavender? Like the flower?"

"Don't knock it 'til you try it."

"I don't normally eat flowers," he said. "And the smell is awful. I tried diffusing lavender oil in Isla's room when her sleeping problems first started because everyone swore it would help."

"Did it?"

"No. All I got was a massive headache."

Hallie picked up the piping bag in one hand and grabbed a cooled lavender-colored cookie from the wire rack at the back of the counter. "It's an acquired taste, but mix it with something like blueberries, and it's delicious."

She smeared a circle of buttercream around the center of the cookie before picking up another half, smooshing it down until a white ring pooled to the edge of the small sandwich. "Try this."

As she held the macaron up to his mouth, her heart thumped hard against her rib cage again. Why hadn't she just handed it to him? Would he think she was coming onto him? With the tension swirling in this kitchen right now, feeding him herself felt way too much like crossing over a line she couldn't return.

When his hands found her waist, she knew he felt it too. Goosebumps skittered across her back as the gentle pressure of his fingers invited her closer. His brown eyes stared back at her with an intensity that surged straight into her soul, a question swimming in their depths. The very question she asked herself.

No, it's not okay. Kissing him would only lead her further into that forbidden territory.

Except she couldn't back away. And for this one moment, she longed to pretend a future was possible between them.

After setting the half-eaten macaron on the counter, she hooked her hand behind his neck, pulling him down to her level. Her eyelids fluttered closed as their lips hovered a fraction of an inch apart, so close their breaths mingled in a tantalizing dance. Anticipation crackled in the air, waiting for someone to make the first move.

Who initiated it, she didn't know, but the next instant, sparks ignited in her brain at this long-anticipated kiss.

Christian tightened his grip on her with one arm, circling around her to splay across her upper back. The fingers of his other hand plunged into her hair, cradling her head. His heart thudded against her as she pressed tighter to his chest.

She shouldn't want this. Everything in her mind screamed for her to step back, create space, think rationally. All while her heart persuaded her to go deeper.

No wonder she was so confused. How could something so wrong feel so right?

"Hallie," he gasped, coming up for air.

"Don't stop," she whispered, not willing to let go of this one moment of pleasure.

Lowering his mouth again to hers, he backed her gently against the fridge. He cradled her tenderly with one arm while the other braced against the stainless steel.

In the foggy abyss of her subconscious, Hallie thought she heard a door shut in the distance. That couldn't be right. They were alone. She refocused her mind on the soft caress of his lips.

"Christian?"

The woman's voice was harder to ignore, though it reached Hallie's ears in a gargled vibration more than an actual sound. Like when someone tried to speak underwater.

Her mind was playing tricks on her, doing whatever it could to stop her heart. But it wouldn't work. She'd like nothing more than to stay in the blissful oblivion of his affections forever.

She slid her hands across his shoulders and down to his chest, basking in the solid realness of him. Clutching his shirt, she drew him closer, closer, until ...

"Oh!"

At the voice, Christian cursed, flying away from Hallie so fast the movement knocked her backward. She bumped her head against the fridge, an inferno raging across her face.

A woman stood in the entrance to the kitchen, her mouth dropped open in a wide O. Multiple reusable shopping bags dropped to the floor. Her light brows raised, and the way she'd pulled back her dark blonde hair gave Hallie a direct view of the shock in her eyes.

The same brown eyes that she'd studied in depth on the man now standing as far as he could get and still be in the room. Christian refused to look at her as his words confirmed what had taken Hallie only a second to understand.

"Hey ... Mom."

Chapter Twenty-Six

"What're you doing here?" Christian asked, his brain still tangled in the aftereffects of that kiss. He rubbed at the back of his neck where the skin burned. His gaze flicked to Hallie over by the fridge. She'd already turned away, hurriedly piping frosting on the macaron halves on the cooling rack.

Mom's whole countenance buzzed with excitement, but thankfully, she kept her evaluation of what she'd just witnessed to herself. She popped a hand on one hip. "I haven't seen my only son for weeks and those are the first words I get from you? Where's my hug?" The fond smile that followed took the sting out of her reprimand.

Giving his head a little shake, he stepped to her, stooping low enough to wrap his arms around her. "It's good to see you, Mom. When did you get home?"

"Late last night." She searched his face for a long moment like she hadn't seen him for years, not weeks. "I would've called when I got back, but I thought you'd be asleep." She dropped her voice to a whisper. "Who's your friend?"

The burning in his neck spread to his face. He shoved his hands in his pockets. "Mom, this is Hallie."

At hearing her name, Hallie set down the piping bag and slowly faced his mother. To the casual observer, she seemed totally at ease except for the white-knuckled clasping of her hands. Christian felt for her. There was no way to make this situation less awkward.

Clearing his throat, he addressed Hallie next. "Hallie, meet my mom."

She fanned her hand out in a wave. "Hey, Mrs. Gustafson."

"It's very nice to meet you, Hallie." Mom took a step toward her and panic sparked in Christian's chest. She was a hugger. And though the younger woman had proved herself calm and rational in every situation, he doubted an embrace would help this one.

Hallie stared at him with wide eyes as Mom's arms circled her shoulders. Then slowly, tentatively, she returned the affection.

"I'm sorry to interrupt," Mom said, after a few long seconds, ending the embrace. "If I'd known Christian would be *entertaining* a guest, I would've called first."

He didn't miss the emphasis on the word entertaining, or the underlying giddiness behind it. A low groan sounded in his throat. He'd be hearing about this later.

"It's okay." Hallie's voice wobbled a bit. "I was about to go pick up the girls." She eyed Christian, and her face turned even more red. "I'm sure you and your mom want to … catch up."

Nope. Definitely not. He'd rather catch up with *Hallie*. All week, Isla and Penelope had dominated her attention up to the minute she'd left for the night. And Hallie had seemed more than willing to give them all her focus. He loved watching the tender way she interacted with his girls, but he couldn't ignore the nagging suspicion that she'd used it as an excuse to avoid talking to him. She'd kept a respectful distance.

He didn't like it at all.

Even though he knew he should prefer it that way.

Mom looked at her watch. "Oh, is it pick-up time already?"

Technically, school didn't end for another two hours. But Hallie gathered her purse from the counter near the back door, throwing it over her shoulder. "It's always good to get to the front of the line. I'll clean up my mess when we get back. It was nice meeting you, Mrs. Gustafson." She beat a hasty retreat from the kitchen. The front door slammed shut a second later.

If only Christian could be so lucky. He ran a hand down his jaw, the facial scruff prickling his fingertips as he prepared to face the music.

"Has she been helping you out with the girls, or something?" Mom asked from behind him after a beat of thick silence. "Why aren't you picking them up?"

He turned around to find her watching him closely. "Yeah," he said in answer to her first question. He didn't mention that he was paying her to do it. That would open a whole discussion he wasn't willing to have.

"She's nice." Mom continued studying him with a curious eye. "How long have you known her?"

"About a month."

"You seemed pretty into her."

Nope, he refused to take the bait. He was twenty-seven years old, for crying out loud. He should be able to make out with a woman in his own house and not be made to feel like a seventeen-year-old caught breaking curfew.

He smothered the smile threatening to break free. Kissing Hallie hadn't been in his plans for coming home early, though no part of him complained about that accident. Guilt wiggled in his chest at how much he enjoyed it. With their situation being what it was, he shouldn't have. He hadn't just overlooked the code of ethics by kissing his kids' temporary nanny, he'd tossed the whole dang book into the fire.

And that was on top of all the other reasons marring the pleasure of that glorious kiss. But he wouldn't be discussing any of that with his mother.

He gestured toward the bags at Mom's feet. "What's in there?"

Some of the sparkle dimmed from her eyes, but she didn't press the issue. She pulled out a chair and lifted one of the sacks onto it. "I picked up a few things for you at the store."

"You didn't need to do that." Judging by the four heaping bags, she'd bought enough groceries to last them a week.

"I wanted to. There are some surprises for the girls in there too."

She pulled out a carton of Penelope's favorite chocolate milk, the expensive brand that Christian never bought. Leave it to his mother to spoil them all. She took the grandma role very seriously. Even after almost a decade of living on his own, she still went out of her way to make sure his cupboards were stocked.

Not that he'd ever complain about free food.

A scratching came at the back door, followed by high-pitched whining. While Mom continued unloading the groceries, Christian opened the back door for Pumpkin. The dog sauntered inside, heading straight for Mom, who paused long enough to give her a few pats.

Christian refilled the empty water bowl and tossed a couple dog treats onto Pumpkin's bed, before helping his mother with the groceries.

"How was your cruise?" He pulled out a loaf of bread from one of the bags.

Mom's demeanor brightened. "Oh, Christian, if I'd known how wonderful the experience was going to be, I would've let Anita talk me into doing it years ago."

She launched into a day-by-day summation of the entire vacation. By dinner of day two, Christian's mind had already drifted back to Hallie.

How was she feeling about the kiss? She'd seemed into their surprise make out, but could she be having the same doubts he did now?

He hated feeling so conflicted. That kiss had been the most incredible, jaw-dropping kiss of his life. In the moment, all his reservations had taken a back seat to the euphoria of it, awakening a part of him that had been dormant for so long.

"We were at sea on Monday, so we spent the whole day relaxing by the pool..."

Christian emerged from his thoughts long enough to nod at Mom's tale. But as he slid a box of Cheerios into the cupboard, he slipped back into his own internal monologue.

For years, he'd stoked the bitter fire clutching his heart. He'd craved it even, convincing himself that it would block out the pain resulting from Sabrina's abandonment. If he never gave his heart away again, he'd never set himself up for the inevitable pain that would follow.

Then in waltzed Hallie, like some mythical fairy who, without him realizing it, started breaking down his walls with every wave of her magic wand. Yet the possibility of surrendering the very weapons that kept him afloat all these years terrified him. Could he really put himself in a position to finish him off entirely?

"And on the last night, we went on this romantic dinner and Paul—"

Christian's head whipped in her direction, and he closed the cupboard door a little too hard. "Who's Paul?"

"The man I've been telling you about this whole time." Mom looked at him, a mixture of amusement and exasperation in her eyes. "Weren't you listening?"

"I am now," he muttered more to himself than to her.

She went back to unloading the final grocery bag. "We met at dinner the first night. I haven't connected with someone like him since your father. He's a widower, in fact, from Fullerton."

Now that Christian had come down from the clouds, he studied her closely as she talked about this mystery man. The slight smile gracing her mouth as she listed his qualities. The twinkle in her eye when recalling some witty conversation they'd had over drinks one evening. She practically radiated giddiness while recounting their nights on the dance floor or talking under the stars.

It was all too much. In the back of Christian's mind, he always knew there'd come a day when Mom might fall in love again, but hearing about it didn't sit well with him.

I don't like it, Dad. "That's ... great, Mom. He seems like a great guy." How many times would he have to say *great* before he started to believe it? More than twice, obviously.

Mom's full smile blossomed. "Thank you, son. We're taking it slow, of course, but I do want you to meet him. In fact, we're planning to get both families together for dinner soon. Isla's birthday is Sunday, so we're thinking about next weekend. Can you make it?"

"Next weekend?"

Mom nodded. "Saturday, most likely."

Christian gaped at her. "That's eight days away. Don't you think it's a little soon to be combining families?" *So much for taking it slow.*

"Well ... yes." Her enthusiasm dipped for the first time, igniting his guilt complex. He hated disappointing his mother. "It may feel a little quick. But our families are important to both of us. Which is one of the things that attracted me to the man in the first place."

Christian squeezed his eyes shut. *Attraction* and *man* were two words he'd rather not hear in a sentence referring to his mother.

"Oh, Christian." She swatted her hand in the air between them. "If I can walk in on you making out with a woman and not get all squirmy about it, you can be a mature adult and recognize that I'm capable of being attracted to someone too."

He choked on a trail of saliva sliding down his trachea. "Thanks, Mom. Somehow, that doesn't help at all."

"I'm just saying." Mom splayed her hands in concession. "Paul is the first man I've met who even compares to your father. It's important to me that you like him."

When Mom put it like that, how could he refuse? She deserved to be happy, and if that happiness came with this Paul guy, who was he to disapprove? It would be unfair of him to project his own muddled feelings about love's existence onto her.

But how could he forget about Dad? If things with Paul progressed further, would he attempt to step into Dad's place? Would Mom let him? The idea of her moving on with someone else besides his father felt a little like being abandoned all over again.

Is this how Isla felt? He'd sensed a change in his daughter the last few days she'd spent with Hallie, as if she was reverting back into the happy child she used to be. Not entirely, but he'd cherished those small glimpses.

What would happen when Hallie eventually left, especially if he did entertain the idea of starting a relationship with her? Because deep down, he had entertained it. And honestly, he hadn't dismissed it.

But if he'd learned anything from Sabrina, it was that romance didn't last forever. And he couldn't string his girls along for some temporary fling.

He sighed. There were so many questions, and so few answers. "I'll keep next Saturday open."

"Wonderful." Mom slapped her hands onto her thighs and stood. "I've got cold stuff in my trunk. Tell the girls that Dani and I will be here to pick them up tomorrow around six for girls' night."

Their special girls' night outing and sleepover had been a celebrated birthday tradition for them all since Penelope's first. Christian would've felt left out if it wasn't a nice break from childcare for him.

"Will do." Christian approached her, sliding an arm around her shoulders. "Thanks for the groceries."

"It's my pleasure, as always. And Christian?"

"Yeah?"

She patted his chest a few times. "Don't be embarrassed about what I walked in on earlier. I've always known there'd be a day when some lucky woman snuck through your defenses."

He swallowed slowly as she started toward the front door.

"And please tell Hallie that I'd love the chance to get to know her better. Maybe next Saturday." Mom winked before slipping out of the kitchen.

Yeah, no. That would definitely not be happening.

Chapter Twenty-Seven

I kissed Christian.

Hallie pushed a gum paste tombstone into the gray-tinted butter-cream that made up the graveyard of Isla's haunted house birthday cake.

In front of his mom.

How had she let that happen? The kiss, not his mom's appearance, though meeting the woman who raised him while making out with him had to top the list of the most mortifying experiences of Hallie's life.

She was barely able to look him in the eye after returning with the girls yesterday, let alone have a normal conversation. Thankfully, Isla and Penelope were so excited to see their dad home early that she didn't have much opportunity to talk to him before leaving for the day.

Tomorrow was Isla's party, and she wasn't looking forward to seeing him again when she dropped off the cakes, knowing that sometime soon they'd need to address that kiss. Hallie didn't usually shy away from the hard topics, but for perhaps the first time in her life, reason had failed her in this situation.

She could no longer deny it. She was falling for Christian. Hard. But as much as she cared for him, she wasn't ready to step into the mom role, no matter how much the girls had grown on her. Watching them for a few hours a day was one thing. Anything more than that seemed so ... permanent. And scary. What if she didn't measure up? What if the arrangement turned out terrible for everyone? What if Christian ended up regretting trusting her with his kids?

Stop overanalyzing this. She couldn't read Christian's mind. That kiss may have meant nothing to him. Why did the prospect of that send a squeamish feeling to her gut? But truthfully, he could've just been caught up in the moment. Hallie had been wrapped up in it too.

Thank goodness for Saturday. She needed this Christian-free day.

A little distraction from her conflicting thoughts was exactly what she needed to figure out the next step. And the ticket to return to her logical self.

If only she could forget about the kiss. She pressed her hands to her cheeks to stop the flush. Never in her life had anyone kissed her like that—so tender, yet with an urgency that made her knees feel like they'd disappeared entirely.

It can never happen again.

Picking up another tombstone, she pushed it strategically into the cake—not in a straight line, but at a crooked angle to add to the spookiness of the scene.

A quiet knock came from the front door.

She frowned. Who could that be? McKenzie had gone to Mexico for the weekend to watch Mitch's tournament, and Beej was on a date tonight. Hallie hadn't seen Kendall all day either, which meant whoever had stopped by wouldn't be for any of them. A deliveryman, perhaps?

Wiping her hands on the towel hanging from the stove, she left the room and made her way to the entryway. When she opened the door, her eyes widened at the sight of the same man that had dominated her thoughts standing on the stoop, his hands shoved deep in the pockets of his jeans. "Christian."

"Hey." He bounced a little on the balls of his feet.

She looked past him into the dusky glow of the fading sun before flipping on the porch light. "Where are the girls?"

"They're out with my mom and sister for a special girls' night. You busy?"

No. I mean yes. Argh! "Sorry, girl's night here too. No boys allowed."

"Oh." His shoulders drooped, as did the hope in his eyes.

She chuckled, despite the nerves swimming in her stomach. "Just kidding. Come on in." She held the door open, ignoring her brain's warning of what happened the last time they were alone in a house together. "Actually, I want to show you Isla's cake."

She led him to the kitchen, stepping aside when they entered so Christian had a direct view.

"Wow, Hal." He approached the island, bending at the waist to inspect the cake more closely. "Isla will love this."

Hallie climbed onto the stool at his side, angling her body to face him. "It still needs a few finishing touches, but I'm close."

"You even have the witch on there," he said without pulling his focus away from the crooked old house. The witch sat on a broomstick suspended from the leafless tree by a wire disguised with spun sugar to look like fog. "I really didn't think you'd be able to pull this off."

"Are you saying you doubted me?" She leaned forward to cross her arms over the countertop.

"It won't happen again." Christian turned from the cake, aiming his smirk on her.

Hallie's breath caught at the intensity in his eyes, his face only inches from hers. His stare burned through her like a wildfire rampaging an entire forest. The overwhelming urge to continue their kiss from yesterday came over her.

Clearing his throat, he straightened to his full height. "Listen, I need to apologize for what happened yesterday."

Apologize? Hallie swallowed, her throat thick. So he did regret the kiss. Shouldn't that be a good thing?

Yes. Yet her stomach dropped.

"It was wrong to come onto you like that." He stared at the cake. "I'd never intend to make you uncomfortable in any way. I feel horrible for taking advantage of you."

Why were her eyes watering? She'd tried all afternoon to figure out how to address that amazing kiss and hearing him indirectly admit to their mistake cut a hole straight through her heart. *You're hopeless, Hal. Stop being so wishy-washy.*

She turned away, afraid that if he looked at her, he'd see her heart traveling through the cheese grater. She should've walked away at the beginning. Should've honored her boundaries before her heart got involved. Because now that it was? Wow, it hurt.

"You're right, it shouldn't have happened." That's all she managed to choke out before her chin wobbled and the first tear dropped to her cheek.

Hopping off her stool, she walked to the sink. The cake pans and mixing bowls she hadn't cleaned yet overflowed from it. She yanked on the dishwasher, and it clattered open.

"Hallie."

She didn't dare turn around.

"I said something wrong, didn't I?"

She shook her head, lifting a ceramic bowl from the top rack of the dishwasher.

His hand on her shoulder stopped her. Why was he touching her?

The seconds ticked past with an urgency that charged the room.

"Hal, what's wrong?" he asked, his voice husky.

His gentle tone snapped the last of her willpower, and she brought her hand up to rest on his. "I'm so confused," she said in a strangled whisper.

As Christian turned her around, she set the bowl back in the dishwasher. Cradling her head against his chest with one hand, he circled his other arm around her waist and held her tenderly. "So am I."

Something about that quiet admission soothed some of Hallie's racing emotions. Maybe his earlier statement hadn't been so black and white as she'd thought.

Warmth flooded her as she brought her hands up to rest underneath his shoulder blades. But not the same kind of heat from a moment ago. This warmth spoke of belonging, like being hugged by a friend, or a sense of camaraderie in this twisted situation.

So much for boundaries.

"Feel better?" he asked, stepping back a minute later.

Hallie blew out a shaky breath. "Surprisingly, yeah."

Chuckling, he ran a hand through his hair. "Me too. Surprisingly."

His repetition of her word choice triggered a round of subdued laughter, quick but purposeful in dispelling the lingering awkwardness in the room. They'd resolved nothing, hadn't really talked about the kiss, and yet, it didn't matter right now. They could have that discussion after they'd both had time to process everything.

"I guess I'll leave you to your baking." He took a step toward the door. "Unless you need a break?"

Hallie didn't miss the hopefulness entering his face. "You want to hang out?"

"Do *you* want to hang out?"

She'd been planning to visit Brad downtown once she'd finished Isla's cake, which gave her an idea. Christian had all but confessed yesterday that he wished he'd had a chance to clear the air with him. And Hallie knew her cousin well enough to predict he'd want the same.

"Actually, how'd you like to run an errand with me?"

He arched one of his brows. "What kind of errand?"

"You'll see. I'll grab my keys and we'll be on our way."

She placed Isla's cake in an airtight container, then pulled a glass Tupperware of leftover lasagna from the freezer. Her cousin knew how to cook, though he'd admitted the last time she'd visited that he'd been mostly avoiding it since the smell of raw meat made Cassie even sicker than usual. After living on cold cereal and sandwiches for weeks, Hallie figured he'd appreciate a home cooked meal—even from the freezer.

"Shoot," Hallie said when she and Christian stepped onto the porch. "I didn't realize Beej parked behind me. Hang on while I go look for her keys. Hopefully, she didn't bring them on her date."

Christian grabbed her arm before she could retreat into the house. Would she ever become immune to his touch? "We can take mine."

"Only if you can trust me. Do you?"

His eyes narrowed. "Are you planning to lure me into a dark alley to finish me off? Because I told my mom I'd pick the girls up tomorrow morning."

"You're such a smart aleck. Just answer the question."

His small smile sent goosebumps dancing across her arms. "I do."

"Good." She held out her palm. "Give me your keys."

"What?" he said through a surprised laugh.

Palm out, she wagged her fingers toward herself. "You said you trusted me, and I'm going to hold you to that. Hand them over, mister."

He considered her for a long moment before huffing out an over-dramatic sigh. Fishing his keys from his pocket, he dropped them onto her hand.

She held her head high in mock smugness, though he still had several inches on her, and started walking toward his SUV parked at the curb. "Okay, let's go."

Chapter Twenty-Eight

"Wow, I never imagined Brad living in such a swanky place." Christian eyed the lady palms lining the front circle drive of an upscale apartment complex in Downtown Los Angeles. The buildings resembled an old Spanish mission with varying shades of brown brick and round windows on every floor. Four levels of balconies completed the look.

Hallie tossed an amused side-eye in his direction. "What makes you think this is Brad's apartment?"

"Let's see. We stopped at a store to pick up the same ginger chews my ex used to eat to ease her pregnancy nausea." He held up the items in question. "And Cassie just happens to be pregnant and nauseated. It doesn't take a genius to put two and two together."

They stopped at the wide glass doors lined with black trim making up the entrance. "Please don't be mad," she said hastily. "You told me yesterday that you wished you could work things out with him. And I was planning on stopping by this weekend anyway. I thought talking would help you take some of the stress off your shoulders."

He bumped her shoulder playfully. "I'm not mad."

How could he be? One by one, she'd been filling his needs, even those he didn't realize he carried. She always seemed to know what to say to quiet the storm churning inside him. She'd willingly stepped in to watch the girls, despite the extra hardship it caused her. And now, she was providing a path to reconciliation with his former friend simply to unburden him. Was it any wonder why he craved her presence even when she wasn't around?

He resisted the overwhelming urge to wrap his arms around her. Their embrace in Hallie's kitchen had been nice, but with everything so uncertain between them, he thought it best to keep the touching to a minimum.

"Hold this." Hallie handed the Tupperware container to him so she could pull out what looked like a hotel key from her wallet-sized cross-body clutch. She swiped it across the reader behind a potted plant. The front door clicked.

"You have a key to their building?" Christian asked as they stepped inside the lobby.

She tucked the card back into the zippered front pocket of her bag. "Brad gave it to me a few weeks ago when I stayed with Cassie while he was out of town. He let me keep it, so she doesn't have to come down to let me in every time I stop by. The buzzer in their apartment has been acting up."

"Do you come often?"

"Every few weeks to help out." She shrugged. "Cassie's been so sick, they could use it."

He shook his head, watching her with awe. "You're amazing. Do you know that? Is there anyone you haven't helped?"

A blush stole across her cheeks. "I don't like seeing the people I care about struggle."

That simple comment made Christian's breath catch. Did that include him?

They crossed the spacious lobby with its plush chairs and chic black-and-white accents. A crystal chandelier hung above the furniture. They took one of the elevators behind the front desk to the fourth floor. Brad's apartment was tucked in a quiet corner on the far side of the building.

"Hal!" A wide grin stretched across his square jaw when he opened the door. He gave his cousin a one-armed side hug. "Cassie said you might be coming."

Hallie held out the Tupperware container. "I brought food. Lasagna from Sunday dinner."

An appreciative growl sounded low in his throat. "You're always welcome when you come with food." His gaze flicked to Christian, a question entering his blue eyes. "It's good to see you, man. Come in."

They stepped inside, and Christian's eyes scanned the open living space of the tastefully decorated apartment. A collage of wedding photos adorned the wall separating the living and dining areas from the kitchen. Along the far wall, thick slatted blinds closed over what looked to be a picture window. The simple, yet elegant accents around the room had Cassie's decorative eye written all over it. Except for the flatscreen television hanging on another wall, broadcasting the USC football game on mute. That was all Brad.

While Brad disappeared into the kitchen with the lasagna, Hallie headed straight to Cassie, who sat crossways on the long side of the gray sectional, her knees bent toward her chest. A powder blue fleece blanket covered her legs, and she wore an oversized USC sweatshirt, one she'd most likely stolen from her husband. A tablet was propped against her thighs.

"We brought the ginger chews you asked me to pick up." Hallie handed her the grocery sack before sitting on the small end of the sectional.

Cassie set down her stylus and peeked inside. "Thanks. My neighbor swears by them when she's pregnant. My body has debunked every other tried-and-true method, so I'm willing to try anything at this point."

Poor girl. As far as he knew, Sabrina's morning sickness eventually wore off. She'd been lucky. But still so unhappy.

Hallie clapped her hands on both her thighs. "I'm here to help, so put me to work. No arguments."

Brad reappeared from the kitchen. "If I'd known you were coming, I'd have saved you the dishes. I could've made some progress on that dumb crib."

Cassie squinted at her husband. "Progress might be a bit of a stretch." She spoke her next comment to Hallie and Christian. "There was a lot of swearing coming from the baby's room."

"Is it too much to ask for some words to go along with those vague pictures masquerading as instructions? Am I supposed to screw the leg into the base, or saw the thing in half? I don't know." Brad crossed the room to drop a kiss on his wife's forehead from behind. Her tired countenance immediately brightened.

"Before long you'll be building these things in your sleep," Christian said.

"Let's hope."

"I'm serious. It only takes a few Christmas Eve all-nighters to turn dads into construction experts."

Brad chuckled, lowering himself to perch on the arm of the couch behind Cassie. She leaned her head back against his thigh, and they shared a look that spoke of mutual adoration.

"Are you ready for dinner?" His fingers stroked her blonde curls.

Christian's brows twitched upward. He'd never seen his buddy like this. The gentle motion, and his obvious fondness were in direct contradiction to the bro-dude persona he'd adopted during his college years.

Cassie scrunched her nose. "Ugh, no. But if you're going to make me eat, I guess I'll try some plain noodles." She glanced at their guests. "My eating habits have become pickier than a toddler's."

Hallie popped up from the couch. "I'll make it. Christian can help with the crib."

He hadn't realized this outing would require his building expertise, but she'd provided this opportunity to talk, so he'd talk. "Sure, I'd be happy to."

Brad placed his hand on his wife's shoulder. "You okay?"

She nodded. "I'll holler if I need you."

He placed another kiss on her forehead before standing. "Let's do this."

They walked down a hallway to the set of bedrooms at the end. An explosion of white wooden planks, screws, and cardboard greeted them in the smaller room to the left. A plush rocking chair already occupied one corner of the room. Next to it, a round nightstand held a lamp with a mini football, basketball, and baseball stacked on top of each other forming the stem. A dresser with changing pad on top stood underneath a circular mirror along the back wall.

Christian knelt amidst a box of screwdriver tips and various sizes of foam packaging. "How're you holding up with all this?" he asked, meaning more than the task of putting together the nursery.

Brad lowered onto his haunches, picking the instruction manual up from the floor. He stared at it, his expression stony. "I'm worried."

"About Cassie."

A single nod confirmed the statement. "It's not a good feeling watching your wife suffer and not knowing what to do about it."

Wow. Marriage really had changed him. Back in college, he had about as much sensitivity as an amoeba.

"I can't believe you're going to be a dad soon." Christian shook his head.

"Pretty wild, huh? I can't grasp it myself most of the time." Brad's momentary grin fell flat. "I'd never say this to Cassie, but sometimes I wish we could go back to before she got pregnant. Does that make me a lousy husband?"

"No." Christian bit back a humorless laugh. "A lousy husband would be at the bar every night with the boys, forgetting all about his sick wife. He wouldn't be trying to make her as comfortable as possible. And let's not forget about building a nursery for a baby who won't be here until March."

Brad's stress was obvious in his rigid posture. "I have to do something. If I can't make Cassie feel better, at least I can give this baby a room rivaling Caesar's Palace. Which, based on what Cassie has planned, isn't far from the truth."

Christian buzzed his lips. "Rotten husband."

A chuckle emerged from Brad's chest as he snapped Christian in the face with the instructions.

Christian grinned, surprised at how natural it felt to talk about Brad's current hardship. Just like old times. Almost. "I'm impressed you're this far along with the nursery as it is. I didn't finish Isla's crib until Sabrina was in labor."

Brad squinted his eyes at him. "I'm new to this whole dad thing, but shouldn't the father be at the hospital for the birth?"

"She didn't want me there," Christian muttered to the screwdriver in his hand. He swallowed the bitterness rearing its ugly head.

"What?"

"She'd rather have her best friend there. I didn't want to rock the boat." Not even Mom or Dani knew that he'd missed both girls' births in an effort to keep the peace.

"That's messed up, man."

Even more messed up was the relief Christian felt during those few days he had at home without her. Like he could finally breathe. Talk about a lousy husband. Not to mention a terrible father for not visiting his children in the hospital.

"You were right about her," he choked out. "Everything you said. I should've listened to you."

Brad ran a hand down the blond stubble lining his jaw. "I admit I could've been a little gentler in my approach."

"A little?" Christian raised his brows.

"Okay, a lot," Brad said hastily. "Cassie has helped me realize that I can be an idiot sometimes."

"She's good for you." Christian nodded. "I could see that at Tyler's wedding."

Brad chuckled. "The funny thing is, we weren't even dating back then. We faked it to get rid of her ex. You know, the drunk guy who crashed the rehearsal dinner?"

How could Christian forget helping to escort the man from the mansion? That whole night made *his* courthouse wedding seem like a fairytale event. "Well, you fooled me."

"I didn't realize it had gotten so bad between you two," Brad said, continuing with their original topic. "I'm sorry for what I said, and for not making a bigger effort to reach out to you after everything went down."

"I appreciate that." A weight lifted from Christian's shoulders. He'd have to find a way to thank Hallie for pushing him to unpack this particular guilt about his past. "If you ever need a breather from all this, give me a call. I'm sure Hallie would be happy to hang with Cassie for a while."

Brad clapped him on the shoulder. "Thanks, man." He handed

Christian the instructions. "Enough chit chat. Let's tackle this beast. I want to finish it tonight."

They worked for several minutes, Christian deciphering the instructions and handing wooden planks to his friend building the crib. Attaching the final leg to the base, Brad looked up from the screw he'd twisted into the wood.

"So, you and my cousin, huh?" he asked. "What's going on there?"

"Don't know." Christian reached for the next plank to ignore the way his neck burned. "She's been watching the girls, so we've spent some time together. That's all."

Brad set down the screwdriver, shooting Christian a disbelieving glare. "Come on man, you can do better than that. Are you interested?"

"I like being with her," Christian admitted. "She has a way of making me feel like things aren't as bad as I've made them seem. I'm not saying it's her job to make me happy, but I am happier around her. She has this presence that's pure ... sunshine. It's peaceful."

Even this rambling didn't feel like enough to adequately describe how she made him feel.

He stared at his outstretched palms. "Even holding her in my arms is enough to give me hope that I can figure out a path to my own happiness. You know?"

When he finally glanced at his buddy, Brad's brows were raised high on his forehead. The knowing grin stretched on his face flipped the switch in Christian's brain. "I love her."

He possibly had all along, he was just so consumed with anger for Sabrina that he'd ignored the subtle stirrings transforming his heart. His muttered curse drew a barking laugh from Brad.

"How did that happen?" Christian asked more to himself than to his friend. "I didn't think I believed in love anymore."

His buddy shrugged. "I didn't think I did either until Cassie came along. The right woman has the ability to change your perspective, I guess."

"Tyler's going to kill me." Christian pinched the bridge of his nose. "I'm glad we could have this talk now because you're looking at a dead man walking."

"I wouldn't worry about Ty. He's a puppy dog."

"Are you saying this because you're planning to get to me first?"

Brad chuckled. "Hallie is one of my favorite people in the world. She deserves to be happy. If that's with you, I see no problem with it."

That's reassuring. At least Christian had a few more days above ground.

"But if you break her heart, I'll break your nose." One side of Brad's mouth tipped up slightly, though a warning hung in his tone.

Christian didn't intend to break her heart. He wanted it for himself. And that required a conversation that sent the nerves coursing through him just as much as the day he'd held his newborn daughter for the first time.

He'd managed to protect his kids all these years. But could he do the same for Hallie's heart?

Chapter Twenty-Nine

Hallie set a folded pair of Brad's athletic shorts on top of the pile of laundry next to her on the couch. "I hope it's okay I brought Christian with me. I wanted to give the guys a chance to talk."

Had they cleared the air? Even if they didn't go back to being best friends, she hoped talking would at least bring Christian an element of peace in his otherwise heavy emotional load.

Cassie waved away the concern with her empty fork. "I don't mind. Brad has always felt bad about what happened between them, but he didn't know how to approach the situation."

"Christian too." Hallie left it at that.

Cassie arched her back to stretch before relaxing against the arm again. "You seem really comfortable with him. Are you dating?"

Hallie didn't miss the eagerness in her friend's tone. She grabbed one of Cassie's blouses from the laundry basket at her feet to disguise her urge to squirm. "No."

Laughter floated toward them from down the hall, interrupting the pointed quiet that followed her answer. Hallie recognized Christian's immediately, erupting warm fuzzies in her chest.

Cassie leaned forward, her perfect eyebrows raised. "You care about him, though. I can see it all over your face."

Hallie hadn't realized she'd been smiling until she touched her cheeks.

"I do." More than cared for him, probably. There was no point hiding it now. "We kissed."

Cassie squealed. "Hallie!"

"Shhhh." Hallie threw the pair of socks she'd balled together at her friend. "They'll hear you."

Cassie tossed her apologetic glance toward the hallway, though her grin didn't disappear. Hallie hadn't seen her this energized since before finding out about the baby. "So ... how was it?"

Good. Wonderful. Fantastic. Awe-inspiring.

Hallie said none of those out loud.

"Okay, I'll guess," Cassie said. "The kiss was bad, and you wish it was good."

"No." Definitely not that.

Cassie tried again. "So, it was good, and you wish it was ... bad?"

Hallie dropped her head into her hands, massaging her temples. In her calculated logic, she'd always thought falling in love would be straightforward. You either loved someone, or you didn't. Easy.

But there was nothing straightforward or easy about this situation.

"I'm confused," Cassie admitted.

You and me both, sister. Hallie pushed out a sigh that ended in a groan. "It was the most incredible kiss of my life, and I want to do it again, but I shouldn't because I can't date him." She paused for a breath. "I'm not ready to be a mom, and I feel selfish for even entertaining a relationship that can't go anywhere. Plus, I'm worried that I've given my heart to an emotionally unavailable man."

She slumped against the back of the couch, a weight lifting from her shoulders by finally speaking her burdens out loud.

"Wow," Cassie said. "That's a lot to unpack."

Hallie pulled her legs onto the couch and hugged her knees. "And on top of it all, I kind of promised Tyler I wouldn't date Christian."

"What does Tyler have to do with it? You're a grown woman. Shouldn't you be the one deciding who you date?" Cassie threw off the blanket, rising slowly from the couch.

Hallie reached for the bowl in her hands. "Let me get that."

Cassie shooed her away. "I need to stretch my legs. My back hurts if I sit too long. But the nausea gets worse whenever I stand up. Seriously, I can't win."

She disappeared into the kitchen, and the clang of the bowl being set in the sink was followed by Cassie's reappearance a second later.

She held one of the two water bottles in her hand out to Hallie. "Want one?"

"Thanks." Hallie took a drink before continuing with her thoughts. "Tyler is just so ... overprotective. I know he means well, and usually I ignore it. But Christian was his friend first. And I can't help thinking that if I'd listened to him at the beginning, I wouldn't have gotten into this mess."

Cassie dropped back onto the couch, pulling the blanket over her legs again. "I won't pretend to know what it's like having an older brother—or any brother, for that matter. But if Tyler were mine, I'd tell him exactly where he could shove his unwanted opinions."

Hallie sputtered out a laugh, water dribbling from her mouth. She dabbed at her chin with the sleeve of her sweater. "I'm so glad you're in this family now." Not only was Cassie's feistiness exactly what Brad needed, she made the perfect addition to the Abernathy/Lucas women.

"I am too. It's fun being part of a big family. When this baby comes, he'll have so many people to love on him."

Hallie gasped. "*He?* You found out? What happened to the big reveal you were planning?"

"The ultrasound tech let the news slip by accident at our last appointment," Cassie said with a smile. "Don't tell anyone. We're still planning a surprise reveal at Thanksgiving."

Hallie slid her fingers across her lips as though zipping them shut. "Oh Cassie, I'm so happy for you." She joined her cousin-in-law on the long side of the sectional.

"Thanks." Cassie returned the hug that followed. "But don't change the subject. We were talking about you. What's this about Christian being emotionally unavailable?"

Hallie sighed. "He told me he didn't believe in love."

Cassie's hand emerged from underneath the blanket to give Hallie's a squeeze. "That's hard. Really, it is. But has he given you any signs that he really believes that?"

Furrowing her brows, Hallie thought hard about the last few weeks. From rebuilding her website, to buying all those cakes, to insisting on paying her to watch his kids even after she'd told him not to, he'd been nothing but concerned about her welfare.

"He even calls me every night to make sure I made it home okay," she said after recapping his kind acts out loud. Last night had been the exception. Her cheeks warmed at the reminder of that glorious, yet overwhelming kiss. "We live less than ten minutes apart."

"Girl, those are not signs of an emotionally unavailable man." Cassie leaned her head on Hallie's shoulder, an unspoken sign of support. "Trust me, I've dated several."

"But he said—"

"I know what he said. And here's what I think about that: Christian has been deeply hurt. He'd probably say anything to protect himself and his kids from letting it happen again."

That rung true but—

Cassie didn't let her finish that thought. "Before you say anything, let me add that your concerns are valid. But if you really care about this man—and you obviously do—don't be so quick to walk away. If it's meant to be, Christian will show you how he truly feels. Don't shut things down before giving him the chance."

"But what about his kids?" Sure, she'd grown to care about the girls, but could she sacrifice her entire life plans to help raise them? Saving for her bakery could take years of focus, hustle, and hard work. And once she realized that dream, it would take just as much tenacity to keep it going.

Cassie made a sound that was part laugh, part squeak. "I'm not sure I'm ready to be a mom either, and Brad and I have talked about this since we were dating. Is anyone ever truly prepared to be a parent?"

She had a point.

"There's nothing wrong with taking it one day at a time. If you're honest with Christian about your fears, I'm sure he'll understand."

Would he? She didn't even know if he felt the same way.

Before she could speak that doubt out loud, the men's voices grew louder, signaling their approach from the hallway. Her gaze locked with Christian's as he came into view, her breath catching at the devastating smile spreading across his mouth.

Cassie's attention landed on her husband. "How'd it go?"

Brad clapped his hand on Christian's shoulder. "Thanks to this guy, our baby now has a place to sleep."

"Hail the conquering hero." She laughed. "We'll think of you every time he goes down for a nap."

"I'd expect nothing less." Christian's eyes grew soft as they landed on Hallie. "You ready?"

One day at a time, she thought, engraving Cassie's words on her heart. One smile, one hug, one conversation at a time.

"Yeah." She hugged Cassie goodbye. "Let me know if you need anything."

"I want lots of details," Cassie whispered so only she could hear. "And remember, it's okay to stay cautiously hopeful."

After saying goodbye, Hallie and Christian let themselves out of the apartment. Alone in the hallway, he pulled her into his arms. His tall frame enveloped her, a relaxing sigh exiting his body. Pressing her cheek against his chest, she closed her eyes, as the steady beat of his heart quieted her lingering doubts.

Cautiously hopeful. If that meant more moments like this, she'd like to try.

"Thank you," Christian murmured. The vibration of the words resonated straight to her soul.

Propping her chin against his chest, she looked up at him. "I take it your conversation went well?"

"We cleared the air, and he helped me figure some things out." He studied her for a minute in silence. "Do you want to get some ice cream?"

"Ice cream?"

A faint blush crept up his neck, and he stuttered out a laugh. "It's been a really long time since I've asked a woman on a date. I think I'm a little rusty."

Hallie's pulse raced. "You're asking me on a date?"

The intensity of his stare cut straight through her, and he bobbed his head slowly. "Yeah."

Warmth pooled inside her. He was trying. And the sincerity of this effort didn't go unnoticed.

Finding his hand, she linked their fingers together. "Ice cream sounds great."

Chapter Thirty

The bell above the door to Scoops and Shakes jingled when Christian opened it, allowing Hallie to lead the way from the shop.

"I swear you let me win," she said, stirring the strawberry cheesecake ice cream in her cup as they walked in the direction of Village Green Park.

Attempting to keep his expression innocent, he dug out a spoonful of double chocolate brownie. "I did not. I'm just really bad at foosball."

He totally let her win. And he didn't feel bad about it one bit.

On the way back to Buena Hills, they'd driven past the arcade on the outskirts of town. Instead of heading straight toward Scoops and Shakes, he'd challenged her to a friendly game of foosball, so they'd joined the weekend throngs of tweens inside the joint.

Christian hadn't been to the place since he was the age of most of the kids buzzing around the coin operated machines. Yet he didn't think he'd ever had as much fun. Talking with Brad had forced him to finally accept his feelings for Hallie, and he silently vowed to give the idea of dating again a fair shot.

Only for her. For them. And maybe for the girls too.

Once he'd made a conscious effort to let down his walls, even flirting with her had been surprisingly easy. And exhilarating.

But along with it came a sense of urgency to figure out where to go from here. He just needed the right moment to start the conversation.

"I don't believe you for a second." She shot him a laughing smile, discernible by the iron lanterns they passed. "I'm the world's worst foosball player and you made me look like Lionel Messi."

He quirked an eyebrow, his spoon hovering above his cup. "Look at you, coming in hot with the soccer references."

Her muffled laugh came around a spoonful of her ice cream. "When you grow up in a family full of sports obsessed men, even the most clueless person tends to pick up a few big names."

"Fair enough."

They fell into companionable silence as they continued their walk down Main Street, looking in shop windows, most of them closed for the night.

"You seem different tonight," Hallie said after a minute.

Christian eyed her sidelong. "How so?"

She stopped walking and faced him. "I don't know. Less burdened. Happier, I guess."

"Tonight has been an unexpected reprieve in a lot of ways." He tossed his cup into the metal garbage can at the curb. "I love my girls —I'd never trade being their dad. But between taking care of them and my job, I rarely have time for myself."

She threw her own cup away, then looped both her arms through one of his. "I'm glad you've had time to reset."

"Me too." He smiled down at her.

They continued walking until they got to the empty store at the end of the street. He watched her studying the *For Sale* sign in the window. She'd once told him she liked to come down here and dream about her bakery. Was she thinking about that now?

"Have you applied for any more bakery positions?" he asked.

She sighed. "A couple, but I don't think they'll amount to much. Don't worry, you're not in any danger of losing your nanny quite yet."

Did she really think that was the reason behind his question? "That's not why I asked. What makes you think they won't work?"

He felt her shoulder shrug against his arm. Her discouragement cut through him as if it were his own.

"They all want someone with years of experience. How does one even break into this business? Even my culinary classes, a lifetime of practice and polishing, and owning a business doesn't seem to fit the requirements these places are asking for. At this point, I've even considered putting my business aside and going back to waiting tables. I know I can get a job doing that. But the idea of letting go of my bakery hurts my heart. I've wanted this ever since I was a kid in Santiago, helping Señor Rosales."

"Who?"

"He was the sweet man at the panadería in our neighborhood. He never had his own children, but all the expat kids flocked to his place after school. He and his wife loved them all like their own." Fondness entered Hallie's eyes as she talked. "I've wanted my own bakery ever since. I just didn't realize it would be this hard."

She rubbed her nose with the back of her hand. For once, Christian followed his instinct to reach for her, and she willingly stepped into his embrace. "This is important to you. It's okay to be frustrated that it isn't happening fast enough. Don't give up. I know you'll figure it out."

She looked up at him, a misty smile gracing her lovely face. "Sorry, I don't know what's up with me lately. I'm not usually this emotional."

"Don't apologize." He dropped his arms, finding her hands instead. "Your feelings are valid."

"Spoken like a true dad." She yawned, covering her mouth with a hand. "Sorry, I got up early to start Isla's cake."

Keeping one of her hands in his, he turned them in the direction of the car. "Let's get you home then."

When they arrived back at her house, Christian walked her to the door, facing her when they'd reached the porch. Nerves bubbled in his stomach. If they were going to have a conversation about where they stood, now was the time to have it.

"Earlier you said you were confused." He shoved his hands into the pockets of his fleece jacket. "Can we talk about that?"

Something akin to panic flashed in her eyes. It was subtle, and gone in an instant, but definitely there.

She lowered her gaze to his chest. "Right. We probably should." Taking a deep breath, she steeled her shoulders. "The truth is, I like you Christian. A lot. But ... I'm scared."

"About what?"

She wrapped her arms around her middle, her focus shifting to the front door. "Don't take this the wrong way. I adore your girls. But the idea of stepping in as their mom is really overwhelming. Dating you would be like saying I'm willing to do that. I just don't know if I'm ready to be all in."

Her admission sent a trickle of dread sliding into his stomach. He understood why she'd feel that way. Heck, he had his own related fears. But it still hurt. "It's a big responsibility."

"But I also feel like maybe I'm jumping to conclusions." She plopped down on the top step, looking up at him expectantly until he joined her. "I don't even know where your head's at. My feelings could be completely one-sided."

Christian set his hand on top of hers where they were balled in her lap. "Trust me, they're not one-sided."

"But you said you don't believe in love."

He wracked his brain. Had he mentioned that when he'd told her about Sabrina? He couldn't remember everything that had come out. "I didn't think I knew what love was anymore. But I'm starting to figure it out."

She sucked in a breath.

"I've tried to fight my feelings because you're not the only one who's scared." He stared at the pavement in front of him, barely illuminated by the glow of the porch light. "Sabrina messed me up, and I'm terrified to put myself in a position of potentially getting hurt again. And I don't want the girls to suffer anymore. But despite all the reasons I've told myself not to, I am falling in love with you. And being with you, I feel ... calm, like everything will be okay."

Silence stretched between them, and Christian wondered what was going through her mind. Had he said too much?

Finally, she turned one of her hands palm up, weaving their fingers together. "The last thing I want to do is hurt any of you. That's why I feel so conflicted. Selfish even."

He pushed out a dry laugh. "You're the least selfish person I've ever met."

Her mouth lifted. "I'm serious. I want to do the right thing, and I'm not saying I'll never get to a point where I'm ready to be their mom. But I feel like if I don't end this now, it'll be a hundred times worse for everyone down the road if I realize I can't get there."

An ache lodged in Christian's chest, the familiar beginnings of his heart shredding apart.

Hallie tugged on his arm until he looked at her. Tears hung in her long lashes. "But the idea of walking away from you hurts me more than anything."

Yeah, he understood that completely. "Where does that leave us?"

She blinked at the moisture, and a tear trickled down her cheek. "I don't know."

Neither did he. So he did the only thing he could think of. Sliding an arm around her shoulders, he pulled her toward him until she relaxed her head on his shoulder. They sat that way for several silent moments, processing the conversation.

Hallie's fears made complete sense, despite amplifying his own. He wanted to be with her, but she was right. If she couldn't get to a point of being ready to be Isla and Penelope's mom, pursuing a relationship now wouldn't be wise.

But the girls already adored Hallie. She'd become entwined in their lives so naturally that even backing out tonight wouldn't save them from collateral damage.

How was he supposed to proceed with that?

"I guess the only thing we can do is be honest with each other," he said, answering his silent question. "Our feelings are out in the open, so we're already in too deep to prevent any of us from getting hurt."

She nodded against his shoulder. "That's true. Cassie told me tonight that it's okay to be cautiously hopeful."

"I like that." He lifted her chin so she could meet his eyes. "I'm willing to try if you are."

She studied him, and he couldn't begin to read the expression on her face. "You want to give us a shot?"

"Yeah," he whispered.

For a moment, he worried she might refuse. Then her whole body relaxed with an exhale. "Me too. But we have to be honest with each other about how we're feeling. The minute something changes."

"Agreed. No more guessing."

"Okay." She furrowed her brows in concern. "What should we tell the girls."

What *should* they tell them? If this thing with Hallie didn't last, they'd be crushed even more than if she just left as their nanny.

"Maybe we shouldn't say anything. At least not yet. I think it's best if we just feel this out for now." He eyed her apologetically. "Which means we should probably keep the PDA to a minimum."

She bobbed her head in agreement. "That's wise. No PDA in front of the children. Which means you have to stop dancing in front of me."

Christian choked on a laugh. "Why?"

She shrugged. "I guess I can't resist a man who can dance. Especially if he's in a certain sequined body suit like the one you wore in one of the videos I watched on YouTube." Her whole face scrunched toward her nose, a clear sign she hadn't meant to add that last part.

"I knew it!" His mouth stretched into a wide grin. She'd known way too much about his college ballroom career to not have snooped around. "Wait, *one* of them? How many did you watch."

Hallie covered her face with her hands, shaking her head violently. Her cheeks were flaming red when she peered up at him. "All of them," she squeaked, squinting one eye.

He barked out a laugh, and she smacked his arm with the back of her hand.

"I'm not a stalker, I promise," she said, the smile evident in her tone. "You just didn't give me very much information to go on that night. Can you blame a girl for being curious? Please don't be creeped out."

Sliding his arm around her shoulders, he pulled her to his side. "I'm not creeped out. In fact, I'm flattered. I'll just have to save the dancing for after the kids are in bed." He winked, reveling at her answering grin.

"I can't wait." She stood, pulling him up with her.

The hug that followed was filled with more contentment than he'd felt in a long time. She kissed his cheek before stepping back.

"I should go." She watched him fondly as she placed a hand on the door. "I'll see you tomorrow when I drop off your cakes."

He nodded. "Sounds good."

"And thanks for the ice cream." A spark of mischief entered her eyes. "Even though I know you let me win."

His mouth quirked upward. "You'll never prove that."

"I'll get you to crack." By the flirty way she wiggled her brows, he couldn't wait to see her try. "Goodnight, Christian."

Stepping to her again, he bent to steal one last kiss on her lips. A goodnight kiss was customary for a dating couple, after all.

Dating. The idea sent goosebumps skittering across his skin.

They were dating.

"Tomorrow then," he murmured, retreating backward toward the steps without breaking her gaze.

Tomorrow couldn't come soon enough.

Chapter Thirty-One

Isla was in rare form the next afternoon when Hallie dropped off the cakes.

"Are you staying for my party?" she asked as soon as she'd thrown open the door.

Hallie hadn't planned to stay. After waking hours before the sun the last two days to work on Christian's cake order, she'd been looking forward to a night of relaxation and an early bedtime. Especially since she'd stayed up way too late giving Beej a full recap of her date with Christian—not by choice—including follow-up questions.

Needless to say, a nap looked a lot more tempting right now than attending a birthday party with a bunch of six-year-olds. Celebrating Isla's birthday with just the family was one thing; managing other little kids seemed more overwhelming than Hallie could manage.

But one look at Isla's hopeful face pushed all that to the side. "I can if you want me to."

"Yay!" Isla hopped a few times before tugging Hallie's elbow into the house.

Hallie shifted the bakery boxes to the side to see as she followed Isla through the living room, already decorated for a Halloween birthday party.

Streamers draped from the ceiling with alternating black spiders and orange balloons hanging from the ribbons. Web-like garlands wrapped around the banister leading upstairs. Isla became distracted by the snacks set on top of the ghost-covered tablecloth lining the coffee table, so Hallie entered the kitchen alone.

Her attention immediately focused out the back window. An array of festive games set up in booths gave the impression of a carnival taking up the entire yard. Christian stood on the patio, front and center of it all, attempting to attach one side of a balloon arch to the deck.

Butterflies flitted about in Hallie's stomach, the events of last night again playing through her mind. Those stolen moments with Christian had been nothing short of heavenly. And the way he'd handled the conversation surrounding their doubts eased some of the guilt she'd carried about unintentionally pursuing something with him.

Of course, things were far from settled. She wasn't naïve to think the pieces would magically fall into place all because they'd talked about their feelings. Love was more complicated than that. And she didn't live in a fairytale. They still had so much to figure out, but after last night, she wanted to try.

Hallie pulled her thoughts away from their date and recognized the young woman occupying the other side of the arch, her honey-colored hair pulled back into a single braid. The same woman she'd seen at the library all those weeks ago—Penelope and Isla's aunt. Standing a few steps from them both, Christian's mom surveyed the assembly.

Setting the cake boxes on the stove next to an assortment of party supplies spilling out of a plastic bag, Hallie headed outside. Penelope's squeal announced her arrival. The child hopped off her patio chair and ran toward her.

Crouching, Hallie caught her, giving her a tight squeeze. "Hey, sweetie. I heard you had a special girls' night last night. Was it fun?"

Penelope bobbed her head. "I sleep at Granny's. We had apple cider."

"Yum." Hallie scrunched her nose as she touched their foreheads together. "Grandmas are the best, aren't they?"

She stood, keeping the child in her arms. Her eyes locked on Christian, and his smile was as warm and inviting as the apple cider his daughter had mentioned. She stepped toward him, but his mom intercepted her before she could say so much as hello.

"It's so good to see you again." Mrs. Gustafson wrapped her in a one-armed embrace.

Hallie had expected a second meeting with Christian's mom to be awkward after the other day, so her warm greeting surprised her. "Hi, Mrs. Gustafson."

"Please, call me Sherry. Any friend of my son's is a friend to me." A twinkle entered her eyes, the only acknowledgement of the very *un*friendlike situation she'd walked into two days ago. Perhaps more-than-friend-like was a better description. Whatever the term, Christian's mom had to know that something other than simple friendship budded between Hallie and her son. But the woman didn't seem mad about it, which helped Hallie lower her walls.

"Have you met my daughter?" Sherry gestured toward the other woman on the patio. "This is Danica. Dani, meet Hallie."

Christian's sister tossed a smile in their direction. "I remember you from the library that one time. I'd give you a hug, but I'm all tied up. Like literally. My fingers are stuck in this twine. Mom, can you help me?"

Sherry rushed to her, giving Hallie the opportunity to approach Christian.

"You've been busy." Her eyes swept the yard as she set Penelope down on the deck.

He finished securing the arch to the waist-high fence and turned to her. "We've worked on this all day, but I think it's finally ready." Bending at the waist, he planted a quick kiss on her cheek.

Okay, that was adorable. After the heated make-out session from the other day—and last night—Hallie hadn't fully appreciated how a sweet gesture like a kiss on the cheek could make her melt just as much.

"Daddy, what are you doing?" Isla asked, suddenly appearing before them. Deep lines furrowed in the older girl's forehead. Out of curiosity or disapproval? Hallie couldn't tell.

Christian cleared his throat, and she could see the wheels turning in his head as he came up with a reason for putting the moves on her temporary nanny.

"In many cultures it's customary to greet acquaintances with a kiss on the cheek." He glanced at Hallie with wide eyes, sucking air through his teeth.

"Acquaintance?" Danica snorted. "Sure. And I'm Miss America."

Hallie stifled a laugh at the eye roll he tossed at his sister. Leaning toward him, she lowered her voice. "Forgot they were watching?"

"Stop being so irresistible," he hissed, shooting her a cheeky grin.

Hallie only had time to grin back before Isla's excitement took over the deck. Bouncing on the balls of her feet, her arms flapped out to the side. "Is it time for my party?"

Christian tugged lightly on his daughter's curly ponytail before checking his watch. "Your friends should be here any minute."

"Come on!" She grabbed her father's hand and dragged him toward the house. "Let's go wait for them!"

He shrugged over his shoulder at Hallie. She smiled back at him, then followed his mom and sister inside to wait for the party guests.

"How many minutes has it been?" Isla asked for the fifth time, popping up from the couch and running to the door. She stuck her head out before coming back inside with a frown. Each time she checked, her spirits dipped a little more.

Sitting next to Christian on the couch, Hallie felt more than heard his dejected sigh as he checked his watch again. She peeked at his wrist, another crack splitting her heart. Almost an hour had passed since the party was supposed to start and still no guests. At this point, it was safe to assume none would be coming.

Poor Isla. She'd been so excited. This rejection would surely send her right back to the despondent child she'd been when Hallie had met her. Why didn't anyone show up?

Christian blew out another breath, rubbing his hands on his thighs before standing. "I have an idea." He crossed the room to the entryway, kneeling in front of Isla. "How'd you like to go out to dinner? Anywhere you'd like."

Her face fell. "What about my party?"

Christian gently placed his hand on his daughter's arm. "I don't think they're coming, sweetheart."

Chills skittered across Hallie's skin at the sadness in his voice. She shared a pained look with Sherry, who sat with Penelope on her lap in the armchair next to the couch. Danica had abandoned the living room completely for the solace of the kitchen.

"Why not?" Isla asked.

He dropped his head. "I don't know. And I'm so sorry."

For a moment, Isla looked as though she might cry. But as Christian moved to wrap his arms around her shoulders, she stomped her foot so hard, her curly ponytail jumped straight up.

"This is all Sammy's fault," she shrieked. "I *hate* her!"

Isla darted around her father and ran toward the stairs, stomping all the way to the second floor. She slammed her bedroom door behind her.

Christian remained frozen in the crouched position. Hallie shared another glance with Sherry before joining him in the entryway. As he stood, she wrapped her arms around his waist. His body sagged around her through his exhale, opening a flood of realizations for her.

How lonely he must be raising these kids by himself. Not having someone to help navigate the challenges of parenting young children had to place even more burdens on his shoulders. The need to fix this latest crisis came over her, and she found his hand, linking their fingers together.

"Do you want me to call Tyler?" she asked. "Or my roommates? They know how to throw a good party. It wouldn't be the same, but it would be something."

Christian smiled sadly at her before raising their clasped hands to his lips. "If I thought that would help, then yes. But I really don't think it will. This is bigger than her birthday party."

"How do you know?"

"By what she said." He sighed. "I should go talk to her. Could you...?" He glanced over her head, and Hallie noticed for the first time that Sherry and Penelope had slipped from the living room.

Hallie turned back to him. "Don't worry about us. We'll handle the cleanup. Your daughter needs you."

"Thank you." He gave her hand another squeeze and slipped past her, disappearing up the stairs.

Chapter Thirty-Two

Christian descended the stairs a few hours later, the living room cast in shadows from the hallway light. Evidence of Isla's botched party had mostly been cleared away, save for a few spider-bedazzled streamers hanging from the ceiling. In the darkness, he could just make out Hallie's silhouette hunched over on the couch. She'd stayed?

Of course she did. She was no doubt the person who'd put the room back to normal.

He headed over to her. "The girls are asleep. Did my mom and Dani leave?"

Hallie nodded but didn't turn around. "They left about ten minutes ago," she said, her voice soft. She swiped at her eyes as he came around the couch.

"You've been crying?" he asked, taking in the tear tracks on her cheeks in the dim light, "What's wrong?"

"Why didn't anyone come?" Another tear fell from her lashes.

Of course she'd be upset over someone else's party. Hallie had shown her heart of gold time and time again. Was it any wonder why he couldn't help loving her?

Leaning back against the couch, he pulled her against his chest. She snuggled into him, wrapping her arms around his middle.

"Unfortunately, I'm not shocked," he admitted. "I had serious doubts about saying yes to a party in the first place. This is why."

Hallie propped her chin against his chest. "What do you mean?"

"She's been having problems with a girl at school. Before she fell asleep, I finally got her to admit that Sammy convinced the other girls that Isla's party idea was stupid, and they shouldn't come. Frankly, I think it's because her mom refuses to let Sammy have any part in

Halloween. Apparently, it's too devilish." He rolled his eyes. "When they were little, those girls were inseparable friends. Now Carrie won't let her daughter anywhere near mine."

"Carrie?" Hallie sat up. "The woman from that monstrosity two doors down?"

Christian didn't bother holding in his snort. The house was pretty massive. "You know her?"

She shrugged. "I met her a couple times. She had some interesting opinions about you."

Had Carrie Pritchard attempted to reel Hallie into the neighborhood gossip? Awesome. "Like what?"

"Things that were completely untrue." Hallie proceeded to explain everything she'd heard from his gossip-mongering neighbor, from his rumored hookups with past nannies to Isla's *psychological problems,* and his tendency to enable them.

Christian groaned. "I won't skirt around the fact that Isla's anxiety makes her misunderstood. She's terrified of people leaving her. Can you blame her, though, after what her mom did? Tell me how a child, already struggling to trust the people around her, deserves to be ostracized by every other kid in her class?"

Hallie pursed her lips, her brows furrowing in a deep V. Her worried expression upended the hairs on the back of his neck.

"What is it?" he asked.

She shook her head. "It just hurts my heart. People can be so cruel."

"Welcome to the world of parenting. One minute, you're bursting with pride watching them take their first steps. And the next your heart is being ripped from your body, stepped on until it's flattened beyond recognition."

His comment only intensified the worry on her face. "That sounds awful. How do you live like that?"

"I don't have a choice."

The way she chewed on her bottom lip amplified his concern. Were his words giving her further doubt about wanting a more permanent role in the girls' lives? They'd promised to be honest with each other about their feelings, but the lingering uncertainty caused by Sabrina's abandonment made it hard to believe Hallie wouldn't abandon them too.

She's different though. He had to trust that she was nothing like his ex.

"Have you talked to her?" Hallie asked finally.

"Talked to who?"

"Carrie. Have you brought up her daughter's behavior?"

Anger flashed through him at the reminder of how those conversations went. "Trust me, I'm not clueless. I know what goes on between those girls. And I'll always advocate for my daughter. *Always.*"

Hallie looked away, her eyebrows creasing. A strand of her blonde hair fell in front of her face. "I didn't mean to imply you were clueless. I just wondered how she'd react."

Reaching out, he fingered the silky lock before tucking it behind her ear. "I'm sorry. I didn't mean to snap. Carrie doesn't like being confronted about things. It makes her … uncomfortable."

Hallie's eyes took on an uncharacteristic gleam. "Being uncomfortable once in a while would do her some good. She's a piece of work."

Her defensiveness forced a chuckle from deep in Christian's gut. She'd never been anything but kind, though the glare in her eye when speaking of his neighbor showed a woman who wouldn't hesitate to protect her people. At least today, that included his little family.

Would it always?

Again, his heart urged him to trust her, even as his head wasn't fully on board.

"Come on." She stood, reaching her hand out to him. "It's been an emotional evening and there are three cakes in the kitchen begging to be eaten."

They walked hand-in-hand into the kitchen. She grabbed two paper plates—jack-o-lanterns and ghosts printed on a plain black background—from the stack on the table while Christian flipped open the lid of the top bakery box, revealing Isla's haunted house cake.

Hallie came up beside him. "Not that one."

He raised an eyebrow at her.

"The birthday girl needs to be present to cut into her cake."

"Good call." Christian slid the box to the side and flipped open the next lid to reveal an all-white cake in the shape of a ghost. "Better?"

She nodded, pulling a knife from a drawer. The easy way she moved around his kitchen provided further confirmation that she belonged here.

"Would you like to do the honors?" She held the knife out to him.

"You made it." He stepped aside, then placed his hands on her upper arms, slowly guiding her in front of the cake. Snaking his arms around her waist from behind, he stooped to kiss her cheek before whispering in her ear. "Have at it."

She turned her head barely enough to flash him a smile before directing her focus back on the cake. While she sliced a small piece for each of them, he retrieved two plastic forks from the cup on the table. With their plates in hand, they headed back to the couch, settling comfortably next to each other.

"I propose a toast." He sliced off a sizable piece of red velvet and held his fork toward her. "To tough parenting moments made easier with something sweet."

"Cheers." She laughed, the sound warming his core as she touched her bite to his. "Cake always makes everything better."

His mouth stretched wide as he looked at her, warmth filling his core when she smiled back. *No. You do.*

Chapter Thirty-Three

"Trick-or-treat!"

Hallie clapped her hands in front of herself in delight, hardly recognizing the girls smiling at her from the porch. "Wow! You two are the best-looking trick-or-treaters of the night!"

That was saying a lot considering the steady stream of kids that had come to the door in the last hour alone.

Penelope couldn't contain her excitement, her pigtail braids bouncing as she jumped up and down. Three pieces of candy flew out of her plastic jack-o-lantern bucket. "I'm a pirate! Surrender da booty, me hearties! Argh!"

Laughter burst from Hallie's gut, and she glanced at Christian's wide grin from behind the girls. "Did you tell her to say that?"

"I may have taught her a few phrases." He puffed out his chest as only a proud father could.

"You're the cutest pirate ever." Hallie tugged one of Penelope's braids. "You'll have no trouble pilfering treasure from anyone."

"If she could only keep it in her bucket instead of eating it all, she'd be golden." He bent to pick up the candies, dropping them back into Penelope's pumpkin.

Hallie took in the sticky blue substance streaked across the child's cheeks. "I can definitely tell she's been enjoying her splendors." Her attention switched to Isla in her sleeveless leotard and leggings. "And wow, Isla. You really look like a zombie gymnast. How'd you make it look so creepy and gross?"

"Grandma did my makeup," Isla said as Hallie gently touched a finger to the lumpy spot on her grayish face.

"It's putty," Christian clarified.

"I love it, Isla. Very spooky." Hallie turned toward the living room where McKenzie was reading a book on the couch. "Zee, come look at this." Moving aside to make space for her roommate in the doorway, she picked up the bowl of candy from the floor.

McKenzie's delight was understated—much like everything about her—but obvious. "You deserve an extra piece of candy." She dropped a chocolate bar into Isla's bucket. "Actually, take a handful."

"Zee's a gymnast," Hallie said while handing Penelope two peanut butter cups to place in her bucket.

The stars entering Isla's eyes rendered the explanation unnecessary. She stared shyly up at McKenzie. "You're my favorite from the Global Elites."

That brought a sincere smile to McKenzie's face. "Aww, thank you. What's your name?"

Hallie introduced both Isla and Penelope. True to her sweet nature, McKenzie stepped onto the porch and crouched in front of the older child. "Are you a gymnast too, Isla?"

Isla shook her head. "I want to be someday though."

"I think you'd make an awesome one," McKenzie said. "How old are you?"

"I turned six two days ago."

Hallie's heart pricked at the mention of that difficult day. Isla hadn't brought up the disastrous party in the two days since, and Hallie knew for a fact that Christian had shoved the cake into the back of the freezer until the sting had worn off. Hopefully, this interaction with her favorite athlete wouldn't be tainted by talk of her birthday.

"Happy birthday," McKenzie said kindly. She glanced up at Christian. "I teach a beginning class of six-year-olds at SoCal Elite. If you're ever interested in signing her up, I can give you the information for the next session. I teach a class for Penelope's age group too."

"Please, Daddy?" Isla pleaded, giving her father a very good impression of puppy dog eyes. "Can I take lessons?"

For a minute, Hallie expected him to refuse. A month ago, she would've interpreted his hesitancy as disapproval. But now she knew it stemmed more from his lack of trust in people, even if he didn't realize it for what it was.

"That would be great," he said to McKenzie. "You can pass it along through Hallie."

"I'll do that." She glanced at her phone buzzing in her hand. "It's Mitch. I'm going to take this." She smiled at Isla one last time. "It was great meeting you. I hope I'll see you in my class very soon."

Once she'd disappeared back into the house, Hallie stepped onto the porch with Christian and the girls.

"I'm glad you stopped by," she said to Isla and Penelope. "I missed you both so much today."

She'd spent all day baking for the Hawthornes' party tonight, preventing her from watching the girls after school. It surprised her how quickly she'd grown accustomed to having them with her in the afternoons. Not seeing them, even for a day, felt off. Like something was ... missing.

She didn't have time to contemplate too much on what that meant right now. She had a party to cater.

"We wanted to catch you before you left," Christian said. "I'm sorry I can't be there to help set up."

Could he get any sweeter? His constant encouragement had provided the boon Hallie needed to keep pursuing her dream. And today, he'd even burned one of his sacred vacation days to help her take care of last-minute preparations while the girls were in school.

She reached out to squeeze his hand. "Don't feel bad. You've already done so much. And Kendall and Zee are helping me. We're heading over there soon."

"You're going to do the best job tonight," Isla said, unwrapping a piece of candy from her bucket. "You're the best baker in the whole wide world."

Hallie raised her brows at Christian, and he chuckled. "I swear I didn't pay her to say that."

"But Daddy, you promised to buy me a—"

He covered up her comment with a forceful cough. Laughing,

Hallie bumped his arm with her side. "Can you come in for a minute? I have something for the girls."

"Sure, we have some time before they start begging for more candy."

She pulled her gaze away from his wry smile and pushed the door open for them. "It's upstairs. I'll be right back."

"I'na come!" Penelope reached up for Hallie.

Christian started to object, but Hallie lifted the child into her arms, touching their foreheads together. "Of course you can come. You all can, if you'd like."

She and Penelope led the way up the stairs with Isla and Christian following a few steps behind. Entering her bedroom, she set the little girl on the bed. Penelope burrowed into the pillows like she owned the place.

Hallie sat down on the mattress, studying Christian as he studied the room. "Look familiar?"

"It's a lot cleaner now than when it was mine. I'm beginning to understand your obsession with my laundry room."

She rolled her eyes but shot him a flirty smile in response.

A plain pink gift bag with white tissue paper exploding from the top sat in the middle of the blue bedspread, but she ignored it for now, reaching for Foxie instead. She ran a hand along the worn orange fur before motioning to Isla.

In the forty-eight hours since her party, Hallie's mind hadn't let go of the hurt look in the girl's face when she'd realized no one would be coming. She'd thought long and hard of ways to help Isla move on from the blow. The plan she'd settled on wasn't much, but hopefully, it would be enough.

"I want to introduce you to my special friend." Hallie held the plush between them so Isla could take a good look. "This is Foxie. My mom gave her to me when my family moved to Chile. Do you know where that is?"

Isla shook her head.

"It's a country far away from here, in South America," Hallie continued. "I was only a little younger than you when I moved there, and I was really scared because I didn't know anyone."

She watched Isla carefully for any signs of distress, but the girl hadn't pulled her eyes away from the stuffy.

"When my mom gave her to me, she said that no matter how far away I go from home, I'd always have Foxie. We've been through a lot together. Maybe she can help you too. Would you like to hold onto her for a while?"

Isla pulled her eyes away from Foxie long enough to look at Hallie in awe. "Really?"

Hallie gave her elbow a light squeeze. "Really. But she's very important to me, and she's old, so I need you to take good care of her. Do you think you can do that?"

Isla took the animal gingerly in her hands for a minute before giving it a hug. "Yes. I *can* do that."

"Good." Hallie accepted Isla's one-armed embrace before pulling the gift bag closer to herself. "And I didn't want you to be left out, Nellie, so this is for you."

Penelope popped up to a sitting position as Hallie pulled out a floppy pink bunny. With a squeal, she snatched it to her chest, squeezing the stuffie tightly. "I love it!"

"What do you say, girls?" Christian asked.

Hallie spared a glance at him for the first time since they'd entered the room. Perhaps she should've checked with him first before lavishing his children with gifts, though he didn't seem disappointed. He just casually leaned his shoulder against the doorframe, watching the scene.

Isla and Penelope each offered an eager, "Thank you."

"You're welcome." Hallie circled an arm around them both.

Was there anything better than tight hugs from these sweet girls? Except those from their father, of course?

She stood, heading over to the closet, but tossing a grin over her shoulder at Christian. "I have something for you too." She pulled out the infamous disco ball, the subject of their first inside joke.

He threw his head back in a barking laugh. "Why do you still have that thing?"

A thrill of pleasure zipped through her at his uninhibited joy. "I found it under the stairs yesterday. It's yours to hang in your house to remind you of all the good times you had while living here."

"I have a better idea." Playful mischief sparked in his eyes as he kicked off his shoes and took the ball from her.

Isla scrunched her face as she watched him step onto the bed. "What're you doing, Daddy?"

Instead of responding, he pushed the hook—still attached to the top of the ball—into the existing hole in the ceiling and flicked on the hidden switch. Hopping back to the floor, he made a show of smoothing out the bedspread. "Just in case wrinkles give you the ick."

Hallie laughed. "You're always thinking of me."

His flirty smolder sucked the air from her as he killed the ceiling light, throwing the room into darkness. Both girls shrieked with delight as pinwheels of neon danced around the walls.

Hallie felt Christian's arms come around her from behind. "Thank you for making my girls feel so special," he whispered, his breath tickling the wisps of hair around her ear. "We're all so lucky you came into our lives."

The sincerity of his gratitude sent giddy shivers racing down her spine. Or maybe it was the sultry way he'd said it. Reaching behind her head, she rested her hand against his cheek.

In moments like this, all her confusion seemed to fade, leaving her with quiet assurances that a life with Christian could work. But she knew that once the moment ended, the same doubts would swiftly return.

Doubts about her ability to step in as a mother, and how she'd manage her business while filling that role. And just as strong, was Christian really ready to give his heart to another woman after the trauma of his past?

But for now, she pushed them all aside. She wanted to enjoy this moment for as long as it lasted.

Chapter Thirty-Four

Christian stepped out of Isla's room on Friday night, prepared to head downstairs when the faint squeak of Penelope's glider chair drifted into the hallway.

Odd.

Had his daughter climbed out of her crib again? Now that she knew how to escape, keeping her in was becoming more impossible by the day. He needed to convert her crib into a toddler bed before she got hurt.

And while he was at it, he'd fix the chair so it wouldn't squeak anymore.

Glancing into her room, the hallway light threw enough of a spotlight near the glider to see. His heart squeezed at the sight of Hallie snuggling Penelope inward against her chest. Passed out on her nanny's shoulder, the girl clutched the pink bunny Hallie had given her in one arm, her favorite blanket in the other.

Seeing the woman he loved cradle his daughter so sweetly, with her cheek resting on Penelope's wispy hair, sucked all the air from Christian's lungs. For someone who claimed she wasn't ready to be a mom, the way she cared for the girls so completely fit the role already.

Her obvious discomfort around them early on had been non-existent for weeks, replaced by a subtle calm that affected not only Isla and Penelope, but Christian too. She wasn't trying to get the girls to like her. They loved her because it was impossible not to. And he trusted her for the same reason. No reservations, no stipulations. She was exactly what they all needed. He wanted her by his side, helping him raise his kids.

If only he could convince her of that. And the fact that he still wondered whether he was setting them all up for disaster terrified him. He had no doubt she *could* rise to the occasion, but she had to believe it too.

Silently, he stepped to them, placing a hand on Hallie's free shoulder. "I thought you'd left already."

She stirred, turning a sleepy-eyed gaze onto him. "She fell asleep before I could put her in her crib. I didn't want to disturb her."

"It happens to the best of us." He'd been nap-trapped with both girls more times than he could count.

Christian lifted Penelope from her arms, *shhhing* the child when she began to whine. He rubbed her back a few times as she settled, then lowered her into the crib. Hallie handed him the pink bunny that had dropped to the floor during the hand-off. He set it beside the girl.

Motioning for Hallie to follow him, he led the way to the door, turning back before stepping into the hall. She remained in front of the crib. The darkness made it difficult to see her expression, but he could've sworn he detected some longing in the soft smile gracing her face as she watched the sleeping child.

"Hallie," he whispered. "She'll be okay."

With one last glance at Penelope, she followed him from the room. Christian's mind still held onto the sweet scene he'd stumbled upon as they headed downstairs to the kitchen.

Plucking a Tupperware container from the dishwasher, he slid the rest of Hallie's homemade chicken tenders into it. He worked in silence, feeling her welcome presence nearby as she cleared away the dinner dishes.

"Hey." Her voice cut into his thoughts. "Are you okay?"

He glanced at her. "Yeah. Why?"

"You're just really quiet." She placed the stack of plates in the sink. "Is work stressing you out?"

Technically, yes, though that was nothing new. But his job couldn't be blamed tonight. He didn't feel right about mentioning the real reason for his contemplative mood, either. The desperate side of his brain urged him to convince Hallie to admit she wanted a permanent place in the girls' lives. But he refused to do that to her. She needed to come to that conclusion on her own. And he had to be patient until she did.

So he went to the other issue occupying his mind. "It's this family thing we're going to tomorrow."

"The barbecue, right?" She placed a ceramic bowl in the cupboard. "You told me about that. You don't want to go?"

He sighed as he moved on to place the dirty dishes in the empty dishwasher. "Honestly, no. My mom planned it specifically so Dani and I can get to know her *boyfriend's* family."

"Ooof," Hallie said, pausing in the act of wiping down the table to pierce him with an understanding glance. "And you don't like him."

Christian turned fully around, leaning his lower back against the sink. "I've actually never met him. I don't know anything about the guy. It's just weird to think of my forty-nine-year-old mom having a ... boyfriend." He slammed the dishwasher closed.

"Do you think you might be a little threatened by him?" Hallie asked gently, coming up beside him. "Because he's not your dad?"

If the words had been delivered by anyone else, Christian would've taken offense at being called out by someone supposedly on his side. But Hallie's tone spoke of compassion and a desire for understanding, making him feel safe to talk about the reservations he'd kept to himself.

"I just don't get it. She goes on one cruise, meets some random dude, spends every waking moment with him and decides he's the one for her. Like some raging hormonal teenager, not a middle-aged woman. I mean, she's only known him for a month."

"We haven't known each other that much longer."

She could've dropped an anvil on his head with that statement. A month. That wasn't a long time. Yet with everything they'd been through together, he was already trusting her with his heart and wanting her to help raise his kids.

Crap, he was just like Mom.

"Technically, we've known each other for years," he said, trying to push away the uncomfortable feeling squirming in his gut. "We met at Tyler's wedding. Remember?"

Hallie fixed him with a dubious stare. "Christian."

That one word, spoken in such a knowing tone, made him stop justifying how their situation was different than Mom's. He blew out a breath. "Okay, I see your point. And maybe I am a little threatened by him. I just don't like the idea of my mom moving on without Dad."

"I get why that would be hard." She wrapped her arms around his middle. He returned her affection willingly, comfort immediately flooding through him.

How did she do that? She challenged his thinking in a way that still showed him full support. No arguments, no need to defend himself. Is this what a healthy relationship looked like? Being able to have hard conversations without the hostility? He'd never had that with Sabrina. Even back when he thought they were in a good place, she'd always become heated in an argument.

"Would it help if I went with you?" She craned her neck to glance up at him without stepping out of their embrace. "For moral support?"

Christian tucked a strand of hair behind her ear. "I don't want to subject you to my family drama."

Her snort turned into a short bubbling laugh. "Christian, I met your mom in the most awkward way possible. It can only go up from there."

"Hey, at least you got to leave after that." He grinned, though heat engulfed his neck at the memory of Mom walking in on them making out. "I had to stay for the aftermath. But let's be clear. She's been Team Hallie ever since."

"At least I have one fan."

Christian pressed a kiss to her forehead. "We're all big fans of you."

Her face softened. Stretching onto her toes, she brushed her lips against his jaw, bursting fireworks all the way down to his stomach. He tightened his arms around her, and she snuggled deeper into his chest.

"I'd love for you to come," he murmured against her hair.

She stepped out of his embrace but slid her hand down his arm to squeeze his fingers. "Then I'll be there with my arms full of goodies. But, if I happen to disappear for a few hours, it's because I'm exploring every nook and cranny of your mom's house."

"Be honest. The only reason you want to come is to see the inside of it."

"Whaaaaat?" She drew out the word unconvincingly. "I don't know what you're talking about."

He laughed. "You might hide it well, but I can feel your giddiness."

"Okay, fine." She turned away from him, tossing a coy look over her shoulder. "Can you blame me? I've coveted that house since my first day in Buena Hills."

He wanted nothing more than to kiss that flirtation right off her mouth. Grabbing her hand again, he twirled her back to him, pleased with the delighted surprise in her eyes. He lowered his face toward hers. "Or we can disappear together, and I'll give you the grand tour."

"Even better," she managed before his mouth covered hers.

Chapter Thirty-Five

Hallie worked hard to reel in her glee as she followed Christian through the door of his childhood home. *You're here to support him, not sneak away to explore your dream home.*

"If I'd known you'd be this giddy, I would've brought you here weeks ago." He dropped back to walk beside her through the entryway. Isla and Penelope had run ahead, searching for their grandma and aunt.

Hallie bit her bottom lip to stifle her grin. "It's still crazy to think you grew up here."

Christian made a noise that she thought was a chuckle but sounded more like a grunt. It was the first sign of amusement she'd managed to pull from him since he'd picked her up ten minutes ago.

He really *wasn't* looking forward to this. She could practically feel the dread radiating from his body. If not for the cake platter she carried in both hands, she would've given the guy a hug.

Switching the plate of pumpkin spice cream puffs to his other arm, Christian placed his free hand along the small of her back to usher her past the entryway.

A simple chandelier lit the hallway leading to the back of the house. They passed a small rectangular table along one wall, holding a porcelain vase of white roses. Hallie slowed to look at the photos lining the blue-and-white wallpaper. A large portrait of the Gustafson family, taken shortly before his father's death judging by the kids' ages, made up the focal point. Pictures of Christian and Danica from infancy to graduation spanned out from it on both sides. Isla and Penelope's baby pictures also held spots of honor.

"You look like your dad," Hallie said, switching her focus from the real Christian to the photo of his father. "It's almost uncanny."

His mouth turned up a bit. "I like when people tell me I take after him. It kind of feels like he's still here."

"I wish I could've met him."

Christian swallowed slowly, studying the picture. "He was a good man." His voice cracked on the words.

"So are you."

They stood silently in front of the portrait for several moments. Hallie didn't push Christian to say more, neither did she tug him away. Understanding inched into her mind. He still deeply mourned his father, and yet his mom's new man was waiting right outside to meet him.

"It'll be okay." She tilted her head to rest against his bicep. "But I understand now why today is so hard."

His arm came around her, and he took a cleansing breath. Then his hand lowered to the small of her back again, an unspoken invitation to continue through the house.

As soon as they stepped into the bright kitchen, Hallie had to take a moment to appreciate the sheer beauty of the space. Granite countertops lined both sides of the room, providing ample space to prepare food. Glass-lined cupboards above displayed several sets of elegant dishware, with more space in the cabinets underneath the counters and center island. The double oven would make baking for customers so much less time consuming.

This isn't your kitchen. Still, her imagination was already latching onto the idea of getting her hands dirty in this room.

"It looks like everyone's outside," Christian said, popping the imaginary thought bubble housing her fantasy.

Sherry was rearranging the plethora of food dishes at a long table set up on the deck when they stepped outside. Her face lit up as Christian headed over.

"Oh, hey guys!" she said brightly as he kissed her cheek. She took the cream puffs from her son but smiled at Hallie. "You made it. I hope you're hungry. We've got enough food to feed an army."

Good thing too. The number of people roaming around the sprawling yard could form a decent-sized platoon. Hallie picked out

Danica, Isla, and Penelope at the wooden playhouse by the fence—the only familiar faces in the group.

Hallie accepted a hug from Sherry, though she was unable to reciprocate due to the cake dish in her hands. "Where do you want this?"

"Let's put both desserts over here." Sherry moved a plate of sliced tomatoes, onions, and lettuce to the side to make room. She removed the tinfoil covering the cream puffs. "Ooh, these look good." Plucking one off the top of the pile, she popped it into her mouth.

Christian arched an eyebrow at his mother. "You never let me eat dessert first."

"Like that stopped you." She winked at Hallie, reaching for the cake. "Let's put that down right here. Thank you for bringing all this. You really didn't have to."

Hallie shoved the tips of her fingers into the front pockets of her jeans. "I wanted to. Family gatherings are so much better with dessert."

Sherry laughed. "I can't argue with that."

A dark-haired woman wearing a navy cardigan over a polka dot ruffled blouse walked up to the table, holding the hand of a small boy in a baseball cap. "Sherry, do you mind if I get Joey something to hold him over until we eat? He skipped his snack."

"Not at all." Sherry smiled at the boy who hid his face behind his mother's straight-legged jeans. He looked to be a little older than Penelope. "It's so hard for the little ones to wait."

"Thanks. Wow, that's gorgeous," the woman said as Sherry took the cover off the platter, revealing the cake's red-and-yellow swirled mirror glaze. "Did you make it?"

Sherry shook her head. "Hallie did. She's an excellent baker. You should've seen the birthday cake she made for Isla."

"I can't wait to try it." The woman extended a hand. "I'm Jenna, by the way. Paul's oldest daughter."

Hallie returned the greeting, but it was Sherry who made the introduction. "Where are my manners? This is my son, Christian, and his girlfriend, Hallie."

Girlfriend? Being addressed that way for the first time bathed her whole body in warmth. She glanced at Christian, gauging his reaction. He met her gaze, the same question hanging in his eyes. She gave him a reassuring smile.

Joey tugged on Jenna's cardigan, and she shifted her attention to his pleading eyes. "Okay, okay, buddy." To the adults, she said, "I better get him a snack."

She walked off and Sherry linked arms with Hallie, speaking to Christian. "Let me introduce you to Paul. He's been anxious to meet you."

As Hallie was being pulled away, she latched onto Christian's hand, dragging him with her. He followed stiffly. Their steps took them over to the man working the grill on the far side of the yard. His jeans and short-sleeved button-down gave him a casually friendly air. Or maybe that was caused by the smile lighting his face when Sherry walked up to him. Whatever the reason, Hallie liked him immediately.

"Paul." Sherry wrapped her arm around his waist. "I'd like you to meet my son, Christian."

Paul pushed his sunglasses up to rest on top of his head. Though his hair was still dark, the gray peppering through it made him look distinguished and polished. "Good to meet you, Christian. Your mom has told me so much about you. I'm assuming those sweet girls belong to you?"

"They do." Christian accepted Paul's offered handshake, and even gave him a smile, though Hallie could sense the discomfort emanating from it. He'd put on his cloak of composure, the mask she now recognized as his way of protecting himself through tough situations.

She feared he was in for a long afternoon.

After most people had finished eating and resumed their chosen activities, Hallie found herself sitting on a lawn chair across from Jenna, matching dessert plates in their laps. Sometime earlier, Christian had disappeared to help Penelope use the bathroom, but the child had already rejoined the unorganized soccer game playing out a few feet from where the women sat. Her father was still missing.

"Hallie, this cake is incredible." Jenna sliced off another bite of the delectable cranberry-orange mousse. "I just want to eat the whole thing."

"I'd probably join you. It's really hard not to sample it whenever I make it." Hallie took her last bite.

"Do you work in a bakery?" Jenna's question caught Hallie with her mouth full, leading to the typical awkward pause as she chewed. "Sorry."

Hallie waved away the apology and swallowed. "I started a home bakery back in college."

"A self-made woman," Jenna said brightly. "I like it."

Self-made? Hardly. More like an insignificant entrepreneur, attempting to figure out her place in the business world.

"Do you still do that?" Jenna asked, scraping her plate clean with her fork.

"Yeah." Hallie set hers on the grass beside her chair before picking up her water glass. "I'm trying to scale up now that I've graduated, but it's a lot harder than I expected."

Jenna hummed in understanding. "I get that. The entrepreneurial world is challenging. Our family is in real estate. My dad managed to build the company from the ground up. He claims he knew nothing about owning a business before he started. He only wanted to be his own boss. And now it's a whole family empire."

Hallie took a drink of water, processing Jenna's words. Was she just making conversation?

The woman answered her question in the next breath. "I'm sure he'd be happy to offer you some advice on how to get things rolling."

"Really?" Hallie could use a little help.

Okay, a lot of help.

"I don't see why not. He's taken a lesser role in the company now that he's close to retiring, so he has more time. And he's pretty passionate about helping fellow businesses. Especially small ones."

Excited jitters danced around in Hallie's stomach. Maybe there was hope for her business after all. "That would actually be really helpful. I've built a decent name around town, but there's only so much I can do to spread the word without a physical location to send people to. I'd like to save up for a space to expand. I just don't know how."

"It sounds like you need an investor to help with the start-up costs."

"Christian suggested that too. I just don't know where to find one of those." Mentioning Christian's name reminded her that he still hadn't come back outside. Was he okay? Maybe she should go check on him.

"I might be able to help," Jenna said.

"How?" Hallie asked, momentarily setting her worry over Christian's whereabouts aside.

Jenna smiled at her eagerness. "When my mom passed, my dad set up a foundation in her memory. She had a real passion for small businesses—she always bought locally, never at the big chain stores. Once I finished my PhD, my dad put me in charge of the committee."

"What kind of foundation is it?" Hallie clamped down on the hope sparking in her mind.

Jenna placed her plate on the grass before leaning forward to rest her forearms on her thighs. "We give grants to small business owners needing a little boost. And we offer mentoring in marketing and other areas to help them succeed. Hearing you talk about your bakery, and after sampling this delicious cake, I think you'd be the perfect candidate."

Hallie brought her hand to her mouth to keep her jaw from dropping. "Really? That's fantastic!"

"We get hundreds of applicants from all over the state of California," Jenna continued, "and we can only award two per year, so I can't guarantee you'll be chosen right away. But you should definitely apply. I can send you an application next week."

Hallie didn't know what to say. "Okay ... I'll do that. Thank you."

"Of course," Jenna said. "In fact, what're you doing next month?"

Next month? "I'm going home to visit my family for Christmas, but other than that, my schedule is pretty open. Why?"

A toddler ran over and patted her mom's legs. Jenna lifted her onto her lap. "Our foundation's Christmas party is the second Friday in December. We'd selected a bakery down in Newport to cater the desserts, but they just backed out this week because of a food handling issue. You have a permit, right?"

"Of course. It's all current."

"Great. How would you like the gig?"

Just like that? Hallie had to take a beat to keep herself from bursting. This was the break she'd been hoping for. Who knew that crashing Christian's family barbecue would lead to the chance of a lifetime? *Just wait until I tell him!*

As she and Jenna fine-tuned the details, her ears picked up on Isla's laughter nearby and she shifted her gaze to the soccer game. Isla kicked the ball past one of Paul's older grandsons, a boy who looked to be around ten. He made a show of missing the save, flopping onto the ground to the girl's delight.

Some of Hallie's excitement dimmed. If this opportunity came to fruition, she'd have a lot of work ahead of her to get things rolling. Sure, the grant wasn't a foregone conclusion. In fact, Jenna had been upfront about the likelihood of her *not* being selected, especially in the first year. But if she did, it had the potential of accelerating her business dreams. And changing her life.

And based on the expectations Jenna laid out before her, the foundation Christmas party next month would be the biggest event Hallie had ever catered.

She'd no longer have the time to watch the girls. Her stomach sank. How would this opportunity affect Hallie's relationship with them in the long run? Would her leaving crush them irreparably? Especially Isla, who'd begun to thrive in only a couple weeks?

And what about Christian? How could she tell him she could no longer help?

It was only supposed to be temporary.

Then why did the idea of pursuing this chance feel like abandoning them all?

Chapter Thirty-Six

Under any other circumstances, Christian would've liked Paul. The man seemed to carry himself with integrity and humility. Every member of his family adored him, and he matched well with Mom's fun-loving energy. Plus, he'd treated her with nothing but respectful reverence all afternoon. In every aspect, the guy appeared to be a saint.

It wasn't that Christian didn't like him; he just didn't like the idea of him dating his mother. Not at the expense of forgetting Dad.

After helping Penelope wash her hands, he'd sent her back outside to play, needing a reprieve from the social crush outside. Alone in Mom's kitchen, he'd occupied himself by emptying and loading the dishwasher. Next, he'd moved onto scrubbing the entire sink, then wiping off the counters on either side of it. Maybe he'd do the windows next.

Man, he really must be stressed if he'd resorted to cleaning to relieve his mind of his troubles. Or maybe Hallie was rubbing off on him.

The sound of the sliding glass door opening caught his attention as Mom stepped inside.

"I'll tell you what." She held up the half-eaten cream puff in her hand. "Your Hallie is a keeper, especially if she continues bringing scrumptious treats like these around." She popped the rest of it into her mouth.

Christian pulled another disinfectant wipe from the container, sparing only the briefest glance in her direction. "Yeah, she's great." He attacked the stove with the wipe.

Mom came up beside him, stopping his cleaning with a hand on his arm. "What's wrong? I've never known you to willingly volunteer to clean my kitchen."

"I'm fine."

His muttered comment earned him one of her signature Mom looks. "Honey, I've had the privilege of watching you grow up for twenty-seven years. I know when you're lying to me. Is it Paul?"

"Paul's great."

"Then what is it?"

Christian sighed, turning to face her. "I don't know, Mom. Everything's just happening so fast. You spend two weeks with the guy and now we're meeting his family? Are you going to call me tomorrow to say you're getting married?" He went back to furiously attacking the burners with the wipe.

Mom stayed silent for a moment before a lengthy exhale preceded her next comment. "I see. You're thinking about Dad."

How does she do that? Her ability to read his mind had always freaked him out. He'd never been able to keep anything from her. If she were a superhero, reading minds would be her power.

"It kind of seems like you're trying to replace him," Christian admitted softly.

"Honey, look at me."

Slowly, he turned toward her, and she gently cupped his upper arms with her hands. "Your father was my first real love. I could never replace him. I'm sorry that's what you think."

Christian swallowed hard, doing a poor job of keeping his sadness at bay. "Do you still miss him?"

Mom touched his cheek. "Every single day. Most nights, I fall asleep thinking about him. When we're all together, I wish he were here too. And I miss him whenever you and Dani do things to remind me of him."

"I remind you of him?"

"So much." Mom smiled. "Especially now that you have your own kids. You'd give anything for your sweet family. Just like your father. Paul's the same way. I think that's what drew me to him so quickly. Neither of us are trying to replace our spouses. But there's a comfort in sharing that grief with someone who understands what it feels like to lose your first love. I am falling for Paul. But it's a different kind of love than it was with Dad. And that will never go away, no matter where things lead with Paul."

Her words hit him like a Mack truck, taking his breath away. For years, he'd doubted that lasting love existed. That emotion, as forceful as it might be at the start, always fizzled out eventually.

But here was his mother, proclaiming her continued love for her late husband, even after fifteen years without him. That realization sent his mind cycling through more examples of lasting love. Tyler had shown his devotion to his wife on many occasions, both in word and action. Even Brad, a guy who Christian would never have expected to settle down with anyone, proved that with the right person, true love could change someone for the better.

Maybe his problem wasn't that it didn't exist. Maybe it was that he trusted the wrong person, including himself. And that one mistake made it impossible to fall in love with the right woman.

Until now.

Feeling lighter, he took his mother in his arms. "I'm sorry I've been such a grump."

"It's okay." She patted his chest. "I handled your mood swings during puberty. I can take a little grumpiness now and then."

"Mo-om," he groaned, smiling at the laugh bubbling from her. "I'll try harder to keep an open mind about all this."

"Thank you, son. I hope you can think of Paul as a friend. That's all I'm asking. I'll never expect you to call him Dad."

"Good, because I'm not going to." He stared out the window at all the people roaming the yard. He spotted the girls playing soccer with Paul's sons and a few grandkids. Hallie sat in casual conversation with Jenna.

Mom followed his gaze out the window. "Maybe one of these days, we can double date with you and Hallie."

Christian tossed a side eye down at her. "There's no way to spin that so it's not weird."

She smacked his chest with the back of her hand, making a noise that was half laugh, half gasp. "Don't get smart with me, young man. I changed your diapers."

"You always hold that over me like I had a choice."

"That reminds me, I need to go find the photo albums. I'm sure Hallie would love to see all those gems of you growing up. Perhaps the one when you got into my mascara and smeared it all over your—"

"Mom!" His indignation didn't prevent the laugh bursting from his gut.

His mother grinned back at him. "It's nice seeing you happy again, son. I've missed your levity."

The lightness brewing in his chest dwindled. "Sometimes it feels like I'm not worthy to be happy after what happened with Sabrina."

"Oh, Christian." Mom pulled him into a motherly embrace. "You're the only one punishing yourself for that. You did nothing wrong. It may not have turned out the way you hoped, but you've done the best you possibly could in a difficult situation. I'm so proud of the way you've handled yourself through all this."

He clung to her, and for a moment, it was as though he were a young boy again, grasping for the safety that only she could provide.

She stepped back enough to look up at him. "There's a pretty fantastic woman outside who seems to think very highly of you regardless of your past. Maybe you should start seeing yourself as she does."

Right on cue, the sliding door opened, and that same fantastic woman burst into the kitchen, bringing all the sunshine with her. She stopped short when she spotted them.

"Sorry." She backed up toward the yard. "I didn't mean to interrupt."

Mom shook her head. "You didn't. I was just heading back outside. I want to snag another of your delicious cream puffs before they're gone."

Hallie laughed. "You better hurry, I think I saw a couple left."

"My name is written all over them." She winked as she left the kitchen.

"What's up?" he asked as soon as they were alone.

Hallie could have lit up a dark runway with the brightness of her countenance. "I got a gig. A big one."

"What? How?"

She bit her bottom lip, resembling an excited Penelope by the way she bounced a little on the balls of her feet. "I've been talking to Jenna about her dad—he's really fascinating. Did you know he owns his own business?"

"No." There was still so much he didn't know about the man. He intended to change that.

She continued talking animatedly. "He built it from nothing. He's actually quite wealthy. Anyway, Jenna asked me to cater their foundation Christmas party next month. Can you believe that?"

"Hal, that's incredible!" Christian tugged on her hand, drawing her closer.

She stepped into his embrace but didn't stay there long, beaming as she continued talking. "That's not all. Apparently, Paul's late wife was the one who encouraged him to branch out on his own. When she died, he set up a foundation in her honor that offers grants to small businesses looking to scale up. Jenna wants me to apply for it. I'm not sure I'm going to, though."

He gaped at her. "What're you talking about? This is the break you've been wanting. Why wouldn't you take it?"

Her shoulders lifted as she began pacing around the kitchen. "I was really excited at first. But then I realized something. If my bakery gets off the ground, I won't be able to keep watching the girls. I'd let them down. And I'd put you in a difficult situation with the whole nanny thing."

Christian's heart dropped. She didn't want to disappoint him?

No. *He* refused to keep her from fulfilling her dreams. "We always knew our arrangement would be temporary."

"I don't want my relationship with the girls to change." She rubbed the back of her hand against her nose as if holding in her emotion. "What if they forget about me?"

Approaching her, Christian stopped her pacing by cupping his hands around her cheeks. "You have no idea how grateful I am to have you in my life. Besides my mom and Dani, no one has ever loved my girls as purely as you have. You might think you're not ready to step in as their mom, but being willing to sacrifice your business for them? Honey, you're already acting like one."

Tears pooled in her eyes. "I don't want to abandon them. But I don't know how to do both."

"You won't be doing either one alone." He brushed his thumb along her cheekbone. "When's the event?"

"Six weeks from now."

His brain began forming a plan. "I have some vacation time I can use that week to stay with the girls while you bake for the party. And I'll help you put together your proposal for the grant. Whatever comes after that, we'll figure it out together."

Her mouth lifted a little. "I like the sound of that."

He pressed a lingering kiss to her forehead, then tugged her to him, wrapping his arms around her. "Me too."

Together.

He hadn't been referring to her potential business opportunities. No, he was thinking in terms of a more permanent togetherness.

Like forever.

Chapter Thirty-Seven

The next few weeks flew by. Work kept Christian even busier than before, and every day he grew more grateful for Hallie's continued help with the girls. With Thanksgiving looming, Jim had gone into a rampage, demanding his team wrap up several projects before taking time off for the long weekend.

Christian still hated his job, but what he had waiting for him at home gave him a special boost to get through each day.

Dating Hallie looked different than any relationship he'd had before, Sabrina included. They couldn't go on regular dates without hiring a babysitter but there was a peaceful comfort in reconnecting with her after the girls went to bed. Having her curled up on the couch next to him while they worked on separate projects had created a contentment within him he'd never felt before. And helping her with her grant proposal had inspired him to take on a new purpose: putting his own dream of starting a business back into motion. At least the idea of it, for now.

The missing pieces of his life were finally coming together.

Two days before Thanksgiving, he turned onto his street, eager to get home. His stomach rumbled as he breathed in the spicy aroma escaping the bags of takeout on the passenger seat.

Since Hallie had driven the girls to their first gymnastics class, he'd beat them to the house for once. Excellent. He had a surprise for her, and the empty house would give him the opportunity to put it in motion.

In the morning, she'd be leaving for Brad's parents' house to spend Thanksgiving with her extended family. He wanted to send her off with something special so she knew how much he appreciated her.

No, appreciate wasn't strong enough. He loved her. Man, thinking that still sent a giddy thrill zipping through him.

In addition to picking up food from Curry & Spice, he'd stopped by the local home goods store for white fairy lights and scented candles. And during the rare hours that Hallie hadn't spent with them last weekend, the girls had drawn pictures to give to her. He had all the ingredients necessary for a cozy family dinner.

Family.

Smiling at the thought, he turned into his driveway, noticing an unfamiliar sedan at the curb. *It's probably for the neighbors.* He pushed his door open, grabbing the food and his work bag from the passenger side. He'd come back for the rest of the stuff after placing dinner in the oven to keep warm.

As he neared the porch, a figure rose from the steps, sending ice cubes down his spine. Her raven ponytail was just as long and thick as it always had been, her skin just as flawless—like she hadn't aged one bit in the time she'd been gone.

The takeout bags dropped from his hands, thumping onto the concrete. "Sabrina."

Her mouth turned upward. "Hey, Christian. I'm back."

He blinked at her. His heart thumped in his ears, muting the words coming from her mouth. She couldn't be back. This had to be one of those nightmares that had plagued him the first several months after she'd left.

He squeezed his eyes shut, rubbing his hands up and down his face a few times to bring himself back to reality. Once he opened his eyes again, she wouldn't be there anymore.

"Aren't you going to invite me in?"

Dang, still here.

And that would be a hard no on the invitation. He'd rather hash it out right here, send her packing, and get on with his evening.

But the longer they stood on the porch like this, the greater the chance someone could see. Providing more fodder to the neighborhood rumor mill was an even worse option. Sabrina coming back? Yeah, the gossips would go to town with that. Especially Carrie.

He made a noise that was half groan, half sigh and picked up the bag from Curry & Spice. One of the Styrofoam containers inside had popped open, spilling rice and chicken through the opening at the top of the bag. Wonderful. He punched the code into the keypad and pushed the door open, wordlessly ushering her into the house.

Princess Pumpkin trotted toward them, sniffing at the bag of food. Christian knelt in front of her, patting her side to calm himself before the negative emotions crashed down on him. It was like he'd been pushed into a time warp that sent him back three years to the day Sabrina had abandoned him.

"You got a dog?" She stared at Pumpkin, who let out a low moan of displeasure. It was telling that the animal who liked everyone found this newcomer suspicious.

You and me both, girl. Without responding, he led Pumpkin into the kitchen, throwing on the lights. He thumped the takeout on the stove as the dog went over to scratch at the door to the laundry room where Christian kept her food.

"Aren't you going to talk to me?" Sabrina asked, entering the kitchen behind him.

Christian whirled to face her. "What do you expect me to say? Why're you even here? Do you need money?"

Her mouth dropped open in stunned silence. "No, of course not. Didn't you hear me? I'm back. I want to be a family again."

He threw his hands up in frustration. "You've been gone for years, and you honestly thought you'd swoop in here, expecting me to be happy to see you? Do you even realize the damage you've caused to us all?"

She took a shaky breath, her gaze dropping to the floor. "Christian, I'm sorry. I was just so ... unhappy. We were practically babies when Isla was born. I'd wanted to do so many things, and I didn't want to regret not being able to experience them."

"And there it is," he muttered bitterly. "Everything has always revolved around you. Your problems. Your unhappiness. Even this house was about you. But what about the girls? What about me?"

"Christian—"

"I bent over backwards, trying to fix our relationship. Nothing was ever good enough for you."

"But I've changed—"

He stopped her by holding up a hand. "So have I. When you left, I had no choice but to move on with my life. And I'm not going back to that situation again. I'm done believing in your empty promises." He spun around, gripping the oven handle to ground himself.

"Is this about your nanny?"

Slowly, he swiveled on his heel to face her again. "What're you talking about?"

Dropping into one of the chairs at the table, Sabrina crossed her arms over her striped cropped sweater. "I saw Carrie this afternoon. She told me all about how you were getting friendly with a woman who'd been watching the kids."

So the gossip mill had already begun to churn. Fantastic. He ground his teeth, his anger nearing its boiling point. Sabrina didn't get to come here and cause chaos, upsetting all the progress he'd worked so hard to make.

"That's none of your business." He kept his voice an icy calm.

"If it involves our girls, it is my business."

"Now you decide to be a parent?" he shot back, unable to stop himself.

His comment plunged them into a chilling impasse, broken only by the creak of the front door opening.

"Christian?" Hallie called from the entryway. "We're back."

Isla and Penelope burst through the house, talking over each other.

"Daddy, Daddy! I walked on the balance beam!" Isla called at the same time Penelope added, "I jump in the pit!"

They skittered to a stop as they appeared in the kitchen. Isla's suspicion immediately replaced her excitement. "Who's she?"

Sabrina turned wide eyes onto Christian. "They're both so big," she whispered, agony marring her voice. Taking a step toward the girls, a tearful smile appeared on her face. "Hi, girls. Mommy's home. Come give me a hug."

Isla backed up, bumping into Hallie, whose gaze darted from Sabrina to Christian. Her furrowed brows asked the question she didn't need to speak out loud.

He bobbed his head once.

The worry plaguing Hallie's lovely face pierced his heart, stabbing some of the air out of his anger. She squeezed the girls' shoulders gently, crouching to their level. "Why don't you go play in your rooms for a bit."

Both girls darted wary glances toward Sabrina before scurrying off toward the stairs. Hallie's gaze followed them before she swiveled back to the tense scene in the kitchen. She teetered in the entryway, obviously not sure whether to stay or go and looking to Christian for guidance.

There was nothing he wanted more than for her to stay. He needed her calming presence right now. But he refused to subject her to his ex's vitriol. Turning to Sabrina, he said, "Will you excuse us?"

Without waiting for an answer, he crossed to Hallie, gesturing for her to follow him from the kitchen. They stopped near the front door. "You should probably go. I need to sort this out."

She studied him, and he suspected the worry in her expression would haunt him for long after she was gone.

"Text me later?" she asked, her voice wobbly.

Nodding, he held her eyes for a long moment, trying to convey that Sabrina's presence changed nothing between them. But with the way his head still spun at his ex's unexpected appearance, the words he wanted to speak only tumbled incoherently in his head.

Hallie slipped through the front door, and Christian closed it behind her, blowing out a deep breath to steel his composure before facing Sabrina again.

"Carrie was right, then," Sabrina said when Christian reentered the kitchen, Hallie's expression still plaguing him. "You're in love with her. I can see it in your face."

Christian didn't deny it. His silence was answer enough.

"But what about us?" Sabrina asked. "We were a family."

"You should've thought about that before you abandoned us." He ran a hand down his face, the exhaustion hitting him with a force that literally dropped him into a chair across from her.

They fell into a silent standstill charged by years of frustration, disappointment, and resentment. Christian stared at his hands in his lap, unable to tune out Sabrina's quiet sniffles but not willing to muster the strength to get her to leave.

"The girls don't remember me." Her voice cracked, and a gasp followed the heavy realization. "They don't know who I am."

"That's the tricky thing about choices, Sabrina," Christian said dryly. "They come with consequences. You can't just pick and choose the ones you want to deal with."

She leaned forward, piercing him with pleading eyes. "How do I fix this? Is there any hope of reconciliation?"

"Any hope of saving our marriage died the day you walked out that door."

"What about the girls? I want a relationship with them."

Over my dead body. He'd sell himself to the devil to protect his girls from the pain Sabrina had caused. And he'd protect Hallie from her too.

But was that the best solution? He couldn't just kick Sabrina out, lock the doors and refuse to answer the phone. What if the girls grew to resent him for refusing to let them get to know their birth mom?

He balled his fists in his lap to keep his anger contained. "If you sincerely want to get to know the girls, we can work something out. But I need time to explain to them what's going on. This will be a big shock for them. We'll talk after Thanksgiving."

"But that's two days from now."

"And you've been gone for three and a half years," he hissed through his teeth. "You can wait a little longer."

Her shoulders slumped, and all indignation fizzled out with the movement. "Okay. After Thanksgiving."

"I need to go check on them," he said, ending the conversation. "Do you have a place to stay?"

Because you're not staying here. And paying for a hotel didn't sit well with him either. But he couldn't leave her with no accommodations. How come after all the damage she'd done, he still felt a pull to make sure her needs were met?

"I'm crashing with some friends in the city." She followed him from the kitchen.

"Okay then."

With nothing more to say, Christian promised to call after Thanksgiving. Once he'd closed the front door behind her, he pressed his back against the wood, sliding to the floor. He desperately needed to check on the girls, to make sure their world hadn't been rocked after the bombshell dropped on them tonight. But with his own world imploding, how could he possibly support them?

Lowering his face into his hands, he let the reality of the situation spin around him. Sabrina was back. She wanted a relationship with the girls. Just when his life was looking up, his ex had managed to send him spiraling back to rock bottom.

Would he ever be free from the demons of his past?

Chapter Thirty-Eight

Three days.

That was how long Hallie had lived with this nagging dread—the kind of dread that camps out in the bottom of her stomach, creating enough nausea to make her uncomfortable but not in any danger of throwing up.

Christian hadn't called her once since she'd left his house on Tuesday. She missed him. But more than that, she worried about him. And them. She'd thought their talk at his mom's house had transformed this relationship into something solid.

But now she wasn't so sure.

And his comment about how she was already acting like a mom changed her perspective. As she'd spent the few weeks since that day with the girls, a miraculous thing had happened. She'd gone from deciding to be open about a more permanent place in their lives, to really wanting it.

So why, at the exact time she'd finally accepted the possibility of being their mom, did Sabrina have to return and seriously undermine that? What did the woman even want?

Hallie contemplated that for the millionth time as she sat at the breakfast table in Beej's parents' kitchen the morning after Thanksgiving. Besides herself, her cousin, Elise, and Kendall, no one occupied the room, a rare feat due to the massive amount of family members attending the holiday get-together.

"Isn't it so fun finally being under the same roof again?" Beej got up from the table to place her cereal bowl in the sink. "It's just like old times."

Elise tugged at the sleeves of her oversized pajama shirt and crossed her arms on the table. "Agreed. Yale is amazing and all, but I've really missed you girls. Too bad Zee's not here."

"We tried to get her to come with us but apparently spending Thanksgiving with Mitch's family was more enticing to her," Hallie said before biting off a piece of the roll she'd made for yesterday's dinner.

"I don't know why she'd think that," Kendall scoffed in exaggerated disbelief. "We're much cooler."

Amused agreement rippled around the table, interrupted by Hallie's phone buzzing in front of her. Heart jumping to her throat, she snatched it up. Had Christian finally reached out?

"You're a little eager for that phone call." Elise leaned over to catch a glimpse at the screen. "Is it Christian?"

Hallie frowned at the unfamiliar number. Setting the device back on the table, she slumped in her seat. "No, must be a telemarketer."

"You've been awfully quiet about him since we've been here." Her sister watched her carefully. "Everything okay between you two?"

Did she have the ability to read minds? How else would she ask the question right as Hallie's worry for him plunged to new depths?

"I really don't know," she muttered.

"I thought things were developing between you two." Kendall stood from her chair, walking her egg-smeared plate to the dishwasher.

Hallie washed her breakfast down with a glass of orange juice before responding. "So did I until his ex came back."

Beej gasped. "You've been holding out on us. When did that happen?"

"Tuesday."

Before she could add more, Brad shuffled into the kitchen, sleep lines creasing his cheeks.

"Morning, sleepyhead," Kendall crooned as she returned to the table.

He ran both hands down the blond stubble on his jaw. "What's up, girlies?" he mumbled, plucking the tea kettle off the stove and heading for the sink.

"Hallie's giving us the dirt about Christian." Elise shot a sympathetic smile in her sister's direction. "His ex is back."

That revelation lit a fire under Brad's half-comatose state. He jerked away from the sink, water sloshing from the top of the kettle. His eyes flashed. "What does she want?"

"I honestly don't know," Hallie admitted amid a fresh wave of worry. She launched into what she'd found when getting back to the house with the girls on Tuesday. "Then he asked me to leave, and I haven't heard from him since."

Why hadn't he at least texted her? Was he having second thoughts? He couldn't possibly have decided to reconcile with his ex.

He wouldn't.

Right?

Brad set the kettle on the stove, turning on the burner before taking a seat at the bar near the table. "She better not weasel her way back into a relationship."

The force of his animosity surprised Hallie. But then she remembered Christian mentioning how much her cousin disliked Sabrina.

Before she could respond, the back door opened, revealing the one person she'd rather not have this conversation with. Tyler, bundled in a thick sweatshirt and joggers with a beanie covering his blond hair, stepped inside. Bags circled underneath his eyes, making him look like he hadn't slept for days. Gemma, carrying Will, entered the house behind him, her dark curls framing her face in haphazardly beautiful waves.

"Whoa." Brad chuckled. "Rough night?"

"Remind me again why we haven't moved this shindig to a larger location?" Tyler pulled a carton of baby yogurt from the fridge while his wife lowered Will into Elise's outstretched arms before plucking a banana and apple from the fruit basket on one counter. "Gem found some really nice vacation homes in the mountains that would fit the family better. Think of it. No one would have to sleep in tents in the backyard. Spending the night outside in fifty-degree weather might've been fun when I was younger, but not anymore."

Hallie wasn't opposed to camping, but not in November. Which was why she was perfectly fine letting her brothers, and some cousins, have the backyard. She gladly claimed the floor of the living room every year.

Their Thanksgiving celebration had been a time-honored tradition ever since Dad and his siblings had moved away from home. It was the one time of year that the whole family invaded the Lucas home, which was bigger than Grandma and Grandpa Abernathy's a few miles away. But although Hallie used to refer to it as a mansion, it was no hotel.

And now that the older grandkids were starting families, bringing in more people to their already overflowing group, the house became more crowded by the year. Perhaps Tyler was onto something. They should start considering a larger location.

"What's the matter?" Brad asked, retrieving a mug from the overhead cabinet as the kettle whistled. "You can't handle camping with a baby?"

Tyler rolled his eyes. "That's some bold talk from someone about to have his own kid. You're in for a rude awakening, pal."

Brad just smirked and shrugged his shoulders. "I'm just saying, for someone as supposedly outdoorsy as you claim to be, I'd think you'd be more up for the challenge. Beej, do you know where Mom put that tea she bought for Cassie?"

"Is it not with the rest of her flavors?" Beej rose from the table. "You're looking in the wrong spot. It's in the pantry." She followed her brother into the walk-in space next to the fridge, her voice rising. "Can we get back to what we were talking about before?"

That would be a hard pass. "Not until Tyler leaves," Hallie muttered.

"Why can't I be here?"

She blew out a centering breath. He'd find out eventually, and it might as well be from her. "Because I don't want to hear you say, 'I told you so' when I admit I've fallen for your best friend."

Tyler blinked at her for a moment, his expression unchanging. "Did he hurt you?"

"No." Then why did her heart feel split in two?

His blond brows furrowed as he lifted his son from Elise's arms, sliding him into the highchair. "What happened?" His voice was strangely calm as he pulled up a chair beside Hallie.

Her chin wobbled, the three days of worry threatening to overflow. If she explained what happened now, she'd lose her composure completely. Seeing her struggle, Kendall caught Tyler up on the details he'd missed before entering the kitchen.

His concern over Sabrina's return rivaled their cousin's in intensity, though without as much hostility. He glanced at Hallie. "How're you feeling about all this?"

She hugged her arms around herself. "I just want him to be okay."

"Oh, Hal," Elise squeezed her sister's thigh. "You love him. I can see it."

A desperate laugh puffed out of Hallie's mouth. "A lot of good that's doing me now. I should've listened to you, Ty."

Tyler slid an arm around her shoulders, tugging her to his side. "I know I can be a bit overprotective sometimes." He laughed when both Elise and Hallie tossed matching side eyes at him. "Okay, a lot protective. I just didn't want you getting hurt."

"I know you mean well." Hallie tilted her head onto his shoulder. "You've always had my back, and I appreciate that. But I need to see this relationship through. Even though it'll hurt if it doesn't work out."

Oh, please let it work out.

She didn't miss the contemplative glance Tyler shared with Brad, but it was Beej who asked the question on all their minds.

"He's not getting back together with her, is he?"

Hallie shook her head. "I don't think he would after the way he's talked about her. And the hostile standoff I witnessed on Tuesday didn't seem like a reconciliation. But what if she wants a relationship with the girls. I don't know if I can handle being a mother figure to them if I'm always having to compete with the real mom."

A grunt from the stove drew her attention to Brad. "Some mom she turned out to be."

"That's really hard." Gemma set a plate of bite-sized bananas and apples in front of her son. Will started grabbing at the chunks with a pincer grasp. "But every couple goes through challenges. Take Tyler, for example. I know he'd never say this, but it has to be annoying living with someone else's grandma."

Tyler pulled his wife down onto his lap as she held out a spoonful of yogurt to their son. "And I'll continue helping you care for her as long as I need to." He kissed the inside of her wrist.

"And look at Brad over there." Beej waved a hand at her brother. "I never thought I'd see the day he'd willingly dote on a woman twenty-four-seven just to make her comfortable. I mean, he's making tea. Who knew he'd ever become the poster boy of wedded bliss?"

Brad rolled his eyes as he dunked a tea bag in and out of the steaming mug of water. "Thanks a lot, sis."

"You already know all the bumps and bruises Rory and I've been through," Elise added. "They haven't magically gone away just because we're getting married."

Hallie didn't believe that for a second. "You guys are perfect together though."

A whimsical smile pulled at her sister's mouth. "While I don't disagree with you, we were still raised in different countries. We've had to adapt a lot to understand each other's perspectives. Besides, English might be his native language, but have you heard the guy talk when he's excited about something? You can't understand a word he says."

The sliding glass door opened, cutting through the laughter echoing off the walls. Rory entered the kitchen, his usually neat dark hair ruffled from sleep. He stopped when he noticed everyone's amused glances on him. "What's so gas?"

"We were just talking about your funny accent." Elise's fond smile made it obvious she loved the way he talked.

Rory chuckled, bending to kiss the top of her head.

As she abandoned her chair to help him find some breakfast, Gemma slid into her spot. "Hal, you can't expect your relationship to be without hardship. If it's not the ex, it'll be something else. That's life. Only you can decide if your love for Christian is worth tackling this challenge."

Elise poked her head out of the pantry. "She's right. But maybe a few days away from Christian can help you figure out what's best for you."

"I just wish he'd tell me what's going on." Hallie picked up her phone again, willing a notification onto the screen. Nothing. "I hate all the unknowns. Are we still together? Is his ex staying at his house? Is he still expecting me to watch his kids on Monday?"

"Wait, you're still babysitting his kids?" Tyler asked. "I thought that was a one-time thing."

"She's the nanny," Kendall answered for her. Hallie didn't miss the ironic humor in her tone.

Tyler's eyes narrowed, though he seemed more confused than anything. "Since when?"

"It's been about a month." Beej looked to Hallie for confirmation.

"What?" Tyler scoffed. "Am I the only one who didn't know?"

A chorus of "yes" came from everyone in the room and his head whipped toward his wife. "Even you?"

Gemma lifted her shoulders in apology. "Cassie told me. She made me promise to keep it to myself."

Tyler pierced Brad with a serious look next. "I suppose your wife told you too?"

"Nope. I heard it directly from the horse's mouth." Discarding the tea bag into the garbage under the sink, Brad picked up the mug in one hand, a bottle of honey in the other. He raised them both in a wonky toast before heading for the door. "Peace out, fools. I'm on my way to deliver my queen her morning sustenance."

"Wait up." Tyler followed his cousin into the hall.

Before Hallie could wonder about all the significant glances the guys had given each other, Elise's arms came around her shoulders from behind. "I wish I could tell you that everything will work out with Christian. But no matter what, I'm always here for you. You know that, right?"

Her sister's support pulled a smile onto Hallie's face. "I do. It's been really nice having you here again."

"It has, hasn't it?" Elise squeezed her tighter. "I miss working through all our problems together."

Together.

Christian had used that word back in his mom's kitchen. Did he still want that?

Or did Sabrina's reappearance change everything?

Chapter Thirty-Nine

Christian tiptoed to Isla's door, sliding it open enough to slip from her dark room.

"Daddy?"

He froze. Hadn't she been asleep a second ago? Turning, he found her propped up against her pillow. He returned to her side. "What is it, sweetheart?"

"Why doesn't Hallie come over anymore?"

His heart pricked at the mention of Hallie. He still hadn't texted her since she'd walked in on his hostile exchange with Sabrina. She deserved an explanation—and probably an apology for his distance—but with his thoughts still in their downward spiral most of the time, he had no idea what to say. Preparing the girls to meet their mother was taking every ounce of energy he had left. But Isla didn't need to know all that.

Kneeling beside her bed, he tugged on the blankets as she laid back down. "She's spending Thanksgiving with her family. You know that."

"But she'll come back?"

Another ache sliced through him at the confusion in her tone. He'd thought she understood that Hallie was just leaving for a few days, not forever. But she'd experienced so much abandonment in her young life. Frankly, he'd been surprised at how easily she'd accepted Hallie in the last few weeks. He hadn't expected a few days away from her to trigger Isla's fears.

"Of course," he said, hoping the reassurance would ease her anxiety. She'll be back on Monday."

"I miss her."

"I do too." So much it hurt, especially after the last three days. So many times he'd wished she were here, supporting him through this latest mess caused by his ex. He'd come to depend on the peace she brought simply by being in the room.

He found Foxie halfway lodged between the bed and the wall and tucked it under Isla's blankets.

She snuggled the animal to her chest. "Do you love her?"

How did she pick up on that? She was only six. "Where'd you get that idea?"

A yawn came over her as she responded, slurring her words. "Grandma said when someone is in love, they smile a lot. You smile all the time when Hallie is here."

Warmth accompanied the painful throbbing in his chest. It seemed the cat was out of the bag, despite the fact that he and Hallie had agreed to keep their relationship from the girls for now.

He needed to call her. But he'd have to worry about that later. Right now, Isla stared back at him expectantly, waiting for his answer.

"I do." He watched her hesitantly, gauging her reaction. Her possible disapproval would put him in an even trickier position. "Are you okay with that?"

She relaxed deeper into her pillow and nodded. "She makes me smile too."

For Isla, that was basically a stamp of approval. He kissed her cheek. "I'm glad. Now, get some sleep."

"Goodnight, Daddy." She closed her eyes.

"Goodnight, sweetheart."

Christian camped out on her floor until her breathing turned heavy, then made his way downstairs. A knock at the front door punctured the quiet. He glanced at his watch. It was after nine. Who could possibly want to come over this late?

Maybe if he ignored it long enough, they'd go away. It could be Sabrina. She'd called a few times in the last three days, demanding a meeting with the girls, but he'd kept telling her he needed more time. Had she finally run out of patience?

Another knock punctured the silence of the dark house, more urgent this time. Okay, ignoring wouldn't work. Dragging his feet, he approached the door and pulled the canvas drape back a crack to peek through the side window. He pushed out a noise that landed somewhere between an annoyed growl and a relieved sigh.

He flipped on the entryway light before yanking the door open. "Do you have any idea what time it is? I was about to go to bed."

"Yeah, right." Tyler breezed into the house, followed by Brad. "I know you better than that. Your night is barely getting started."

That doesn't mean I want company.

"We would've been here sooner if someone hadn't insisted on stopping for a burger on the way." Tyler slugged his cousin in the shoulder.

Brad rubbed at the spot, scoffing as though offended with the roughhousing. "I was hungry. Do you know how hard it's been not eating meat? I need my iron."

"What're you doing here anyway?" Christian asked, leading the way to the kitchen. He grabbed a protein bar from a box on top of the fridge and tossed it to Brad, who made himself at home at the square table. "Shouldn't you be at your family thing right now?" Brad's parents lived a good two hours away.

Joining his cousin at the table, Tyler held up a hand, a silent request for his own protein bar. "You would've known we were coming if you'd answered your phone."

Christian tossed him one too, then rested his hip against the counter by the sink. "I think I left it upstairs. I needed a break from it after all of Sabrina's calls."

"It's true then?" Brad asked around a mouthful of protein bar. He swallowed. "She's really back?"

Neither he nor Tyler seemed surprised by the news, which could only mean that Hallie had already told them. Forcing out a deep sigh, he leaned his head back against the cabinet behind him. "Yeah, she's back. She wants a relationship with the girls."

"And you're encouraging it?" Brad's hostility didn't go unnoticed.

But this time, his buddy's opposition didn't rankle Christian. He agreed with it even, that being the main reason for putting off the introduction. "What other choice do I have? As much as I hate it, she gave birth to them. Can I realistically keep her from being in their lives if she sincerely wants a place in it? The girls don't deserve to be caught in the middle of our problems."

"What about my sister?" Though subtle, Tyler's tone held a slight edge. He'd adopted his protective older brother persona.

"What about her?"

Tyler peeled back the wrapper of his protein bar, though his eyes remained fixed on Christian. "I think you know."

Christian sighed. He couldn't keep playing dumb about his feelings in front of his friend. It was time to come clean. "I'm in love with her."

His buddy's expression remained unchanged. "Duh."

"You knew?" After being so protective of Hallie, Christian had expected some kind of reaction from his friend.

"Of course I knew." Tyler pushed back his chair. "Shall I present Exhibit A?" Tugging open the freezer door, he waved his hand in front of the shelves where Christian had crammed Hallie's two remaining cakes. Isla's haunted house had already been eaten. "How many cakes did you buy at the Autumn Festival?"

Christian ran his hand down his face. "Three." The word escaped as a low growl.

Brad barked out a laugh, almost falling out of his chair. "Welcome to the club, man."

"What club?"

"The Smitten Guy's Club." Tyler shut the freezer before reclaiming his spot at the table. "Only a fully initiated member would go to those lengths for a woman."

Christian dropped into the chair across from him. "If you already knew, why didn't you call me out when she showed up that day you were at my house?"

"I know I'm protective of my sisters. But believe it or not, I really do respect their ability to choose for themselves." Tyler leaned back on his chair's hind legs. "Plus, Gemma told me not to."

That pulled a chuckle from Christian. He was looking at the president of the Smitten Guy's Club. "And you're not mad?"

His buddy crossed his arms over his chest as he pondered the question. "I'm ... concerned. My sister is important to me. Her *happiness* is important to me. But she told me, in no uncertain terms, to back off and let her figure things out herself."

A smirk tugged at Christian's mouth. "I can't picture Hallie ever saying those words."

"That was more my interpretation of it." His eyes lit with mischievous amusement.

"The question is," Brad said, placing his elbows on the table and steepling his hands together, "now that your feelings are out in the open, what're you going to do about it?"

"I don't follow."

His buddy rolled his eyes. "Why are you here while she's at my parents' house wondering where she stands?"

That gave Christian pause. He'd been so wrapped up in his own crumbling world, he hadn't considered the possibility that she needed to be reassured that his feelings for her hadn't changed. Actually, not being with her had made him even more sure about where they stood.

Boy, did he mess up big time. He wouldn't blame her for considering it a deal breaker. Or at least a humongous red flag.

Tyler must have recognized Christian's sudden panic. "Can you blame her for being confused? She gets to your house to find you in the same room as your ex, and instead of explaining the situation, you ask her to leave and ghost her for three days. See why I'm concerned?"

"I have to make this up to her." Christian jerked to his feet. "I'll call her now."

Brad arched one of his dark blond brows. "Don't you think this conversation should be done in person?"

The amount of nervous energy pulsing through Christian's veins sent him pacing across the kitchen floor. "She's not getting back until Sunday." He snapped his fingers. "As soon as the girls wake up in the morning, we'll drive up there so I can talk to her. Do you think your parents will mind?"

Brad's mouth quirked up in approval. "There are so many people swarming that house right now that three extras wouldn't make a difference."

"Good," Christian mumbled, his mind already forming the heartfelt apology he'd give to her in the morning.

"Do you mind if we crash here tonight?" Tyler asked. "I need a few hours of shut eye, so I don't fall asleep behind the wheel."

Christian emerged from his thoughts long enough to answer. "Sure thing. I've got a couch with your names on it."

"Rock, paper, scissors for it?" Brad lowered his chair to the floor, shooting a smirk in his cousin's direction. "Loser gets the floor."

Tyler put one fist on top of his flattened palm. "Best out of three."

It almost felt like old times watching his friends battle for the couch—just three nineteen-year-olds messing around after a full day of classes.

But they were no longer those guys, and he couldn't keep living in the past. He could only look to the future with the hope of sharing it with Hallie.

Chapter Forty

Late Saturday morning, Hallie carried a giant popcorn bowl in her arms on her way to the basement prior to the start of the family's annual Christmas movie marathon. She passed through the Lucases' entryway just as Tyler and Brad came through the front door.

"Where have you two been?" She shifted the bowl enough to grab the handle of the door leading downstairs.

"We were on an errand." Brad glanced at Tyler.

"That was a long errand." Hallie looked back and forth between the two, their guilty expressions triggering warning bells in her brain. "No one has seen either of you since yesterday afternoon."

Tyler shrugged, though he struggled to hold back a smile. "Duty called, and we had to answer."

Duty? What duty?

Before she could contemplate their strange behavior, tiny, erratic taps came from the front door, more like scratches than actual knocks.

"It looks like someone's at the door." Brad sounded like a bad actor in a low budget film. "I wonder who that could be?"

Tyler choked on a snort. "Maybe you should answer it, Hal. Here, I'll take that." He snatched the popcorn bowl from her arms before booking it down the stairs after their cousin.

What was up with them? They seemed eager that Hallie get the door for this mystery guest. But why should she care who it was?

Unless ...

Had they magically talked Christian into driving all the way up here?

They didn't.

Did they?

Insides buzzing, Hallie yanked opened the door. Christian wasn't on the porch. In fact, he was nowhere in sight. Yet her heart still burst at the two small figures bundled in thick sweaters and hats. They each held a piece of paper, and Penelope also clutched the last few stragglers from Aunt Claire's white daisies still going strong despite the late season.

"Hallie!" She shook with excitement, dropping her picture. The flowers were practically goners in her tight fist. Isla, though more understated in her reaction, smiled so big her brown eyes almost disappeared.

The warmth charging through Hallie threatened to bubble over, and she laughed. "I'm so happy to see you!" Crouching to the girls' level, she took them both in her arms for a tight hug. "I've missed you both so so *so* much! What're you doing here?"

"We surpise you!" Penelope squeaked.

"You sure did." Hallie scrunched her nose, touching her forehead to the child's. "This is the best surprise." She sat back on her heels to study their angelic faces. "And you brought me flowers?"

"I pick them for you." Penelope held out her fist with pride.

Hallie relieved her of the wilted bouquet, and the flowers fell over her hand. "That's so sweet. Thank you."

"We drew pictures too." Isla bent to pick up her sister's from the cement.

Hallie took both drawings, Penelope's on top. It was only a series of multi-colored scribbles, but Hallie saw a priceless work of art she'd cherish forever. She gave the child another squeeze. "I can't wait to go home and hang it in my room."

She flipped to Isla's picture next. Four stick figures took up most of the page. Two small ones stood on the outside, holding the hands of the ones in the middle. A slightly larger one with yellow hair and oversized blue eyes came next. And the fourth was so long, Isla had run out of room for more than a tiny circle for the head at the very top of the page.

"It's us. There's me and Nellie, and you and Daddy." She pointed at the indecipherable words written in crayon along the side. "And this says thank you for being my forever friend."

Hallie didn't think her smile could grow any bigger. "I'm so happy to be your forever friend. Awww, you've even got Princess Pumpkin in there." She studied the brown doodle somewhat resembling the golden retriever. "I love it."

The lopsided sketch of Christian caught her eye. Where was he? Hallie glanced past the girls, scanning the yard. Unless he hid behind the trees to the side of the driveway, he wasn't nearby. "Where's your dad?"

Isla turned over her drawing, pointing at the words scrawled across the back. "He left a note."

Immediately, Hallie recognized Christian's handwriting scrawled hastily in pencil.

Meet me at the creek in 10?

Hallie knew the exact spot. Nestled in the foothills of the San Bernardinos, the Lucases' property backed a miles-long thicket of scrub oak with pine trees becoming denser further down the trail. "The Woods," as all the cousins called it when they were little. They used to love taking the five-minute walk to the clearing where the small stream passed through, spending hours skipping rocks and splashing around the ankle-deep water.

How did Christian know about that? And what was he up to?

Tyler and Brad had to have a hand in this. No wonder they couldn't keep a straight face.

"Come inside, girls." She ushered Isla and Penelope into the house.

It took longer than ten minutes to get them settled in the familiar company of "Uncle Tyler." She was anxious to discover what plan Christian had concocted, but she wasn't about to leave the girls—especially Isla—without being completely confident of their comfort.

Once they were seated next to her brother on the couch with plates of snacks, eagerly watching *How the Grinch Stole Christmas*,

Hallie slipped on a thick sweater and left out the back door. She weaved through the numerous tents set up in the spacious backyard until she got to the gate.

She hadn't been to the creek in years, but she still knew the way by heart. Her pulse pounded a jagged rhythm in her neck in time to each step. The nerves buzzed stronger the closer she got to him. After four days of silence, what could he possibly have to tell her that he couldn't say over the phone?

It had to be something good. He wouldn't drive the girls all the way up here, lavish her with hastily picked daisies and drawings if he planned to get back with his ex.

Right? The very possibility gave her pause.

What if everything had changed for him?

Light musical strains floated through the air to her, easing her doubts. She knew that melody; had danced to Jason Mraz's proclamation of not giving up on loving someone. The sweet strains of the chorus brought her back to the night of that wonderful, glorious, beautiful dance she'd shared with Christian.

Peace spoke to her soul. Everything would be okay. *They* would be okay. More than okay. She increased her pace.

His back was to her when she stepped into the clearing. A small smile tugged at her mouth. "What're you doing, Christian Gustafson?"

He turned, sliding his hands from his hoodie pocket as he approached her. "I was up all night trying to come up with the perfect grand gesture." His voice was husky, uncertain.

Hallie held her breath, studying the glassy shine in his brown eyes, the way his brows furrowed like he was holding back emotion.

"I couldn't think of anything that came close to being worthy of what you mean to me," he said. "So, I've come here to ask this one question. Will you dance with me?"

Maybe it was the sweet reminder of that night. Or the sincerity of his tone. Whatever the reason, the simple question spurred her into action. She lunged at him, throwing her arms around his neck. Burying her face into his chest, she breathed him in, already comforted by his familiar essence. He pulled her into his strong embrace, holding her tenderly as though refusing to let her go.

They didn't dance. The music drifted into the background, mixed with the breeze rustling the trees around them and the water bubbling in the brook. All that mattered was him. His embrace, his presence, his love.

"Christian." She backed up enough to look at him. "Why did you need a grand gesture?"

His hands ran down her arms, tangling with her fingers. "I know I messed up, Hal. I shouldn't have shut you out. I left you with doubts, and I wouldn't blame you for deciding to walk away. But please let me explain. Not to make excuses, just to help you understand."

Hallie led him to a boulder overlooking the tiny stream. She sat, pulling him down next to her before nodding for him to continue.

"Seeing Sabrina again really shook me." Christian stared at their interconnected hands on his thigh. "It sent me right back to that guy desperately trying to fix his marriage only to come home to his wife gone and his world in pieces. I spiraled. I'm sorry. You have every right to be mad."

"I was never mad." Tears stung her eyes at hearing the agony of his last few days. "Just worried about you and the girls. I want you all to be okay. Even if that's without me."

Christian leaned forward to rest his forehead on hers. "That's the last thing I want. I don't want to be that jaded guy anymore. I don't want to be driven by the bitterness over what Sabrina did, unable to see the love right in front of me. You've shown me what a healthy relationship looks like, and you deserve that in a partner."

Hallie swallowed past the thickness in her throat.

"You told me once that every problem has a solution." He brought his hand up to caress her neck. "Hallie, you're my solution. Not because I expect you to solve all my problems, but because I want to go through life with you. The highs, the lows. Everything. I want to help you get your bakery and walk with you when you're stressed. I want to dance with you in the kitchen while we're cleaning up dinner and relax on the couch together after the girls are in bed. I love you. And I won't give up until I become the man worthy of you."

"Oh, Christian." She closed her eyes, savoring his soft caress. "You already are. I see the way you selflessly care for your daughters. And you've been nothing but supportive and kind to me. That's why the last few days have been so hard. I was worried your ex coming back had changed everything."

"What?"

Hallie blinked the moisture away. "I'm not the girls' mom. I only recently realized that I wanted to be. But how can I compete with the woman who gave them life? That's a leg up I'll never have."

Christian took hold of her hand again, resting it in his lap. "You've been more of a mom to them in the last month than Sabrina has in their entire life. They love you. Isla asks repeatedly when you're coming back. Penelope walks around the house, calling your name. Even Pumpkin waits by the door for you."

"Really?"

His mouth lifted in an ironic smirk. "Please come back, Hal. I can't take her constant whimpers anymore."

"I miss them," Hallie admitted. "Even Pumpkin has grown on me. I never thought I'd say that about a dog."

His chuckle sent happiness trailing down her spine before he sobered. "If Sabrina really wants a relationship with the girls, I'll always have a connection with her. It's just the way it is. But Hal, there's no competition. You're the standard that no one can ever match."

"Is that what she wants? A relationship?" Hallie had suspected as much, yet it was still a lot to process.

"Yeah." He blew out a heavy breath. "I'm not convinced she'll stick around, so I'm being cautious about giving her time with the girls at this point. We'll see what happens. But I doubt she'll make it easy for either of us."

Even a week ago, the idea of navigating a relationship with Christian while dealing with his ex would've made her run for the hills.

But not anymore. She knew what she wanted. And she'd willingly walk through this trial if it meant being with him.

She repeated the words he'd said to her in his mom's kitchen. "We'll figure it out together."

"I like the sound of that." He kissed her forehead. "For whatever reason, my kids needed to come when they did, and I wouldn't change that. But my heart belongs to you. I can feel it. And you're the only partner I want with me to raise the girls. If you're willing."

Hallie touched her hand to his cheek and nodded. "I'm ready." She no longer had any reservations about that. "But if this is going to work, you're going to have to teach me to dance."

"Of course." Christian lowered his face to hers. Their lips hovering a breath apart, he murmured, "I'll make a dancer out of you in no time."

The kiss that followed was soft and tender at first before growing in urgency. Hallie pressed into his embrace as his hand slid around her waist, drawing her closer. Every caress of his lips echoed his devotion, sealing the words he'd spoken with sweet assurance that he knew—as she did—that this love between them was the kind that would last forever.

"Ew, Daddy! That's gross!"

A giggle followed Isla's loud pronouncement, as did a pair of bird caws and the flapping of wings. Hallie threw her head back in laughter. She turned to find both girls staring at the scene before them, with her brother standing in between, his face scrunched in disgust.

"I agree with Isla on this one." Tyler shuddered.

Christian groaned. "I think we can take it from here. You can go."

Tyler's gaze darted from his friend to Hallie and back several times before they narrowed theatrically. "Fine. But remember, you might be together now, but she's still my sister. And I'm keeping my eye on you, pal."

"Oh, you're looking for a show?" Sliding his hand around Hallie's waist again, Christian pulled her closer, his smile full of mischief. "We've got more where that came from."

Hallie cackled, shoving him away playfully. Penelope giggled. And Isla shouted more objections.

"*Okay,*" Tyler said, holding his hands up in surrender. "Fine, I'm leaving."

Hallie grinned as she watched him turn in the direction of the house. Dating her brother's best friend would certainly be interesting.

When he'd disappeared through the trees, Penelope climbed onto her lap, placing her small hands on both of her cheeks. "Are you my mama?"

Hallie's heart melted at the sweet question. "Not yet." Though her next comment was still directed to Penelope, she glanced over at the child's father. "But hopefully soon."

With one arm around Isla at his side, Christian leaned over and kissed Hallie's temple.

Penelope snuggled into her. "Mama," said said, resting her head on Hallie's shoulder.

Warmth pooled inside of Hallie's stomach, radiating outward until it had engulfed her entire body.

Mama.

There was no sweeter sound than that.

Christian's arm came around her, and she leaned into his side, knowing this moment was the start of something life changing. They were together. She and Christian. The girls, who she'd grown to love so much.

Her family.

Always and forever.

Epilogue

Three Years Later

"It's time to put the book down, kiddo," Christian said, entering Isla's room and flipping the switch by the door to turn off the ceiling light. The lamp on her nightstand bathed the area around her sleeping space in a soft glow. He knelt next to her mattress.

"Just a few more minutes, Dad?" She gave him a pouty look he hadn't seen on her in ages. "Hallie isn't home yet."

Placing her bookmark on her page, he closed the graphic novel and set it on her nightstand. "I'm afraid not. It's already late. But Hallie promised to come in and say goodnight as soon as she gets home."

Tonight was Buena Hills' annual Christmas tree lighting festival, and both girls had loved helping out in Hallie's booth throughout the evening. It took a lot of convincing to get them to come home for bed instead of going back to the bakery to help clean up after the event.

Christian picked up Isla's pink stuffed jack-o-lantern, holding it out to her. "Okay, we've got Jackie."

Isla put the stuffy in its assigned spot against the wall.

"And here's Lanny." He reached across her legs to grab the purple jack-o-lantern, popping his daughter gently in the face with it. She giggled, so he did it again.

"Da-ad." She grabbed the plush, swinging it behind her head to use as a second pillow. "Lantern doesn't like being called that. She's grown-up now."

Christian splayed his hands in front of him as he spoke to the pumpkin. "I'm terribly sorry, Lantern. I failed to see the sophisticated gourd you've become. Please accept my heartfelt apology."

"She says you're forgiven." Isla arched a single brow. "This time."

"Thank goodness for that." He booped her nose before straightening the rest of the stuffed animals on her bed.

"Where's Foxie?" Isla lifted her pink-and-purple bedspread and leaned over the side of the mattress to look underneath. "I think she fell off last night. Will you get her?"

"Sure." Christian went onto his hands and knees to search under the bed. He pulled Foxie out, tucking it into his daughter's waiting arms. "Here you go."

"Thanks, Dad." She slid further under her blankets, snuggling the stuffed animal tightly. She'd slept with it every night since Hallie had given it to her ages ago.

The animal had seen her through some big changes this year—Christian's marriage, a new school, and moving, to name a few. After Mom had married Paul, she'd agonized over selling the house that held so many memories of Dad. In a solution that still thrilled Hallie, she'd passed the house to Christian to continue the family legacy in the place.

"The lights look good," Hallie said from the doorway, her purse still slung over her shoulder as though she'd just returned home.

Christian watched her enter the room, his mouth lifting. "Tyler and Brad came over before the festival to help hang them up."

"Carrying on your father's reputation, I see." She planted a quick peck on his lips. "Surprising your wife with the Christmas lights on the house." A strand of her blonde hair had escaped her chunky braid, and she looked tired after her early wake up call to bake for the festival.

Standing, he tucked the hair behind her ear. "That wasn't my intention, but now that you mention it, I might make this a yearly thing."

She gave him a playful smile before kneeling beside Isla's bed. "You ready to sleep, sweetheart?"

Isla nodded, holding Foxie out to her. "She needs a hug."

Hallie gave the animal a squeeze. "Goodnight, Foxie. Watch over Isla tonight and keep the bad dreams away. Can you do that for me?"

She screwed her voice into a squeaky one to mimic the animal talking. "You can count on me, Hal."

Christian smiled at Isla's giggles. He never tired of watching their sweet relationship blossom. It was like they'd formed an exclusive girls' club with Penelope. One that he was lucky enough to be admitted as an honorary member.

Hallie's peaceful influence had been vital to Isla's progress, especially with Sabrina's continued struggle to be a constant presence in the girls' lives. His ex was trying; he'd give her that. But she had issues of her own she still needed to address.

Hallie handed Foxie back to Isla. "Now you can expect nothing but sweet dreams all night long." She kissed the top of her blonde curls.

Isla tucked Foxie underneath the blankets again. "I love you, Mom."

Christian's breath hitched, and his eyes darted to Hallie, gauging her reaction to their daughter's simple endearment. She'd never pushed for either of the girls to call her mom, though Penelope had given her the title from the beginning. But despite Isla's growing attachment to her stepmom, tonight was the first time she'd used the title.

Hallie kept her face even, though her mouth lifted in a soft smile. "I love you too, sweetheart." She gave her one last hug before smoothing the blankets over the child. After stroking her hair for a moment, she stood, stepping away so Christian could move in to say goodnight.

"Sleep well, kiddo." He planted a quick kiss on her cheek, then switched off the bedside lamp, leaving only the weak glow of her haunted house nightlight.

"'Night, Daddy."

As Isla drifted off, Christian backed away from the bed. He hadn't needed to stay in her room for months, another way Isla's challenges had improved. And watching her thrive provided even more healing for him.

Hallie was already in their bedroom when he entered, lounging in the blue plush armchair by the window overlooking the front yard. She stared out at the darkness, her fingers softly stroking Princess Pumpkin, whose head rested in her lap. A quiet sniffle reached his ears.

"Hal?" He came around the chair, nudging Pumpkin out of the way. Kneeling before his wife, he lifted her chin gently. The evidence of tears pricked at his heart. "What's wrong?"

She waved away his concern, assuring him that these were not tears of sadness. "She called me Mom." Her voice cracked on the last word.

Christian brushed the moisture from her lashes before pulling her from the chair. "A most deserving title." Circling his arms around her, he held her close to him. "You've woven your magic over all of us, and we're all so much better for it."

She nuzzled her cheek against his chest. "I don't know why I'm so emotional about it though. It must be the extra hormones."

"Hormones?"

She nodded, keeping herself entangled in his arms. "From the baby."

Baby? His heart stuttered, and he backed up a step to look in her face. "You're pregnant?"

Hallie snagged her bottom lip with her teeth. "Mmhmm."

"We're having a baby?" He shook his head, not fully comprehending the possibility.

She nodded, new tears lighting her already expressive eyes. "I found out this morning. It's been so hard keeping it from you all day, but with the festival, I didn't have a chance to tell you."

Lowering himself to sit on the side of the bed, he took her hands in both of his. "Wow. Another baby."

"Are you happy?" The uncertainty in her voice surprised him.

He pulled her down to sit on his lap. "Oh, Hal. Of course I am. I'm just surprised. I didn't think it would happen this fast." They'd only agreed to start trying a few weeks ago.

"I know." She dropped her head to rest on top of his. "It surprised me too. But I'm excited. And a little terrified. Three kids. Can you believe it?"

He chuckled. "I can't wait. You're already an amazing mom. This little one is the luckiest baby in the world."

Placing her hands on his cheeks, she lifted his face up to hers. "I love you, Christian," she said, sealing the words with her lips on his.

"I love you too," he whispered against her mouth before deepening the kiss.

She was his life, his entire world. And now their love had culminated into adding another beautiful addition to their family.

Their family.

Man, he'd never get tired of saying that.

"This place is going to get a lot crazier next summer," she said after they'd broken apart. She rose from his lap, a lightness crossing her features as she flashed him a radiant smile. Her stomach didn't show signs of their impending arrival yet, but she already glowed. How had he not noticed it earlier? "Are you up for that?"

Christian quirked a brow as he pulled her back down to him. "Honey, with you, I'm up for anything."

Thank you so much for reading! If you enjoyed *Surrendering His Heart,* I'd love for you to leave an honest review.

Buena Hills Series

Discovering Her Heart

Book 1

Chasing Her Heart

Book 2

Champion of Her Heart

Book 3

Surrendering His Heart

Book 4

Stand-alone Bonus Book:

Risking His Heart

Stay up-to-date on all my new releases by following me on Amazon.

Acknowledgments

Here we are ... another book and another chance to thank everyone who had a hand in making it shine.

First and foremost, I couldn't do this without the support of my husband—my biggest cheerleader. Every time I feel like throwing in the towel and doing something else with my life, he's always there to remind me of why I'm doing this. He's my sounding board when I need to talk through ideas that aren't exactly right, he's quick to offer feedback that I may or may not listen to, and he talks me down when my ambitions get a little too unattainable. Being married to an author is an adventure, and he is the perfect partner in crime.

I couldn't let an acknowledgment page go without again thanking my amazing editor, Raneé. Her insights and ideas have been invaluable in taking this book from a first draft with potential to the incredible story you hold in your hands. And can we talk about the gorgeous cover she designed? I love it!

My proofreader, Roxana, has been wonderful to work with again. Her sharp eye for details caught all those pesky little errors to make this book shine.

I couldn't have finished another book without the constant support of my critique partners: Sarah, Judy, and Danyelle. These ladies are more than just fellow writers, they're my best friends. I'm so glad they're with me to celebrate the completion of another book.

And last but certainly not least, I have to thank you, dear reader. If this is the first book of mine you've read, I appreciate you taking a chance on Christian and Hallie. And if you've been with me since the beginning, thank you, thank you, thank you from the bottom of my heart for coming back to Buena Hills book after book. Your support of this series and of my author career means the absolute world to me.

About the Author

Allison Gygi wrote her first official story in third grade from an old word processor in the computer lab of her elementary school. Since then she has crafted countless tales both on paper and in her head. As a mom, her days are spent trying to find a few minutes to write in between the never ending dishes, meal prep, and helping kids with homework. She loves fairy tales and gravitates towards books with happy endings and swoony kisses. Allison enjoys reading, hiking, and traveling the world. She lives with her husband and three children in a cute suburb of Chicago.

Learn more at https://allisongygi.com

instagram.com/authorallisongygi

bookbub.com/profile/allison-gygi